HUNTER'S DESCENT

Praise for the Works of Lisa MacTague

Demon in the Machine

...is an exquisite steampunk and paranormal mashup permeated with action, mystery and romance! This book had my heart thundering in my chest on so many levels! One of the many things I love about MacTague's writing is her ability to create strong, complex and "real" characters and the wonderful dynamic she develops between them. This book is no exception! All great steampunk features wonderful gadgets and contraptions and this novel is rife with such inventions as multi-functional goggles, powerful jump suits enabling the scaling of tall buildings and, of course, the new horseless carriage. My favourite aspect is how MacTague adds her own flair to these gadgets in terms of how they are powered. I also love how she brilliantly captures the atmosphere; the romance, etiquette and manners of the Victorian era and then pumps it full of grotesque imps and demons! However, what really draws me in to Lise's novels is her fantastic characterization. So, if you enjoy layered, well realized and imperfect but enticing characters, then this book is definitely for you!

MacTague is really suited to steampunk! She excels at writing stories with strong women and Briar and Isabella are no exception. *Demon in the Machine* is a wonderful mélange of mystery, steampunk, paranormal and romance that is appealing on so many levels!

- The Lesbian Review

Five Moons Rising

MacTague completely knocks it out of the park with this one, one of the best lesbian paranormals I've read. This book blew me away. Not just for the imagination MacTague demonstrated around the different creatures that haunt the darkness and the work Malice and her colleagues have to undertake to defeat the rogue ones, but also because of the underlying themes and threads that hit on so many subjects. Family, commitment, what it means to belong, what it means to trust—MacTague covers them all and in writing that's so powerful it took my breath away at times.

It's another winner from MacTague, who is rapidly becoming one of my all-time favorite lesfic authors.

-Rainbow Book Reviews

This book is absolutely brilliant. It is filled with memorable characters and a plot that will keep you coming back to it even when you know you should be working or sleeping or doing something else. MacTague really got into her head and gave us a beautiful account of what it would be like to be a werewolf. It was so wonderfully done that I now have a massive book crush.

- The Lesbian Review

Heights of Green

What a rip-roaring sequel this is to *Depths of Blue*! There are layers within layers in this book, and the subtle ways they are revealed is brilliant in its execution. It's clear something is going on, but MacTague teases this out, strand by strand, and brings it all to a stunning ending. There's politics, intrigue, action, and lots of emotion. Both Jak and Torrin's actions and reactions are explored in just the right amount of detail alongside the story itself, and it's a fantastic blend. The book finishes on a great cliffhanger, ready for book three, and I can't wait to get started on that.

-Rainbow Book Reviews

The ending had me standing on my feet. Reading it had me pumped and the teaser at the end did nothing to slow my heart rate down. The way Jak's and Torrin's journeys split apart and then come back together had me turning pages so fast I got a digital paper cut and those SOBs hurt! But it was worth it.

-The Lesbian Review

Vortex of Crimson

I thoroughly enjoyed the story and the characters that Lise MacTague has drawn in *Depths of Blue*. The world building is top-notch and the back stories of the characters are told in such a way as to move the story along and not in a pedantic, expository way. I would recommend anyone who likes a good sci-fi book give this a try.

-Lesbian Reading Room

Depths of Blue

This is a proper sci-fi/action/adventure story with two very strong female leads and I absolutely loved it! Both Torrin and Jak are kickass women, and that was such a refreshing change—there's no tough butch here rescuing a weak femme damsel in distress. They can both look after themselves and they therefore have a lovely tension between them from the start. This is part one of a trilogy and I cannot wait to get into book two—I love MacTague's story-telling, her narrative and descriptive skills, and the universe she's created. Excellent lesbian sci-fi, of which there isn't enough, so this is a brilliant addition to that genre.

-Rainbow Book Reviews

…absolutely a must-read novel. Lise MacTague has a really refreshing take on this genre. Her world is well created and different enough to make it interesting. Her story moves at a good pace, lingering only on important moments. Her characters are both gorgeously written, full of insecurities and real.

-The Lesbian Review

Other Bella Books by Lise MacTague

Five Moons Rising
Demon in the Machine

On Deceptions Edge Trilogy
Depths of Blue
Heights of Green
Vortex of Crimson

About the Author

Lise writes speculative lesbian fiction of all flavors. She has written a space opera trilogy, a steampunk novel, and this paranormal urban fantasy series. She grew up in Canada, but left Winnipeg for warmer climes. She flitted around the US, before settling in North Carolina where the winters suit her quite well, thank you very much. Lise crams writing in around her wife and kids, work, and building video game props in the garage, with the occasional break for D&D and podcasting. Find some free short stories and more about what she's up to at lisemactague.com.

HUNTER'S DESCENT

Lise MacTague

BELLA
BOOKS
2019

Copyright © 2019 by Lise MacTague

Bella Books, Inc.
P.O. Box 10543
Tallahassee, FL 32302

All rights reserved. No part of this book may be reproduced or transmitted in any form or by any means, electronic or mechanical, including photocopying, without permission in writing from the publisher.

This is a work of fiction. Names, characters, businesses, places, events and incidents are either the products of the author's imagination or used in a fictitious manner. Any resemblance to actual persons, living or dead, or actual events is purely coincidental. The publisher does not have any control over and does not assume any responsibility for author or third-party websites or their content.

Printed in the United States of America on acid-free paper.

First Bella Books Edition 2019

Editor: Medora MacDougall
Cover Designer: Sandy Knowles

ISBN: 978-1-64247-072-7

PUBLISHER'S NOTE
The scanning, uploading, and distribution of this book via the Internet or via any other means without the permission of the publisher is illegal and punishable by law. Please purchase only authorized electronic editions, and do not participate in or encourage electronic piracy of copyrighted materials. Your support of the author's rights is appreciated.

Acknowledgments

Thanks as ever to my small but mighty army of alpha and beta readers: Lynn, Christina, Amy, Brooklyn, and Fern and Shari. Thank you especially to Brooklyn who has taken on the unenviable task of alpha reading my manuscripts. I couldn't do this without your excitement and demands for the next chapter.

Many thanks to my amazing editor, Medora MacDougall, for being willing to take a look at the manuscript while it was definitely less than polished, and again after I was finally able to figure out the plot. Not that there weren't a few holes, but it is thanks to your eagle eye for inconsistency that we were able to fill those and create what I hope is an entertaining yarn.

Thanks to the entire crew at Bella for giving lesbians their own voice in publishing, and for including mine in that chorus. Our stories deserve to be told and I'm honored to be a part of that.

Thank you to Sandy Knowles for being willing, once again, to work with me on the cover. This one took my breath away when I saw it.

Lynn, thank you for putting up with my writer brain and for guarding my writing time. I love you more than I can say, and your support is a big reason I continue to write. Your feedback is always invaluable. My stories and my life would be all the poorer for your absence.

Finally, to my readers: thank you so much for reading my work, and for reaching out and letting me know what you think. I love hearing from you. Your feedback and enthusiasm are contagious and keep me coming back to the keyboard to start on the next story.

Dedication

For Amanda McLoughlin and Julia Schifini of the Spirits Podcast. I listened to your podcast heavily while researching this book, and many of the creatures and mythological beings found within are based on folklore you discussed. Liberties and inaccuracies are all my fault. Thank you for inviting me and your listeners along into a multitude of worlds every week.

CHAPTER ONE

Malice struggled forward, her hands groping through the darkness. She reached toward something, but what, she didn't know. Pale hands clamped down around her wrists. The skin sloughed off the unyielding digits in chunks. They pulled at her, but she resisted, trying to dig her heels into the hard ground. She knew where this led. She didn't want to move ahead anymore.

Tears prickled at her eyelids, then rolled down her face.

"Mal," a soft voice said. It stretched out her name, the syllable becoming something dark and malevolent. It was definitely not how Ruri said it.

"Mal," it said again.

She yanked back on the hands that were pulling her forward inch by inch.

"Did you miss me?" Stiletto's face filled her vision, a crazed grin spreading from ear to ear. Her skin was chalky and so dry it had cracked, revealing something dark and moist beneath.

Malice tried to scream, but all that came out of her mouth was a pitiful moan. Hands grabbed her upper arms. In vain, Malice tried to shake them off. Stiletto couldn't be stopped. She wouldn't be stopped. Malice raised both hands to strike, depending on every ounce of extra strength her altered physiology afforded her.

"Holy crap!" Ruri threw herself to the bed as Mary Alice's open hand knifed through the air where her head had been a second before.

"Oh no," Mary Alice said. The words were stupid, she knew that, but there was nothing else to say as her world coalesced around her. The loft was bright, lit by the winter sun through the loft's row of windows. She blinked, trying to get her eyes to adjust to something other than impenetrable darkness.

"Are you back?"

"I…think so?" Mary Alice shook her head, then looked down at her hands. "Did I hit you?"

"Not for lack of trying."

"Oh." She pulled in a deep breath, centering herself in the moment and allowing the last of the dream to slide away. *If it's a dream, why does it feel so real? Why can you remember it so clearly? Stiletto is gone. She can't hurt anyone anymore. You saw to that.*

Warm arms wrapped around her shoulders and Ruri pulled her close. "Bad dream again?"

Mary Alice nodded.

"That's the third time this week. Maybe you should find a therapist to talk to. Or a shaman."

"No." Mary Alice shook her head with as much emphasis as she could muster. "No religion. Of any kind." Shrinks were far worse than priests in her estimation. Both peddled a sad sack of tricks, none of which would help her. Sleeping after a run was supposed to be the cure. She'd been trying to work herself to exhaustion over the past few weeks. The dream didn't come when she was so tired she was ready to fall over, but no longer, it seemed. Ruri helped. She wrapped her hands around her lover's forearms and held her in place, taking comfort in the feel of Ruri's skin warm against her own.

How quickly she'd learned to rely on the strength that Ruri loaned her without thinking about it. Her golden wolf-woman made it easy, but what would happen if that crutch went away? *Am I in love with her?* It wasn't the first time the question had crawled through her brain. It had a tendency to crop up at the most inopportune times. She squeezed her eyes shut, not wanting to examine any of the thoughts more closely? *Why can't I just relax and take what she's offering me?* Lord knew, she wanted to.

"Do you want to talk to me about it?" Ruri nuzzled her face down into the crook of her neck.

"There's nothing to talk about. I was trying to get through the dark, but there was something awful in there with me." Her subconscious wasn't exactly subtle. Mary Alice didn't have to dig too deeply for the root of her nighttime restlessness. It was ironic. Killing Stiletto was supposed to bring her some peace of mind. Instead here she was trying to pull herself together after yet another night of fractured sleep. For all intents and purposes, the woman had disappeared off the face of the earth. Uncle Ralph had seen to it. The fiery ambulance wreck had been a bit of overkill as far as Mary Alice was concerned, but when it came to her handler, she had long since ceased being surprised by the lengths he would go to keep their existence a secret. No hint of the Hunters, one of the US Army's elite monster-hunting soldiers, could make its way to civilians. Not even to those who might mourn them.

"It's fine. I'm fine." She tried to push Ruri's arms away gently, but Ruri tightened her arms, holding her tight.

A spiteful buzz on her bedside pulled her out of Ruri's comforting arms.

"Now what?" Mary Alice reached over and snagged the phone. She froze as soon as she saw the laughing death's head on the display. She angled it so Ruri could see it. "Uncle Ralph." She took a deep breath and drew her thumb across the screen. "What do you want?"

* * *

Even if Ruri hadn't seen the phone screen, she still would have known "Uncle Ralph" was on the other line. No one else could bring such unhappiness to Mal. Anxiety flowed off her in a spiky wave. Contact from Mal's government handler usually meant a major disruption to the fragile routine they'd started. Ruri had only met the man once. She made sure never to come under his eye again. If he found out that a wolven was carrying on a relationship with one of the Hunters designed to wipe them out, it would go badly for Mal. And yet, every time he called, Mal picked up the phone and went right back to work.

"I hear you." Mal's normally expressive voice was flat. "Yes. No. I'll need a couple days." She paused, waiting for Uncle Ralph's response.

As hard as Ruri tried to listen in, she couldn't quite make out what Ralph's response was. Her wolf might have had a better chance of it, but her human ears weren't quite up to the task. She hoped he was merely checking in, but she suspected it was another job. They'd had scarcely a moment to rest these past few months, and she'd hoped they might have a few days just the two of them. Now that didn't seem likely. The strain was starting to show; Mal had barely touched her latest sculpture. It hadn't been difficult to figure out that the artworks her mate created were as much therapy as they were cover.

She got out of bed and pulled a loose robe around her naked body. There was no point in waiting around if she couldn't listen to both sides of the conversation. Her stomach rumbled, an artifact of their long run only a few hours before. Ruri puttered around the kitchen, pulling together a warm breakfast of scrambled eggs and ham. Mostly ham for her, with only a few spoonfuls of eggs. She made sure the ham didn't come in contact with Mal's breakfast. The Hunter refused to eat meat, though Ruri had seen her nostrils flare on more than one occasion when she'd had a particularly rare cut of steak.

Mal Nolan. Even after living with her for months, Ruri felt like she'd only scratched the surface when it came to her enigmatic mate. Oh, she was attentive and warm, but always at a remove. So often, when they were together, her eyes gazed at something deep inside her own mind. Mal wasn't quite distant, but neither was she completely present.

That wasn't how it was supposed to be. Mated pairs practically lived in each other's pockets. She'd been longing for that type of closeness with someone for so long, but with Mal, it was completely one-sided. She had to feel the bond. How could she not? Mal blazed like a beacon on her internal landscape. Ruri would never lose her; it wasn't remotely possible. But if Ruri was gone, would Mal notice?

She poked at her half-eaten slab of ham and sighed.

The clatter of a plate against the granite of the kitchen island pulled Ruri out of her funk. Mal sat across from her; she nodded her thanks for the eggs before scooping up a big bite.

Ruri stared at her, using the weight of her gaze to push Mal into talking about her conversation with Ralph. Watching Mal was never a chore. Her dark hair was loose at the moment, a state it was almost never in. It fell forward, brushing the tops of her shoulders and conveniently obscuring chocolate brown eyes that Ruri never tired of looking into.

"Uncle Ralph has a new assignment for me," Mal finally said. "I'm going to go away for a few days. I don't know how long exactly. You'll stay behind to keep an eye on Cassidy."

No way. This isn't happening. How could Mal even suggest such a thing? A knot expanded in Ruri's chest, driving breath from her lungs and keeping her from pulling a full breath. The wolf bristled beneath her skin, and she had to relax her mouth after her lips peeled away from her teeth. Ruri drew herself away from the wolf, maintaining enough mental separation to keep her from forcing the shift into wolf form. The wolf resisted her efforts, trying to muscle her way into Ruri's body. Her muscles trembled on the edge of cramping, just short of initiating the transition. It was a testament to how worked up the wolf was that it was this difficult to resist her, even with the full moon still a few days away.

This won't work, Ruri tried to tell the wolf. *I have to talk to her, convince her this isn't the way.* The wolf paced within her, not content to listen to her words, not when it meant their mate would be far from them. *Let go.* All at once, the wolf stopped fighting. Ruri looked down. Mal had leaned across the table and had her hand wrapped around Ruri's arm. The wolf quieted at her touch, and Ruri took advantage of the lull.

She sat up straight while watching Mal closely. She had no doubt that her eyes glowed the brilliant gold that betrayed how close she'd come to shifting. Well, let them glow. Mal needed to know that what she'd just tried to propose had no chance of succeeding.

"I don't think so," Ruri said. "There's no way in hell."

"It's not up for discussion." Mal let go of her arm and looked back down at her plate. She scooped some eggs onto her fork but didn't lift them to her mouth.

"You may not think so, but I go where you go. You're not leaving me behind." The wolf shifted restlessly within her. They were in complete agreement.

"I can't take you with me on assignment. You know that."

"I don't see why not. I've gone with you on other hunts."

"That's different." Mal placed the fork carefully back down on the plate. "There are all sorts of people here. Where I'm going is much less populated."

"And where is that exactly?"

Mal cut her a sideways glance, then turned her gaze back to her plate. "Wisconsin."

"Wisconsin? There are still people in Wisconsin?" Ruri shook her head. "Why on earth would you go there?"

"It's part of my territory. I do venture outside of Chicago, you know. I'm responsible for a large chunk of territory."

"Then why haven't you been out there before?"

"I have, only not recently. Smaller incidents are handled by Black Ops squads. There doesn't tend to be a large concentration of supras outside of large population centers. Your people don't like to be far from food sources."

"They're not my people." The denial was automatic, but true. Her people had disappeared after Dean was killed. Her Alpha had held their pack together, and though most of them now acknowledged Cassidy as Alpha, she wasn't included. The kicker was that most of that was Mal's fault. Maybe not directly. She doubted Mal had set out to be her mate. *How nice would that be?* a small voice in the back of her head asked. The wolf whined in agreement, and sorrow washed through them, carrying away the words she'd been planning to say.

Mal shrugged. "Either way. The point is, I don't often leave the city, but it happens. Something's going down in the North Woods. I need to look into it. You need to stay behind."

"Don't tell me what I need." Ruri struggled to keep the fury from her voice. Despite her best efforts, heat still colored the edges, enough that Mal glanced her way, an eyebrow raised. *What I need is you*, she wanted to say, to scream until Mal finally understood. "You can't leave me here."

"What's to stop me?"

Does she even realize how cruel her words are? Ruri looked out the front window, not really seeing the lines of grey concrete that stretched out in front of them. *She must not*, Ruri decided. *She can't.* "I can follow you to the ends of the earth. I will follow you to the ends of the earth. You *can't* stop me." It wasn't a threat; it was a simple statement of fact.

"Someone needs to keep an eye on Cassidy."

The shift in tactics wasn't unexpected and Ruri almost smiled. This was a much easier argument to overcome. "Your sister doesn't want or need an eye kept on her. She has two dozen wolven at her back. If anyone needs someone at their back, it's you." Mal took a breath to respond, but Ruri refused to yield her advantage. "How pissed off do you think Cass will be when she finds out you set me to 'watch over her'?"

"Pissed." The response was quiet. Mal gnawed at her lower lip.

"You know it. And you know I'm coming with you."

"I'll think about it."

"Think about it all you want." Ruri pulled her robe more snugly around her. "It doesn't change the fact that I'm coming along. You can't order me around. You're not my Alpha, you're my…" She stopped before saying "mate." Mal got nervous when she used the word, though she didn't understand why.

"Girlfriend." Mal sighed deeply. "You're my girlfriend, and I don't own you."

"No, you don't."

"Fine, you can come. But you can't get in the way."

"I won't. So what's going on in Wisconsin that we need to take care of? Demons? Vampires?" *Please, let it not be wolven.*

"All I know is kids are dying. Teenagers. Five of them so far, and no one knows why."

"No one there knows, or your people don't know?"

"Both. Uncle Ralph has no idea what's going on, but he doesn't think it's normal. So I get to check it out and see if it's related to supra activity."

"Were there injuries?"

"I don't think so. He's going to send me the dossier. We'll get the details then."

"All right." No injuries means it was unlikely wolven were involved. Wolven kills tended to be messy, especially for ones newly turned. So there was that. The woods sounded nice, and her wolf enjoyed the snow. She'd wanted time with just the two of them, maybe this was it.

CHAPTER TWO

The loft seemed empty when they got back from picking up supplies for their trip. Mary Alice closed her eyes and extended her senses, feeling her way for anything different, out of place. Nothing registered. Of all the changes the government's program had wreaked upon her body, that was the strangest. Heightened senses and increased strength and endurance all made sense for someone in her position, but her other "gifts" weren't so obviously helpful. Even the lab-coated ghouls who'd created them hadn't been aware of all the abilities her cohort would end up with. She'd been trained on some, but others had been left for the Hunters to figure out on their own. This extra sense of touch was one of the latter. Sometimes it felt like she was mapping an area on her skin, or at least that was the best way she had of explaining it. But there were no suspicious itches or dead spots that would indicate her home had been penetrated. She tossed her keys into the small bowl on the kitchen island. The burner phone she used for work sat in its cradle next to the bowl. It was dark, without the blinking light that would indicate she had a message.

"We need to leave soon," she said. "Pack what you'll need for a few days."

"That won't be hard." Ruri shook her head slightly and headed for the bedroom. She'd shown up those months previous with her possessions in one small duffel bag and had only added a few items since then. Her stuff took up one and a half drawers in Mary Alice's dresser.

Mary Alice watched after her for a moment. She'd been withdrawn since their argument. She wasn't sure why Ruri was surprised she'd tried to leave her behind. It only made sense, after all. She'd had a point about Cassidy, however. Should she call her? She was going to be out of town for a few days. If Cassidy needed her, she wouldn't be able to drop everything and come to her aid. *How many times has that happened since the time you couldn't save her?*

Ignoring the voice in her head, Mary Alice pulled out her phone and swiped her thumb across the screen. Her contact list held two numbers, one for her sister and one for her mother. Ruri didn't have a phone and had ignored all her hints that she might want one. Her finger hesitated over the two contacts for a moment, then she stabbed down at Cassidy's name.

The phone rang and rang. Before the events this past Halloween, it would have been beyond imagining that Cassidy would be without her phone. Things were different now. Cassidy was different now. They were only a few days out from the next full moon. She could easily be in wolf form, out with her pack at that very moment. The sun was above the horizon, its winter-weak rays barely penetrating the frosted glass of the loft's windows. Surely her sister wouldn't be so silly as to be on a run at this time of morning.

"Hello, Mary." If Cassidy's voice had been any more neutral, Mary Alice might have mistaken her for a robot.

"Cass." Mary Alice smiled wide, desperately trying to inject some warmth into her tone. "Hi, how are you?"

"I'm fine," Cassidy said warily. "What's up?"

"Nothing much. Have you talked to Mom since Christmas?"

"No. Did you call to tell me to call her?"

"Well, no—"

Cassidy broke in before she could finish. "Good, because I don't need another lecture about missing out on family stuff since I'm not going to visit her for Easter break."

"I wasn't going to lecture—"

"It's not like I'm not busy here. There's a lot of shit to handle running your very own pack of wolven, you know."

"I know that—"

"So I don't need to hear about how I'm letting the family down. I'm keeping my new family together, no matter what happens or who comes sniffing around."

"Sniffing around? Who's been—"

"I may be young and new to being Alpha, but I'm not an idiot. I know when someone's messing with me."

Enough was enough. If Mary Alice let this go on much longer, Cassidy was liable to work herself into a froth, then hang up.

"Cassidy." Her sister didn't seem to hear her and kept on ranting. "Cassidy. Cassidy. Cassidy." She kept her voice steady, making sure not to raise it. Yelling at her would only put her in a worse mood, which wouldn't help anything. Maybe it was good she wouldn't have to try to set Ruri on watching her.

As if the thought had summoned her, Ruri stuck her head around one of the dividers that served for walls in her home. Mary Alice smiled faintly at her, as she continued to repeat Cassidy's name. Her girlfriend certainly was easy on the eyes. The way her honey-blond hair, barely long enough to touch the top of her shoulders, glowed even without the benefit of the sun's rays made her want to dig her hands through it. Amber eyes caught the light and flashed a hint of gold back at her, and an answering smile hovered around the corner of her mouth. Ruri's jawbone demanded Mary Alice assault it with kisses, and the barely perceptible pulse along the column of her throat was almost impossible to resist. Mary Alice wanted to cover it with her mouth and nibble on the supple flesh until Ruri moaned in her ear.

With a start, she realized there was no sound at the other end of the line.

"Are you quite done?" Cassidy asked dryly.

"Uh, yes."

"Is Ruri there?" Laughter lurked along the edges of Cassidy's tone. Try as she might, Mary Alice couldn't find it in herself to be offended.

"Maybe."

Cassidy barked out a laugh.

"Now that I have your attention," Mary Alice said, choosing to ignore her sister's amusement, "I'm heading out of town for a few days."

"For work?" All traces of amusement were gone now, as they always were when Cassidy had to confront the reality of her sister's job as a Hunter.

"Yes. What's this about you being messed with?"

"Oh that." Cassidy sighed. "It's nothing. Just some probing to see if I'm strong enough to hold onto my pack, or so I've been told."

Mary Alice sat up, her eyes locked with Ruri's. "I can see about putting off my trip if you need me." Ruri padded into the room, barefoot as usual. She leaned against the island and watched Mary Alice closely.

"There's no need. I can handle this. If I can't, then I don't deserve the pack."

"Maybe Ruri could—"

"No." The response came from two mouths at the same time. Ruri pushed herself away from the island and left the room, her back stiff.

"Fine. I'll be back when I'm back. Call Mom." Mary Alice terminated the call and followed after Ruri. It felt good to get the last word in for a change, even if she'd done so by hanging up on her sister. She had to get a handle on her life. If she continued like this too much longer, something was going to get the drop on her while she worried about Cassidy or Ruri.

"Wait." She reached out for Ruri's hand but missed when her girlfriend twitched it away.

"Why should I wait?" Ruri spun around and continued walking backward. "It's obvious you want me out of your hair."

"That's not true." Did she want Ruri out of her hair? Things would be simpler, that was for sure. She could go back to the way things were before Ruri had come into her life. That was what she wanted, wasn't it? Simple. Lonely. That's what waited for her without Ruri. "I do want you."

"How can you ask me to stay away from you then?" Unshed tears trembled in Ruri's eyes.

Sorrow reached up and grabbed her by the throat. Mary Alice swallowed hard, but couldn't force out the words she wanted to say.

"I mean it. Literally. How can you ask me?" Ruri lifted her arms to cradle the back of her own head. "You shouldn't be able to. You shouldn't even be able to think it. We're mates, Mal. You. Are. My. Mate." Her voice trembled as she bit the end off each word. "How can you not know what that means?"

Mal. The nickname hung between them. No one else called her that. It was Ruri's name for her, no one else shared it. The single syllable was almost unbearably intimate, hanging between them as a symbol of everything she would lose when her time with Ruri came to an end.

"I'm not…" The words were raw, squeezed around the bundle of razor blades taking up residence in her vocal cords. "I can't be your mate." Oh god, but that hurt to say, but no matter how much it hurt, it was true. Mary Alice swallowed and was surprised not to taste blood.

Ruri bent forward as if Mary had just buried her fist in her belly. When she looked up, her face was wet. "You are," she whispered. "You will always be. Wolven mate for life."

"Ruri," Mary Alice said quietly. She reached out and scrubbed tears from Ruri's cheek with her thumb. "I care for you. A lot. But I can't be your mate. I'm not wolven. I'm not fit to be anyone's partner. I've done things. Terrible things."

"You're wolven enough." Ruri grabbed hold of her hand and held it to her face. The tears continued unabated. "I can feel it. My wolf can feel it. You have to let yourself feel it."

"I would love nothing better, but you're not safe around me. No one is."

"Safety is an illusion. You aren't."

"I don't deserve what you're offering me." Mary Alice pulled her hand back. She turned away, biting down on the inside of her lip hard enough for flesh to crunch beneath her teeth and hot blood to bathe her tongue. If she really cared for Ruri she would say something to drive her away, but as much as she wanted to, as much as she believed it was the right thing to do, the words wouldn't come. "I don't deserve you" was all she could say in a broken whisper.

Ruri wrapped warm arms around her. They felt so good and Mary Alice longed to let herself relax into the refuge they promised, but she couldn't.

"Tell me," Ruri whispered in her ear. "Tell me what's got you so wound up. What you've been hiding from me since that night."

"I can't." Ruri would never look at her the same way again if she knew. Mary Alice could not handle seeing the love Ruri felt for her turn to hatred or, worse yet, disappointment. The wolven put so much stock in pack, in family. Stiletto hadn't been family, but she was a compatriot, a sister-in-arms, and Malice had ended her. It hadn't even been an honorable death. She'd suffocated her while Stiletto was unconscious through the actions of another. If there was a more ignominious way to die, Mary Alice wasn't sure she could think of one. Killing Stiletto was supposed to bring her some peace of mind; instead Malice couldn't get her out of her head. When Ruri left her, her isolation would be complete. She would be left all alone with her ghosts, and her squadmate would lead the pack. *What did you expect after killing Stiletto? Puppy dogs and rainbows?* She shook her head in a vain attempt to silence her own mocking question.

Ruri didn't push it. She simply held Mary Alice against her until the tears stopped flowing. It was times like this when she thought she might be able to love the wolven. And that only made Ruri even more dangerous.

"That email from Uncle Ralph is probably in my inbox." With infinite care, Mary Alice extricated herself from Ruri's embrace. "I need to get the logistics nailed down so we can get out of here."

Ruri squeezed her closer for a moment, then let her go. "You have to talk to me sooner or later," she said.

Mary Alice lifted one shoulder in noncommittal response. It was unlikely, and right now what she really needed was to be alone to gather herself and try to figure out what she was going to do with this whole mess.

She made her way to the living area to pull up her email. The exposed beams overhead provided something to stare through while her mind wandered, not seeing the screen of her laptop. Toenails clicking against concrete pulled her away from her thoughts. Ruri's golden wolf settled herself in front of the couch. Mary Alice slipped her feet into the tiny gap between Ruri's belly and the floor, allowing her feet to become nice and toasty. She sighed and relaxed against the beat up back of the sofa and opened up her marching orders.

CHAPTER THREE

Ruri shifted again and pulled at her seat belt for what had to be the fourteenth time in the past half hour. Wind whistled through the window cracked open on her side of the truck. Mary Alice set her jaw and glared through the windshield. If Ruri squirmed once more, she swore she would yank the steering wheel from the column, toss it out the window, and consign them both to a fiery wreck in the trees lining the road. It was sunny, which was nice enough but made for treacherous patches of black ice along the two-lane highway through this stretch of Wisconsin's woods.

Ruri put one foot against the dashboard and pushed back against her seat.

"Do you have to do that?" Mary Alice tried to smile to take the sting out of the clipped question, but she was pretty sure all it looked like was a baring of teeth.

"Do what?" Ruri started bouncing her knee up and down. She turned to look out her window and tapped her fingertips against the door.

"Move. Constantly." Mary Alice firmed her grip on the wheel, being careful not to crack it. "It's very distracting."

"Sorry. I'm not very good being cooped up for a long time." She stopped tapping her fingers, but the knee kept bobbing away.

"Clearly."

Ruri's grin was cheeky. "We could stop at the next gas station. Get some snacks, give me a chance to stretch my legs."

"That'll be the third time this trip. We've only been driving for four hours."

"I wouldn't say no to some cheesy poofs."

"Another bag?"

"Or I could go back to entertaining myself."

"No. That's fine. We'll stop at the next one I see."

"Or we could talk."

Mary Alice froze, then rolled her shoulders to cover her discomfort. "About what?"

"Anything you want. We don't have much in the way of conversation. Usually your mouth is occupied doing…other things."

"I don't recall you complaining." Mary Alice bit her lower lip and shot Ruri a sideways glance. Ruri's grin had gone from cheeky to positively wicked, and it kindled a fire low in her belly.

"I'm not. But since you can't do anything like that now, we might as well get some different uses from that talented mouth of yours."

"If you want." As long as they didn't talk about the night they took down MacTavish, Mary Alice was willing to discuss most things. "What do you want to talk about?"

"So here's something I've been wondering for a while. Why do you call us supranormals? Pretty much everyone else refers to us and the other groups as supernatural. Or paranormal."

"Umm." Mary Alice chewed at her lip. She was never sure how much of her work she should share with her lover. The question seemed fairly innocuous and she couldn't see how it would hurt to answer it. Ruri already knew about her existence and that she answered to a government handler. "It helps weed out those in the know among humans. When paranormal became popular, people started talking about it a lot more. And then there's that TV show. From what I gather, the term helps ping on people who might know things they shouldn't."

"How would your bosses even know what people are talking about? Are they trolling Tumblr looking for people posting about supranormals?"

"Among other things, I'm sure."

"Other things? Like what?"

"I don't think I should answer that question."

"Oh my god, they're listening in on phone conversations, aren't they?"

"I have no idea." But she had her suspicions. It was vanishingly unlikely they weren't. She certainly operated as if they were.

"They totally are." Ruri shook her head. "That's awful. Your bosses are assholes."

"You won't hear me disagreeing." Time to change the subject before Ruri started pressing her on even more sensitive topics. "How did you get changed?"

Ruri didn't say anything for a long time. "That's not a question wolven ask each other," she finally said.

"Why not? It seems pretty basic."

Ruri smiled, but it didn't touch her eyes. "The question is basic, the implications…less so." She sighed heavily. "There's an unspoken bias in a lot of packs. Like an idea that wolven who were born that way are somehow better than those of us who were made."

"Interesting. Like cradle Catholics."

"Cradle Catholics?"

"Same idea. Catholics who were born into the church are more Catholic than those who converted. It was a whole big thing at my parents' church when we were kids. It always seemed backward to me. Like how is lucking into something by being born to the right parents better than going out and intentionally doing it?"

Ruri smiled. "That's a decent analogy then. Though I doubt it leads to many brawls in the middle of mass."

"Not so much." She had a mental flash of Father Antonio rolling around on the floor with one of his parishioners. "It would have made church a lot less boring."

"I bet." Ruri went silent again. She stared out the front windshield for a while. "I'm not ready to talk about it with you."

"Oh." The pang of disappointment went deeper than Mary Alice had expected. "That's okay." It didn't feel okay, but what else was she supposed to say?

"So what's your origin story?"

"Origin story?" Mary Alice raised an eyebrow. "You've been reading too many comics, you know that?"

"You're the big badass Hunter. I'd like to hear it."

"It's going to have to wait. Here's the gas station I promised you." They didn't need gas, but Mary Alice needed a few minutes to get her head on straight before telling this story. She pulled into the small gas station. It looked just this side of rundown. If the pumps took credit cards, she'd have been surprised. "Go get some snacks, then we'll get back on the road. I want to get there before dark."

For a moment, she thought Ruri was going to argue, but the wolven stalked from the car and into the shabby convenience store.

She stood next to the truck while the tank filled. The sun wasn't nearly far enough above the trees for her. In the dark it would be even harder to see patches of ice on these roads. Still, she'd have stopped twenty more times if it meant Ruri wasn't so twitchy. Her eyes staring into the darkness of the trees across the road, Mary Alice chewed on a cuticle and tried not to think about Cassidy and who might be hassling her. She sighed and waited for the pump handle to click off, then followed Ruri inside.

Her girlfriend leaned on the sales counter across from a woman who had to be pushing fifty. Her round face was animated as she chatted with Ruri. She had that effect on people, Mary Alice had noticed. Well, most people. Some unfortunate souls realized deep down inside that they were within arm's reach of a predator. Likely, they never realized exactly what put them off about her. This woman apparently had no such awareness.

"Oh yeah," she said with barely a glance in her direction before turning her attention back to Ruri. "The folks up in Hawthorn County are powerful strange."

Mary Alice gravitated toward the snacks while trying to look like she wasn't paying attention. Hawthorn County was hard to pin down. She'd done her research. She knew it was the least populous county in the state, with barely more than 3,000 residents. Apparently that population swelled a bit with summer tourists, but not as much as other counties in the area. It was full of trees, but the logging industry was practically nonexistent. As far as she could tell, the economy was extremely depressed, which is probably how the county had been picked for a juvenile reformatory camp.

"Really?" Ruri sounded like she was hanging off the clerk's every word. "How so?"

"They're just queer is all. Keep to the themselves. I know people call this the ass end of beyond, but they really live up to that name." She tsked. "You need to watch yourself up there. Why you heading up again?"

"It's a bit of a vacation for us."

Mary Alice cringed, wishing she hadn't said that. The less anyone could associate her and Ruri in a way that suggested they were in a relationship, the safer the wolven would be. She snagged a bagged snack and brought it up to the cash register.

"This, the gas on the pump outside, and whatever she's having," Mary Alice said.

"The two of you, is it?" The woman gave them a long look.

They didn't have time to deal with her rural homophobia. "We're sisters," she said, sounding bored.

"Adopted," Ruri said with a wide smile.

"Oh," she said. "Of course." Still, something had thrown her off. She rang them up quickly but offered no more conversation.

"Thanks," Mary Alice said after getting her change. "Come on," she said to Ruri and left, not waiting to see if her girlfriend followed her.

CHAPTER FOUR

"I wish you hadn't done that." Ruri said as she pulled on her seat belt.

"Done what?" Mal bent forward and took a long look at the rapidly darkening sky. Dusk was almost upon them.

"Shut down that conversation. She was telling me about Hawthorn County. That could have been useful, but instead you came stomping up and got all glowery. Do you even realize you do that?"

"What do you mean? I was perfectly polite."

"Sure you were, in that 'I'm going to rip out your tongue and feed it to you' way you have. I don't know, Mal. There's something about you that puts off humans sometimes. It's like they know you could take them out without even thinking about it."

Mal got very still. She tightened her grip on the steering wheel and glared into the pools of light the headlights left on the asphalt. "Other humans," she said.

Ruri blinked at her. The comment made no sense to her.

"Don't you mean I put off other humans?"

"Oh, that. I mean sure. I just think of you as one of us most of the time." She held up her hand as Mal took a breath to refute her. "It's not a bad thing. You know more about us than almost any other human alive." She stressed "other" slightly. "That's all I mean. Don't get too bent out of shape about it."

Mal's shoulders slumped. She seemed to deflate in front of Ruri's eyes.

"I don't even know how human I am." The words were so quiet that without the benefits of her wolven side, Ruri might have missed them.

She waited for a follow-up, but Mal stared fixedly through the windshield at the empty road in front of them.

"What do you mean by that?" she finally asked when the silence had stretched to breaking.

A grim smile twisted Mal's lips. It was a relief that none of it touched her eyes. "You don't know about Hunters at all."

"Of course not. It's not like I have anyone who will tell me about your little club." *Including you,* she thought at Mal with all the fierceness she could muster. Surely she'd proven her trustworthiness by now.

The smile warmed into something more genuine. "I'm going to catch fire if you keep glaring at me like that." Mal sat up straighter and shifted in her seat, unlimbering herself as best she could in the confines of the truck. "It's not pretty. Are you sure you want to know?"

Ruri opened her mouth to say "Of course," then closed it. Mal wasn't asking as a piece of useless formality, of that she was certain. The question deserved serious thought and she paused to give it just that. Try as she might, she couldn't think of anything Mal might say that would change how she and the wolf thought about her. Mal had kidnapped Ruri to help her sister, who she was keeping in a metal box to "protect" her. There wasn't much worse than trapping a fledgling wolven in a cage, no matter how pure her motives had been.

"I do," Ruri said. "And thank you."

"Don't thank me until you've heard the story. Here goes then." Mal took a deep breath.

"I was recruited away from my Army unit after we saw combat with some things that took out half our platoon. I survived, but I got a good look at them. Said some stuff I shouldn't have during my debrief. A few weeks later, I was transferred to a new company. They said we were an experimental Special Forces unit." She laughed. "They weren't lying. They really put the experiment in experimental." Her knuckles were sharp under her skin from the force of her grip on the steering wheel. Discomfort rolled off her in spiky waves.

Ruri reached over and placed her hand gently on Mal's thigh. She rubbed the tense muscle in slow circles.

Mal continued. "It was fun at first. We worked in small teams, did a lot of hand-to-hand work. That's always been some of my favorite. Then it got weird. They brought in a whole bunch of old bladed weapons. That's when I wielded my first sword. Machete first, then I got a liking for the katana. Stiletto went for long knives. She picked up dual-wielding like she'd been born with blades for hands. There were four of us in our team. We bunked together, ate together, trained together. Hell, some of us even fucked together.

"Then the docs arrived."

The muscle under Ruri's palm went from tense flesh to stone. She sneaked a quick glance at the dashboard. The needle on the speedometer was rising rapidly.

"Maybe you should slow down a little bit, babe," she said quietly, accompanying the suggestion with a gentle squeeze to take out any hint of censure.

Mal twitched, then eased off on the gas until they were back down to something resembling the speed limit. She took a deep breath. "So the docs came about a month in. At first they just ran a bunch of tests. Some of the other recruits were reassigned. My team was so proud because all of us had made the cut. We weren't proud for long. Our team was in the middle of the group. They started with Alpha and worked their way down. The mess hall was emptier every day as each team went back in for more 'testing.' No one came back. By the time they made it to us, the remaining teams were seriously discussing going AWOL.

"We knew when it was our day. We'd seen it coming for a week and a half. They loaded us into the back of a van and drove us off base. There were no windows, we had no idea where we were going, but we were in there probably an hour. Cerberus timed the route and marked the turns, but it didn't end up doing him any good. We were let out in a loading dock, no way to see where the building was. They had us change into hospital gowns and put us on gurneys, then wheeled us into a big operating room. They pushed the sedatives."

Mal stopped talking. A muscle in her jaw jumped rhythmically as she wrestled with her memories. Her hands flexed on the wheel and the muscles in her leg twitched.

"Maybe you should pull over," Ruri said.

"Maybe I should." Mal slowed, then pulled onto the shoulder of the highway where the snow didn't seem too deep. Her movements were jerky as she engaged the truck's parking brake. She grabbed Ruri's hand in her own and held on tight.

"Are you going to be okay? If it's too much, you can tell me another day."

"I'm not okay, but we're halfway there. I don't know if I'll be brave enough to tell you again. We might as well take advantage of what courage I have now."

"If you say so. But I'm right here. You're not doing this alone."

"I know." Mal nodded and loosened her grip on Ruri's hand. "It's the only thing keeping me going. Here goes. It's all downhill from here." She let go of Ruri completely and took another deep breath. "The sedatives weren't enough. I came awake halfway through. The pain…" She squeezed shut her eyes and clenched her fists.

If Ruri hadn't known better, she would have sworn Mal was feeling that agony right then. She took one of Mal's hands and gently pried open the fingers, then laid the palm against her chest. She took a deep breath, then let it out slowly, followed by another, then another.

After a few cycles, Mal matched her breathing. The deep creases around her eyes softened. "The pain went on and on. I started screaming and someone rushed over and gave me something else through the IV hooked up to my arm. I wasn't in a place where I could take much in, but I know I was surrounded by bags. There were tubes going into me in more places than I could count. I wasn't the only one screaming.

"When I woke up, I felt like I'd had food poisoning for a month. I could barely move. My muscles were pretty much useless. Every sense was in overload and I couldn't separate things out. The first time they brought me food, I threw up all over the bed. Eventually, I was able to handle things better. I started to eat again and regained my strength faster than I could imagine. I went from being as weak as a newborn to walking in two days. I started up physical training again two days after that. That's when I found out me and Stiletto were the only ones to survive from our team. Cerberus and Mangonel were the biggest and in the best physical shape of us, but neither of them made it.

"After that, we were reunited with the other teams who had gone before us. They'd all lost at least half their members, some more. From then on, we trained as individuals. They pitted us against each other at every turn. Instead of working in groups, everything was a competition, and the punishment for losing was…intense and administered by our opponents. I did what I could to get through it. When they told us the truth of what we would be fighting, we all just went with it. It was easier than thinking about what they'd done to us, what they were still doing to us. Our days were training, class, more training, then bed. No breaks. No downtime. I guess they were trying to get us used to our new capabilities and out in the world as fast as possible."

"Do you know what it was they shot you up with?" Ruri had a feeling she knew the answer to the question, but she wanted to hear Mal's hypothesis. Heat grew behind her eyeballs as her anger threatened to burst out of her control. The wolf paced within her. She wanted to latch on to the neck of whoever had hurt their mate and not let go until they were dead. Ruri didn't disagree.

"Best we could figure, when they would let us talk without supervision, is that it was a cocktail of supra DNA. Set a supra to catch a supra." She shrugged. "It makes a certain amount of sense. We couldn't go to toe to toe with any of you physically without it."

"That's insane." Now it was Ruri's turn to moderate her own breathing. Her wolf still shifted inside her and she was almost angry enough to let her out. "So they juiced you up physically, but made no efforts to figure out what makes us tick."

"What does that have to do with anything?"

"Everything! You once told me that almost all you Hunters have some sort of addiction, right?" Mal nodded and Ruri bit the inside of her lip to keep from losing her temper completely. "They built you up into teams, then put the DNA of pack creatures inside you and forced you to become solo killing machines. Does that sound like a good idea to you?"

"Over half of us died. I don't think they ever planned on having us work on our own, but circumstances dictated otherwise."

"How can you make excuses for them? They *killed* your packmates. They took your brothers and sisters away. Losing their pack can drive wolven insane. Sometimes they get better, sometimes they don't." Ruri wanted to hit someone, preferably Uncle Ralph. She was unlikely ever to see him again, but if she did there was a good chance he wouldn't survive the encounter. Her wolf wrapped around her core in agreement.

"I…" Tears welled up in Mal's eyes. She rubbed her palms into them, obliterating the teardrops before they could fall. "I…"

Ruri pulled Mal into her arms. It was a little awkward in the truck's cramped cab, but Mal buried her head against Ruri's shoulder. Hot tears dripped onto her skin, but Ruri paid them no mind. The wolf rubbed herself along the underside of her skin where it touched Mal. She swore she felt an answering echo of fur from her mate. Or did she want to feel it now that she knew some part of Mal was wolven?

It didn't matter. All that she needed to do was offer comfort to the woman who cried against her, shoulders heaving with bone-deep sobs. Mal's reaction to Cassidy's predicament made even more sense now. There was no way she would have permitted the loss of another pack member.

After a while, Mal's sobs subsided. Somewhere along the way, night had fallen. Not even a hint of blue colored the western horizon anymore. It was a good thing the engine was still running, or they would have been quite cold by now.

"Are you all right?" Ruri asked. She brushed a lock of hair back from Mal's forehead.

"Probably not," Mal said. She sat back into her seat. "But I feel better. I guess I needed that."

"What you need is to pop Ralph on the chin next time you see him. Better yet, let me lure him into the woods. I'm sure I know a few wolven who would love to take care of him. We can supervise, make sure it's done right. And slowly." Her jaws ached at the thought.

Mal laughed, a surprised hiccup that was half sob. "You're a bloodthirsty thing, aren't you?"

"He has it coming if he knows half of what they did to you. If he was there…" Ruri made a show of cracking her knuckles. "Let's just say we won't need any other wolven to do what needs to be done." She smiled, showing sharp teeth.

"He wasn't," Mal said. "Not that I know of, anyway. I'm pretty sure if he had been there, he'd be happy to lord over me what he knows of the process that I don't. Knowledge is one more pressure point."

"Lucky for him."

Mal looked around, taking in the darkness outside the truck. "We need to get going. I don't plan on bunking down in the woods tonight, not when I have a hotel reservation."

"If you say so. If you need more time, we can stay here as long as it takes."

"No, I'm good." She smiled and seemed looser than she had in weeks, but already Ruri could feel her walls going back up.

Would she ever let her guard down completely? They'd gotten close, Ruri could feel it, but they still weren't there. Still, she was cheered immensely that Mal had made the effort to tell what was obviously an incredibly difficult story. They would be all right, and she had another piece of the puzzle that was her mate.

CHAPTER FIVE

Ruri turned over to get away from the hand shaking her shoulder. The hotel bed was soft and she had no particular desire to leave her cozy nest.

"Get off," she said into the pillow, but the hand paid no attention whatsoever.

"Time to wake up," Mal said all too sweetly. "Come on, sleepy-butt."

"Sleepy-butt?" Ruri peered up at her mate through one eye. "What time is it?"

"Almost six a.m." Mal shook her again. "Come on, we have work to do, and we need to go over our game plan."

"So early." She tried to pull up the comforter, but Mal wrested it from her hands.

"This isn't like you. Usually you're up before I am." She sat back and studied Ruri carefully. "Are you coming down with something?"

"I don't think so, but then I haven't had a cold since I was turned." Ruri pushed herself up. "I'm exhausted. Must be the car ride. Or the talk."

"Maybe." Mal completely ignored the mention of her revelations in the car. "I can leave you here if you're not up to joining me, but I could really use your nose on this one."

"I'm up." She stretched, reaching toward the stucco ceiling above them. The vertebrae along her back popped almost as one. "Oh, that's good."

"I'll say."

"Lecher." Ruri tossed her pillow at Mal's head. She hadn't missed the look Mal raked down her naked chest.

Mal leaned to one side and allowed the pillow to go whizzing past her. "I can't help it. You're amazing to lech over. You'd better get some clothing on or we aren't going to head out to the camp any time soon."

"Is that such a bad thing?" Ruri arched her back. Delight filled her at the look on her mate's face.

"The sooner we wrap up the job, the sooner we can head home." Mal leaned forward and gently bit Ruri's collarbone. "Then I'll pay some very close attention to you, for a very long time."

A shiver emanating from the bite made its way down her spine and found a home low in her gut. "I can't wait," Ruri said, her voice raspy.

"Then get dressed. Hopefully this is a natural occurrence, if a strange one."

"I'm going, I'm going." At least the room was fairly warm. Ruri snagged her bag on the way to the small bathroom. She hadn't engaged in anything active the previous day so there was no need to take a shower, but a good tooth brushing was in order. She'd skipped it before bed, and now her mouth tasted like the inside of a boot. After that, she attacked her hair with a brush and combed out any budding snarls in quick order. A shirt and pants were next. After a moment of thought, she pulled out a plaid flannel. She'd stolen it from Mal, and it still smelled of her. Ruri's wolf stirred at the deep whiff of their mate as Ruri held it to her nose.

Finally feeling a little more awake, Ruri stepped back into their room. Mal hovered over the papers spread across the table in the corner by the window. Ruri tried to keep her mouth closed, but the wide yawn was too much for her.

"I hope this won't be too boring," Mal said without looking up.

"I'll manage." Ruri craned her neck to see what was going on. Mal hadn't said much yet. All she knew was that some kids had died. "Is this them?" She leaned in to get a look at the five photographs in a row at the top of the table.

"It is. Carlo Diaz, Simeon Sawyer, Latawna Cummins, Jermayne Tremaine, and Shejuanna Jackman. Each died of natural causes overnight, Jackman most recently. Each was found in his or her bed by the camp staff."

"What kind of camp has campers in the middle of winter?"

"The kind of boot camp that caters to the justice system. This is a juvenile detention camp, one of those 'tough love, last chance' kind of deals. From the files, they have a combination of private clients with parents who can't control their teenagers and court-ordered campers."

"That explains why they look so surly, then." The photos were mug shots. One boy had an amused look on his face, but the rest of the pictures held the same mix of anger, fear, and resignation. They were painfully young for such a combination of emotions.

"I want to interview the camp staff. Obviously, I can't tell them who I am, so Uncle Ralph's gotten me some ID for the CDC."

"CDC?"

"Centers for Disease Control. You haven't heard of them?"

"Wolven don't get sick much, so no." Ruri shrugged. "We don't pay much attention to government types unless they're actively interfering with our lives."

"I guess not." Mal shook her head and pointed at the papers. "Here's the layout of the camp. There are the kids' barracks, staff cottages, admin building, and the training field. The whole place is surrounded by an eight-foot fence. I'm sure the staff thinks the place is impenetrable, but in my experience, if there's a way out the inmates will have found it. I want you to keep an eye on everyone I talk to. Make sure they're telling the truth, that sort of thing. Also, keep your eyes open for anything that looks out of place."

"Do you want me in fur or in skin?"

The look Mal gave her made her insides quiver, but her voice was mild when she answered. "Let's start with skin. I'm going to tell them you're my assistant. If you see anything that requires a closer look, we'll come back later for a good long sniff." She shrugged. "Like I said, this could be nothing."

"How often does your handler send you out for nothing?"

"Not often, but it has happened. I don't know if you've noticed this, but he can be a little paranoid."

"Just a little."

"Great. So I'm Marion Tipple and you're Annie Smith for our little jaunt. Try not to say too much."

"Marion Tipple? What are you, British?"

"Leave off. I don't control what Uncle Ralph gets me. Chances are there's an actual Marion Tipple at the CDC and she's conveniently out of the office right now."

"All right, Miss Tipple. It is Miss, isn't it?"

"See, this is why I need you to stay quiet. You start snickering at the wrong time, and they'll know something's up for sure."

Ruri stifled another yawn behind her hand. "Yes, Miss Tipple, ma'am."

"Now that we have that figured out, let's head out. I want to catch them before they settle into their daytime routine." Mal scooped up the papers with efficient motions and stashed them in a nondescript manila folder. Ruri had no doubt that everything was in perfect order.

"I'm right behind you," she said.

* * *

Ruri and Malice sat quietly in the waiting room of the administration building. It was far older than the barracks they'd seen on the way in. It seemed likely that it was an old farmhouse, converted to its current state without too much effort, and the clapboard barracks had been thrown up fairly recently. The guard at the front gate hadn't given them too much trouble, though he had insisted on checking their credentials and calling ahead to announce them. The middle-aged woman at the large wooden reception desk watched them as she spoke into the phone in hushed tones.

"Mr. Shockley will see you in a few minutes," she said after she hung up. "I'm Mrs. Brewster, his assistant. May I get you something to drink? Coffee, water?"

"I'm fine," Malice said. "How about you, Miss Smith?"

"No, thank you, Miss Tipple. Mrs. Brewster." Ruri smiled faintly.

"Thank you for your hospitality," Malice said. She smiled, trying to look like she was grateful. "You don't sound like you're from around here. Have you been in the area long?"

"Only a year or so," Mrs. Brewster said. "I'm from Milwaukee myself. I lived there all my life before moving up here."

Malice nodded. "I thought so. You don't have the North Woods on your tongue."

"And thank goodness for that."

"I bet the locals were glad for the jobs you brought to the area, though. Can't be too much to do around here, employment-wise."

"You'd think so, but they keep mostly to themselves. We've had to hire from further south or over Twin Cities way." Mrs. Brewster looked over at her computer screen. "It doesn't really matter, though. We all stay here, and our supplies get trucked in, mostly from Tomahawk."

"Is that so?" Malice pulled out a small notebook and scribbled down a quick note to herself. "You don't get them through La Pointe?"

"No." Mrs. Brewster stared at her for a moment. "Is that important?"

"Could be." Malice shrugged. "Or it could mean nothing."

"You're here about the tragedies, aren't you." It wasn't a question. Mrs. Brewster watched them both levelly.

"We are."

"I'm glad you're here. We have nothing to hide, and we did nothing wrong. Those poor kids died on their own. We run a tight ship, but we don't do anything to hurt anyone. We're trying to save them, not harm them."

That was a strange tack to take for someone trying to cover something up. In Malice's experience, if there were shenanigans going on, people didn't express enthusiasm for the presence of authorities. Maybe they'd be able to shut this down quickly and head back home.

"That's enough, Mrs. Brewster," a male voice boomed. "I'm ready to see our guests." A tall man whose muscle had run somewhat to fat at the onset of his middle years paused next to her desk. He clapped Mrs. Brewster on the shoulder and nodded to them. Silver hair caught the light from the lamp on the desk. He walked toward Malice, his hand extended. "I'm Brandon Shockley. You must be the representatives from the CDC."

"We are." Malice stood and took his hand, not blinking when he tried to crush it. "I'm Marion Tipple, and this is my assistant, Miss Smith."

Shockley nodded at Ruri. "Very good. Why don't you come into my office and I'll see what I can do to convince you that nothing is amiss and put this whole sad mess to bed."

CHAPTER SIX

From everything Ruri had seen and smelled, Shockley and Mrs. Brewster were genuinely concerned for the kids in their care. They truly believed their influence was the only thing that could turn their lives around, and the recent deaths had shaken them both to the core, especially Shockley. As he gave them the background of the facility, it never seemed to bother him that he'd seen Mal's credentials, but Ruri hadn't produced any. They took Mal at her word that Ruri was her assistant.

"I'll need to see everything," Mal was saying, "especially the sleeping quarters and the mess hall."

"Of course," Shockley said. "Whatever I can do to help."

She wouldn't have put money on it, but Ruri would have sworn before two packmates that Shockley was innocent. So far, it all looked like this was some freak circumstance. With any luck, they'd be leaving soon.

Shockley held open the back door and gestured for them to precede him. A group of teenagers in matching sweats strode past them in two columns, their breaths combining in a cloud of vapor that dispersed quickly in the cold air. They didn't quite march, but they moved almost as one. A few faces turned to watch them but quickly turned back to the front when they saw her looking. Not surprisingly, the majority of the kids weren't white. Humans put too much stock in the color of skin. Wolven didn't have that problem. The color of the fur meant next to nothing. What mattered was loyalty and willingness to cover the backs of the wolven to your left and right. Or in her case, to make sure her mate knew she was there to support her no matter what.

The campers had disappeared around a corner when the sound of running feet crunching through the snow reached her ears. A young human careened around the corner, using one hand to push off the side of the building. The other hand was clapped to her head to keep her from losing her too-large knit cap. She skidded to a stop in front of their little group, her eyes wide. They darted guiltily toward Shockley, then away.

"Late again, Rabbit?" His voice was stern.

"Not yet, sir." She bobbed up and down on the balls of her feet. "I will be if I don't move."

"Then move," Shockley said. "But don't run." He had to raise his voice to reach her as she broke into a sprint.

Rabbit slowed down to a pace a hair slower than her previous breakneck pace, then was gone around the corner.

"You'll want to speak with her," he said. "Shejuanna's bunk was next to hers. The latest…unfortunate."

Ruri pulled out her notebook and scribbled *Talk to Rabbit* halfway down the page. Mal nodded approvingly. So far, this undercover stuff was pretty easy. All she had to do was keep quiet and let Mal do the talking. That made it easier for her to keep an eye out.

"We'll inspect the mess first," Shockley said.

There was nothing amiss in the mess, nor in the rest of the buildings they surveyed. Neither Ruri nor her wolf smelled anything that seemed unusual or out of place. From everything Ruri could see, Shockley ran a tight ship. She sensed no particular animosity toward him from the staff they ran into and far less than she would have expected from the teenagers here. There was certainly some resentment, but that was to be expected. They were being held here; no matter how much Shockley talked about saving them, it wasn't their idea.

Their last stop was the barracks. Ruri noticed nothing untoward there either. Mal stopped to take samples every now and again, running a cotton swab over various surfaces, then passing them over to Ruri who dutifully played her part, noting each one in her little book and then placing them in labeled snack-size plastic bags. By the time they reached the last of the barracks, her jacket's front pocket bulged with them.

"Here is Shejuanna's bunk." Shockley stopped in front of a pair of bunk beds in the middle of the long room. "I had Mrs. Brewster pull Rabbit from class to answer questions."

The short teen they'd seen earlier pulled herself to something approximating military attention. She stared past them at the far wall.

"Thank you, Mr. Shockley." Mal held out her hand to him. He took it, engulfing it in his much larger hand. "You've been very helpful. We'd like to speak with—Rabbit, is it?—privately. I'm sure you understand."

"Ah, well." He withdrew his hand and wrung it in the other. "As she's a minor and I'm technically her guardian while she's in our facility, I can't allow that to happen. You recognize that, don't you?"

"I do." Mal chewed her lower lip, mulling over the problem. "I also can't have you influencing a witness." She raised a hand to forestall his objection. "Not that I think you would. Why don't you take a seat over there? You'll be able to hear any questions I ask, but I don't have to worry you'll try to intimidate her."

"That's very reasonable, thank you." Shockley took a seat on a footlocker a couple of bunks away.

Mal smiled at Rabbit. "You can take your ease. Is Rabbit your given name?"

"No, ma'am. It's Julietta, but that doesn't really seem to fit." She smiled, teeth white against light brown skin. "Rabbit Romero has a ring to it, ya know?"

"That it does." Mal indicated the bunks with her chin. "You shared that bunk with Miss Jackman?"

"Sure did. Hers is the upper, she offered to take it and everything." Rabbit's face took a downward cast that looked foreign on her face. Her lips had looked more natural when smiling. "She was a good bunkmate. Never snored."

Ruri took a discreet step closer to the bunk.

Mal looked over at her. "Good idea, Miss Smith. Why don't you take some samples?"

"All right." She took the proffered swabs and did a thorough examination of the mattress and sheets. Someone had made the bed; it looked like no one had slept there since then.

"Were you the one who found her?" Mal asked Rabbit.

"I did. Shook the bed to get her up for reveille, but she didn't move. When I climbed up to get her, her eyes were open, staring at the ceiling."

"Did you touch her?"

"Course I did. She was cold."

"But you didn't feel sick or funny in any way after that?"

"No. I felt fine." Rabbit shrugged. "Still do."

Ruri leaned closer and inhaled the combined scents of the sheet, mattress, and detergent. She sniffed again, more deeply, but there was still no sign of anything untoward. "When was this?" she asked.

Mal looked up, startled that she'd said something.

"Three mornings ago." Rabbit closed her eyes.

If the girl had died in this bed that recently, there should still be some sign of her passing, but Ruri couldn't smell even the smallest hint of death. "Is this the same mattress she was found in?" She directed the question at Mr. Shockley, who looked down at his hands.

"I'm afraid so. There were no fluids on the mattress, so we left it."

"I see." She studied the offending mattress a little longer.

"Anything else, Miss Smith?"

"Not right now." She stared at Mal for a moment, willing her to understand what she'd discovered. Or rather the lack of anything she'd discovered.

Mal didn't appear to notice and went back to grilling Rabbit. Over the next fifteen minutes they established that Shejuanna hadn't acted sick, hadn't eaten anything strange, and had participated fully in the physical conditioning that seemed a staple of life at camp. Occasionally, Shockley would have something to add, but mostly he let Rabbit talk. He didn't seem concerned that she might let something slip. Finally Mal sat back and looked at Shockley.

"I think that's everything I need from Miss Romero."

"Very good. Rabbit, head on back to class."

"Yes, Mr. Shockley." Rabbit crammed the knit cap onto straight black hair and didn't wait to finish pulling on her jacket before trotting out the door.

"Is there anything else you need to take a look at?"

"Nothing here," Mal said. "How often do you take your campers outside the fence?"

"They go for long runs only once a week, with the way the temperature is right now. In warmer weather, they go out two to three times a week."

"Is there a chance Shejuanna picked something up in the woods?"

"I suppose anything is possible," Shockley said. "The staff keeps a close eye on them when they're outside the fence, though."

"We should still take a look. Is there any way you can mark the typical routes your campers run? Say on a map."

"Absolutely." He stood and headed for the door. "I'll be right back."

"Do you have Shejuanna's things around? We need to gather samples and eliminate them as a possible vector."

Mr. Shockley pointed to a footlocker barely visible under the bed. "Her family hasn't been up to collect her or her things. Everything she had is in there."

"Very good. We'll take a look."

He hesitated for a moment, but when it was clear Mal had no more requests, he continued out the door.

"What do you think?" Mal asked when he was out of the room.

"I don't think they're hiding anything. Everything seems legitimate. Shockley is a little overenthusiastic, but there's no indications he has something to hide." Ruri hesitated.

"What is it?"

"Shejuanna's bunk."

"I was going to ask you. You seemed really interested in it."

"It doesn't smell right. There's no way anyone died in that bed, especially not three days ago. Either they switched out the mattress or something else is going on. And it wasn't a new mattress. It smelled like someone had been using it. I don't know if it was Shejuanna or not. I can check her stuff against the mattress to find out for sure."

"Good call." Mal chewed over her revelation. "I didn't expect that. We need to figure out if that's the right mattress."

"And if it is?"

"I wanted to take a look at the corpse anyway. It should still be at the morgue, but I imagine not for much longer." Mal straightened, her mind made up. "Why don't you check out the mattress again, then we'll take a look around the perimeter. I was going to say we should check the woods, but that can wait for another day. The morgue will be our next stop after the perimeter. I'll keep an eye on the door while you sniff out what's going on with the bed. You should probably shift."

Ruri tried not to roll her eyes but wasn't as successful as she could have been.

With a grin, Mal reached out and punched her upper arm. "I saw that. Guess I shouldn't be telling you how to do your business."

"I think I can handle it," Ruri said, her voice so dry it was a good thing there were no open flames nearby.

Mal fished the long wooden case out from under the bed. She rooted around for a minute, then tossed a T-shirt over to Ruri. "Will that work to get her scent?" At Ruri's nod, she headed for the front door of the barracks. "Just hurry. I don't want anyone catching us. I'll send him off, then let you out."

"Okay." It could get dicey, but she trusted her mate to be true to her word. At least Mal wasn't telling her that she couldn't help. It was progress, however small.

Ruri left the shirt on a chair, then poked around until she found the showers. There was no reason to shift in the middle of the common area where the girls who bunked there would have to clean it up. The fluid from the change would be easier to clean here.

"Hey, Mal, I mean Miss Tipple, we should make sure we run the showers before we take off. I'm about to leave some traces that can't be avoided." Ruri pulled off her clothes and stacked them in a small pile in the corner.

"Good point." Mal grinned. "I'm glad you keep me around for my opposable thumbs."

"And other things." She spared a quick glance at her mate over her shoulder as she readied herself for the wolf, who was strangely excited to emerge. She barely had to coax her out. Ruri dropped to all fours as her muscles cramped all at once.

"Oh god—" She barely had time to gasp before her muzzle had lengthened past the ability for human speech. Fluid burst from her gums as teeth lengthened and shifted. The fur rippled from her skin in a continuous wave from her nose to her tail, pushing more liquid from the skin. Not having had the time to brace herself, she toppled awkwardly to her side when the change abruptly ended.

"Are you okay?" Mal hissed from the doorway. She spared a glance for Ruri, then went back to watching for Shockley.

Ruri whuffed quietly in assent. She scrabbled to her feet, finding it challenging to get a grip on the slick porcelain tiles. Globs of fluid stuck to her fur and she shook herself with contained violence. Mal was far enough away to avoid being tagged with the spray. She'd learned through experience to give Ruri room. The fluid from the change wouldn't hurt her, but it was sticky and viscous and the Hunter didn't appreciate having to clean it off.

Ruri made her way back to the bunks, then sniffed the floor by Rabbit and Shejuanna's bunk, getting a flavor for the two girls. Rabbit's scent was dry and light, reminding her of snake scales. Shejuanna's scent wasn't as distinct, having had days to dissipate. It was strange: darker, of the depths of the forest and blooming flowers. An odd combination. Ruri stood still, rolling the girl's scent over her tongue as she panted. She stuck her nose in the shirt on the chair and got another whiff of blossoms and loam. Satisfied that she had a read on the dead girl's scent, Ruri sat back on her haunches and looked at the top bunk.

"Shit, I didn't think of that," Mal said from where she stood. "No sight of him yet. I can lift you up."

The wolf's annoyance at the suggestion matched Ruri's. She shot Mal a look of disgust and leaped to the top bunk, landing gracefully.

"Message received." Amusement danced below Mal's serious response.

If Ruri had been in skin form, she would have shaken her head.

Mal turned her head, then opened the door. "There you are," she said as she went out the door. Ruri felt exposed in the middle of the large bunk room, standing on top of the bed. Still, Mal said she would keep him out and she could only trust that she would.

Time to get back to work. She bent to inhale the covers. Shejuanna's scent lingered here, though the detergent on the sheets confused the scent somewhat. It was even more floral. Ruri stuck her nose into the sheets, inhaling deeply. The smell of flowers clogged her nose, overwhelming all other scents until it was difficult to make out anything else. They sneezed violently, trying to drive the invasive scent from their nostrils. It didn't work. Ruri felt like she was being drowned in an avalanche of petals. The wolf had also had enough, and she jumped from the bed. Pawing at her nose, Ruri tried to clear the cloying smell.

Finally, something else came through. Mal stood next to her, and her scent filled her nostrils, soothing them both.

"Is it hers?"

Ruri nodded.

"Then why doesn't it smell like her death?" Mal stared out a nearby window. "It doesn't make any sense, unless there's something about where she actually died that they're trying to hide. The photos showed her on the bed. I'll have to ask the coroner if there's any evidence she was moved. Let's get out of here."

Ruri and the wolf were in complete agreement on that front. Best to leave the scent of flowers behind. Damn humans and their need to perfume everything to the edge of beyond and back. Ruri waited while Mal retrieved her clothing. The Hunter turned on the showerheads above the worst of the fluid from the change while the wolf made her way to the door, still following Rabbit's scent. Rejoining her, Mal opened the door and she stepped out into the cold. It didn't penetrate the wolf's fur in the least. She lifted their head and inhaled deeply, the crisp wind washing away the final remnants of flowers. She turned to follow Rabbit's trail. It led away from the rest of the compound. Ruri stared at the nearby fence. Why would Rabbit head that way when she'd been told to go back to class? She doubted very much class was being held in the woods.

"What is it?"

Ruri didn't respond, couldn't respond. She put her nose down and inhaled Rabbit's scent. The notes of snake were more intense, pushing away the light and dry overtones until the snake was dominant. That was exceedingly odd. People's scents didn't change like that, not usually. Something was going on. They stepped out onto the packed snow. It was time to find out what Rabbit was up to.

CHAPTER SEVEN

Mary Alice hadn't expected Ruri to hang a left out the door. There was nothing to grab onto aside from her tail, an option which she doubted would have been well received. The wolven bounded over a low snowbank and into snow marred by lines of footprints. Those met up with more footprints. There was quite a path worn into the snow around the inside of the fence. The guards made rounds there frequently, it appeared. Ruri kept her head down, nose hovering above the ground, and followed the path for a short way, then stopped. She looked back at Mary Alice, then stared pointedly at the fence. Mary Alice joined her but couldn't see anything. With a look that could only be one of exasperation, Ruri leaned forward and nosed at the chain links. They shifted. Instead of being attached to the post, someone had been careful to cut the links where the damage wouldn't be noticed.

Mary Alice pulled back the fence and Ruri eeled her way through the opening. Mary Alice, her five-foot-three frame being closer to that of their quarry, followed easily, replacing the cut fence as best she could behind her. When she turned around, Ruri was already quite far down the trail, following a narrow path of footprints that disappeared into the underbrush.

Mary Alice hustled to catch up with her girlfriend. The woods were quiet around them. That in itself wasn't unusual. When

Ruri was around, the forest often seemed to hold its breath as the animals who called it home went to ground to avoid attracting her attention. Something about the silence felt more watchful than she was accustomed to, though. Her hand strayed to the hilt of her katana; she cursed when she encountered only fabric. Of course she didn't have the sword; that would have been difficult to explain to Shockley.

"Ruri," she hissed. "Wait up."

Ruri flipped an ear back toward her but kept going. If anything she picked up the pace. Mary Alice swore under her breath and hustled to catch up to her.

"If you want to go poking around out here, you should really wait until I can get a weapon."

Ruri sniffed and glanced at her ankle without stopping. Sure, she had a knife strapped there, but that wasn't going to help much against anything large. Of course, anything they came up against would also have to contend with an angry wolven.

They continued further, following the trail that by now only Ruri could pick out. The snow under the trees was harder for Mary Alice to read, and it was old enough that it had been tamped down in places by the relentless freeze-thaw cycles of winter. Ruri didn't hesitate and showed no sign of pausing. Whatever she'd found, she was determined to pursue, and all Mary Alice could do was follow along.

Fifteen minutes into their unscheduled hike, Ruri stopped. She perked both ears forward and stared deeper into the woods.

"What is it?" Mary Alice crouched next to her and strained her eyes to see what had finally stopped the wolven. "I don't see—" A flash of movement stopped her mid-sentence. Something slipped between the trees up ahead. It was grey, and if she didn't miss her guess the same shade as the sweats worn by the kids from the camp. "Ah." *What are they doing out here?*

That was likely the same question that had motivated Ruri. She moved her hand over to caress Ruri's chest for a moment before moving slowly forward. It was harder to stalk when snow covered the ground and obscured sticks that would break underfoot, but the snow also muffled those same sounds. She moved as quickly as she could to close some of the gap between them and the figure ahead. She didn't want to tip whoever it was off. Ruri flowed soundlessly over the ground and around a small stand of trees to her right, keeping pace easily. As they got closer, Mary Alice was surprised to see that the figure wasn't alone. There were two other teenagers a little further on down the path. The one they'd seen first was the tallest of the bunch, the other two were shorter, one by quite a bit. Straight dark hair hung down her back.

"Rabbit," Mary Alice breathed. So that's what had set Ruri off.

The kids made their way through the woods without any thought of pursuit. They probably figured that since they'd cleared the area around the camp, they were home free. They arrived at a narrow stream and made their way down onto the ice that covered it, then followed it west.

The ice cracked alarmingly under Mary Alice's feet when she stepped down onto the slick surface. It felt like her feet might slide out from under her at any moment. The snow and dead leaves on top only served to make her footing even more treacherous. She took a couple of experimental steps forward. Ruri passed her on the right, the ice not slowing her down a bit. It would have been nice to have claws at a time like this. Mary Alice found that the edge of the frozen rivulet was rougher and she did her best to stick to that and not to lose her balance. The kids had still shown no indication that they knew they were being followed, and she wanted to keep it that way.

They made their way downstream for another six or seven minutes. She and Ruri kept far enough back that they could barely see the kids, but they didn't dare get closer. When the stream curved and they lost sight of them through the trees, Mary Alice had to fight the urge to rush ahead. Ruri's nose would keep them from falling too far behind. She had to trust the wolven. She could trust the wolven. It was a luxury she was still coming to terms with.

Ahead, the trees thinned out, then disappeared altogether. They'd followed the three kids to the bank of one of the many small lakes that dotted the countryside. This was going to be a problem; there was no cover out there on the frozen lake. Mary Alice stopped at the tree line and knelt, holding her hand flat and lowering it. She hoped Ruri would understand the hand motion. They hadn't practiced with this one. It was the same one she'd been taught in basic. Ruri didn't hesitate, going right to her belly.

They were in luck; the kids hadn't gone far. In fact, they walked to the edge of the ice. The only thing that distinguished the shore from the water was the end of the shallow slope. The tall teen pulled a string sack off his back. The three huddled for a moment while he distributed the contents. As one, they turned and placed the objects from the sack on the ice. The bright red of a can of Coke stood out like blood on bed sheets. The other objects were harder to make out. One was in a rectangular box of bright teal, the other in a squat bottle, perfume maybe?

The kids settled back on their heels and waited, staring out over the water. Then, in response to a signal Mary Alice couldn't see, they stood and walked forward onto the ice. Between one step and the next, they disappeared.

They reacted at the same time, Ruri slingshotting forward as Malice yanked the knife from the sheath at her ankle. They sprinted down the shallow incline to the water's edge.

* * *

There was nothing in front of them, except for a thin slit in the air that shimmered like waves off hot pavement in the dead of summer. Ruri and the wolf didn't think twice. She launched herself at the strange disturbance, then stumbled when her paws encountered rock instead of slick ice. Bare stone rose around them, from floor to ceiling. Water dripped in the distance and reverberated back to her. A moment later, Mal appeared beside her, going to one knee and pausing to take everything in. She took the change of scenery in stride. Her head snapped around in the direction of the three youngsters.

Two of them knelt, heads bowed, the third stared back at them.

Rabbit's eyes were wide. "Oh shit," she mouthed.

"Who dares?" The words resounded around them, the syllables overlapping in echoes that grew louder with each repetition until the cave hollered outrage at them. The youngsters raised their heads and shifted to the side, giving Ruri a good look at the being whose anger threatened to deafen them.

A naked woman shifted and swayed; with each movement shells and bells clacked and jangled. Lines of pale beads contrasted sharply with her dark skin. More beads festooned her hair, wrapping it around and holding it down at the front in defiance of where it sprang to life at the back, surrounding her head in a nimbus of kinky curls.

Ruri started forward, then paused when she realized what accounted for the woman's strange movements. Instead of legs, from the waist down she had the body of a large snake. The coils brushed against each other, raising a dry susurration that replaced the fading echoes of her voice. It sounded like they were surrounded by snakes, but when she looked to one side, then the other, there was nothing but damp rock.

Mal moved more quickly than Ruri thought possible. Every time she thought she had a bead on her mate's abilities, something would happen to prove her wrong. The woman was layers upon layers, and one day Ruri hoped she would find what was at the center. Ruri got low to the ground and circled wide, around the kneeling younglings. She made sure to keep in line with Mal. The creature would have to split her attention between them, leaving one of them free to strike.

Nothing could have prepared her for the column of water that spun itself into existence from the pool behind the snake creature. The small waterspout unspooled itself and slid sideways, cutting through the air and striking Mal in the side. It lifted her as it continued and dashed her against an enormous column of rock. The creature turned and hissed at Ruri, her mouth wide, displaying human-like teeth. There were too many of them to be completely human, never mind the snake body.

She stayed low. If the waterspout came back, it wasn't going to get her. Ruri dodged to one side, watching the snake-woman as she swiveled to follow her. She was quick, maybe even as fast as Ruri was in fur-form, but she didn't have eyes in the back of her head. Mal was picking herself up, looking no worse for wear.

Ruri feinted toward the snake-woman, teeth pulled back and a warning growl rumbling deep in her throat. The snake-woman pulled away from her, then struck in a blur Ruri couldn't dodge. Strong arms bore her up and up, then back. The surface of the water rushed toward them. It shone from within, a bottomless glow that promised to take her down into the depths forever. Ruri uttered a panicked yelp, then the water closed over her head. The wolf wanted to thrash her way toward the surface, but Ruri exerted herself, forcing steely calm upon them. She was still being borne deeper, and each thrash, each struggle cost her oxygen she couldn't afford to lose. The water lit her from below, illuminating the bubbles that sprang to life around her and made their way upward. Ruri used that to orient herself, turning around to keep an eye on the surface. As soon as the force dragging her down ceased, they would be on their way.

Should she shift? Her skin form was much better in the water, and with the wolf ascendant it was even more difficult to overcome her instincts. She struggled to clear her mind, to find the peace that would allow the wolf to recede back inside her. It wasn't happening. Her lungs burned and the edges of her vision had already started to darken. Still the wolf wouldn't let her in; she was going nowhere.

They were together for whatever happened. It seemed fitting. Together and never alone.

The piece of her that was Mal's pulsed, giving her the energy needed to stay conscious a little longer, then that too was gone. The edges of her vision collapsed. She needed air. Her jaws unlocked in one last desperate attempt. Even knowing what it meant, she dragged in a breath and choked.

Without warning, the force dragging her down was gone. No longer was she being pulled into the brightly lit depths of that impossible pool; she was being propelled through the water toward the surface that still seemed impossibly far away but was getting closer by the second. Ruri broke the surface in a fountain of froth and was borne to the edge where she was deposited almost gently. Her world snapped into focus as oxygen filled her lungs.

She shook her head and took in the tableau in front of her. The snake-woman hovered protectively in front of Rabbit and the tall youngster. Across from them, Mal held her knife to the throat of the third youngling. Distress smoothed the snake-woman's face into something far softer than the hiss with which she'd confronted Ruri.

"Are you all right?" Mal asked, not taking her eyes from the creature's face.

Ruri pushed herself to her feet and shook the water from her fur. She gave a short bark of assent.

"Good." She pulled the knife tighter to the child's neck. "Now send over the other two."

The snake-woman slid her tail around them. Her face hardened. She was never going to let them go. The youngsters clung to her; they had no desire to go anywhere. The child in Mal's grip fought to get closer to her and Mal had to clamp her arm around the insistent boy.

This was going to end badly.

Now that they were no longer fighting for breath, the wolf didn't hold to her form nearly so tightly. She allowed herself to be pushed down. Ruri collapsed to the ground as the fur pulled back, revealing her bare skin. Her gasp of pain was loud in the suddenly quiet air of the cave. All eyes were on her as muscles twisted themselves back into human shapes and her bones lengthened and shifted beneath her skin.

"Maybe we can talk this over," Ruri said, as much to her mate as to the snake-woman.

CHAPTER EIGHT

Malice gaped at Ruri for a moment, then returned her attention to the snake-thing wrapped around the two kids.

"What are you doing?" she asked Ruri. "Get her."

"Get her?" Ruri walked closer to the snake-thing. "That's your plan? I think we have this all wrong, Mal."

The creature watched Ruri, its torso weaving warily on top of the snake body. It spread its arms behind it, keeping the teenagers contained.

"You're protecting them from us, aren't you?" Ruri said to it. "We won't hurt them. We thought we were rescuing them."

Snake-thing cocked its head to one side. It didn't blink, and with a shiver, Malice realized its eyes were slit and devoid of whites. Pale brown the color of amber stretched from eyelid to eyelid, broken only by a band of dark green through the center. The green matched the color of its scales, Malice noticed with revulsion.

Ruri sat on the floor in front of it. Malice hissed in irritation. She was well within the thing's reach. She readied herself. If it struck at Ruri, Malice would be on it in a second. She might not be able to save her girlfriend, but she would certainly avenge her.

"You're hurting me," the teen in her arms whined. "Let me go. I need to go to Mami Wata."

Mami Wata? What the hell is that? She'd never heard of such a creature. "We're here to take you back. We won't let her keep you."

"She doesn't keep us." He struggled against her. "She loves us."

Ruri had turned her head enough to hear his words. "Is that true? Do you love these children?"

"They are not children." Its voice was accented, one Malice wasn't familiar with. "Your world does not permit them to be children, but I love them as if they are my own nonetheless."

Ruri gestured back toward her. "If we let you have him, will you speak with us? Will you allow us to speak with them?"

"They aren't who they say they are," Rabbit said. She peered around Mami Wata at them, her eyes accusing. "They said they were with the government."

"That part actually isn't the lie," Ruri said. "We aren't with the branch we said we were, though. Or at least she isn't. I'm not government at all."

"Ruri." Malice couldn't keep quiet any longer. None of this was anything close to protocol.

"We had it wrong," Ruri said. "She isn't holding them here. The only ones threatening violence are us. We should hear what they have to say."

Reproach lay heavy in Ruri's voice, chiding her for not thinking of…something. Malice was damned if she could figure out what that was. She'd covered her bases as best she could and had secured a hostage. The snake-woman watched them but its eyes pierced at her, if Malice would let them.

"I will harm neither of you for the duration of your visit if you release my acolyte to me," Mami Wata said. "We can talk, and I will answer your questions truthfully."

Malice hesitated. If she let the boy go, she would have no recourse should the snake-woman attack Ruri. Her girlfriend motioned at her, impatience in the stiff lines of her arm. Malice could almost hear her exasperated "Come on, already" in her head. She took a deep breath and let go of the teen. He stepped forward uncertainly. When she made no move to grab him back, he darted away and around Ruri, settling himself with the others behind Mami Wata.

"Very good," Ruri said. She stood and joined Malice, who finally realized Ruri was completely nude.

"Do you want my jacket?" Malice asked quietly.

"I'm fine. It's plenty warm in here."

"If you say so." It was balmy in the grotto, despite the damp stone walls.

"Why have you chosen these children?" Ruri turned back to Mami Wata.

"They have been discarded by their families. Why should I not take them up when they have been abandoned?"

"Is that what they've told you?" Malice asked.

"It's true," Rabbit said. She ventured away from Mami Wata, but not so far that she couldn't dart behind the creature if Malice made a move. "I was in foster care. The state took me from my grandparents, and they never tried to get me back."

"My mom is more interested in her man than in me," the tall boy said. "When I got in trouble, she let them put me here. She don't care what happens to me."

"And you, what's your story?" Malice asked the third teen.

"He can't talk," Rabbit said. "His daddy beat him when he found him with another boy. Kissing."

The boy balled his hand into a fist and slugged Rabbit on the arm. "Hey."

He scowled at her and shook his head.

"I don't care about that," Ruri said. "I know what it's like to be on the outside." She looked up at Mami Wata. "What do you get from taking them in?"

"Do you find it so hard to believe I would do so out of the goodness of my heart?"

Malice laughed, the sound harsh in her throat. "You're some kind of fae, aren't you? Your kind never does anything for free. You're almost as bad for bargaining as demons."

Ruri's brow furrowed into a faint frown of disapproval. She shook her head.

"You appear to know enough about those on the fringes of human habitation to know how much of an insult that was," Mami Wata said. "Why should I not teach you a lesson here and now? You will not equate me to the fae nor to demons again at peril of your own humanity. Our agreement protects you now, but one more insult and it will no longer do so."

Malice blinked. If Mami Wata wasn't fae or demon, then what was she? She certainly wasn't vampire or wolven, which didn't leave much.

"The question could have been worded more diplomatically, but she has a point," Ruri said. "What do you plan for the children?"

"I will tutor them in the ways of water and healing. When they are of an age, and should they choose, they will put on red and white and be my voice and eyes in the world of humans."

"And have you tried teaching other kids from the camp?" Malice asked.

"I have not. These are mine and no others."

"How did they find you?"

"They came to the shore of my lake. I watched them for a time as they played along the shore. When I revealed myself to them, they were able to overcome their fear and converse. It is refreshing to spend time with mortals who have not yet lost their sense of wonder. They bring me gifts and their love, and I return that love and keep them safe." Mami Wata smiled broadly. "Our pact is mutually beneficial."

"Do you know what killed the other kids?"

"I know of no dead children." Mami Wata shrugged. "But I am not the only one in these woods. I am Mami Wata of Lake Labette, but others make this area home. I should look to them, were I you."

"Others?" Malice leaned forward, watching Mami Wata's face for signs of dissembling or lies. "What others? Others like you?"

"Like me, and yet not like me." She cocked her head, unblinking eyes staring into hers. "Do you have the sight?"

"The sight? What does that mean?"

"It means you can see magic," Ruri said. "I don't have it. Do you?"

"You have more than you think," Mami Wata said. "If she has to ask, she has it not. I can assist in that area." She leaned over to Rabbit and spoke quietly. The teen nodded and made her way to the back of the cavern, past a row of stalactites that reached almost to the floor. Mami Wata turned back to them. "You will want to speak with Reese the Hand for assistance. No one knows the woods and its denizens better."

"Reese the Hand." That didn't sound suspicious at all. "Sure."

Mami Wata inclined her head to Rabbit when she returned. "Take them back to your camp," she said. "Give it to them when they are back." She looked back at Malice.

"All right." Rabbit knelt quickly, her knee barely touching the floor before she jumped up.

"Nothing will help you see clearer, and with that I have no more to tell you," Mami Wata said. "I have answered your questions and truthfully. If you enter my domain again without invitation you shall do nothing more as humans," she inclined her head toward Ruri, "or close to human."

That was obvious enough. If she ever had to come back here, Malice was going to make sure she was armed seventeen ways to Sunday. Mami Wata hadn't even broken a sweat when taking them out. Did snakes sweat? She didn't think so.

Ruri got up and padded across the cave floor to the entrance. "Do you have my clothes?" she asked when they got to the entrance. A blanket of stitched together furs held back the cold.

"They're outside. I dropped them when the kids disappeared."

"I'm not going out there in skin-form." Ruri crouched down and touched her palms to the smooth floor. Her shift into her wolf form was preceded with the usual snap of bone and tendon.

Rabbit stopped dead, her mouth agape as she witnessed Ruri's transformation. "Holy crap," she whispered, her eyes almost bugging from her head. "That is amazing. And disgusting. I didn't notice it so much earlier. I was a little…busy." She shot Malice a look, then backed up when Ruri shook the remaining fluid from her shift off her fur. A slightly iridescent puddle marred the spotless floor.

Nice touch. Mami Wata wouldn't be thrilled about the mess, Malice imagined. She couldn't bring herself to trust the snake-woman. Whoever this Reese the Hand was, she would be damned if she'd look up someone who would probably report their every move back to her.

"Let's get out of here," she said to Rabbit.

Rabbit rolled her eyes, then pushed back the skin blanket. Bright light spilled out around it, outlining her figure, blurring it until there was nothing left, then the blanket fell back into place.

Teenagers are so much fun to deal with. Malice remembered how much of a pain Cassidy had been at that age, and she hadn't even been in a juvenile reformatory camp. She was less of a pain now, but some things never really changed. *Here goes nothing.* She walked forward, Ruri at her side. She held the blanket back for Ruri, then stepped into the teeth of the frigid wind. Ruri seemed not to notice as the wind rustled her fur about. Her ears twitched at the breezes that tugged at them, but she showed no other indication that she felt anything.

Ruri's clothes lay in an untidy heap at the tree line. Malice picked them up and did her best to shake the snow out of them. "Lead on," she said to Rabbit.

"I said I would." She took them over a small hump where a snow-covered sand dune separated the ice from the trees. "This way."

She led them back on a circuitous route, even Malice could tell that, though her woods-craft wasn't the best. She'd gotten training in basic and then some more as a Hunter, but she was much more accustomed to maneuvering in cities. Give her steel and concrete and she was right at home. The trees with their muddled lines of sight were a much greater challenge.

"Wouldn't it be faster to go right through that way?" she asked Rabbit. Malice pointed in the direction she was sure the camp was in.

"It might be more direct, but it wouldn't be faster," Rabbit replied. "Lots of brambles and swampy stuff that way. In the summer, it's completely impassable with the water and everything. It's a little better now, but we'll make better time avoiding it."

"You're the expert."

Rabbit swelled a bit with pride at the compliment. "So is she a werewolf?" she asked, apparently taking Malice's comment as invitation to chat.

"She doesn't like that term. Her kind prefer 'wolven.'"

"But she's like a werewolf, like on TV."

"Close enough." Protocol indicated she should be making sure the girl was in no position to talk about the presence of supranormal beings, but it seemed like they were far past that. Besides, if she broke Rabbit's neck or bundled her up for "reprogramming" at a Hunter black site, Mami Wata was likely to be irritated. Not to mention that it seemed like a crappy thing to do. The kid hadn't done anything wrong that she could tell. Mami Wata might be a strange surrogate mother, but she knew what it was like to look for someone to take the place of a parent in her life. The best choices weren't always obvious, and the worst ones were usually only distinguishable in retrospect.

"How often can she change? If she bit me, would I turn into a werewolf? Is her fur as soft as it looks?"

"Why don't you lead on and can it with the questions? There are things you don't want or need to know the answers for." Malice chose not to notice the eye-roll she got for her pains, but Rabbit desisted and directed them ably back to the camp.

* * *

The youngster's questions didn't bother Ruri, though she couldn't answer them. Mal was the one who seemed offended, having gone all stiff and refusing to answer. Rabbit smelled annoyed for a few minutes but quickly regained her composure as they got closer to the camp.

"Here we are," she finally said. "The fence line is on the other side of those trees."

"Are you coming back?" Mal asked her.

"No, Mami Wata needs us now. We'll be back before curfew and no one will be the wiser."

"How does that work?"

Rabbit shrugged. "Dunno, but I never get yelled at for missing class or maneuvers or anything. It beats running around in circles." She dug around in her pocket. "Here. Put it on your eyelids when you need to see. That's what Mami Wata says." She pressed a small earthenware vial into Mal's hands. A whiff of spices and herbs drifted to their nose, but Ruri couldn't distinguish any particular one. Rabbit turned and disappeared back into the trees.

"You should probably change now," Mal said. "I don't have any way of explaining where you went and where the big-ass dog came from if anyone stops us."

The prospect of losing her fur-form wasn't one Ruri relished, but Mal was right. She shot Mal a look.

"I have your clothes right here," she said. "I tucked the shirt and socks under mine so they'd be warm." She grinned suddenly. Her cheek pulled a little higher on the right, crinkling the skin around her eye.

When Mal smiled like that, Ruri was powerless to resist her. She wondered if her mate knew that. She certainly pulled out that cheeky smile when she wanted something. She pushed down the wolf, who went with poor grace. She'd loved being in the woods and snow. If they hadn't had work to do, she would have been gamboling in it. Before they left, they would have to go for a long run.

Cold shot through her and shocked the air from her lungs with a forceful cough. "Give me the shirt," Ruri gasped as soon as she was able. She snatched it from Mal and yanked it over her head so fast that a stitch popped in complaint. "Pants and socks," she ordered. Mal handed over each piece as soon as she pulled on the previous one. Soon she was bundled back up and trying to force the shivers to dissipate.

"Let's get you into the truck," Mal said. "I'll blast the heater." She put an arm around Ruri and they jogged the rest of the way to the fence. By the time they got to the chain link barrier, the worst of Ruri's chills were gone, thanks to the movement and Mal's body heat. She held up the fence while Ruri scooted under it, then scrambled under it herself. "Hopefully nobody notices us."

Ruri wasn't sure what would happen if they were noticed. They might have some explanations to make, but that would be the worst of it. Mal's cover was built for snooping around. No one stopped them, and soon they were back in the pickup.

"Do you still want to stop at the coroner's office?" Ruri asked. "Or should we try to look up Reese the Hand?"

"No way are we going to get help from anyone *she* suggested." Mal put the truck in gear and backed out of the spot. She stomped on the brake before shifting into first and peeling out faster than was really necessary, especially in the frozen parking lot. "He probably reports right to her. We have no way of knowing how much she's involved."

"She said she didn't know anything about the youngsters' deaths."

"And you take her word for it that she didn't?" Mal shook her head.

"I didn't notice any signs that she was lying." Ruri took a deep breath and decided to broach a topic that had been bothering her since that morning. "Tell me, if Shockley or Brewster had been supras, would you have bothered asking them so many questions?"

"What do you mean?" Mal shifted her eyes over, then back to the road. "They *are* human, so what does that have to do with anything?"

"If they'd been vampires, or my kind, chances are we'd be waiting for a cleanup crew right now. Isn't that right? That is how you operate."

A furrow creased the skin between Mal's eyebrows. She looked truly confused. "They aren't. From what I can tell, they have nothing to do with the deaths. I'm not prepared to count them out completely, but I'd be very surprised if I'm wrong on this one. Why? Do you think they had something to do with those kids dying?"

"Not at all. I agree with you, for what it's worth." She paused, trying to find the right words. "It's just that you treat supras differently than humans, and I don't think you realize it. You didn't slow down to figure out what was going with Mami Wata, you just attacked."

"So did you."

"True. But I was also able to pull back and look at the situation. Some supras need to be taken out, MacTavish was the poster child for that. But how many of my kind or the others out there weren't so deserving of your…services? Would you even know? Do you ever stop to wonder about that?"

"I don't choose who I go after. You know that. They give me a target and I take them out." Mal shrugged, but the motion was jerky. "I haven't known them to be wrong yet."

"But you wouldn't, would you? All you have to go on is the trust that they're not abusing your willingness to follow orders."

Mal's face flushed a dark red; she was clearly struggling not to lay into her. Ruri smacked her open palm on her knee in frustration, took a deep breath and gentled her tone. "How much do you really trust Uncle Ralph? Would you trust him to handle my life? I know you don't trust him with Cassidy's. We may not be human, but we're still people. You know that."

"I know that now." Mal wasn't quite as flushed and the vein down the column of her throat was no longer throbbing visibly. "What do you want me to do? If I question every single order or target, supras who need to be dispatched could get away."

"I don't know. Maybe talk to your targets? Ask more questions of Uncle Ralph? If you don't have evidence of their crimes, maybe you should do something to make sure you're not taking out someone who doesn't deserve it. I'm pretty sure Mami Wata doesn't deserve it."

"I'm pretty sure I'd need a lot more firepower to take her on." Mal relaxed. "I'll think about it. That's all I can promise right now."

"And that's all I ask," Ruri leaned over and placed one hand over Mal's where it rested on the gearshift. "I trust you, and I know you're capable of coming to the right decision when it comes down to it. I've seen it."

Mal didn't respond, but she didn't smell angry anymore. She kept her eye on the road even though they hadn't seen any other cars.

"Next stop, the coroner's office?"

Mal nodded. She took Ruri's hand in her own and squeezed.

They were going to be all right. If they could get through that discussion, maybe they could get through others. Ruri smiled. Things were looking up.

CHAPTER NINE

A feeling of dread settled in Ruri's bones. She looked around and realized they were back in La Pointe. Something about crossing the town limits was enough to freak her out. Her wolf stirred, responding to her agitation, and she couldn't help but twitch.

"You're not going to start doing that again, are you?" Mal asked. "We've only been in the car for twenty minutes."

"Don't you feel it?"

"Feel what?"

"Like something is about to go terribly wrong." She shook her head. "I hate this place."

"Well, the good news is that if everything checks out at the morgue, I think we can head home."

"That would be fantastic."

"I think so too." Mal smiled, then looked her up and down before returning her attention to the rapidly approaching stoplight. The light seemed superfluous. Even though it was red, there were no other cars in sight beyond the handful parked in front of businesses along what passed for the main drag.

"What was that look for?"

"Just thinking how amazing you looked without your clothes on in the woods." Her smile widened to a full grin. "When it's warmer, we need to find somewhere outside where we can go for a romp. Or two."

"Mal!" Ruri swatted the side of her arm. "I was freezing."

"I could tell."

"So in my moment of discomfort, all you could focus on were my nipples?"

"Among other things."

Ruri opened her mouth but was interrupted by a mechanical chirp from Mal's pocket.

"Looks like we finally have some cell service," Mal said. She hauled the phone from her pocket and handed it over to Ruri. "Who called?"

Ruri powered on the phone and checked the lock screen. Mal had push notifications from… "Uncle Ralph and Cassidy, it looks like."

"Cassidy?"

"That's what it says." Ruri held the phone away from her when Mal reached for it. "Why don't you wait until we're parked before checking your messages. No point in burying your car in the front of that horrifying little antique store."

"Fine." Mal checked both ways, then moved through the intersection. "What? There weren't any other cars."

"Aren't you the one who always says those with the most to hide should follow the rules the hardest?"

"Yeah, but not when there's a message from Cass on the phone. You know she'd have to be literally on fire to call me right now."

A siren wound up behind them. Ruri glanced into the side mirror and noted the flashing red and blue lights. "Looks like you'll have to explain that to local law enforcement."

"Dammit." Mal steered the car to the side of the road.

"When the cop asks where the fire is, I'd leave out the part where Cass is a wolven new to her pack who doesn't want her big sister to swoop in and fix everything."

"Very funny. Hand me the registration and insurance cards from the glove box, would you?"

The time to needle Mal for this one would be later, Ruri decided based on the dangerous gleam in her eye. She pulled the top set of documents out and passed them over.

By the time the sheriff made his way over to the car, Mal had regained her composure. She assumed a smile Ruri knew she wasn't feeling when he knocked on the window.

"I know why you pulled me over, officer," Mal said as soon as the window was open. "I shouldn't have gotten impatient waiting for the light, but there was no one else there, so I didn't think it would be an issue."

"From Chicago, is it?" The sheriff's voice was deep for a woman's. She gazed through the cab at Ruri, then back to Mal. "The pace may be different up here, but the law is still the law."

"Yes, ma'am. It's only that we're on the way to the county coroner's office and I'm sure it closes soon. I didn't want to make anyone stay after hours on our behalf."

"You must be the CDC inspector everyone's talking about."

"Everyone?"

"It's a small town, Mrs. Tipple."

"It's Miss."

"Of course." She handed Mal her papers. "Everything seems to be in order. I'm letting you off with a warning this time. Next time, CDC inspector or no, you'll get a ticket. We take our rules very seriously here. Remember that." She glanced at Ruri again. The last part of the message felt like it was being directed at her, though Ruri had no idea what she was getting at.

"Thank you, officer."

"Coroner's office is in the county admin building. I'm headed that way. You can follow me. Wouldn't want you to get lost."

Mal laughed, but Ruri didn't think the sheriff had been joking. The statement should have been laughable. If the town had more than 800 people, Ruri would have been surprised. That they could get lost sounded impossible.

With a tip of her hat to them, the sheriff left Mal's window.

"It's a good thing we really were headed to the morgue," Mal said. "We'll have to leave the poking around town to a different day."

"If we have to stay," Ruri said.

"If we have to stay," Mal agreed. Ruri didn't think she meant it.

The sheriff's SUV passed them, then slowed down. Mal carefully checked her mirrors, then pulled into the cruiser's wake.

* * *

Mary Alice gripped the steering wheel and glared at the sheriff's tail lights. The blasted woman was driving much too slowly. She had a message from Cassidy to listen to, and the sheriff was in her way. They adhered exactly to the posted speed limit but every time Mary Alice tried to push things a little faster, the sheriff tapped her brakes, bright lights sending a message she couldn't ignore. There wasn't room to pass, and if they were pulled over for speeding, as Mary Alice had no doubt the sheriff would do, it would be even longer before she could listen to that message.

Finally, after what seemed like an eternity of narrow, snow-crowded streets, the sheriff pulled off the road into the small lot of a municipal building. The concrete block screamed local government with its spare grey walls and tiny windows. Mary Alice pulled off and parked a few spaces down. She watched the sheriff walk through the glass doors in the front of the building.

"My phone, please." She held one hand out while she put the truck in park.

Ruri dropped it in her palm without a word.

"Thanks." Mary Alice swiped open the lock screen and perused her missed calls. Uncle Ralph had called a few hours previous, Cassidy not thirty minutes ago. She'd barely missed her. Mary Alice pressed the icon for voice mail and put the phone to her ear.

"It's Ralph, kiddo. I have a new number, I'm texting it to you. Don't call me here again." The message ended abruptly, and Mary Alice frowned slightly. There was little attempt at joviality; he was all business. Still, that wasn't important. She'd keep an eye out for his new number. The important one was the next one.

"Mary, it's me." Cassidy's voice paused long enough that Mary Alice checked the phone, wondering if her sister had disconnected the call before finishing her message. The message picked up after a few moments. "It's not that important, so don't freak out, but I need to talk to Ruri. Can you have her call me? Thanks, bye."

Mary Alice stared at her phone. The first message she had from Cassidy in weeks, and it wasn't even for her? And why shouldn't she freak out? Her molars squeaked and she quickly unclenched her jaw.

"I heard," Ruri said. "Do you want me to call her now?" Her voice was gentle, as if she knew the hurt that Mary Alice was trying to tamp down. Who knew, maybe she did. She certainly was adept at reading her moods.

"Go ahead." Mary Alice passed the phone over. "Just hit the phone icon next to her number. It'll call her right back."

Ruri's look of annoyance would have been highly entertaining if Mary Alice hadn't been so put out with her sister. She said nothing, pressing the icon instead, then turned to stare out the truck's window while the phone rang.

"Mary?" Cassidy's voice was tinny through the phone's tiny speaker, but Mary Alice could hear it well enough.

"No, it's Ruri. You said to call?"

"Yeah…" Cassidy's voice trailed off. "Are you alone?"

Ruri cut her eyes over toward her. Mary Alice nodded, telling her to let Cassidy know she was by herself.

"No."

Mary Alice lifted both hands off the steering wheel and looked up at the roof of the truck.

"Can you be?"

"Sure, give me a second." Ruri slid out of her seat belt and opened the truck door. She closed it firmly behind her, the snap telling Mary Alice not to follow.

Over the space of a few breaths, Mary Alice wrestled with herself. She wanted nothing more than to follow, even if it was only to hear Ruri's side of the conversation. She was on the edge of getting out of the car, her fingers closed around the handle, when she made herself let go and lean back. Ruri was on her side, she knew that, she had to trust that. If something needed her attention, she had no doubt her girlfriend would say something. Right? Surely she would.

Thinking about it and what those two were talking about was going to make her crazy. Instead, she ran over the day's events in her mind. The humans at the juvie camp were clean, she was almost certain of that. That Mami Wata was hiding something, despite her protestations otherwise. The fae were tricky to deal with. She'd had run-ins with their kind only three other times. Once in training and twice in Chicago. Only one had been full-blooded, the others had been faerie-human hybrids. The truths they dealt in were rarely what they sounded like, but try as she might she couldn't figure out Mami Wata's angle. Should she have treated her more gently? Was Ruri right? But if she started handling supras with kid gloves, they'd roll right over her. She had to maintain herself as someone to be respected, and the best and fastest way to do that was through fear.

Still, she needed to know more about the fae. Mami Wata was pure fae for all her protestations, but she'd never heard one fae like her. If she was going to get Uncle Ralph to hook her up with one of his experts, then she'd need to get his new number out of her texts. Mary Alice sighed, her breath wreathing her face in the truck's cab. Now that the engine was no longer running, it had gotten cold and quickly.

As much as she wanted to believe that the death of those teens had been natural, it was looking less and less like that was the case. They were going to be in this damn town for a while yet.

The sound of shoes crunching on packed snow heralded Ruri's return. She pulled open the car door and tossed the phone back.

"Here you go," Ruri said.

"Good." Mary Alice unbuckled her seat belt. "Anything I should know?"

"Not really. Cassidy had some questions about what kinds of challenges to expect as a new Alpha."

Mary Alice's mind raced. Someone was challenging Cassidy? Did that mean some sort of showdown?

"Not like that." Ruri reached across the passenger seat and laid a hand on her arm. "There's nothing like an official challenge going on, more like factions pushing a little on the edges of her territory." She shrugged. "It's not unusual when there's a new pack or a new Alpha. The other players will poke at the newcomers to get their measure. I told her what I think she needs to do. She'll be fine."

"We should go back so I can be there if something serious does go down."

"That's a terrible idea." Ruri squeezed Mary Alice's arm and gentled her voice. "All that will tell the others is they should wait until you're not around to protect her. She's more than capable of standing on her own and pushing back. Let her."

"Fine." Mary Alice squeezed her eyes closed, then opened them and stared out the windshield. "It's so hard."

"I know, but you won't be doing her any favors."

Mary Alice nodded. "And I'm not doing those dead kids any favors by sitting around in here and worrying about Cass. Let's get this rolling."

Ruri smiled, her face lighting up, eyes almost glowing from within. When she smiled like that, Mary Alice wanted to take her to a secluded corner and wrap herself around her. To cover Ruri's scent with her own until they no longer smelled different, but like the combination of the two of them. She shook her head. That was a strange thought. *What the hell was that with smells, anyway?* She pushed open the car door and stepped out.

Two frosted glass doors glowed with light. It was starting to get dark already, the sky deepening to indigo. Wisps of clouds streaked the sky with splashes of orange stretching out from the west. It seemed much too early, and yet there it was.

The interior of the building was as featureless as the exterior promised. Mary Alice and Ruri found themselves on carpeting of nondescript grey in front of a long reception desk of generic wood laminate. After spending much of the day in the woods where the trees still held the texture of bark and dormant moss, the bland approximation of wood was nearly an affront.

"We're here to see the coroner," Mary Alice said. "I'm Miss Tipple with the CDC." She slid her false credentials across the desk to a bored-looking receptionist. He was likely counting the minutes until his shift was over. "This is my assistant, Miss Smith."

"Sheriff Corrigan said you'd be here," he said. He picked up her badge and perused it closely before handing it back to her. "One moment." He picked up the phone and pressed a few buttons. "CDC is here to see you," the receptionist said. He listened for a few seconds, his eyebrows dipping with annoyance. "I know what time it is, but Sheriff said to see them. They'll be right down." He hung up without pausing to see if the person at the other end had anything else to say.

"I don't want to make any trouble," Mary Alice said, trying to get into her CDC persona.

"No trouble. Seamus is always trying to slip out early. He doesn't usually get this much excitement." The receptionist pushed a couple of badges with prominent red Vs on them. "Clip those on over your coats and no one will hassle you." He leaned across the desk as Mary Alice passed one badge to Ruri. "Head down the hall and take your second left. The stairs will be on your right. Head down to the basement, the morgue is the first door." He wrinkled his nose. "You can't miss it."

"You never can," Mary Alice said.

"Guess you're more used to them than I am." The receptionist shuddered. "I never head down there if I can help it."

"Thanks for your help." Mary Alice headed down the hall. The receptionist's directions had been very clear, but the urge to explore was a powerful one. She lingered in a doorway to see if there was anything interesting. A room full of filing cabinets greeted her curious gaze.

"Come on," Ruri said, tugging at her elbow. "This place makes my fur itch."

She allowed herself to be guided past the open door and down the stairs. The smell of antiseptic grew stronger the closer they got to the basement.

Her phone vibrated against her leg with the insistent buzz of an incoming call. She pulled it out and glanced down, then stopped. It was Cassidy again. Two calls in one day? That couldn't be good. Her finger hovered over the screen before coming down on "Ignore." They had a job to do. She would call her sister back as soon as they'd finished.

The stairwell door opened onto a long white hallway, lit with banks of fluorescent bulbs. It looked as sterile as it smelled. Sure enough, the door to the morgue was right in front of them. Mary Alice reached forward to push it open, but before she could do so the door was snatched out from under her hand.

"It's about time." The perturbed greeting came from a cadaverous man whose deep-set eyes glared down at her. "I've been waiting for you to grace us with your presence."

"Us?" There was nobody else around that Malice could see. She extended her senses, but felt no other presence in the room except the man who was still giving her the stink eye. His presence pressed into her, buzzing against her skin. She wondered if she might be missing someone because his force of personality was so strong.

"Miss Jackman and I," he said. He ran one hand through thinning hair, then pushed thick glasses up on his nose. Between the hair now sticking up and the glasses, he had the look of an extremely scrawny owl, an image that wasn't dispelled when he thrust his head toward her. "Well, what do you need to get this inspection over with?"

"Just to take a look at the body for now, doctor." She held out her hand in his direction while giving the interior of the morgue a thorough once-over. It was clean, though not quite as spotless as the scent of antiseptic might suggest. Wear showed on most surfaces. Malice had no doubt that they were clean, but scuff marks dimmed the tops of counters and the floor. Corners were dinged and edges chipped. This had been a cutting edge lab thirty, maybe forty years ago.

"Chernowicz," the doctor said, ignoring her extended hand. "I'll be in my office if you need anything. And CDC or no, if you plan on cutting into the poor girl's body, I must insist on being present."

"If it's necessary." Malice wasn't about to tell him that there was no way either of them were about to do any autopsy work on top of what he'd already done. "I'd like to take a look at your report, if you please."

"Surely you already have a copy."

When she folded her arms and stared at him without saying a word, he threw both hands up in the air and stomped away, muttering to himself. He banged open the wooden door in the corner hard enough that frosted glass rattled in the frame, then he disappeared through it. From the ruckus, Malice expected clouds of dust and debris to spew forth from the doorway. She exchanged a glance with Ruri, who looked as bemused as she felt. This was certainly a contrast to the helpfulness Shockley had demonstrated at the camp.

A minute later, Dr. Chernowicz emerged from his office. He blinked at the lights as if their brightness bothered him.

"Here." He slapped a thin manila folder down on the stainless steel examination table. "She's in drawer three." With those words, he disappeared back into his office, closing the door behind him with a snap. If Malice hadn't watched him go back into the small room, she wouldn't have been able to tell he was in there. No light escaped through the glass on the door nor the windows that lined the wall. He must have some amazing blackout curtains for not even the barest hint of light to shine through.

Malice passed her phone over to Ruri. "Take pictures of all the pages in the report," she said. "I'm going to have a look at the body."

Ruri nodded and scanned the screen, looking for the camera icon. After far too long, she found and pressed it. As she opened the folder to take the first picture, Malice headed over to the four hatch-like doors in the far wall. There weren't many compared to other morgues Malice had been in, but then she supposed that Hawthorn County didn't have too much in the way of deaths that required further examination. Most deaths were probably handled by the local funeral director.

She found drawer three without any trouble and pulled its door open, then grabbed the edge of the metal drawer and yanked on it. Cool air spilled over her hands, and the tray with Shejuanna Jackman's sheet-covered body slid freely toward her. Malice pulled the top edge of the sheet down far enough to see the girl's face. She could have been asleep, save for the faintest hints of blue and purple shadows that had gathered under her eyes and at the corners of her mouth. Malice leaned in for a closer look. She checked behind the girl's ears, in her hairline, anywhere someone might try to disguise a needle stick. She'd died in her sleep. To Malice that usually meant poison, likely delivered using a needle.

"Does the tox screen flag anything?" she asked. She pulled the sheet lower, exposing the upper torso, with its classic Y-incision. To her admittedly inexpert eyes, the incision looked pretty decent.

"It says levels are normal," Ruri said from beside her.

Malice gripped the edge of the tray to keep from jumping a foot and a half in the air. "Great," she managed to say between gritted teeth. "Would you mind not sneaking up on me like that?"

"Yeah, yeah." Ruri showed no sign of having actually heard her request. She stared intently at the teenage girl before them. "Mal— I mean Miss Tipple, if she's dead, shouldn't she smell like it?"

"What do you mean?" Malice swung back to look more closely at the girl's body. "Of course she's dead. He autopsied her."

"Then why don't I smell any kind of decay? All I'm getting is flowers, just like at the camp."

CHAPTER TEN

"Flowers?" Mal sounded confused and Ruri shook her head, realizing she hadn't passed that particular tidbit along.

"I don't know what it means, but there was a strong floral smell instead of the smells I'd normally associate with a dead body. It's the same here."

"So you're saying this isn't a dead body in front of us."

"It sure looks like it, but it doesn't smell right. I don't think this is the right time to shift and find out more, do you?"

Mal hesitated for a second, then shook her head. "That would be difficult to explain. I suppose we could come back later."

"And break into a government building? That seems risky. The sheriff's office is in here, isn't it?"

"Yes." Mal chewed on her bottom lip. Ruri could practically see her brain trying to twist its way through the problem in front of them.

While waiting to see what her mate might come up with, Ruri leaned forward and took another whiff. Still no hint of decay. The body had been stored in cool, not cold conditions. There was no way it hadn't started to decompose. Her eyes and her nose were not at all in sync on this one.

"What about the cream Mami Wata gave us?"

Mal's eyebrows drew together, gouging a deep furrow between them.

"She said when we needed to see we should use it," Ruri said before Mal could say anything to the contrary. She'd learned from experience that it was easier to talk her mate around on something before she'd verbalized her objection. Mal hated seeming like she wasn't in full control of a situation, and nothing bothered her more than being wrong. The Hunter wasn't the first hard case Ruri had had to work around, simply the first who was also her mate.

"How can we trust it?"

"I don't think she's going to poison us with eye cream." Ruri very carefully kept the exasperation she was feeling from her voice. "She was doing just fine physically. If she wanted to kill us, I imagine we'd already be dead."

Mal nodded slowly. She'd frowned further at the reminder of Mami Wata's prowess, but her forehead was smoothing out.

"Worst comes to worst, we'll have greasy eyelids. I think we should give it a go."

"All right." Mal pulled the small earthenware vessel from her jacket pocket and handed it over to her. "But only put it on one eye."

"Smart." Ruri cracked the wax seal with her fingernail, then popped the small cork from the bottle's neck. She tilted it slowly. "How much do you think I should use?"

"I have no idea. I'm not a faerie pharmacist."

"Too bad. You'd look cute with wings." A small dab of a thick pearlescent liquid glopped onto her fingertip. Ruri brought it up to her eye to take a closer look at it. Mal leaned forward as well, then pulled back before they knocked foreheads together. It was a little thinner than hand lotion, and when she moved her head to one side, a hint of iridescence spangled the surface. A pleasant tingle suffused the tip of her finger as if blood was rushing to the area. "Here goes nothing."

Ruri swiped the tip of her finger to the skin covering her right eye. The eyelid promptly tingled. It felt warm, but when she carefully touched her finger to it, the skin was still cool. She looked down at the human girl's body and blinked. Not believing her eyes, she closed the left one, then opened it, before closing it once again. No matter how much she blinked, the image stayed constant. That wasn't a human on the metal tray. It was a bundle of sticks wrapped up in cloth and tied with red string.

"What is it?" Mal asked.

"You're not going to believe this." Ruri looked up, then back down again. "I wouldn't if I wasn't seeing it." There seemed to be bits of dried petals in amongst the twigs. Finally there was an explanation for the near-constant smell of flowers.

"I'm not going to believe what?" She sighed deeply when Ruri handed her the bottle instead of answering. She upended the bottle against a finger and shook until a dab coated her fingertip. Mal dabbed it on her left eyelid and looked down. "Oh." She grabbed the edge of the sheet and swept it off the strange bundle. It was fabric-swathed twigs all the way down.

"Yeah."

"That's not Shejuanna Jackman."

"No. No, it isn't."

"So if she's not dead and on the slab, then where is she? And what about the other dead kids? Were they replaced by bundles of sticks too?"

"How could the coroner not notice this?"

Mal bent forward to examine the bundle of sticks more closely. "It has to be a glamour or something." She ran her fingers over the exposed twigs. "I haven't dealt with the fae much, but it sure looks like some of their work." She pulled her hand back and left it hanging at her side as if not sure what to do with it. "It's very possible he didn't even notice."

"He did an autopsy. He cut her open. He sent her blood out for analysis. If he didn't notice, surely whatever lab he sent it to had questions when they ended up with a couple test tubes of water and bark."

Mal's fingers twitched. She cut her eyes up and over, giving the room the most thorough once-over Ruri had ever seen. She was in full-on Malice mode.

The smell of flowers was stronger than it should have been. The petals in with the sticks were dried out, but it smelled as if they were in the middle of a field of blooming wildflowers. Ruri glanced around the room trying to pin down where the perfumed air was coming from. The coroner's office door swung slowly open, pushed by an impossible breeze.

"Mal," Ruri murmured. "Behind you."

Mal turned, bending down to pull the combat knife from the holster on her ankle. "Chernowicz is in on it, whatever this is," she said through gritted teeth. "Let's see what the good doctor has to say for himself." She stalked toward the door, closer to the sickly-sweet stink.

Ruri stayed at her side. Whatever came through that door, she was going to be there to cover Mal's back.

* * *

The space beyond the door looked completely normal. The corner of a desk and a battered filing cabinet were all Malice could see. Light from a lamp painted the top of the desk. She flexed her hand around the combat knife in her left hand, wishing she had something more substantial. Ruri stared at the door. If she'd been in wolf form, Malice was sure her fur would have been sticking up at all angles. She had to agree with her girlfriend's instincts. Her skin prickled and she licked lips gone suddenly dry.

"Chernowicz," Malice said, trying to inject as much authority into her tone as she could. It wouldn't do to have it waver in time with her apprehension. "Come out. We have some questions."

"Just a moment" came the doctor's voice after a long pause. They waited, but there was no sign of the coroner.

"Chernowicz."

There was no answer.

"Damn it, Chernowicz! You're going to answer our questions."

Still nothing.

Malice stared at the doorway, trying to decide if she should go in. She shook her head. *This is ridiculous.* She'd been in far tighter situations than this one and had jumped in without thinking about it. Was her hesitation because Ruri was with her? No, that couldn't be it. Ruri could handle herself and then some. She took a step toward the door.

"Don't." Ruri grabbed her arm and yanked her to a stop without ever looking away from the door.

"I'm going to pull him out of there. He's hiding from us, which doesn't look good for him."

"Let's wait here until he comes out. He can't stay in there forever."

"I'm done with this. We'll be fine as long as we watch each other's backs." Malice gently pulled her arm, back then strode forward, each step striking hard and loud against the linoleum floor. The sound of running footsteps filtered to her ears from the hall. Something was going down, and she had a feeling they were right in the middle of it. No one was going to stop her from finding out what had happened to Shejuanna Jackman. "Last chance, Chernowicz. Come out or I'm coming in after you." Without breaking stride, she stepped through the doorway to the coroner's office.

Everything pitched to one side and went dark. Malice flung out an arm to keep from falling, but her hand flailed through nothing and she kept tipping without ever hitting anything solid. She tried to open her eyes, but realized they were already open. Her eyes weren't closed, they were picking up everything just fine, there was simply nothing to see. With a start she discovered her feet weren't on anything either. She cast about, looking for Ruri, but couldn't see her.

The ground firmed up beneath her feet with such suddenness, she thought she must have fallen from a great height, only there was no pain. Sharp crags sprang into focus around her, jagged rocks reaching up toward a sky where clouds swirled by at breakneck pace. The sun set in the distance before her and above it, almost lost in the dying brilliance of the sun's rays, hung a swollen crescent moon.

Feet hit the ground behind her and she whirled, combat knife out, lunging at whoever was trying to sneak up on her.

"Whoa!" Ruri dodged to one side. "It's me."

"Sorry." Malice lowered the knife.

"What is this place?" Ruri looked around. Her voice was tight and her eyes looked within herself as much as they took in the twisted landscape around them.

"I don't know." Malice turned in place to take everything in, her eyes catching more details of this place that practically vibrated with wrongness. With a start, she realized the rocks reaching toward the sky were backward. Or upside-down. Or something. Their tips penetrated the ground and they widened the closer they got to the sky. It looked as if a gigantic child had plucked rocks from the dirt and then stabbed them back in upside down. Small pale roots grew upward on their tops, quivering gently as if searching for sustenance.

For how quickly the clouds moved in the sky, the corresponding breeze was anemic at best. It was warm where it caressed her skin and only the movement of it cooled the sweat that sprang up on her forehead. The wind smelled floral, with a side of damp earth tinged with rot, as if something had decomposed in it recently. The bones and flesh might be gone, but the decay remained.

Snapping bone pulled her attention back to Ruri. She was down on all fours, muscles writhing beneath skin that already blurred with the tips of golden fur. In moments, her girlfriend was gone, replaced by the wolf who stuck her nose to the sky and inhaled deeply. She didn't even try to shake off the fluid that clung to her fur, matting it with a moist sheen. Malice couldn't recall the last time Ruri had gone through the transformation and hadn't bothered to remove the slime from the change.

Ruri pawed at the ground, stuck her nose into the rocky soil to take a deep sniff, then sneezed. Her ears were flat to her skull. Malice couldn't blame her. She wished she could do the same. As it was, she was starting to feel exposed. She turned all the way around and noticed a small door.

"Here." It was sunken into the hillside behind them, a sheer face that went up twenty or so feet and was topped with more of those strangely broken rocks. The door came up a little higher than her waist, and she had to bend low to grasp the crudely fashioned wooden handle. They must have come through there, somehow. It seemed strange that there was an ordinary office behind the door, but what else could it be?

The bottom of the door scraped along rocky ground. A grinding sound echoed hollowly back to her. Malice looked through the widening crack and saw only gloom. That made sense, they'd come through the dark to get here. There were many things she'd rather have done than enter back into the darkness they'd traversed to get to this place, but if it was the only way, she'd take it.

To her disappointment, the space behind the door was neither the coroner's office nor the emptiness of the space they'd so recently crossed. A tunnel ran into the side of the hill, illuminated by the setting sun behind her, casting her shadow deep under the rocks. Ruri stuck her nose into the empty space and snorted. The sound echoed back to them, overlapping and growing louder into a booming cough that cut off suddenly. The sun's light glinted off a wet rock down past where its rays reached. Two points of light reflected back at them. Malice shifted, letting more light in, and a dozen or more points of brightness sprang to life further down the tunnel.

Malice stared, trying to figure out yet one more paradox in this place. The sun was glinting off things it couldn't reach. That didn't seem likely, but plenty of other things were off here. As she tried to puzzle it out, Ruri took another whiff and whined, the sound bouncing around the tunnel, striking sparks off the side until hundreds of points of light gleamed at them. The points were all doubled and once they winked into existence, they didn't wink out.

"Eyes." Malice winced when her word careened around the inside of the long cave, echoing back to her again and again until her own voice shouted at them: "Eyes. Eyes. Eyes. Eyeseyeseyeseyes." Ruri's whine layered in and around it until it all disappeared in a wave of sound, one long note, high-pitched and grating that descended upon them and crashed about them. The eyes rushed forward with the wall of sound. She backed up, letting the door snap shut on whatever was coming for them.

"Run!" she hollered at Ruri.

The wolf jostled up beside her, bumping her leg with an urgency Malice felt deep in her marrow. She wound her fingers in the dense fur around Ruri's shoulders and held on as the wolf bunched herself up and sprang away. She ran alongside Ruri, her legs eating the ground as the wolf pulled her along. The world blurred around her and each stride got her further away from those things in the ground.

She forced herself not to look back when the door in the hillside slammed open. The sound of wood splintering against stone told her all she needed to know. Whatever they'd seen in that tunnel was after them.

CHAPTER ELEVEN

Small stones and rocks slipped past Malice's feet as they devoured the ground at a pace she couldn't believe. Yet, for all their speed, the nightmarish sounds from behind them grew steadily louder. The avalanche of footfalls on the hard surface wasn't nearly as terrifying as the scrabble of something hard on rock and the sounds of pebbles being knocked loose.

She spared a glance up and to her left. The triangular boulder they skirted glowed golden in the rays of the setting sun before the back edge was blotted with first one, then two, then dozens of shadowed spots. They poured over the edge and flowed down the boulder toward them. The darkness was interspersed with curious flashes of small beings with pale grey skin and black-tipped fingers. The faerie ointment was still doing its job. If only she'd slathered it across both her eyelids.

"Faster," Malice yelled.

One of Ruri's ears twitched back toward her in acknowledgment. The muscles beneath her skin bunched and released, then bunched so much that they pulled the skin nearly taut around her shoulders. Malice firmed her grip, hoping she wasn't pulling on Ruri's fur, hurting or, worse, distracting her. They hurtled forward. Malice quickened her pace to keep from slowing down the wolf. She tried to keep her eyes ahead, to shift with Ruri around boulders and rocks, but her eyes kept straying to watch what harried them.

She had to scramble to stay with Ruri as the wolf dodged to one side to avoid a massive boulder that sprouted up in their path. Had it been there the moment before? She couldn't tell. Those things were closer now, no matter how much more speed they'd put on. Her lungs strained and her heart pounded, feeling like it might burst free from her chest. Malice was accustomed to the feelings of intense physical stress, she could put them from her mind and she did, but she knew she couldn't maintain this pace indefinitely.

Her eye burned with sudden fire, her vision going blurry. Malice swore as more sweat contaminated with ointment dripped into her eye. Without breaking stride, she scrubbed desperately at her eye with her palm. After too long, the pain and blurriness receded, but with them went any ability to see through the shadows around the pale beings.

The shades rushed over the surface of a monolith to their right, pausing as they filled the shadows on the other side to overflowing, then bursting free and skittering over the next spot of light, pulling ahead now.

"Left," she shouted at Ruri's pricked ears. They had to get away. Who knew what would happen when those things caught up to them.

Ruri responded immediately, throwing herself between the gap at the base of two inverted boulders. Malice leaned down and wrapped her free arm around Ruri's chest, ducking her head to keep from giving it a dreadful knock. She made sure not to cut Ruri with the knife she still gripped hard in her left hand.

As they entered the gap, the sun's rays winked away, cut off by the stones' bulk. Glints of light sprang up around them in pairs.

"Oh shit," Malice whispered. They'd been neatly trapped. She had no doubt that the way back was closing behind them, but she could still see a glimmer of sun on stone ahead of them. There was still a chance they could shoot this gap. "Move it!" She dug her toes into the rocky ground, trying to provide more forward momentum, to push their way through the shadows that worked to swallow up that last bit of light.

As they careened forward, Malice felt dozens of touches along her sides and back. Whether they were fingers or claws, feathers or scales, she couldn't tell. Her mind shied away from briefly glimpsed images of pale beings with obsidian fingers as her skin crawled. They burst through and she was free of the touches. She moved to plant her next foot, to help Ruri again with a strong push.

Her toe caught on something and she fell, burying her face in Ruri's fur. Her weight transferred to her girlfriend and Ruri leaned away from her to counteract the sudden shift in weight, then toward her as she was unable to compensate.

No! Malice let go, unwilling to pull Ruri down with her. The wolf slipped free from her grasp, fur sliding out from beneath her fingers. She ducked her shoulder, rolling to lessen the shock of the fall. She firmed her grip on the knife. It was her only defense, and she was going to need it.

There was no time for a mental rundown on what injuries she might have sustained in the tumble. Malice pushed herself up and backpedaled, putting her back to the nearest boulder, making sure that it was bathed in full sun. She crouched and flexed her fingers, glaring back into the gap. Whatever was in there was probably going to kill her, but she was damned if she would let that happen without taking some of them with her. She might be beaten, but that didn't mean she was going to make it easy.

Blots of shadow oozed out from the gap. They circled, hugging the areas of darkness until more arrived, shoving those in front out of the gloom and into the light. Those shoved into the sun's meager rays hesitated and shied away as if the light hurt them. The closest one hissed, the shadows around it pulling back to display needle-sharp teeth. Her eyes tried to resist focusing on it, but she forced herself to watch this strange thing of nasty teeth that glinted from the darkness. It was something from a nightmare. In fact she didn't doubt her subconscious was taking notes and would serve it up with a side of zombie Stiletto the next time she tried to sleep.

A blot separated from the group and skittered apart from the others, mounting a boulder twice its size as easily as walking. The skull of an animal with too many horns poked out of the darkness around the top of its head. The darkness around it shifted and it howled to the twilit heavens above.

As if the call had been a signal, the others took it up. They screeched and hollered, then flowed toward Malice. There was no doubt what they wanted. Ruri would have to forgive her for not trying to negotiate this one. She braced herself, but they were already upon her. Malice grabbed at one, her hands plunging into the shadows and grasping solid flesh. She sent it spinning around and pulled her knife across what she thought had to be its throat in one motion. It fell, but the next one clambered over its falling body and was on her before she could bring her arms up to stop it. She stabbed the knife viciously into its back as it tore at her with lethally sharp claws that she could feel but not see. Steel parted its flesh like paper, slicing it almost in two with the barest amount of pressure. Two more replaced it. One she was able to elbow free. The other she grabbed by a convenient body part and flung as far away from her as she could manage.

Something landed on her back and sharp fingers tangled in her hair, yanking her head around. She pushed back into the boulder, trying to squash whatever it was into submission. The ground was covered with shades, the darkness a roiling mass as they fought amongst themselves to be the first to reach her, to rend her flesh from her bones, to tear strips of skin to use as belts. Glittering eyes looked up at hers, surrounding her as she flailed to get them away, to take them down, but there were too many. Too many were hanging from her arms, tearing at her clothes, wrapping her legs around, claws hooked into her skin.

If she went down, she was finished. Malice tried to keep her footing, but it was too much. One of the things launched itself off the boulder onto her back. That last bit of momentum was more than she could compensate for and she toppled forward, that one on her back. It was joined by another, then another, until she feared she would die of suffocation. Each breath was more difficult than the last and the sides of her vision collapsed in on her.

Then all at once she could breathe again. Space opened up around her. She looked up, grateful for the ability to breathe again, filling her lungs with sweet, cool air. Her heart stuttered at the first glimpse of golden fur.

Ruri stood over her.

* * *

It had taken Ruri precious seconds to realize her mate no longer clung to her side after making her way between the two boulders. When she got turned around, her way was blocked by scores of ashen-skinned little almost-human shaped things. Her mate was on the other side, up against a boulder. Ruri could see Mal, holding off the pasty beings. Their skin was sallow, a milkiness of flesh that rarely saw the sun, over which they wore tattered rags of grey and mottled green held together with strips of cloth or ragged bits of rope. The ends of their fingers and toes were black and angular. Ruri had no doubt that they could use their obsidian claws to devastating effect despite only coming up to Malice's knees. She didn't have to second guess what they wanted. Unlike during their tangle with Mami Wata, she saw nothing that implied the pale ones wanted anything other than to flay the flesh from their bones.

She wasted no time. Ruri wanted to bull her way through the gathered mass, but the wolf counseled cunning over brute strength. It wasn't that far, maybe a dozen yards, yet hundreds of the Pale Ones filled the space between her and her mate.

She was fast, faster than they were. Ruri snatched one out of the air as it threw itself at her. Strange though it looked, its bones crunched as easily as those of a rabbit's between her teeth. The creatures weren't as eager to attack her as they were her mate.

Ruri dropped the no-longer-struggling body after giving it a quick shake to ensure it wouldn't come back to bedevil her. The blood that bathed her tongue was strange and sweet. It tingled along her teeth and gums and down her throat when she swallowed. Warmth spread from her stomach, pushing fatigue from her muscles and leaving renewed energy in its wake. She practically trembled with a surfeit of energy.

Up, the wolf whispered. She looked to the boulders around them. There were fewer of the creatures up there. Mind made up, she sprang, toenails giving her purchase on rough sides of stone, allowing her to bounce from the side of one boulder to the next, then on top. Up here, the broad tops of the boulders formed a kind of highway. The gaps from one stone to another were not so large that she couldn't ford them with ease.

The creatures below scrambled, trying to get up there to block her way, but she was already gone. She landed on the next boulder, then bounded to the one after that. The roots that stretched toward the sky were tougher than they looked and caught at her paws but were little more than annoyances. Before the Pale Ones could regroup, she flung herself from the top of the boulder, just in time to see her mate disappear beneath a tide of pallid bodies.

Ruri surged forward, snapping in midair to snatch away body after body, flinging them away from Mal. Colorless bodies made solid contact with the stones around them or flew off into the gathered masses, taking more Pale Ones with them.

She grabbed the last one from her mate's back and bit down into it, savoring the sweetness of its juices as it coated her muzzle and flowed down her throat. Vigor burst through her muscles, and she turned with speed she could scarcely believe to face down the rest of the creatures.

As one, the gathered Pale Ones shrank back from her. Triumphant, she pointed her blood-drenched muzzle to the sky and howled. The creatures drew back further. To one side, Mal pushed herself up, then slowly clambered to her feet. Blood ran down her arms in bright rivulets of shocking red. A cut above one eye painted half her face in a curtain of crimson and soaked the side of her head. Hair matted with blood stuck to her face.

Ruri cataloged each injury, each insult to the skin of her beloved. A low rumble started deep in her chest, and she pulled back her lip in a snarl to reveal their teeth. A collective groan rippled through the Pale Ones. On a rock to one side, one wearing the strange skull of an animal on its head waved its hands in the air. Sparks like those from a campfire rose from it and descended over the creatures, disappearing into their skin.

As one, they turned their heads, locking eyes upon Ruri and her wolf.

Ruri bared her teeth and waited. This fight would come to her, and she would make these small ones pay for each cut on her mate.

With a cry that should have shattered the stones and boulders around them, the Pale Ones moved forward, but oh so slowly. Each moved as if trapped in molasses. A cub could have picked them off as they unwisely moved within range of her jaws. With each pasty body she crushed between her teeth, Ruri's energy grew. The dance was deadly for the creatures, and if the occasional scratch or cut from talons of black stone made it through, it wasn't worthy of notice. She didn't slow down, not even when a dozen spots along her sides bled into her fur.

A Pale One dropped in front of her. She hadn't touched it. She shook her head and picked off one to its side. Another one went down, a long shaft appearing in its back. Then another, and another. Ruri looked around her as the Pale Ones dropped off the boulders around them. Something was taking them out, something that wasn't her or Mal.

The Pale One atop the boulder looked over its shoulder, then scrambled down the rock headfirst. It disappeared into the shadows of the gap between the two boulders that had led them to this place. Without that one to exhort them on, the remaining creatures drew back into the shadows, then were gone. In the space of seconds, Ruri and her wolf were the only living things left with Mal.

"Ruri?" Mal whispered. "Are you all right?"

She picked her way around the bodies to stand at her mate's side. Ruri licked Mal's hand, getting a little zing from the blood there. It wasn't all hers.

"Good." Mal threw her arms around them and pulled them close. "I don't know what I'd do if…" Her voice trailed off and she slumped to one side.

Alarmed, Ruri pushed at her with her nose. Mal shifted limply, but didn't respond. She hadn't passed out; her eyes were open, but unseeing.

Something hit the ground near them and Ruri looked up. Then all went black.

CHAPTER TWELVE

Mary Alice opened her eyes and blinked, trying to focus. Stiletto's grinning face swam before her eyes before resolving into blocks of pale grey stone. She blinked dully, not registering what was in front of her. It was the dream, that damn nightmare that had been cropping up for a couple of weeks now. Usually Ruri woke her up before it went on that long.

Ruri! The last time she'd seen her girlfriend, she'd been tearing up dozens of shadowy little beasts with her teeth. *Wait, was that part of the dream?* Mary Alice sat up and looked to her side. Ruri was there, on her back, one arm under the pillow. The covers were far enough down her torso that Mary Alice could tell she was naked. Her hair spread across the pillow and Mary Alice found herself reaching for it. As always, it was as soft as it looked. There was no sign of the blood and gore that had streaked her fur in that other place. Maybe it had been part of the dream. But then how had they gotten from the coroner's office to … where exactly?

With a start, she realized that she had no idea where they were. Walls of stone surrounded them, broken by four tall tapestries that reached from a gleaming wooden floor all the way to the ceiling, one on each wall. She saw no doors, but there seemed to be a window. Lavender-tinged light seeped past heavy drapes, offering the room's only illumination. It seemed brighter than it ought to have been. Were they still in that same place? The place with those shadow things who'd tried to attack them?

She pulled back the covers with deliberate care, trying not to disturb Ruri. As soon as she eased her way out of bed, Ruri turned toward her and opened her eyes.

"Mal? Are you all right? Did those things hurt you?"

"I'm fine." She traced a fingertip down Ruri's cheek. "How are you?"

"Good." Ruri winced and shuddered for a second.

"That was convincing." Mary Alice scooted closer to Ruri, inspecting her carefully. She didn't see any sign of injury. Wait, was that a new scar? She'd spent a lot of time getting to know the vestiges of Ruri's cuts and scrapes. Most of them healed without any trace, but those that had been significant tended to leave light scars. Injuries that would have killed a human left very obvious marks. There were more of those than Mary Alice would have liked.

"I'm fine." She brushed Mary Alice's hands away.

A pang of sudden hurt shot through her chest and settled in her belly. That was unlike Ruri. "What's the matter?"

"I can't feel my wolf." Her face twisted into a despairing grimace that bore not the slightest relation to a smile, even if Mary Alice could have ignored the pain in Ruri's eyes.

"Is that even possible?"

Ruri sat up and curled in on herself. "Apparently so, but it shouldn't be." She flexed her hands on the bedspread, then stared down at her fingertips when they did nothing but scratch lightly against the felted fabric.

A glint of metal caught Mary Alice's eye. Around Ruri's upper arm was a delicate band of filigreed metal that gleamed too brightly to be silver. She reached for it.

"This is new." It was warm to the touch. "I wonder if it has anything to do with your situation."

"I don't know," Ruri said. She lifted her hand and caressed the band carefully.

"I don't see anything else it could be. Not unless you're wearing some werewolf-inhibiting pants under those covers."

The joke fell so flat Ruri didn't acknowledge it. Instead, she kept running her fingers over the intricate design. Even though her head was down, staring at the bracelet, one tear dropped from her eyes and splashed onto her shoulder. It glittered in the strange light.

"Let's get that off you," Mary Alice said. Seeing Ruri in this much distress ate away at her insides. She wanted to punch something, but she settled for reaching for the bracelet. She hooked one finger around it, sliding it down Ruri's arm toward her elbow.

"I wouldn't do that." The voice was familiar, a woman's voice in a deep register.

Mary Alice turned, not removing her hand from Ruri's arm. A tall woman stepped away from one of the tapestries, a ball of cool light hovering above her hand. She waved it away, almost negligently, and the ball flew away from her and attached itself to the wall by the bed.

"Sheriff Corrigan?" Mary Alice asked, squinting at the new arrival. Granted, the last time Mary Alice had seen the sheriff, she'd hadn't been over six feet tall and wearing bright red hose and a dark grey tunic covered in silver embroidery. Nor had her hair been arranged in a stiff crest that revealed ears that came to a graceful point. She hadn't seen the color of the sheriff's hair, covered as it had been by her hat, but she would have bet her last dollar it hadn't been a bright cardinal red that matched her leggings too perfectly to have been accidental.

The woman nodded. "Don't remove the bracelet," Corrigan said.

"And why the hell shouldn't I?" Mary Alice moved to place her body between Ruri and the strange woman. "It's hurting her."

"It's protecting her. Any pain she may feel is a price she must pay."

Ruri laughed, a short sharp sound that was almost a bark. "Why don't you let me decide what prices I will and won't pay?"

"The bracelet hides your wolf from those who would kill you for having it."

"What do you mean by that?" Mary Alice demanded.

Corrigan moved until she looked down at them. Her face was calm. She could have been examining a museum exhibit of mild interest. "If you weren't who you are, the wolf would be dead. Of course, if you hadn't brought her here, she wouldn't be facing a choice between death and identity."

The words came as almost physical blows, each one driving into her how much danger she'd put her girlfriend in and how much Ruri was paying for her poor decisions.

"I know what you are," Corrigan said, tipping her head to one side as she continued to examine them. "What you both are. I've known since you showed up in my town. Seamus summoned me when you discovered the glamour in the morgue. I followed you through one of the portals in my station. I arrived barely in time for that one to change her form. I did what I had to to keep the realm from knowing a cur had penetrated into the kingdom. I made a choice to protect my people at the expense of concealing the presence of one of our historic enemies. If it wasn't for the fact that your people would come looking for you if you turned up dead, I wouldn't be treading the thin edge of treason to protect my home. The home you've invaded."

That was a lot. Mary Alice blinked at the sheriff, then homed in on the only part of the word salad that had been important. "And you thought your best option was to steal Ruri's wolf?"

"It's not the first one we've taken." Corrigan spread her hands when Ruri shifted toward her. "Do you know why you even have a wolf? Why your people were created?"

"As far as I know, we've always just been," Ruri said. "That's what the stories say."

"Much has been lost. I suppose that can be placed at our door. We grew complacent in our dominion over humans. It never occurred to us that you might employ our own methods to counteract that."

"Methods?" Mary Alice asked. "What kind of methods?"

"Magic, of course. What did you think I was talking about?"

"There's no such thing as magic." Her denial was flat and absolute. So far, everything she'd dealt with had a logical scientific explanation. *What about where demons come from?* a pesky voice in her mind asked. *And how did we end up here? And what about the ball of light on the wall right by your stubborn head?*

"Wishing won't make it so," Corrigan said. Her eyes crinkled a bit at the corners in a sudden burst of amusement. "At least it won't make it so without the proper ring, the right phase of the moon, and a completely still pool inhabited by a naiad."

"You're kidding."

"Only a bit. One of the three forms I mentioned is inaccurate. I can't have you wishing your problems away unprepared. Many of your fairy tales capture the dangers of that particular scenario. And yet you are doubtless completely unprepared for the realities of this place."

"And what are those?" Mary Alice asked.

"You are in a land of magic and chance, far from your world of technology and reason. You are as children in the wilderness. To survive, you must do as I say. Much will seem familiar to you. The day lasts as long. The sun rises in your east and sets in your west." She grimaced. "With one notable exception."

"Why does any of this matter?" Ruri's voice was raw with frustration. She'd wrapped her arms around her torso, fingers pushing deep indents into the skin at her shoulders.

"Because I want you to know why it's so important that the bracelet stays on." Corrigan shifted around the end of the bed until she was directly in front of Ruri. "You werewolves were created to hunt us. You're the specific answer to our Wild Hunt." She shook her head. "There hasn't been a Wild Hunt outside of Faerie in centuries, so it's not surprising that you don't know. Your shamans decided they needed guardians who could match what the fae could do, who could see through our magic, and who could stand toe to toe with all but the most powerful creatures of our world."

"Huh." Ruri sounded troubled.

"What the hell is this Wild Hunt?" Mary Alice asked. "Why should we care?"

"The Wild Hunt is how the fae kept upstart humans in check within their ancient territories. If one of you offended one of us or if your settlements encroached too much on our lands, we unleashed the Hunt. It swept away mortals in front of it and fouled your land with uncontrollable magics in its wake. It was the main tool we used to remind you of our dominion over you. Eventually, though, humans proved too adaptable. You used our own Wild Magic against us."

Mary Alice reached a hand over to touch her girlfriend and calm some of the agitation she was feeling. Her hand rubbed soothing circles between Ruri's shoulder blades. She didn't relax, not completely, but Mary Alice felt when she let go of some of the tension.

"How did you feel when you fought those kobolds?" Corrigan asked.

"The pale men with obsidian fingertips?"

Corrigan nodded. "You felt energized when you fought them, didn't you? I watched you and her for a while. You held your own, much better than most would when facing down a clutch of those particular fae."

Ruri nodded, her face troubled.

"Did you see them easily, or did they appear as shadows in your vision?" Corrigan asked.

"No, I saw them pretty well. They overwhelmed us in a massive wave. It would have been hard to miss them."

"That's because your wolfish form can see through our glamours. I haven't dealt with your like in centuries, but I still know every inch of our ancient enemies." She smiled down at Ruri. "In some ways, it's good to see you again, though your people have been responsible for the deaths of uncounted masses of my kind."

"Ancient enemies, is it?" Ruri's question was polite, but there was an edge to it.

"Oh yes." The sheriff nodded. She didn't seem too worried to be sharing the same room with something she termed an enemy. "And I'm not the only one who will know you're here if you're not very careful." She pulled open her tunic to display a pendant that glowed with a soft, cool light. "Moonstone. It enables me to recognize and track your kind. Most fae of my station own at least one piece of moonstone jewelry. These days, they're prized for the light they give off, but with the presence of a wolf nearby, it blazes forth in an incandescent beacon that's impossible to ignore. Luckily for you, I came through the portal before you transformed and was able to keep the stones from alighting and alerting my people to your presence."

Mary Alice broke in. "So we'll leave. No one will know we've been here, and we'll get back to our own world without any of the rest of you being the wiser."

"If only that were true. You've shed the blood of the king's subjects. You are now tied to the land, and only his permission will grant you leave to depart." She shook her head. "No, as much as I would prefer to avoid having you interact with my liege, you must attend to him. Only then will he release you, once he realizes you aren't a threat to his kingdom."

"Are you serious?"

"Deathly so." Corrigan moved away from the bed. "But I'm certain you won't take my word for it." She walked over to one of the tapestries and pulled it aside, revealing a narrow wooden door. "I shall create a portal back to my offices in your world." She pushed the door open. On the other side was a small room of the same stone as the walls surrounding them. Clothing hung from pegs on the wall and a small window looked out onto that alien twilit landscape. Before Mary Alice could object, the doorway's interior glowed with a pale light. The room beyond shimmered as if it had suddenly gotten very warm. The heat shimmer continued, growing stronger until the adjoining room disappeared and was replaced by a drab modern office. The fluorescent bulb overhead bathed a spartan desk in light that pulsed in time with the flickering bulb. The walls were standard government off-white, and on the floor was an unremarkable grey carpet just this side of threadbare. The sheriff stepped through the doorway and walked into her office.

"This is my office." She picked up a nameplate from the desk, then stepped back into the room and tossed it on the bed. It landed on the covers face up. Sure enough, it read "Sheriff Corrigan" in white letters etched through a fake wooden background. "You may attempt to cross through the portal as I did, if you don't believe that you're bound to this land."

"I'm not exactly dressed to show up in your office," Mary Alice said. "Neither of us is."

"It won't matter, but you may garb yourself. I had to dispose of your clothing. It was too damaged to salvage. And of course your mate didn't have any."

"She's not my mate," Mary Alice said absently, staring intently through the door.

"Nevertheless." Corrigan indicated a stack of soft garments on a nearby chair.

"Let's get out of here," Mary Alice said to Ruri. "We'll get home and dump that bracelet. Then we can head back to Chicago and I'll tell Uncle Ralph to shove this mission so far up his ass he'll belch fairy dust for a week."

Her sally had its intended response. Ruri cracked a small smile, slipped out of bed, and moved to the chair with the garments. Neither of them had any particular problem being nude in front of someone else. The clothes were a little unfamiliar. It had been years since Mary Alice had last worn tights, which was the closest thing she could liken the hose to. The top was a simple flowing shirt that tied at the wrists and neck. Soft shoes with flimsy soles completed their garb. They would look out of place in the sheriff's office, but at least they wouldn't be naked.

Beneath the stack of clothes was her knife in the ugliest sheath she'd ever seen. It was thick dark leather and tooled with blocky runes. A sleeve hinged at the back to cover the hilt, encasing it completely. That wasn't going to be particularly useful, but she planned on ditching it as soon as they got out of here. She slipped it through the back of her belt and felt slightly better for being armed.

Mary Alice extended her hand to Ruri, and together they stepped through the doorway while Corrigan looked on.

CHAPTER THIRTEEN

Mal's fingers twined around hers and Ruri took solace in her mate's presence. The loss of her wolf had already torn a gaping wound inside her, but at least she still had Mal. They walked through the doorway. A brilliant flash left lingering shadows on her retinas. When her vision cleared, they were not in Corrigan's office but in a room that appeared to adjoin the bedroom they had been in, walls of grey stone still around them. A large wardrobe took up most of one wall, and large trunks lined the other two, one open to reveal folded clothing. Ruri had recognized Corrigan's scent there as soon as they'd arrived. Even without her wolf, the good sheriff's odor was easy enough to pick up. Oddly, she found herself wanting to drop Mal's hand and curl up among the clothes.

"Now that you're in here," Corrigan said, breezing through the doorway after them, "we can get you prepared for your audience with the king."

Ruri turned away from her and stared out the small window. The setting sun highlighted everything in shades of rose and gold. Shadows stood out in dark relief of purple and blue, in shades somehow too vibrant for her eyes. Clouds whipped past, flashing in front of the sun so quickly the landscape seemed to flicker fitfully.

"So why didn't that work?" Mal asked. She still gripped Ruri's hand tightly.

"You have deprived my king of his subjects. Until you meet with him and he absolves you of this trespass against him and the land, you are bound to it. Believe it or not, I am working to get you out of here. Your presence here threatens my people almost as your absence from your world threatens them. I want you to attend King Connall, gain absolution, and leave this place. Fortunately for you, the kobolds are not subjects he holds in high esteem." She looked them up and down. "I have summoned someone to help you prepare." She watched them closely.

Ruri couldn't tell if she was waiting for a sign of resistance, but she wasn't going to get it from her. She had no idea what to do. She waited for the slightest feel of fur against her insides, but there was nothing, not even when Mal put a hand against the small of her back. Normally, the touch would have been reassuring, but without the feel of her wolf rubbing against the point of contact, it only reminded her of what she was missing.

"I'm sorry," she whispered before pulling away. Even with the apology, a brief spasm of pain flashed across Mal's face. She felt an echo of it in her breast, but it felt like it was swathed in layers and layers of muffling fabric.

"It's okay," Mal said softly. "We just need to get through this audience and then we can head home."

Home. Desperate for some distraction, Ruri looked over at the sheriff, locking eyes with her. "So where are we anyway? What is this place?"

"This is the Kingdom of Flower and Bone," Corrigan said. "Good King Connall rules over it absolutely, as is our way."

"But *where* is it?"

Corrigan tilted her head, her stiff crest accentuating the angle. "It is a pocket world that exists half a step to the left of your world. Think of our worlds as echoes of each other. The rules are different here."

"I could tell," Mal said. "Those were upside-down mountains, weren't they?"

Corrigan nodded. "The roots of the mountain reach to the sky in that area of the realm."

"Mountains don't have roots," Mal said.

"Maybe not on your world."

"So then this is all part of Faerie?"

Her eyes widened slightly. "Then you do know of it."

"I know about the fae. It stands to reason that they come from somewhere." Mal leaned forward to watch Corrigan's face. "So where's Chernowicz?"

"Chernowicz?" Corrigan looked confused by the sudden shift in topic. "Oh, you mean poor Seamus. I'm afraid he's going to be unavailable for some time. When you demanded his presence after your discovery of the changeling, he panicked and fled. I felt him kindle the portal and came to see what had gone amiss, but you'd already stepped through. I followed you through the portal, but twisted the exit so I wouldn't come out on top of you. Our master was more than a little disappointed when his carelessness allowed you entry to his domain. He's probably regretting that decision right now." She looked over at one of the tapestries. "It sounds as though our assistance is here." She crossed the room, then moved the hanging drape out of the way, exposing a tall door of dark wood.

The door swung open. Before them stood a diminutive man whose curly brown hair, almost the same shade as his skin, peeked out from under his soft hat. "Reese," he said to the sheriff, bowing so low the long tail of his hat swept the stones beneath their feet.

Ruri took a closer look at the sheriff. Was she the one Mami Wata had suggested they contact? She didn't seem exactly hostile to them, but neither was she being overly helpful, not with the shackle she'd so blithely locked Ruri's wolf into.

"Billy, be so kind as to clothe my guests for an audience with King Connall." Corrigan motioned Ruri forward.

"Of course." Billy looked them over critically from the dressing room doorway. "They'll need a lot of work before they'll be fit for His Majesty."

"I shall cover any expenditures you must make."

"Very well then." He swept into the small room, then looked around critically. "Where's the rest of it?"

Corrigan snapped a finger. Ruri tried not to jump as the far wall suddenly shot away from them and furniture leaped into being in its wake. The room they now viewed was sizable, with other doors of varying sizes and richness of carving leading from it. Ruri followed the small man to the center of the chamber. As she ogled the suddenly expanded space, she realized there was no way this room or the doors could be here. The windows looking to the outside had butted up almost to the doorframe on either side.

"Let's see what I have to work with," Billy said. He reached out to stop her, then walked a large circle around her. Ruri had no doubt that all her shortcomings were being noted and cataloged. She was certain her wolf would have impressed him. Mal stood to one side and watched Billy closely.

"You are summer sunshine, my dear," Billy said, still walking around her. "All eyes should be on you while they bask in your presence."

"Nothing too dressy, please," Ruri said. "Or confining."

"Your audience is with His Majesty. Dressy it will have to be."

"Fine. But not too complicated."

"Very well. Andra!" he called out.

One of the smaller doors opened and a small woman maybe an inch or two shorter than Billy emerged. Her skin was a brown similar to his, if a few shades darker. Her short curls were uncovered.

"What is it?" she asked, her voice sharp. "I was busy."

"The Hand wants them dressed for an audience with Him. I need you to provide the base, and I'll make her shine."

Andra looked Ruri up and down in much the way Billy already had. "No gowns for this one."

"It is traditional," he objected.

"And will look ridiculous on her. Look at the set of her jaw, the tilt of her head. There is little submission in this one." She cast a look over at Malice. "Or the other. Pattern them both after the Heir. That will be more appropriate for their demeanor." Andra tilted her head. "And it will better accommodate that one's weapon."

"There is that." Billy stepped to the side and perused the items on an ornate wooden side table. A series of bowls and boxes of varying sizes covered the top. He picked up one, then put it down after peering inside. As he poked through the boxes, he muttered to himself, not quite loud enough for Ruri to hear.

She thought perhaps she ought to have objected to being discussed as if she were an odd mannequin, but she had no idea what she was objecting to. So far Billy looked like he was going to make a soup rather than get Ruri clothed.

"Here we go," he said as he returned to where Ruri and Andra waited.

Andra had said nothing to her while they waited and had instead watched them with those sharp and careful eyes. "What do you have?"

"A head of sun-ripened wheat, the wing of a dragonfly, two sky stones, and a drop of morning dew."

"Very nice." Andra nodded approvingly.

Billy pretended to ignore her approval and dropped a handful of items into her palm.

Andra looked up at Ruri. "Close your eyes and turn clockwise three times."

Her head already spinning, Ruri complied. She felt no different when she stopped, but when she looked down, her arms were covered in sleeves the color of the sky at noon. Diaphanous cuffs stuck out from the end of the sleeves. Colors danced across them as she turned her hands one way, then the other. Golden breeches covered her legs. The color should have been gaudy, but she was reminded of her wolf's fur. She bit the corner of her mouth to keep from crying.

"It will do," Billy said critically. "One little adjustment." He twisted his hand in a peculiar, almost backward motion.

"An excellent touch," Andra murmured.

"I thought so," he said. "Now for you." They turned to look at Mal as one.

"The knife is non-negotiable," Mal said. She closed her hand over the dark sheath at her belt.

"Yes, yes." Billy waved his hand, brushing aside her objection. "With your complexion, something dark and cool would be best."

"May I suggest spider silk, a magpie's feather, moonstone, and coral?" Andra said.

"What color coral?"

"Green."

"That could work." Billy turned away and rummaged through his boxes and drawers.

She held out her hand impatiently and Billy dropped more things into it. Andra looked up at Mal. "Close your eyes and turn clockwise three times."

Mal closed her eyes and turned.

"The other way" came Andra's swift correction.

Ruri could hear Mal grinding her teeth, but she did as she was told. She turned in her three circles.

"Keep your eyes closed," Billy said when she finished turning. "Now turn the other way. I shall tell you when to stop."

"Is this really necessary?" Mal asked while turning, the bite of impatience heavy in her tone.

"If you wish to be presentable to His Majesty," Andra answered. "Those who despoil his presence with inferior clothes don't always survive intact. Now hush, my father's working."

Malice squeezed her eyes harder and kept turning. She twirled long enough that Ruri worried she might get dizzy. She'd never seen Mal off balance, but if anything could do it, it was this. Between one turn and the next, clothing sprang into place on her body. The style was centuries out of date, and Mal should have looked ridiculous in the tight breeches and doublet with its slashed sleeves, but she didn't. Jewel-green silk peeked through the slits in the black doublet, which managed to shimmer green and purple. Soft boots the same dark grey as her belt rose to her knees. Silver embroidery embellished every surface, winking back at her more brightly than should have been possible. The chunky brown sheath still hung from her belt.

"Stop now," Billy said.

Mal opened her eyes, looked down, and gasped aloud. Ruri gaped openly, but she couldn't help herself. She wanted to push Mal against the nearest wall and run her fingers through the hair that brushed the top of her shoulders. She wanted to peel those amazing clothes from Mal and help herself to the body presented so stunningly before her.

"There's a mirror over there," Andra said, voice smug.

Malice turned and stopped, stunned. "How did you do that?" she asked, running a finger around the bottom hem of her doublet. More pale stones weighted it down.

Ruri stepped up to stand beside her. Her outfit was more severe than Mal's, which matched the anguish she was keeping from seeping out by the skin of her teeth. They made a handsome couple, she thought. Like night and day. She took Mal's hand.

"Magic, of course," Andra said. "It's a heavy glamour. Over time, each outfit will revert to its original appearance. If you need to get rid of them more quickly, turn the clothes inside out. Of course the knife can't be covered by illusion as it's…steel." Her voice dropped at the word.

"You won't disgrace us at least," Corrigan said from behind them all.

Ruri had forgotten the sheriff's presence in the excitement of gaining a suit of magic clothing, like something out of a story. She hadn't realized how much she relied on the wolf's constant watchful presence. That Corrigan could disappear from her radar was proof positive of exactly how crippled she was right now. She raised her chin and stared into Corrigan's eyes.

The sheriff nodded gravely to her. "Come, my dears. His Majesty awaits."

* * *

"Follow me," Corrigan said. She passed Malice, leading her and Ruri down the hall. Wide windows lined each side of the corridor, looking out onto the strange lands of Faerie. There was no sign of the upside-down boulders and choppy hills of their entry point to this land. Instead, they looked out onto the tops of trees. Malice tried not to think of how high above the ground they must be to walk among the canopy of those trees.

A railing carved with roses and bluebells ran the length of the hall. Malice looked again; the flowers seemed to be on the edge of blowing in a nonexistent breeze. She couldn't stop herself from running a finger over the nearest flower. It was only carved wood. At a sharp pain in her fingertip, she jerked her hand back. She stared at it. In the middle of her index finger was a dark thorn. She pulled it out easily and dropped it, only to watch it disappear into a sliver of mist before it hit the ground.

"Be careful," Corrigan said. "Not all is as it appears here."

"You don't say," Malice said, fighting the urge to stick her finger in her mouth and suck on the spot that throbbed slightly. "I suppose I should avoid eating and drinking the food or I'll wake up in my world twenty years from now."

"Of course not." Corrigan smiled, showing her a little too much tooth. "The food does nothing to affect the passage of time."

To their right, a large brightly plumed bird with a long trailing tail burst from the leaves. It trilled loudly, then dove back into the branches. A second later, a swarm of lights broke the surface of the canopy where the bird had emerged. They hovered for a moment, then one headed to the spot where the bird had disappeared.

There was a commotion within the leaves and the large bird burst through again, trilling with all its might. The lights surrounded it, diving in toward it. Its sharp beak clacked together on air, narrowly missing a bright one. Another bright one zipped in, then out again, a tail feather twice as long as it was clutched to its body.

More bright ones surged in, harrying the poor bird until all its tail feathers had been harvested. The lights vanished back into the canopy. The bird flapped heavily along, its flight no longer the easy flutter and surge it had been moments before.

"Pixies," Corrigan said before Malice could ask. "They can be quite bloodthirsty. The fundevogel is lucky all they were after were tail feathers."

"I see." She didn't, not really. She wished she'd had the chance to talk to Uncle Ralph's fae expert. It occurred to her that she didn't have her phone. Would it even work in the Kingdom of Flower and Bones? It seemed unlikely her cell provider had a satellite out in these parts.

"Where are the rest of our belongings?" Malice asked. "I'm going to need my stuff, sooner than later."

"Are you referring to the faerie ointment you had?" Corrigan said. "I'm afraid you won't be getting that back, though I'm curious how you came into possession of it."

"Mami Wata gave it to us," Ruri said. She stared hard at the sheriff.

Malice cringed. That was a tidbit of information she would have preferred to keep to herself.

"Indeed." Corrigan turned her head to look at Ruri. She didn't seem particularly surprised. "In any case, you can't be permitted to have it here."

"Why is that?" Ruri asked. "We were told this place is built on illusions. Seems to me this is the perfect place to be using it."

"That's exactly it. Deliberately peering through glamours and illusions is the height of bad manners here. Many are nude beneath their glamours. If everyone could see through them, there would be no point in garbing ourselves so."

"So no one looks through glamours?" Ruri looked doubtful.

"Of course they do, but not so obviously. Being so obvious would lead inevitably to a duel. You already have a large black mark against you for being human—or nearly so. Manners and pretending not to notice anything untoward will keep you alive."

"Great," Malice said.

"I take it tact isn't your preferred way of dealing with people, Hunter?"

"I'll say so," Ruri said. She flashed Malice an amused grin that didn't quite mask the shadows of her pain. "You'll have to be on your best behavior."

"I'll do my best." She focused on Corrigan. "Speaking of glamours, illusions, whatever. What did that one fae mean about the illusion not being able to cover my knife because it's steel?"

The sheriff considered her out of the corner of her eye for a long time before responding. "Iron and, by extension, steel are toxic to us. It affects some fae more quickly than others. The sheath you bear the knife in mitigates the effects enough that most of my people could handle it. It's to keep you from accidentally poisoning one of us, which would not help your case with the king." She sighed. "I suppose I should tell you about the protocol around meeting the king." She paused, seeming to gather her thoughts as she drifted serenely down the hall with its unlikely windows on both sides, passing impossible doors at irregular intervals. Not only were the doors strangely placed, but they varied in size, shape, and composition.

Malice caught sight of one on the ceiling. When she looked up, the door closed, as if someone had been peeking through it at those passing below.

"There's not much opportunity to meet royalty in Chicago," she said, craning her neck back to keep watching the ceiling door.

"More than you'd believe." Corrigan folded her hands into the sleeves of her tunic. "The first rule is never to try to pierce his glamour. Trying would end in a duel among lesser fae. With him you'll likely lose your head, possibly on the spot."

"I guess it's just as well we don't have that cream." Ruri wiped at the back of her neck.

"Precisely. If you look directly at him, he may assume you are trying to see through to his true self. Fae have occasionally been executed for less, humans certainly would be. There are mirrors to either side of his throne that you may use to observe his countenance. Do use those, so he will know you are looking upon him and appreciating the face he chooses to reveal to the world."

"So don't look right at him but still look at him, so he knows he's pretty," Malice said. "Got it. Anything else?"

The sheriff looked pained. "Do try for some manners. You may get some consideration for your race, but the ignorance of humanity will only get you so far."

"Noted." Malice wasn't going to promise anything, certainly not to a member of the fae. From what little she remembered, promises were considered binding, a short step behind blood oaths, and the fae had ways of ensuring promises to them were kept to the letter. Not that she could trust what she remembered. She'd completely forgotten about the iron thing until Corrigan had revealed it.

"Do not speak unless spoken to. Do not directly disagree with His Majesty. Remember that he holds your life and that of all around him in his hands. This pocket of Faerie is a direct extension of his will, and if it is set against you, there is little chance of surviving his anger."

"So we're inside his mind?"

"Not exactly, but this reality is a reflection of him."

"What happens if he dies?"

"Then this pocket and all within will be plunged into eternal nothingness. It's an effective way of thwarting assassination. Before he dies, he abdicates the throne to his heir. The realm then shapes itself to the new sovereign." Corrigan gestured at both sets of windows as the sun managed to set on either side of the hall at the same time. "His sun sets, as it has for decades now. He is afflicted by some sort of wasting sickness of the soul, one the court physicians haven't been able to diagnose. No one is certain how much longer he has, but when that sun dips below the horizon, power will pass to his heir, and a period of uncertainty will begin. His court has thinned as those who attend him become concerned for their own skins. They have abandoned him for courts not so fraught with uncertainty or even for the mortal world. Some of their places have been taken by those whose agendas are suspect. He will pass his power on, though whether it be tomorrow or in a hundred years, not even the augurs can tell. We are in an interesting period, but there still remain those who would see that some order continues to reign in these halls."

"So the sun is what?" Malice struggled to understand the implications. Language and metaphors had never been her strong point as straight Cs in high school English could attest. "It represents him?"

"The sun is a reflection of his power. As it ebbs, so does it."

"I see." She didn't, not exactly, but from what she could tell, they were in a tense political situation with a leader who was unpredictable and could lash out at any time. Not so different from dealing with the vampire Lord of Chicago. If she could manage that, then surely she could manage this faerie king.

"Well, I don't," Ruri said. "What do you mean his sun sets? And how do you have two suns if this is supposed to be an echo of our world."

The sheriff took a deep breath. "You don't know our ways, but I'm uncertain how much to tell you of us." The sheriff paused, chewing at her lower lip. "Think of the sunset as a representation of the king's decline. In a healthy realm, the sovereign's magic waxes and wanes with the sun. My liege no longer waxes and wanes. Instead, it is the dull glow of a fading fire, one that dare not be allowed to go out for fear it may never rekindle. Does that make sense?"

"A bit, I guess." Ruri didn't sound completely convinced, Malice wasn't sure she was either, but if that's the way things were, she would roll with them.

"So what can we expect from Connall?" Malice asked.

"*King* Connall," Corrigan admonished. "I am unsure. We have treated only rarely with humans. Some mortals are taken on in different capacities, but almost never in a position where they might come to the king's notice. He may require you to make amends, possibly in the performance of a task. Technically, you may refuse a request from him, though that is inadvisable. However, if you do accept a request, you are within your rights to request something in exchange. Make sure it does not exceed the magnitude of his request, however, or you may end up owing him instead."

"All right. I'm to be on my best behavior, don't look right at him, flatter him at every turn, and return any requests with one of my own. I think I've got it."

Corrigan shook her head. "Doubtful, but hopefully you have enough to avoid death or dismemberment."

That was a cheerful thought. Malice was glad for the combat knife at the small of her back. At least she'd have something to fall back upon if she made an irretrievable diplomatic faux pas.

"We have arrived." Corrigan stopped them in view of the double doors at the end of the hall. Sentries in shining golden armor edged in lavender stood on either side of tall bronze doors filmed with a layer of blue-green patina. Each carried a tall polearm of shining silver, the heads a fantastic combination of cutting and spearing implements. They looked as impressive as they did impractical.

She turned and looked them up and down. "You look the part, remember to act it. By bringing you here, I vouch for your behavior. Any disgrace you bring upon yourself will reflect upon me as well." She moved closer until her face was inches from Malice's. "I do not suffer disgrace lightly."

"Got it." She placed a finger against Corrigan's shoulder and moved her out of her personal space before she could start to feel like a threat.

Corrigan dipped her head briefly, acknowledging the invasion of Malice's space. She stepped away from her and brushed at the arms of her coat.

"Then we shall proceed." She took Ruri's hand and threaded it through the crook of her arm. When Malice refused to do the same on the other side, she turned them back toward the door.

The sentries said nothing to them as they approached. They bent down and grasped the handles in the middle of each door and pulled them open, revealing a glittering hall. The low hum of a hundred quiet conversations rolled out over them only to still into immediate silence as they stepped through the doorway.

CHAPTER FOURTEEN

They paused inside the open doors and Corrigan nodded to a small woman with pointed ears visible against green hair pulled back in an elaborate set of braids. She stepped forward and lifted her head, exposing what could only be gills. She placed a brass instrument that looked like a French horn with an impossible number of curls to her lips and blew an elaborate fanfare. It echoed loudly in the silence.

"Reese the Hand, Heir of the Land, Duchess of the Broken Moon," she proclaimed in tones only slightly less carrying than those of her instrument.

Corrigan stepped forward half a pace and gracefully inclined her head to the room at large.

"Hunter Malice of Chicago and consort Ruri," the herald said. She waited expectantly.

Malice held out her hand to Ruri, who took it with only slight hesitation. They stepped forward to stand next to the sheriff. Malice was overwhelmed with the uncomfortable sensation of dozens of eyes upon her. She could feel each set on her skin. There would be no indent on her flesh, but it felt like there ought to have been. She smiled widely, allowing Corrigan to draw her forward, while distancing her attention from what her sense of touch was telling her. The presence of so many fae in the room felt like carbonation on her skin: first a little swipe, then another, until she felt like she was drowning in club soda, except that she could breathe just fine.

The long carpet through the middle of the chamber with its glitter and sparkle was deep blue verging on purple, the color of the sky on the opposite side from the setting sun. The floor to either side was buttery yellow marble, a shade that reflected from the mirrors and baubles festooning the chamber. Figures of all description pressed in toward them, none setting foot on the carpet. She caught glimpses of feathers and tails, of fur and scales, and other things she couldn't describe nor quite recognize. It was all quite overwhelming, and she concentrated on putting one foot in front of the other, ignoring those who gawked at them like they were a zoo attraction.

The room was longer than she had expected, though why she continued to have expectations of this place, Malice didn't know. Corrigan continued down the long carpet at a stately pace they were forced to match. The stares weighed on her, making her feel like she was pushing through sheer material, though there was nothing that she could see. By the time they got to the end of the carpet, the muscles in her legs were starting to feel the first pinches of fatigue.

The indigo carpet ended in a wide swath of marble. A dais of carved stone rose in front of them. There were no steps up the front and the implication was clear. No one at floor level was fit to join the man on the throne. Corrigan dropped to one knee, sweeping her arms out to either side. Malice remembered not to look up at the man seated above them. She wondered what the proper etiquette was. Politeness was definitely called for, but she would be damned if she would go down on her knee for a supra she'd never met before. Even Carla wouldn't have expected that much. A curtsy was ridiculous in an outfit like the one she was wearing. She bowed at the waist, splitting the difference between kneeling and curtsying. A muted murmur went up among those who watched.

She held the bow for the space of a few breaths, aware of Ruri echoing the pose to her right. Corrigan stayed kneeling, one fist pressed to the carpet, the other on the pommel of the rapier at her waist. She didn't move. Finally, Malice had had enough and unbent. Another whisper of surprise rippled through the crowd. They must think her terribly uncultured. They were right. If this so-called king wanted to deal with Malice, then he would deal with her as she was.

The sides of the dais swooped up and around. Light winked back at her from the dozens of mirrors that seemed to grow out of the stone.

She looked into the nearest one and had to stop herself from pulling back. A pair of electric lavender eyes regarded her. Malice blinked and transferred her gaze to another mirror, this one larger than the first. The same eyes still watched her. Skin almost as pale as that of a corpse made the color of his eyes all the more striking, and against it the gold of his eyebrows and hair shone. She'd seen blond hair before. Ruri had fur and eyes she'd often thought of as golden, but here was a being whose hair looked as if it was spun from the thinnest possible strands of pure metal. Even his eyelashes were the same color, she realized as he blinked at her. As brilliant as his eyes were, there was a curious matte quality to them, a deadness that persisted even with the beauty that surrounded them.

"So you are the one they call Malice." His voice held hints of a fanfare of trumpets. It should have been disconcerting, but Malice felt herself wishing he would speak more.

With a start, she realized he was waiting on her to speak. "Ah, yes, I am. Your Majesty."

"And your lovely consort." His eyes flicked over to Ruri. Malice tried to figure out what he meant by the statement, it was so bland it had to mean something, but she had no idea what. Ruri wasn't going to like the consort thing. With a sinking feeling in the pit of her belly, she realized she might be in way over her head.

"What business does the Hunter of Chicago have in our domain?"

Corrigan got to her feet. "With greatest respect, Your Majesty, I believe her intrusion Underhill was accidental."

Those dead eyes left hers. Malice took a deep breath when the weight of their regard lifted from her. Corrigan dropped her eyes.

"You may be our most favored," the faerie king said, "but it is still possible to try our patience."

"Yes, my king." Corrigan bent at the waist. She stayed that way until the king turned his attention back to Malice.

"I'm investigating the mysterious deaths of five young humans," Malice said. "My investigation took me through a door in the coroner's office and I ended up here. Or somewhere here." She smiled, lips tight. "I hadn't expected the trip to be quite so…hazardous."

"Seamus's blunder has been dealt with," King Connall said. "His error in leading you into danger is being rectified as we speak."

"I'm glad to hear it." Or maybe she would be if the pronouncement hadn't sounded quite so dire.

"You may return to your world with the answers you seek," the king said. "Your children are not dead, but they are now ours. Those who have been cast off by mortal men have been born anew into our court." He looked away from her.

Was that supposed to be her cue to go? The king's blithe pronouncement gave her more questions than answers. Where were the kids? Had it really been their decision to come here? And wasn't he supposed to be upset about the kobolds they'd killed? Malice waited for the king to elaborate, but he seemed to have forgotten she existed.

"Um, hello?" Malice cocked her head. She rested her hands at her waist, her hand groping the air where the hilt of her katana would normally be.

Corrigan stiffened. She reached toward her but dropped her hand before it was halfway to her as Malice stepped off the carpet onto the marble in front of the dais. Ruri gave her a startled look, then moved with her. It warmed Malice to the core to know her girlfriend had her back. Emboldened, she raised her voice.

"'They're fine, take my word for it.' That's what you have to say about five missing teenagers I thought were dead until twenty seconds ago?"

The buzz that had started through the onlookers dropped away to nothing when the king rose from his throne. No one spoke, no one breathed. Corrigan took a step to the side, away from her.

The production might have intimidated another, but Malice had faced down demons and vampires. She'd gone toe-to-toe with the rabid Alpha of a werewolf pack. She'd had enough. Those kids were her responsibility. The rest of the world might have given up on them, but she wouldn't leave them to dance attendance to this puffed-up supra.

"Is our word not enough, little human?" The brassy edge to the king's voice was sharper now. It threatened to slice her if she wasn't careful. Malice had been cut before. The threat of a little blood wasn't enough to scare her off.

"Actually, it isn't. Where are they? If they're so happy to be here, let's hear those words from their own mouths."

"Is that your request of us?" His voice was silky; it practically oozed reason and conciliation.

She wouldn't have called it a request, more like a demand, but if that's what he wanted to call it, then fine. "Yes. I wish to see the five human teenagers who disappeared from human lands."

The king clapped once. Figures pushed their way through the crowd to stand on either side of their little group gathered before the throne. There were two girls and three boys. Malice recognized them from the file photos. Carlo Diaz, Simeon Sawyer, and Jermayne Tremaine were on the left, Shejuanna Jackman and Latawna Cummins on the right. They looked almost at home among the glittering horde around them, though they lacked a certain lightness of step and seemed somewhat shadowed compared to the sparkle of the beings who watched them all.

The king turned toward Malice. "As you can plainly see, your children are well. Now, as we have granted your request, you owe us a boon. Until you repay our kindness, you will enjoy the hospitality of our court."

This faerie was crazy if he thought Malice owed him anything. All he'd done was to wave his hand. She opened her mouth, but the sheriff leaned in close.

"Don't argue with him unless you wish to remain here longer," Corrigan murmured into her ear. "Find out what he wants and provide it to him. Nothing else will permit you to leave."

Malice opened her mouth to argue, but the sheriff gripped her upper arm. The gesture must have appeared friendly enough with the grin plastered on her face, but she squeezed hard.

"If you want to see your world again, attend to my words," she said.

"We should listen to her," Ruri said quietly from her other side. Apparently having lost access to her wolf hadn't dulled her hearing much, if at all.

Ruri's words broke through where Corrigan's had only made her want to push back. She gritted her teeth and met the king's gaze through the nearest mirror. "As you say, Your Majesty. Perhaps you'll be so good as to tell me what kind of boon I can do for you."

"Perhaps," he said. "Or perhaps you'll learn for yourself what your new lord requires from those who serve us, no matter how grudgingly." He sat down, brushing the material of his long coat out of the way as he did so. "You may speak with our children," he said. "You have many questions for them." With that final decree, he looked away.

Carlo bowed and reached out for her hand. "Come on," he said quietly. "I know somewhere we can talk."

Latawna and Shejuanna both nodded. Shejuanna took her other hand. To the side, Simeon took one of Ruri's hands while Jermayne tried to take the other. Ruri avoided having both her hands occupied, but smiled slightly at Jermayne when she pulled her hand back. Malice allowed herself to be drawn away from the king's presence. She glanced back once to see Corrigan on the floor in front of the dais. She was in deep conversation with the king. Without the entertainment they'd provided, the beings in the crowd began to move again. As if someone had flipped a switch from "watching" to "merriment," music started up and the gathered throng began to move in time to it. Her own feet wanted to join them, but she forced herself to tune out the sound of fiddles and drums. She lost her view of the throne as dancers flitted back and forth.

"You can't make us go back," said Jermayne as soon as they entered a small alcove. It was silent; not even the faintest note of music penetrated back here. He crowded himself to one side of the table that took up most of the space and sat down. "I don't want to go back there."

"You don't want to go home?" Ruri asked. "What about your family?"

Shejuanna laughed harshly, tossing glossy black ringlets over her shoulder. "What family? We have better family here than we ever had back in your world."

"Do you all feel that way?" Ruri looked around the table at the other three as they settled themselves carefully in chairs that looked like they might shatter if the softest breeze touched them.

Malice sat back and watched the teenagers, trying to get a read on them.

"We do," Carlo said. "We have everything we want here. Besides, we're dead back there. How could you bring us back now?"

"Are you sure?" Ruri asked. "What if you're enchanted? If they've put some glamour on you?"

"Glamours don't work that way," Carlo said with the unshakeable certainty only an adolescent could muster.

"And even if they did work that way, the fae wouldn't do that to us." Jermayne sounded dead certain too; his voice was solid as a rock.

"And even if they had, it's safer here than out there," Latawna said, her voice soft. "Two of my brothers were shot. One died in the street, the other in the hospital two weeks later."

"Everyone's been real nice to us," Jermayne said. "They treat us like adults, like real people."

Ruri looked across the table at her.

Malice leaned forward. "I won't force you back, but I have to be sure. If any of you changes your mind, I don't know if I'll be able to help you."

"We won't," Carlo said, looking around at the others. They all nodded. "We have a place here."

"What place is that?" Ruri asked.

"We care for the beasts of the Wild Hunt."

CHAPTER FIFTEEN

"The Wild Hunt?" Ruri perked up at the mention. Sheriff Corrigan had mentioned that. After what she'd said, Ruri definitely wanted more information.

Carlo shrugged. "It's no big thing. Apparently they're much more docile when tended to by humans. I guess a lot of courts have humans who look after the beasts."

"What do they look like?" Ruri asked.

"How many courts are there exactly?" Mal said at the same time. Carlo and Latawna looked at each other. Mal pointed at Ruri, indicating they should answer her question first.

"They're all different types," Latawna said. "From the size of a small dog to animals bigger than a pickup truck."

"And how do they need to be cared for?"

"Do you want to see them?" Shejuanna asked. "A lot of this is hard to explain."

"I would like that very much." Ruri looked over at Mal. "You want to check it out?"

Mal nodded but was still watching the kids. "Is the work hard?" she asked. "Do they take advantage of you?"

"It's not easy," Shejuanna said, "but it isn't like they're working us to the bone. We get time off, we're allowed to come here and dance. They even spin up fancy clothes for us, like they did for you."

"So about those other courts?" Mal prodded.

"I don't know how many there are, exactly," Simeon said. "I don't think any of us do." The kids each shook their heads or spread their hands to indicate their ignorance. "I know there are other kingdoms."

"And queendoms," Shejuanna said.

"And queendoms." Simeon nodded. "There are some portals here that go between them, but we're not allowed anywhere near them. Mostly the higher up fae use those. Lower fae who want to go to those realms have to make their way through our old world. I guess that's why not many of the lower fae leave."

Mal pinned Simeon with an intense look. "Not allowed to go near them? What else are you not allowed to do? How do they keep you in line? Physically?"

"Of course not," Shejuanna said. "It's nothing like that. Usually it's just magic that turns us aside, or we forget why we were there or how we even got there. They don't do anything bad to us."

While the teens reassured Mal that they were there of their volition, Ruri took the time to look around the alcove. Rough stone walls made it look natural, in contrast to what she'd seen in the main room. Glowing crystals poked through the walls, softening the rough angles on the walls.

When Mal stopped grilling them, Carlo and Simeon disappeared back into the glittering throng, leaving the others to keep them company.

"You can go if you want," Malice said.

"I'm good," Latawna said. Jermayne nodded and placed his arm around Shejuanna's shoulders.

"Then why don't you show me around this place." It wasn't a request. Mal was clearly looking to get the lay of the land. Ruri couldn't fault her, not if they were going to be stuck there for an unknown while. Either the kids could help or they could go back to dancing or whatever else it was they had to do all day.

"We can do that." Jermayne stood and offered his hand to Shejuanna who took it. She blushed faintly and looked down when he helped her up. Latawna scooted off the seat behind them.

Ruri stood up first, and she grinned at Mal with her hand outstretched, waiting for her mate to take it. Together, they stepped from the alcove back into the bustle and music of the throne room. Fairies jostled and spun around them. Mal kept her hand at Ruri's waist. For all the fun it looked like they were having, she couldn't relax. Every inch of her body told her she needed to be on alert.

"This is the throne room," Latawna said over the wailing fiddles.

"I got that," Mal said.

Jermayne grinned at them, teeth flashing white against his dark skin. "If she's bored, there's always the stables."

"Yes, please," Ruri said.

Shejuanna's eyes lit up and her smile matched Jermayne's. "Yes, the stables!" She was still holding his hand, and she took off, pulling him behind.

Mal and Ruri moved to keep up with them, but it wasn't long before their supposed guides were lost in the crowd.

"I think they went that way," Mal said in her ear. She dropped her hold on Ruri's hand to gesture to the right. Almost immediately, the eddies and currents of the dancing fae surrounded them and pulled them apart.

The glittering throng whirled around her. Ruri went to her tiptoes to see if she could find Mal, but there was no sign of her mate. She could feel her off to the side, but whenever she made her way in that direction, it seemed as if a wall of dancers sprang up in her path. She was carried along with them. Hands reached out and took hers, twirling her, then passing her off to another of the dancers, who dipped her so low her hair brushed the floor before snatching her up and tossing her to yet another.

The music of the fiddles urged the dancers along, faster and faster as the tempo rose. Finally, Ruri planted her feet and refused to be moved. More hands tugged at her, then moved on when they realized she'd stopped playing. A gap opened in the crowd, and Mal was there, staring at her with her hands on her hips.

"If you're done dancing, let's go down to the stables," she said, her voice raised to carry over the music.

Ruri opened her mouth to dispute the statement but closed it with a snap. It was too loud to plead her case. With a glare, she shook her head and followed Mal out of the throne room.

* * *

With Ruri back at her side where she belonged, Malice followed Jermayne, Latawna, and Shejuanna through dimly lit halls of carved stone. Unlike the throne room with its glitz and flash or the wide window-lined corridors Corrigan had walked them down, these halls were narrow and verged on dingy. There were no windows and the few doors they passed were small and unprepossessing. When Malice looked closer, she realized it wasn't that the hallway was dirty or dusty, they were simply dark. Some corners did hold some truly impressive spider webs. The teenagers gave the webs a wide berth. Ruri slowed down once to get a closer look at the intricate patterns woven into them.

"I wouldn't do that," Jermayne said from up ahead. He'd turned around to watch them while continuing to walk backward.

"It's really pretty," Ruri said. She stopped and leaned forward to take a closer look. This web looked as if someone had woven a series of constellations into it. Each "star" shone faintly, lending the corner where wall and ceiling met a ghostly luminescence.

Malice walked up to Ruri, just in time to see her pull back, her movement sharp from shock. "What is it?"

"I think those are pixies or something." Her mouth twisted in disgust.

"They built that?"

"No. They're the glowing points. Something caught them and trussed them up. I think they're bleeding out."

"Oh."

"The webs belong to the djieien," Shejuanna said. "They prey on other fae. They're tolerated back here because these are servants' halls. We learned to steer clear of them early on. Carlo found that out the hard way."

Ruri backed away from the web, keeping her eye warily on the other webs that dotted the hall.

Malice grabbed her hand again and they hastened to catch up with the kids. This place had her on edge. She was under-armed and knew next to nothing about the creatures that populated this place. Drop her in a nest of newly turned vamps and she would clean it out without a second thought. She knew what she was dealing with when it came to vamps and lycans. This place was a perfect example of the problem with fae and demons. They were too unknowable, too far removed from humanity. *How much of them run through your veins?* the little voice in her head asked. She shook her head, trying to dispel the damning words. No, they could not get out of here too quickly for her.

"What do they do?" Ruri was asking Shejuanna.

"It's great," she replied with a wrinkled nose that indicated it was anything but. "Their bite injects a hallucinogenic venom. Carlo got nailed on the shoulder and spent two days trying to get outside. The djieien who live in here are juveniles and survive on smaller fae. After a couple of their bites, bigger prey usually ends up wandering into the forest where the older ones snack on them." She shuddered. "I've heard there are djieien as big as horses."

"And you're okay with staying here," Ruri said. "How does that work?"

Latawna shrugged. "We have to be careful, but we know the dangers now, and we're trusted to deal with them."

"Besides," Jermayne said, "we have cold steel." He pulled something from a leather pouch at his waist. With the flick of his thumb, he revealed a pocketknife. He held it up to the nearest web which blackened as if burned and shriveled away from the metal blade.

Shejuanna laughed. "Yeah, that really helps. The fae sometimes forget we have it. If we feel threatened, all we have to do is remind them. It works best on the more animal-looking ones, but even the others slow down if they see we have it."

"Then the king's protection means nothing?" Malice asked.

"Of course it means something, but not everyone here remembers," Latawna said. "I think a lot of fae have really short attention spans. He'd totally kill anyone who hurt one of us, and he has. The djieien who bit Carlo was thrown into the fire. It got what was coming to it."

Malice stared at the girl for a moment, taken aback by her completely matter-of-fact tone. "I'll keep that in mind," she finally said.

"It helps," Latawna said. "Survive and report, that's what works best here."

"And how did you end up here at all?"

Jermayne and Latawna laughed, but nervousness colored their tone. They looked over at Shejuanna.

"I met the most beautiful man in the woods. He said there was a place for me, far away from the crap we had to do at the camp, and all I had to do was go with him." Shejuanna shrugged. "His voice was…"

"Seductive," Jermayne said, his voice dreamy.

Shejuanna smacked him on the arm and he seemed to snap out of his reverie.

"What? It was, or you wouldn't be here either."

"Mine was a gorgeous lady. I took her up on the offer," Latawna said. "Anything sounded better than what I'd been doing. She brought me Underhill, and I've never been happier." Her eyes glowed with an edge that bordered on manic. The other two nodded, a similar gleam in their eyes.

"What do you mean by 'underhill'?" Ruri asked.

"The way in is basically a door in the side of a hill," Shejuanna said. "How did you miss that?"

"Apparently, we came in through the side door," Malice said.

"Well, that's what they call it when you come from the mortal world to this place. It's called being Underhill, like we're down below the surface of the Earth or something."

"And they just crooked a finger at you and you came over? Sounds to me like they were affecting you somehow." She wouldn't use the term magic. It might be all around her, but that didn't mean she had to be happy about it. "Have they tried to affect you this way since then?"

Shejuanna tilted her head to one side. "It wasn't quite like that. I made a deal. I hold up my end, and the one who sponsors me keeps up his. He doesn't try to influence me, or anything like that."

"So you work for this sponsor looking after the animals? What do you get out of it?"

The teens all gave her the same incredulous look. "We get to stay here," Jermayne said as if the answer was obvious.

"Room and board. In exchange for looking after dangerous beasts. That's all." It wasn't a deal Malice would have made, but she had to be sure the kids weren't being manipulated into accepting it. Not that she could ever know for sure.

"It's more than that," Latawna said. "The mounts are fun to work with in their own right. Besides, the Wild Hunt doesn't go out that often anyway."

"If you say so," Malice said.

They turned another corner. The corridor ended at a set of double doors as tall and as wide as the hallway itself. It was the first door tall enough that Malice wouldn't have to duck to get through.

"We're here," Jermayne said. The three teens quickened their pace as though they were eager to be at their destination.

As they drew closer, Malice realized each door was split in half. Shejuanna let go of Jermayne's hand and pulled open the top half of the door on the right. Light spilled into the hall, casting her silhouette back toward them as she looked first one way then another.

"It's clear," she announced, then opened the door's bottom half. Latawna slipped past her, followed closely by Jermayne.

"Clear of what?" Ruri asked.

"Mostly the mounts," Shejuanna said. "Some of them are pretty good about getting out of their stalls. You wouldn't want to come up on them by accident. They know us, but they're not great about strangers wandering around on their own."

Shejuanna waited impatiently as Malice paused in the doorway. At first glance, the place looked like no other stable she'd ever seen. Admittedly, she hadn't been in many, but if they hadn't walked through the ubiquitous divided doors, there would have been little to indicate that this was a place to keep horses. There was no straw. Instead, a wide, clean-swept hall with dark wooden floors and whitewashed walls punctuated by all manner of doors stretched to either side. Ruri stepped into the hall, pulling Malice along with her.

An audible sigh punctuated by the soft thump of the door swinging into place betrayed Shejuanna's irritation at being kept waiting.

Latawna and Jermayne had split, each heading the opposite way down the hall. Jermayne had a door open and was leaning against the doorway, looking for all the world as if he was chatting with someone. Latawna was stretching over the bottom half of another barn door and seemed to be reaching toward something.

"This is it," Shejuanna said. "We take care of everyone in here who can't do for themselves."

Ruri lifted her head and flared her nostrils. Malice squeezed her hand and shook her head when Ruri looked over at her. If Corrigan was right, they couldn't let anyone know Ruri was wolven, not even the human children. They'd bought in to whatever was going on here and could no longer be trusted.

"Samson is my favorite," Shejuanna said as she turned away from them. "If you want to meet him…" Her voice trailed off as she made her way in Latawna's direction but stopped short of her friend. She leaned down and opened a door that came barely up to her waist, then sat cross-legged on the wooden floor.

Still hand-in-hand with Ruri, Malice walked up on the girl. She made sure they took their time, which wasn't difficult as Ruri seemed to want to stop every other second to surreptitiously sniff at something. It was probably just as well she was wearing the armband Corrigan gave her. From what Malice could tell, without it Ruri would have shifted to wolf form not long after they entered this so-called stable.

They had just gotten up to Shejuanna when a small furry head peeked out around the door. It was much smaller than the door would have implied. It appeared to be a small terrier, covered with rough grey fur and with a curiously square muzzle. Large bat-like ears unfurled from its head when it looked over at them.

"It's all right," Shejuanna said. "I know them."

The ears folded back along its head. It inched closer to Shejuanna while continuing to watch both of them. There was something strange about its eyes, and it took Malice a moment to put her finger on it. She stopped dead in her tracks when she realized what was putting her back up. Unlike a dog's eyes, which show very little white unless the animal is in distress, this creature's irises were surrounded by the white of a cornea in much the same way a human's were.

"Isn't he adorable?" Shejuanna said. She reached forward and pulled the human-eyed terrier into her lap. It cuddled down against her and raised its head to lick the bottom of her chin. They weren't close enough that she could tell, but Malice could have sworn the tongue was thicker than a dog's would usually be. She was quite well acquainted with the tongue of Ruri's wolf form, having received many tongue baths to the face when her girlfriend was feeling frisky. As a wolf, Ruri's tongue was wide and flat. Malice decided not to look too much more closely.

"What kind of hunt has such tiny coursers?" Ruri asked. Malice was glad for the distraction from her disturbing thoughts.

"A hunt that chases all variety of game," replied a dry voice from behind them.

Shejuanna put the terrier-thing aside and bounded to her feet. "My lord," she said, bowing low.

Malice looked up to see the other two doing the same. Ruri stayed unbent and regarded the slender man who was their height but still managed to look down his nose at them.

Like Corrigan, he had pointed ears that poked out from under his long hair. To say his hair was brown was too simple. Shades from mahogany to a golden honey shade covered his head in strips not entirely unlike the coat of a particularly gorgeous tabby cat. With every shift of his head, his hair revealed another shade of brown—now auburn, now chestnut. Eyes of palest lavender regarded them closely, seeming not to pay any attention at all to the teenagers. The terrier-thing trotted up to him and sat by his feet, staring up at him with intent eyes that seemed much too intelligent.

"Who are you?" Malice asked.

"I am the Jaeger," the man said. His demeanor unfroze and he offered them a smile that warmed his entire face. "I lead the Wild Hunt, and I think you and I can help each other, Hunter."

CHAPTER SIXTEEN

"The Jaeger?" Ruri watched this strange man closely. "What does that mean?"

"An excellent question," he said. "It means I am the king's huntsman. I, and I alone, decide what game the Wild Hunt will pursue."

"Doesn't your king have a say?"

"Of course he does," the Jaeger said. "But the beasts of the Hunt respond to me alone. He directs me, but I alone direct the Hunt."

"And how can you help us?" Mal said. "More importantly, why do you want to?"

Ruri nodded, heartened by her mate's healthy skepticism. Nothing about this place rang true, she could tell as much even with senses blunted.

"Simple, you are a Hunter, as am I," he said. "I currently have no second for the Hunt. Our numbers have diminished since traversing the ocean to these lands. Without a second, I'm unable to hunt more dangerous game. With your aid, we can clear the realm of the more dangerous predators who have threatened King Connall's subjects. I'm certain he'd consider that a mighty boon and would permit you to leave as a result."

"What kind of game are you talking about?" Ruri asked. "Are they dangerous?"

The Jaeger laughed, a disconcerting sound that reminded her vaguely of deep-toned bells. She supposed the sound was beautiful. From the smile that spread across Mal's face, she definitely thought so.

"My dear, of course they are. Everything is dangerous here. You are in the land of the fae, after all." He tsked at her while shaking his head gently from side to side. "And so human."

Ruri tried not to bristle at the condescension. She managed to keep from correcting him, but she couldn't keep from crossing her arms in front of her chest.

"Ruri, it's all right," Mal said. "This could work out for both of us." She smiled and turned to face him. "She's an excellent hunter in her own right."

"Is she now?" The Jaeger looked her up and down. Ruri felt like a calf being sized up for slaughter. "She's fit enough. I'm happy to take her on as well."

"That's fantastic." Mal grinned and clapped her hands together, rubbing them in glee. "We'll be out of here in no time. How do we sign up?"

"I'll send word when the Wild Hunt will ride again. I must confer with His Majesty." The Jaeger bowed to Mal, the courtly action seemingly second nature to him. He turned on his heel and walked off down the long hall of the stable, past Jermayne.

"He invited you to be part of the Hunt!" Shejuanna's whisper was harsh with excitement. "Humans aren't allowed to participate. Simeon asked and got yelled at for daring to presume or whatever."

The no-humans allowed rule didn't exclude either of them, but Ruri wasn't going to elaborate. Instead, she smiled tightly. "I guess… if it gets us out of here."

"Yes," Mal said. She watched the Jaeger's departing back with a bright smile, one that faded slightly when he turned a corner and was gone from sight. She turned back toward them and gripped the bridge of her nose between thumb and forefinger for a second. "I'm sure it'll be fine."

"Of course it will," Shejuanna said. "That's the Jaeger." She sighed. "He's kinda…"

"Kinda what?" Jermayne asked, coming up on their little group. "Do I need to worry?"

"What?" Shejuanna said. "Of course not. He's hot and all, but it would be like dating the sun or something. Someone like him is never going to be interested in someone like me." She paused and stared down the hall. "Besides, I have you," she said, seeming to realize that her initial reassurance might not be what Jermayne was looking for.

"Yeah, you do." He pulled her into a loose embrace and nuzzled where her neck met her shoulder.

"That's great," Ruri said. "Let's get out of here. I think I've seen enough of the stable for today, especially since it seems we'll be seeing it again."

"Are you sure?" Mal asked. "We might as well look around while we're down here."

"Look around if you want. I need some fresh air." She stalked down the hall, away from her mate. Each footfall echoed sharply against the stone walls of the corridor. She managed to keep from stomping her feet, but it was close.

At the far end of the hallway was a set of double doors, taller even than the ones they'd passed through to get here. If Ruri had been the wagering sort, she would have bet all of her meager savings that those opened onto the outside. Even as she stormed away from Mal, she listened for some sign that she was following. When no footsteps followed her, the anger she'd been holding in her breast since the Jaeger had accosted them threatened to burst into searing flames. She broke into a run. It wasn't the easy lope of four paws on loamy forest floor. Her wolf didn't quicken within her, straining against her bonds of skin. Tears flowed down her cheeks as she thrust her arms forward, shoving her way through the doors, which flew open under the assault of her palms.

Fresh air tickled her nostrils. Ruri did her best to ignore the lack of wolven response. She inhaled deeply, letting the scents of wildflowers coat the inside of her airway. The smell was familiar. She'd been smelling it for a day, after all. This was the smell that had been all over Shejuanna's bunk and her false corpse. She opened her eyes to the twilit sky, her view partly blocked by tall walls of gleaming white that reached halfway to the sky. Crenellations marched evenly across the top of the walls, in contrast to the royal blue and lavender of the sky. Her feet came down on flat rocks, not ringing nearly as loudly now that she was out of that hall.

She veered off to the right, heading for the grassy lawns spreading out before her. Beyond were trees and beyond those more walls. She made a beeline through the grass and into a stand of trees. It couldn't rightly call itself a forest, but it was too wild to be a garden. The branches closed around her, welcoming her into an embrace that was at once comforting and made the hairs on the back of her neck stand on end. It was familiar, but subtly wrong. It was all she had.

She inhaled deeply again, seeking the smell of the trees in a vain attempt to block out the cloying sweetness of the flowers. It didn't work. With a deep sigh, she sat herself down beneath the nearest spreading boughs and leaned back. She looked up toward the canopy, trying not to notice the lavender-tinged light that filtered through the lattice of boughs and leaves.

Why am I so angry? She asked herself. *He didn't say anything wrong. Sure, he was kind of dismissive, but all I have to go on is a feeling.* The wolf would have known and would have either confirmed her vague suspicions or dismissed them. Her fingers twitched as she fought not to succumb to the urge to pull off the armband Corrigan had saddled her with. Would anyone really know?

Not within the walls. Ruri put her hand down. As soon as she could make her way beyond those ridiculously bright walls, though, she'd shift and go for a run. She might even clue Mal in to her plans.

Leaning against the rough bark of the tree, Ruri was finally able to relax. If this place hadn't felt so subtly alien, she might have fallen asleep. That wasn't going to happen anytime soon. Would she be able to sleep here at all? That would make for a fun stay as she grew progressively more sleep-deprived. Would Mal notice, or would she be too busy being all "we're Hunters now" with that Jaeger fellow?

He was using Mal, that was as obvious as the muzzle on her wolf's face. But to what end? She had problems believing his reasoning. There had been plenty of fae in the throne room. Surely some of those could help out on their little hunt. Why did it have to be Mal?

She shifted irritably against the trunk behind her as if the rigid roots would somehow shift to accommodate her. They didn't.

Well, if she had to save Mal from herself, it wouldn't be the first time. Ruri would simply have to keep an eye on her mate and redirect her when necessary. She laughed aloud. If they were back in their own world, Mal would go back to fretting about the fact that Cassidy never called her. That particular habit was rather aggravating, especially when Ruri got the distinct impression that Mal blamed her for being the one Cassidy reached out to. Yet there she was, wishing for that very same distraction.

A soft sound to her left broke Ruri out of the tangle of her thoughts. She couldn't place it at first, not until she picked out the source of the noise. There, not more than a few trees from where she sat, a young man with a curtain of black hair was trailing his hand along the trunk of one of the trees. His clothes were simple, and what she could see of them appeared to fade into the background, blurring slightly around the edges.

She waited as he leaned his forehead against the tree's trunk and closed his eyes. His lips moved as though he was talking, but Ruri heard nothing. He stayed like that for a few minutes, then stopped speaking. He didn't move at all for a few moments after that. Finally, he heaved a long sigh that was echoed in the breeze that sifted through the boughs of the grove's trees.

He stepped back and looked over at her with such sadness that she wondered how he wasn't in tears.

Ruri stayed seated. She didn't know what else to do. So far, most of the fae she'd met here had put a whole lot of stock into formality. But they'd also been dressed for the fanciest prom parties of their lives. He wasn't.

Ruri smiled hesitantly. "My apologies," she said, keeping her voice quiet, but loud enough to carry to his ears. "I didn't realize anyone else was out here."

He smiled in return, but the sadness didn't leave his eyes. "There is no need to apologize. This area is closed only to a few. As far as I know, Connall has not yet added humans to that list."

"That's good. We only just got here, but already I've managed to put my foot wrong with at least one person."

He laughed a joyous burst of sound that was surprising given the anguish Ruri could practically feel coming off him in waves. "Was it someone in the castle?"

Ruri nodded.

"I'm not surprised. Most folk among the Seleighe are quick to take offense."

"See-lee?" Ruri rolled the unfamiliar word around on her tongue.

"Seleighe," he repeated, his pronunciation a hair different than hers. "Do you mind if I come over to you?"

The request was strangely phrased, but Ruri nodded.

"I am called Nagamo," he said as he made his way over to her. He dropped into a sitting position with unconscious grace. "The one you rest against is called Azaadi."

"I'm Ruri," she said before the second part of his statement had a chance to sink in. "Wait, who I'm sitting against?" Ruri scooted forward, looking first at Nagamo, then twisting to stare at the dark grey bark of the tree behind her. "I'm so sorry. I had no idea this was a person. Is a person." She squinted, looking for a face or hands, anything to indicate this was some kind of fae. "Is he a dryad?"

"She, and not exactly," Nagamo said. He placed a hand on the nearest root to him. "She says she isn't offended and that your presence is welcome as it demands nothing from her." He paused, his brows furrowed, then withdrew his hand and sat up straight. "She is surprised to feel such peace from one of the wendigo."

"Wendigo?" Ruri had some vague knowledge of the term. If she remembered correctly, it was a villain of some sort from comic books. Somehow she didn't think that was the dryad's frame of reference.

"A malevolent spirit that sometimes possesses humans and leads them to do heinous acts against others, especially of their own kind."

"That doesn't sound like me." Though it did sound like the more misinformed stories about the wolven. It also sounded a lot like MacTavish.

"Nor do you have the look." Nagamo relaxed slightly. "We are constantly surprised by new forms that aren't quite like those we're used to."

"How do you mean?"

Nagamo watched her for a long time, the seconds stretching uncomfortably between them. He caressed the root that ran past his leg. "She trusts you," he finally said. "Though she is less certain of the other. I was in the throne room when you came in, though you would not have seen me. I told them of the arrival of strange human-looking mortals. It is up to me to keep them abreast of happenings in this realm and in yours." He stood and offered her his hand. "Let us walk deeper among my people and I will tell you our sad story. If you are to stay here, even for a short while, you deserve to know what kind of folk you are dealing with."

Ruri took the offered hand and allowed him to pull her to her feet. His palm was rough against hers. Standing next to him, she was surprised at his height. He was easily as tall as Sheriff Corrigan and likely taller. He smiled down at her, the skin crinkling at the corners of eyes so dark the iris was impossible to distinguish from the pupil. His hand was cool, though not distressingly so. He squeezed her hand encouragingly, then let it go.

"This isn't a long tale," he said as he moved away from her, hands clasped behind his back. "In retrospect, it shouldn't have come as a surprise, but at the time it did. I suppose that is one reason hatred burns so strongly between kin. It always surprises us when those like us hurt us."

Ruri had to lengthen her stride to keep up with him, though he wasn't moving that quickly. She didn't think he was trying to get her to scurry along, rather that he was unaware how much longer his legs were than hers.

"You called Azaadi a dryad, a word you've no doubt heard from human stories," he said.

"I've heard it a few places. My parents used to talk about those who could take the form of trees, but they called them *hulderfolk*."

"Quite so," Nagamo said. "My extended family spans your world, and when your ancestors came to these woods, they brought along those who call themselves fae, though your kin knew not of their presence. At first the fae recognized us as their own. We taught our cousins the ways of what they called the New World, though it was ancient to us. All was well until they realized that we live wholly in your world while they have one foot in the human realm and the other here."

"What does that mean?"

"It means we do not go 'Underhill,' as the European fae would call it. After a time, the fae were able to reestablish their portals and went Underhill once again. Apparently there are certain places where portals may be set up, places where the mortal world and this one are close enough to breach using their magics." He shook his head. "I do not understand it completely, though it has been explained to me more than once. If these worlds are echoes of each other, they look for places where the echo overlaps so closely it is indistinguishable."

Nagamo laughed softly at Ruri's confused expression. "You understand. They think it is a simple thing, but not to those of us who do not share in those gifts.

"My family was given the option of joining as repayment for the hospitality we showed upon their arrival. That consideration has rarely been shown to those who have since arrived. Time passed and they began to call those of us who make their homes in the mortal world by one term: Unseleighe, in contrast to the term for Seleighe, which means The Shining Ones. By calling us what they did, they made clear their opinion of us. Originally, there were Seleighe and Unseleighe courts and they would share control of the fae world, one in summer, the other in winter. Now there are only those who live in Faerie and those who live without, whether by choice or by decree."

Ruri nodded as she walked alongside him, wondering how long his story was going to take. He'd said it was a short one, but the background alone was taking a long time. At least she hoped this was the backstory and not the background to the backstory.

"So this is perhaps a way of saying that we are alike, our extended kin and we, but also unlike, sometimes in surprising ways. Take the dryads as an example. The dryads, our cousins, now live in their trees and leave them but rarely. They are powerful guardians as a result. My people are tree spirits as well, but our nature is much more fluid. We inhabit trees, yes, but we leave them frequently to roam the forests that are our homes.

"Not long after the European fae settled here, the tree bodies of their dryads were destroyed by human settlers. Have you ever wondered why this county is called Hawthorn?"

Taken aback at the sudden question, Ruri blinked twice before finding her voice to answer. "Uh, no?"

"When human settlers moved to this area, they were surprised to discover a grove of small-flower black hawthorn trees and an old one at that. Hawthorns of that variety were native to portions of Europe, not to what they called North America. They did what humans do when presented with something rare: they destroyed them. Every last tree in that grove was chopped down." He looked down at her. "I do not mean to give offense."

Ruri shook her head. "I'm well-versed in the sins of humans. You don't have to apologize to me."

Nagamo nodded. "The retribution of my kin was swift and fearful. They called on their Wild Hunt that very night and rode down every last human settler within fifty miles. Those who weren't pulled screaming from their beds and summarily dispatched were afflicted with a terrible wasting sickness. Within two weeks, no living human remained in the area. Despite his flaws, King Connall is wise in his own way. He knew more humans would come. Some would arrive despite the stories of a cursed land, and others would come because of them. With the grove of guardian trees gone from the main entrance Underhill, he needed new sentinels, which is where my people came in. We were as horrified at the destruction as they and offered aid. It is my long-standing regret that Connall took us up on the offer.

"You see, we did not fully understand them nor they us. We had no knowledge that we were expected to be constant, silent sentries, allowed to leave our trees only during the equinox. We expected to render aid in the form we chose, but the forms of agreement Connall used were binding to *his* will, not to our intentions. My people suffer, bound inside their trees for such periods of time as they were never meant to endure. Some have ceased responding to me and do not come out in the spring or fall. Those who do must exist here, for Connall insisted they be bound in both realms. It was for our greater protection, he said. What he meant was that he could not have them leaving this place to take over their forms in the mortal world and wandering the forests, leaving the entrance short even one guardian. Should hostile humans encroach on the grove around the entrance Underhill, they would be confronted by a force of vengeful forest guardians propelled by the power of the king's bargain back into their true bodies.

"I fear I will never hear their voices again." He stopped in front of a massive oak and gazed at the limbs that stretched forth above their heads. Small lights drifted between the boughs. "I was the one who agreed. I was the one to doom them to this existence. I alone remain free to walk where I may."

"Oh, wow," Ruri said. She had no problem believing the arrogant fae she'd met in the throne room was capable of such a deception. "What are you doing about it?"

"What I can." Nagamo ran a finger over the oak's roughened bark. "I address the throne when Connall will permit it, which happens less frequently now than it did."

"What changed?"

"Other beings arrived, carried along by the beliefs of humans from different parts of the world. He feels threatened, outnumbered, though his fae still count many more than the so-called Unseleighe. There are those within his court who encourage his paranoia in the name of their own personal power."

"Why tell me all this?"

"So that you may know who it is you bargain with. The deal you make may not be the one you perceive it to be. The one with the power decides what shape any bargain will take. They work for their advantage, and if they are working with you, it's because the benefit to them outweighs any favor you may think they're doing you. They aren't all the way Connall and those who would use him are, but each seeks advantage."

Ruri had no response. On the one hand, she wasn't surprised to hear such a thing. It lined up with all the stories she'd been told and what she'd seen so far. It was surprising to hear it laid out so matter-of-factly.

"Do well, my young friend," Nagamo said. "Continue to treat my people kindly. I'm afraid I've overstayed my welcome." He put a finger to his lips. "I was never here."

At her nod, he moved the finger from his mouth to his earlobe, which he tugged upon once, then he disappeared from sight in a soft pop of displaced air.

CHAPTER SEVENTEEN

Mary Alice watched Ruri storm off down the hall.

"What's her problem?" Jermayne asked.

"I'm not sure," she answered. She thought about going after Ruri. Her girlfriend was obviously having issues, and who could blame her? It was probably best to give her some space. There was nothing Mary Alice could do to bring back her wolf, at least not at the moment. But who knew about the future? "Where does the Wild Hunt ride?"

"All over," Shejuanna said. "They come back covered in mud and sticks. Sometimes other things."

"What other things?"

"Blood," Jermayne said. He watched her as if gauging how she would take his blunt answer. "Bits of flesh and fur."

"That makes sense," Mary Alice said, her voice deliberately bland. "They are hunting things, after all."

"And with some of what we've had to clean off, they're definitely things." He grinned down at Shejuanna, who was rolling her eyes at the delight he was taking in recounting the gruesomeness of their task.

"Maybe I should take one of the beasts out, get to know it," Mary Alice said.

The teens exchanged glances, then shook their heads as one. "Better not," Shejuanna said.

"You should wait until the Jaeger assigns you a mount," Jermayne said. "He's particular about who gets to ride what. You can tell who's in good with him by what mount they're assigned. There are more mounts than riders, so when he assigns you to something lame, you know he's pissed."

"Then where would I go if I wanted to just go for a nice ride? Can I borrow an ATV or a car? Anything like that."

Jermayne shook his head, the grin on his face barely short of outright laughter.

"Not so much with cars," Shejuanna said. "There's a regular stable, though. They can't keep horses near the beasts. Some of ours can open latches on their own. If we left something that tempting around, they'd get eaten up for sure." She pointed the opposite direction from the one Ruri had just stomped away down. "Through there and across the courtyard is the horse stable. Tell the brownie there that you're with Reese. The Heir gets what she wants around here."

"Got it. Stay out of trouble, all right?"

Jermayne rolled his eyes while Shejuanna grinned widely. "Are you kidding?" he said. "They want us to get in trouble. Think it's the best thing ever."

"Fine then," Mary Alice said. She was suddenly very tired. The kids had made it clear they didn't need rescuing. She wasn't their mother. If they wanted to get up to mischief, that was on them.

She made her way down the hall, past the doors and windows. She couldn't help but peer into some of the pens. The term "beast" was too tame for many of the things she saw. Animals in combinations of every conceivable type watched her with too-intelligent eyes as she walked past. The thing that seemed to be equal part trailing shadows and tentacles sent a chill down her spine that threatened to settle in her bones. After that one, she kept her eyes front and ignored the things that watched.

The courtyard on the other side of the double doors was bright and cheerful. Mary Alice slowed to take in her surroundings as she passed through. The cobbles were white and regular, marred only here and there by wear. Thin strips of manicured lawns lined the edges and were planted with bushes sporting sprigs of colorful flowers. The external walls rose high into the sky, towering above her. In the middle was a massive portcullis. She stopped in her tracks. It was easily five stories tall or so it looked from here. Why on earth would the King of the Fae need a door that tall into his castle? She wasn't certain she really wanted an answer, so she kept going.

The horse stable looked much more like she imagined one would. It smelled sweet, of straw and dust.

"What have we here?" A short man popped out from around a corner. His skin was dark brown, almost the same color as the chestnut horse who watched them curiously from a nearby stall.

"I'd like to borrow a horse," Mary Alice said.

He looked her up and down. Her fancy getup got an approving nod, which vanished when he reached her face. "Who claims you?"

"Claims me?" She lifted an eyebrow in what she hoped was cool disdain.

"Cor but you're new, aren'cha?" He shook his head. "Your keeper should have given you the talk before letting you roam around free."

Malice smiled widely. The little man backed up a step. That was fine. Malice stepped closer. She leaned down, getting a feel for his personal space before deliberately invading it. They were practically nose to nose when she inhaled sharply to speak. He flinched.

"I can assure you that no one claims me."

"I–I'm sorry." He actually wrang his hands in distress. "B–but someone has to. Humans don't get to wander around here."

"Maybe I'm the first."

"M-maybe." He squared his shoulders and stood up defiantly. "I can't let you borrow a horse if someone here isn't good for it."

"I could take one. Who would stop me? You?"

"If I have to." He brought his hands up and started to weave his fingers together in a complicated gesture.

"Hold on there, spark plug," Malice said. "I'm messing with you. I'm with Corrigan. I mean Reese. You know, the Heir."

Apparently, the clarification had been unnecessary. He ceased the finger gestures as soon as Corrigan's name came out of her mouth. "Why didn't you say so? Of course you can borrow a horse if you're one of Reese's."

"Maybe I don't like your attitude."

"Maybe the feeling is mutual." He glared at her, a muscle jumping in his jaw.

Malice returned his venomous look with interest. The longer they stared at each other, the more ridiculous the situation began to seem. She was having a death stare-off with a man half her height in a place where magic was real. Her lips started to twitch and try as she might, she was unable to keep the first chuckle inside. The harder she tried not to laugh, the more guffaws burst from her. She laughed until her sides ached, her hands on her knees, trying to stay upright.

When she finally looked up, the little man was watching her, an expression that could only be described as consternation on his face.

"I like you," Mary Alice said. "You're feisty."

"If you say so," he said, not looking any less worried.

"So, about that horse. Can I get one?"

He hesitated. "I guess so. Try not to lose it."

"Great. Which one can I have?"

He sighed and preceded her down the row of stalls, stopping in front of one about a third of the way down. He looked her up and down. "Yeah, this one will do." He reached up and unlatched the stall door, then stood to one side.

Mary Alice strode into the stall and stopped. A horse with a dusty grey coat stood in front of her, more interested in the contents of her feed bag than with the human who had entered her space.

"There's a problem with the horse," Mary Alice said.

"What?" The little man stuck his head into the stall and looked the mare up and down. "No, there isn't."

"It doesn't have a saddle on it."

He pointed at the saddle hanging off a hook on the wall. "It's right there. Reins are next to it."

Mary Alice stared at the saddle. It seemed simple enough to figure out, but the reins looked like so much leather spaghetti. "Yeah, that's not going to work for me."

"You don't know how to saddle a horse."

Mary Alice bristled at the judgment in his tone. "I grew up in New York City. We don't have horses. I can teach you all about taking the subway, but I don't know how to get a horse kitted out."

"Oberon save me," he said to the ceiling.

"I can make that necessary," Malice offered.

"I will saddle the horse once. Pay close attention to what I'm doing because I won't do this for you again, no matter if the Heir claims you or not."

Malice chose not to respond. She watched everything he did closely and was reasonably certain she'd be able to do it again if she had to. The man muttered to himself the entire time, though the mare didn't seem to mind. In fact, she spent half the time with her head in the feed bag and only raised her head when he kneed her in the belly while trying to cinch down the saddle's belly strap. The horse wasn't as disinterested as she seemed. The knee forced a lungful of air out of her chest. The sneaky thing had been holding her breath. Mary Alice took note of that particular technique.

He made the reins look particularly easy, paying little attention to the large teeth that his tiny hands were so close to. The horse took the bit easily. As soon as it was in her mouth, her entire demeanor changed. She shifted toward the door, clearly eager to be out and about.

"There you go," he said, slapping the ends of the reins down in her hand. "Wait until you're outside before mounting. And head back before dark. There are things out there that love to snack on horseflesh."

"Got it." Mary Alice started to walk toward the entrance, the horse clopping eagerly at her side. "What's your name, anyway?"

"You can call me Geffron." He nodded.

"It's good to meet you, Geffron. I'm Mary Alice."

"Well, then. Don't fall into a ditch, Mary Alice."

She laughed. "Words to live by." She stopped the horse outside the stable and considered her. She looked much taller than she had in the stall. Mary Alice was no equestrian. There had been the pony ride for her birthday when she was six and a ride at the New York State Fair when she was twelve, but aside from that all she had to go on was what she'd seen on TV.

"All right," Mary Alice said. "I just need you to hold still while I get up there, all right?"

The mare watched her with dark eyes. It was impossible to tell what she was thinking.

"Here goes nothing." Mary Alice kept the reins in one hand and put her left foot up to the stirrup. So far so good. The next step was to get up top. She experimentally put her weight on the stirrup. The horse shifted away from her.

Mary Alice managed to keep her foot in the stirrup, but she had to hop forward to keep up with the mare. "Enough of that." The horse stopped. Mary Alice took a deep breath. Going at the problem tentatively wasn't giving her the results she wanted. It was time to damn the torpedoes, as her father used to say.

She gripped the sides of the saddle and used her momentum to pull herself up. At the last moment, she remembered to lift her right leg over the horse's back. It bounced off the top of the mare's back, but she kept going, carrying the leg over to the other side. She was able to stabilize herself on top of the horse fairly easily, no matter that the mare shifted under her again.

"I did it." A wide grin spread across her face. It was too bad Ruri wasn't there to see it. Farm girl that she was, riding a horse was probably no big deal, but she would have liked to share the moment with her.

"Now to make you go." Mary Alice dug her heels carefully into the horse's sides.

The mare shot a look over her shoulder, then took a step forward.

"Yes, that's it," Mary Alice said encouragingly. "Now take another, please." She touched her heels to the horse's sides again.

The mare broke into a reluctant trot that jostled Mary Alice up and down uncomfortably. She gritted her teeth and went with it, guiding the horse through the portcullis.

No one tried to stop her. The horse's hooves echoed loudly as they made their way across the wooden drawbridge. Mary Alice tugged at the reins to stop her when they'd crossed. A road meandered down the hill in front of them. To their right were trees as far as the eye could see. There were trees on the left also, but beyond them she could make out the angular wedges of the strange mountains where she and Ruri had appeared. It would be best to avoid those. The road had plenty of clearance on either side. That seemed like a good enough place to start.

With a gentle touch, she urged the horse down the hill.

CHAPTER EIGHTEEN

Mary Alice steered the horse back up to the castle. She'd eventually figured out a pace between the incredibly uncomfortable trot and an all-out gallop, and that was where they were now. Her thighs burned in a way they hadn't since basic training, and the inside of her legs were more than a little chafed. Horseback riding was much more taxing than she'd anticipated. She stretched in the seat, knuckling at the small of her back to loosen some of the tension that was settling there.

She'd wondered what Geffron had meant about nighttime here. With the constant twilight she had wondered how she would know when night fell. There seemed to be some sort of light source that was unmoored from the setting sun. The sky had darkened perceptibly as it started to wane. Fortunately, she hadn't left the road.

Now that they were crossing back over the drawbridge, the sky was almost completely dark, except for the persistent lavender in the west, or what she assumed was the west. Even at night the sunset was still visible, if slightly dimmer than it was during the day.

"Where have you been?" Geffron demanded when she entered the courtyard. He hopped down from a set of stairs heading up the side of the gate tower. "It's dark out. There are plenty of things that come out at night. Maybe in your world you can stay out until all hours, but not here."

"Sorry," Mary Alice said. "I didn't realize it would get dark so quickly."

"I'm missing the start of the evening reel," he said, his voice testy. "I suppose you don't know any more about turning a horse out for the night than you did about saddling one."

It wasn't really a question. Mary Alice shook her head, trying not to get her back up over his tone. It was difficult.

"Figures." He darted forward and grabbed the reins from her hand, having to reach up almost to his tiptoes to do so. "I'll tell you what to do, but you better hop to. I'm not missing any more of the festivities than I have to just because you don't know how to do the most basic things."

You might need him later, Mary Alice told herself. *Don't piss him off now.* "Whatever you say," she said, trying to sound as cheerful as possible. It was something Ruri had mastered, managing to sound as if whatever was being asked of her was the most interesting and natural thing in the world and that there was nothing she would rather do. From the sideways glare Geffron gave over his shoulder, she'd failed to impart that.

For all his moaning about the situation, she was able to get the mare unsaddled, rubbed down, and groomed out reasonably quickly.

"About time," Geffron said in a low grumble. "After this, you're on your own." He turned on his heel and left the stall.

"Well, then." Mary Alice looked over at the mare whose head was back in her feedbag. "I think that was a little much."

The horse didn't respond, which Mary Alice took as assent. There was no point in getting angry. In fact, she didn't think she could have if she wanted to. At that moment she could only describe herself as relaxed. She wandered toward the door. Relaxed didn't typically apply to her personality. She came by it honestly at least. Her parents' genes combined with her upbringing, her training, and her job had conspired to make her one of the least laidback people she knew. Not that she knew that many people. This was an unusual feeling, one she usually experienced right after she and Ruri had made love or after one of their joint runs in the park.

Where was Ruri? Surely she'd gotten over her pique from earlier. It occurred to Mary Alice that this was a big place. Ruri could be pretty much anywhere. However, if she had to guess, and she did, she would say Ruri was wherever there were the most trees. She looked around the courtyard. Shining lights dotted the walls. They were too constant and cool to be torches, but she was pretty certain they weren't light bulbs either. She hadn't seen anything as mundane as a wall plug. It seemed likely electricity wasn't a thing. Still, the lights revealed no trees. The shrubs around the perimeter definitely didn't qualify. She crossed the courtyard, heading for the only other door she recognized, the one to the Wild Hunt's stables.

Inside there was no sign of Shejuanna, Latawna, or Jermayne. There were only a few lights, and they were much dimmer here than they had been in the courtyard. As she walked down the hall, though, more burst into brightness around her, lighting her way forward. It wasn't eerie at all, she tried to tell herself. At the other end were the double doors Ruri had busted open in her anger. That was somewhere to start.

When she came through the doors and saw the large grove of tall trees, Mary Alice knew exactly where Ruri had ended up. She made a beeline through the columns of thick trunks to where her girlfriend lounged, cradled between the massive roots of an ancient oak.

"You found me." The look of quiet joy on Ruri's face was something Mary Alice knew she would treasure for a very long time.

"Of course I did," she replied, not thinking of the words. "I'll always find you."

"That's some smooth talk," Ruri said. "And not at all like you. Who took my big, bad Hunter, and could you hold onto her, please?" She grinned up at Mary Alice. "I like this version better."

"Well, this version needs a long bath." Mary Alice held out her hand to Ruri, who accepted it and allowed herself to be pulled to her feet.

"You do smell a little...odd." Ruri wrinkled her nose. "Is that horse I'm smelling?"

"It is."

"You know how to ride a horse?"

"I do now. I had some vague notions and they panned out after some trial and error." She kept hold of Ruri's hand as they walked through the trees.

"Poor horse."

"You're hilarious."

"It's true." Ruri was quiet for a few moments as they continued to walk.

Mary Alice was content to stay quiet, Ruri's hand warm in hers as they continued forward.

"I have a question for you," Ruri said a little while later. The trees had thinned out around them and the shining walls were visible between their trunks. The brilliance of the ramparts was only slightly diminished by the fall of night.

"Go ahead," Mary Alice said.

"How are you so okay with all of this?" Frustration pulled at the edges of Ruri's voice.

It was a good question. Mary Alice probed at it, worrying it like a six-year-old with a loose tooth. "I'm not sure," she finally said. "I should be right royally pissed. And I am." She lifted her hand to forestall Ruri when she opened her mouth to respond. "What Corrigan has done to take away your wolf is terrible. I can't even imagine how awful that must be. This thing with their dick of a king shutting down the portals for us sucks too, but it feels like a problem with a solution, especially since that Jaeger guy talked to us."

"If you say so" was Ruri's dark response. "I don't trust him."

"Neither do I." Mary Alice laughed aloud at the idea. "I trust you and I trust me. Everything else is suspect."

"Oh, Mal." Ruri tucked a lock of Mary Alice's hair behind her ear. "That is such a lonely way to live."

"Not as much as it used to be." That was definitely true. As much as she chafed at the changes Ruri's presence brought to her life, now there was more to look forward to than the next mission. They were both in uncharted territory, but Mary Alice knew she wouldn't want to be there with anyone else. They were walking a tightrope blindfolded. A stray gust of wind could send her tumbling to her death, but she knew that without Ruri, that tumble was assured. She would anchor her girlfriend and Ruri would stabilize her. She already did.

"What are you thinking?" Ruri asked.

"About how stiff my legs and back are getting thanks to that damn horse." She should have said something about her fears, but she didn't know how to put them in words. Mary Alice had spent so much time keeping Ruri at a careful distance that now she wasn't exactly sure how to let her in closer.

Ruri laughed. "Uh huh. In any case, I'm glad you don't trust him. Promise me you'll keep that in mind."

"I promise." Mary Alice stepped toward the outskirts of the woods. "Now let's go find a bath and our stuff."

"Sounds like a plan to me."

* * *

Ruri wasn't having any luck falling asleep. Oh, the bed was certainly comfortable, and the room was more opulent than any she'd stayed in before.

When she and Mal had made their way back into the castle, they'd been set upon almost immediately by a small woman in a diaphanous dress so perfectly matching her wings that it had taken Ruri a moment to notice them. From her exclamations, they'd been the subject of her search for quite some time. Mal had been whisked away down one corridor when she'd asked after bathing facilities. Ruri had been led to this room.

On a heavily carved and gilded table had been Mal's belongings, including her phone and the few items she'd had in her pockets. There was no sign of Ruri's notebook and the "samples" they'd taken at the camp. They'd gotten to the bottom of the mystery, so she didn't really need them, but she still wondered where they'd ended up.

She'd been unable to settle down and had divided her time between watching out the window and pacing between it and the door, over and over. There were twenty-seven steps between them. Mal had come back full of rapturous details about the baths. According to her, the waters must have had healing properties as her pain had almost completely diminished. She'd fallen asleep not long after glancing at her phone to see if they had any cell service. They hadn't.

Oh, she'd made every effort to keep her eyes open and talk, but Ruri had told her it was all right to go to sleep. Mal had been breathing deeply within minutes.

That had been a couple of hours ago and Ruri was still awake. The pale lavender light from the window was simply one more reminder of where they were whenever she opened her eyes. As if she really needed the reminder. The absence of her wolf was more than enough for that. Curling up around Mal helped a bit, but even that couldn't completely fill the void within.

Her skin felt too tight, that was the real problem. Not being able to sleep wasn't helping.

Ruri slithered out from under the heavy covers, her feet hitting the plush rugs on the floor without sound. The cool air caressed her naked skin. It was a far cry from the cold winter's touch she'd endured since leaving Chicago. Still, she didn't take her time in pulling on one of the loose-fitting tunics and a pair of leggings she'd found stacked in the wardrobe. They were much less fancy than what she'd worn to court. In any case, as promised, that outfit had disappeared when she'd turned it inside out in the course of taking it off. She'd been left with a handful of random items that wouldn't have been out of place in a toddler's pocket.

Mal stirred while she was getting ready and Ruri froze. She reached out for Ruri in her sleep, and for a few seconds she was able to forget about her wolf. Mal settled back into her pillows and the slow rhythm of her breathing resumed. Ruri smiled down at her, then quietly let herself out the door.

The sourceless light in the hall had dimmed. The strange night sky was visible through the windows that lined both sides of the hall. Not sure where she was going, Ruri started out in a brisk walk down the hallway to her left. Hopefully she could wear down some of the jumpiness that rode her.

A door opened as she walked past it.

"I suppose I shouldn't be surprised you're wandering about tonight," Corrigan said. "You've had a lot to deal with today."

"You could say that." Ruri knew her voice was cold and made no effort to warm it.

"I deserve that, from your point of view, I know." The sheriff moved out into the hall and shut the door to her rooms behind her. She was no longer in the insanely fancy court clothes Ruri had last seen her in. It looked like she was wearing her sheriff's uniform pants and a plain white T-shirt. "Why don't we find somewhere to talk?"

"You're the princess or whatever."

Corrigan cringed a bit at the title. "I'm the heir to King Connall, long may he reign." In her mouth, the words sounded like a fervent wish and not the rote declaration it likely was to most people.

"It sounds like your life is really hard."

"Not as hard as it will become when I do inherit the throne." She led the way down the hall and stopped in front of a sturdy wooden door built into an arch. The ring of keys she produced from a pocket was much larger than the pocket should have allowed. The keys ranged from modern house keys to ancient skeleton keys. Corrigan flipped through them quickly, then inserted a skeleton key into the lock. "Through here," she said.

A stone staircase spiraled up into darkness. Ruri stepped through, her eyes adjusting easily enough to the shadows. "Where are we going?"

"Somewhere we can talk without prying ears. Keep going until you reach the top. There's nowhere to stop along the way."

"All right." As much as she didn't want to speak with the sheriff or spend any time with her at all really, she had no other notion of what to do. The path of least resistance felt like the best one at the moment, and for all her anger at Corrigan, the fae woman didn't irritate her the same way the Jaeger had. So despite her misgivings, she ascended the spiral stairs. It took a while and her legs had started to burn by the time she hit the last step. That took a lot, and she wondered how high up they were. Corrigan climbed behind her so quietly that Ruri couldn't stop herself from checking to see if she still followed. Every time she looked back, Corrigan was there, watching her.

Another heavy wooden door greeted her at the top of the stairs. It too was locked. She moved back so Corrigan could get at it with her ridiculous pile of keys. The door opened onto a flat roof. A tall flagpole stretched out from the middle of the space. At the top of it two pennants, one gold, the other lavender, snapped and danced in a stiff breeze.

Ruri inhaled deeply. The wind smelled less strongly of wildflowers up here. She imagined the tension on her skin loosening somewhat.

Corrigan closed the door behind her. "I thought this place might appeal to you."

"It isn't terrible," Ruri said. She closed her eyes and drank in the scent of the wind.

"It's more difficult to see the terrible." Corrigan walked past her toward the crenellated edge of the tower. "Come see what the kingdom has to offer."

Intrigued despite her misgivings about the sheriff, Ruri followed her. Even up here and in profound darkness, the stones of the castle still exuded a faint glow. When she looked up, Ruri discovered a spray of strange stars. They peppered the heavens above them, except to the west where the violet sunset lingered perpetually.

"You already know the shattered mounts of Aventhar." The edges of the familiar upside-down crags glowed in the darkness. "It's home to the kobolds you already met, among others. The kobolds have treated with the king. They provide him with metal ores and gems, and he turns a blind eye to the travelers that disappear on their way through the passes."

"Doesn't your king care about his people?"

"Of course he does. For those who know the forms, avoiding the kobolds is child's play. Those who don't should have done better research before attempting such a journey." She shook her head. "Or so he thinks."

"Okay." Ruri strained her eyes to bring the distant mountains into focus. All she could make out were their odd topsy-turvy shapes. "Why do they look like that?"

"The mountains? Connall inverted them to entomb an attacking army of fire giants."

"And he didn't bother to put them back after." So far, she didn't think much of the fae king's leadership abilities.

"Doing so would have released the giants from their prison. Besides, it was millennia ago. To do so now would destroy the homes of many of his subjects. The mountains might look strange to your eye, but they're part of the landscape here."

"Oh." Ruri thought on that for a bit but couldn't think of anything to take fault with. "Is that a river?" She squinted at the thread that wended its way through the landscape reflecting the uneasy purple of the sky.

"Ah yes, the Ayregad Sneethe. It runs the length of the kingdom and ends in a cascade of silver into oblivion. The journey duskward to the edge is full of peril, but the beauty of its final descent is something to behold. Especially these days as it descends through the violet signs of our king's decline."

"Is everyone here a poet, or is it just you?"

A genuine smile crept across Corrigan's face. She looked more... human, though Ruri hated to use the term.

"There's something about being here that does that to me," the sheriff said, sounding much more like the person they'd met in town. "It really is beautiful here, for all its other faults. English doesn't allow me to do it justice, no matter how flowery I get. It would be rude of me to wax on in a language you don't understand."

"Rude of you." Ruri cocked her head and stared at the sheriff. "Rude. Of you."

"Well, yes." To her credit, Corrigan noticed that Ruri had an issue with her phrasing. Her brow crinkled slightly as she tried to figure out exactly what the problem was.

"You trap me in this form, away from the other half of myself, but you're worried that slipping into a different language would seem 'rude'?" Ruri hooked her fingers savagely against the air in the largest, most sarcastic air-quotes she could come up with.

"Well, when you put it that way, it does seem more than a little—"

"Don't you even say 'rude.'" Past caring that the woman in front of her was what passed for royalty in this place, Ruri breached Corrigan's space. She used her presence for all it was worth, beyond considering what the lack of her wolf might to do to her dominance. All that Ruri was bore down on Corrigan, and she was angry.

Corrigan hesitated for a moment, then gave ground.

Ruri followed. Her prey wasn't going to elude her. "I wake up in a strange place, and I'm stripped of all my defenses."

"Clearly not all of them…"

Ruri ignored the muttered response. "You take something from me. Maybe it's a little thing to you. 'Oh, the human's pet wolf, she won't miss that.' Well, guess what. I do miss her. So far, the only thing keeping me from taking off this fucking armband is your story that it'll bite Mal and me in the ass. I am losing patience here. You'd better get real convincing and fast or I'm stripping this thing off. How happy do you think my wolf will be with what you've done?" She leaned in further, closing the distance between them until her nose almost touched Corrigan's. Her lips curled off her teeth in an unholy cross between snarl and smile. "I'll give you a hint," she said in a voice that emanated from deep within her chest. "If you think I'm angry now, you haven't seen anything."

"You're not wrong." Corrigan stood her ground and reached up past Ruri's elbow. "I figured it would come to this eventually, but I'd hoped we could find somewhere more remote for the demonstration. Allow me a moment to prepare myself." She guided Ruri to the center of the tower, then sat on the ground. She closed her eyes and lifted her face to the stars above for a moment. Ruri looked up but saw nothing except the star-speckled heavens.

Corrigan opened her eyes, then withdrew something from her pocket. "Watch this moonstone." She tossed a pale pebble that glowed faintly to the floor between them. As Ruri's eyes followed the movement, she grabbed the armband and pulled it down the length of Ruri's arm.

CHAPTER NINETEEN

As the armband skimmed down her arm, the wolf rushed into Ruri's head. A howl of exultation split the inside of her brain and came out of her mouth in a protracted moan. Gooseflesh erupted on her skin, pierced through by fur in the next instant. The tissues of her gums filled and split as teeth forced their way into her mouth. Her jaw was overtaken by a pain too fierce to be an ache. Her knees buckled as her legs started to reform; the snapping sound of her joints was whisked away by the night breeze. Bright light bathed the top of the tower.

Corrigan held her up when she threatened to keel over, but Ruri scarcely noticed, distracted as she was by the being who shared her soul.

Then the wolf was gone. This time Ruri did howl, a long sound of disappointment and loss. Corrigan pulled her hand away, having secured the armband once more around her bicep. It took a moment to realize the brilliance that had shone around them was gone. The moonstone the sheriff had left on the ground was back to a fitful glow.

"This was the only moonstone to light up," Corrigan said. "I... negotiated a limitation of its effect for a short period of time. The closer the moonstone is to you, the brighter it gets. It would have been safer to do it further from the castle, but I didn't think you would be willing to follow me out to the woods, so I found another way. You needed to know. I am not doing this to torture you."

Ruri tried to laugh, but all that came out was a strangled grunt. "If this isn't torture, then you need a new definition." Her body still felt the energy of the change, but now she had nowhere to go with it. Was this how Cassidy had felt during her first shift? Her own was so long ago that she could no longer remember. She pushed Corrigan's hands away from her and promptly collapsed into a heap.

"I regret any discomfort you feel, but I really am trying to keep you as whole as possible. My goal is to get you and your Hunter back to your world as soon as possible. The last thing we need is for her people to come sniffing around after her."

"That's all well and good for you, but you're not the one feeling like your insides got flipped to outsides then back in again." Ruri shook her head. "Seriously, if you ever try that again, I will kill you. It doesn't matter which form I'm in."

Corrigan smiled, her lips thin. "I'm certain you'd try."

"Whatever. We can stay here and thump our chests at each other some more, or we can help each other. What's our best way to get out of here?"

"Your Malice needs to stay polite and composed around the king and members of his court. I've been doing my best to determine what Connall would consider enough of a boon to atone for the insult she gave him when she questioned his word on the safety of the human children."

Ruri pushed herself carefully back up. She eyed the sheriff carefully. "Did you send the Jaeger to us, then?"

The look Corrigan gave her was sharp in the extreme. "I did not. When did he approach you?"

"When we were in the stables of the Wild Hunt. The human kids gave us a tour. I was curious."

"The Jaeger is well respected in court," Corrigan said slowly, "but he is feared outside these walls and even more outside Connall's kingdom. For good reason. You should stay away from him."

"He says he can help Mal with the whole boon thing."

"Doubtless he can. I can't stop you from working with him, but exercise caution. He is my main rival in court and would give next to no thought to using you and your Malice to replace me as heir."

"I don't get a great vibe from him," Ruri said. "But then you're not one of my favorite people right now either."

"I understand that. Just be aware of him. It's possible his motives are pure and he simply sees your Malice and her skills as an opportunity to get some work accomplished that he hasn't been able to. Titania knows, the Wild Hunt hasn't had its full complement since it stopped making incursions into your world. The hunters thrive on the possibility of death, and there's less of that here, for all that our beasts are quite different from your own. Perhaps Malice can lend an edge that's been missing. Mortals often do. All I ask is that you and she stay vigilant and don't enter into any bargains with the Huntmaster. The only transaction in play right now is between your Hunter and my king." She cocked her head. "Do you realize you could leave at any time?"

Ruri shook her head. "That makes no difference. I won't leave her alone in this place."

"Even knowing you'd be able to have your wolf back."

"She would drag us back in here so fast your head would spin."

"Ah. Probably not a good idea then."

Ruri grinned, showing more teeth than mirth. "All you have to remember is I'm the level-headed one."

To Ruri's amusement, Corrigan paled slightly at her comment. "Maybe you should stay here."

"Lucky for you, that was already the plan." Ruri stretched, feeling the buzz of electricity down her limbs. She wished she could have had a little more time with the wolf, long enough to work out some of the kinks. A thought occurred to her. "Where's the moon?"

"There is none tonight."

"Like it's the new moon here, or you don't have one at all?"

"Connall doesn't wish to see her face tonight, so we don't."

"Aren't there fae creatures who are tied to the phases of the moon?" She thought she remembered some among the stories her parents used to tell.

"There are," Corrigan said. "Some of them stay Underhill to avoid the tyranny of your world's moon as much as possible. Our moon doesn't have the same effect, likely because it's an extension of Connall's will. Those who remain here are in the minority, however. Many of our celebrations are tied to the moon. On those nights, the court celebrates in your world. It's one reason so many of us keep homes in both places and why we have so many portals. Your world is also a useful refuge from Connall's court in these times of upheaval."

"Good for you," Ruri said. She didn't mean it. In fact, at that moment she seethed with resentment at those who could move freely back and forth. The only good news in the sheriff's explanation had been that she shouldn't be subject to the moon's demand that she shift. The wolf wouldn't be forced from her and expose them.

"You can come to me whenever you have questions or problems," Corrigan said. "I've claimed you both as my own. All that means is other fae aren't permitted to exert their gifts over you without my express permission."

"How ever did we get so lucky," Ruri said in her most monotone drawl.

"It's for—"

"—our own protection, I know." Ruri sighed. "Look, I get that you think you're doing the right thing by us, but it's really hard to appreciate that at the moment. I'm heading back to bed. Maybe I won't want to rip your throat open with my very human teeth by morning." Her teeth almost itched with the urge to bite something and her body tingled with the need for some sort of release. There was one thing that might help, since she couldn't shift to fur form and hunt down some poor animal.

"Very well." Corrigan seemed to sense her agitation. She wasted no time in trying to talk further. Instead, she crossed the top of the tower to the door and opened it for Ruri, giving her a peculiar half bow from the waist. Ruri ignored it and her as she trotted down the stairs. She made her way into the hall and back to her room without seeing anyone else. The door didn't so much as creak when she opened it, and Ruri slipped into the room.

"Where have you been?" Mal asked from the bed.

"I'll tell you about it later," Ruri said. She stalked toward her mate, a grin of anticipation rising on her face.

Mal sat up in bed and watched her approach. She pulled back one corner of the covers so Ruri could get into bed.

Ruri seized the blankets and threw them back, exposing Mal's body to the cool air. Her smile widened as she watched Mal's nipples harden at the sudden chill.

"You're in a mood."

"You have no idea." Ruri lay down next to Mal, running her hands down her mate's ribcage. "God, I need you right now."

"Is that so?" Mal smiled up at her, then leaned forward, pulling down the edge of Ruri's tunic. Before she realized what she was up to, Mal had given the skin over her collarbone a sharp nip.

Ruri crushed Mal against her and bent her head back. She captured Mal's lips with hers, running the tip of her tongue over the oh-so-soft skin. She drank Mal's taste in, licking and nibbling until Mal opened her mouth to allow her tongue to dip in briefly. Mal moaned into her mouth as Ruri tasted her, sliding her tongue against Mal's, then pulling back. She wanted to leave Mal wanting more, needing more.

Her hands roamed over Mal's back, marveling over the smoothness of her skin.

With a suddenness that surprised her, Mal slid her hands up into Ruri's hair, gripping hard and pulling her head back. She gasped. Mal nibbled and sucked her way down the column of her throat. Ruri no longer had the upper hand, Mal was in charge, taking over with an ease that should have galled her, but didn't. Instead, she thrilled to the feel of Mal's mouth on her, claiming her, making her Mal's and only Mal's.

Mal let go of her hair with one hand and got to her knees, pulling Ruri along with her. Her other hand slid down Ruri's back to her waist.

"These are in the way," Mal said, tugging at the waistband of her leggings.

Ruri disengaged long enough to skim off the tight pants. She shucked the tunic over her head and into a dark corner of the room with one motion.

As soon as the shirt was off, Mal was on her again. She nipped along Ruri's collarbone. Each bite added to the answering ache between Ruri's thighs. Wetness gathered there until Ruri was certain it would start dripping down the inside of her leg. Mal let go of her waist and hair. She placed a hand on Ruri's sternum and pushed.

Ruri fell back, landing on the soft mattress as she watched her mate. Mal's eyes gleamed, almost matching those of a wolven for luminosity. She knew exactly what she wanted. Ruri shivered as Mal devoured her with her eyes. To be wanted with such ferocity by this woman who had the wherewithal to take it and more made her weak in the knees. Or it would have had she not been lying down already.

The shivers increased as she yearned for Mal to touch her, to cover her with her body, to feel Mal's skin on hers.

"I need to feel you inside me," Ruri said, her voice cracking. She licked dry lips.

"In a bit." Mal smirked. "I'm busy." She knelt where Ruri's legs dangled over the edge of the bed.

Ruri cried out when Mal grasped her knees and spread her legs. Cool air brushed over the wetness of her arousal. It should have cooled her, but instead she found herself further inflamed. When Mal's fingers gently spread her lips and her hot breath bathed her clit, Ruri grabbed the comforter to keep from coming right there.

Mal's lips closed around her clit and Ruri clenched her teeth to keep from screaming. There was no point in announcing to everyone else in the castle what they were up to. She did her best to muffle her cries, but when Mal's gaze met hers over the swell of her mound with a look of pure mischief in her eyes and she sucked Ruri into her mouth, she couldn't be quiet any longer. The pleasure Mal nursed from her in long, deliberate sucking strokes sent her out of her head in an explosion of light and sound. She screamed her release at the ceiling and imagined her wolf howled along with her.

Ruri peaked once, twice, and again as Mal refused to let her come down. She slid one long finger within Ruri's slick canal while she continued to lick her clit. When Ruri felt like she couldn't possibly come again, she hit another crest. Another finger joined the first one, stretching her wider, sending her past her limits once more. She screamed again as the pressure that had been building finally burst out of her.

She drifted slowly back down to the bed, coming lazily back to herself. She settled back into her body, delicious lassitude swallowing her. When she opened her eyes, Mal lay next to her on the bed. She smiled at Ruri. That line of silver throbbed between them. Mal's love cradled her, free of the stain of guilt.

"Pleased with yourself?" Ruri asked. She couldn't help but smile back at her mate.

"Shouldn't I be?" Mal said.

"Mm…" Ruri stretched, every muscle in her body oozing relaxation. "You definitely should be."

"Then I am." Mal put her arms behind her head and looked up at the ceiling, radiating smugness.

"Good for you." Ruri turned on her side and reached for Mal. "Now it's my turn."

Mal squeaked when she was pulled on top of Ruri. She looked down at her, straddling her hips.

"And once we're done with that, you can fill me in on what all you've been up to," Mal said, her voice raspy as Ruri rolled her nipple gently between two fingers.

There'll be time enough to get up to speed, Ruri thought. *First things first.*

CHAPTER TWENTY

Mary Alice stretched as she did every morning, looking to dismiss the weakness of sleep from her muscles as quickly as she could. When her hand didn't hit the bedside table as usual, her eyes popped open. Instead of the loft ceiling with its exposed rafters and ducts, she saw stone and timber. She was halfway out of bed when she remembered where she was.

She willed her racing heart to slow and after a few moments it did. Ruri's hand groped toward hers under the heavy woolen blanket. Mary Alice took it. Her heart rate slowed even further. From what she could tell, her girlfriend wasn't actually awake. She watched Ruri's sleeping face peeking out from under the covers with a pillow jammed up against the top of her head. Last night had been nice. A wide smile crept across Mary Alice's face as she remembered how Ruri had looked below then above her. She reached forward and gently pushed back an errant lock of blond hair.

We have to get out of here.

Her stomach took that moment to remind her that it had been quite some time since she'd eaten. She rubbed her belly in a vain attempt to quiet the tortured sound that wavered back and forth between a rumble and a squeal.

Do fairy castles have cafeterias? The loud groan of her stomach propelled her from the bed. Where should she go? It didn't really matter. She had to find something.

Mary Alice reached over and located Ruri's shoulder through the covers. She gave it a gentle shake.

"Mmph" was Ruri's response. She snugged the blankets more closely around herself.

"I'm going to find breakfast," Mary Alice said quietly. "Do you want to come with?"

"S'allright," Ruri said, voice slurred from sleep.

"Okay then." Well, she'd tried.

The clothing in the wardrobe was unfamiliar, but not difficult to figure out. She wasn't pleased with how exposed her behind felt in the leggings with the tunic that didn't cover it completely. The discomfort was alleviated when she found a coat that came down almost to mid-thigh. It had belt loops through which she threaded a plain leather belt. Some rummaging turned up a belt pouch, which she threaded onto the belt along with her knife. Her phone went into the pouch.

The coat's puffy sleeves, slit to allow the tunic to show through, felt awkward, but less so than the soft-soled shoes she donned. Even on the piles of rugs strewn around the chamber, the ground felt distressingly close.

There was a full-length mirror next to the wardrobe. Mary Alice looked at herself critically. She felt like she was cosplaying a character from a movie she neither knew nor cared about. What she really needed was a full set of tac gear, down to the combat boots and her katana. She was heading into who knew what and she was woefully unprepared.

Her stomach spoke up again, letting her know that ill-prepared or not, she needed sustenance. At this point, all she was doing was delaying meeting her insecurities head on. That wasn't like her. It was time to jump into the unknown.

Mary Alice pulled her shoulders back and strode across the room. Grasping the door handle, she pulled it open, and Malice stepped out into the hall.

A man of middling height stood up from where he'd been leaning against the wall. At least Malice assumed he was a man. His face was broad and flat, the eyes set wide from each other. He reminded her uncomfortably of a frog, an impression that wasn't the least bit alleviated by the seaweed decorating the lower half of his face. No, after a closer look, Malice realized he was sporting a goatee of green hair. His skin was dark grey verging on black. It shone, but whether it was from dampness or from the multitude of tiny scales covering his skin, she couldn't tell.

"Can I help you?" Malice asked. She dropped her hand to the knife at her belt.

He chuckled, a wet rumbling sound that echoed through his barrel-like chest. "I'm here to help you, as a matter of fact." He nodded his head at her. "The Heir has requested you and your lady be attended by the palace pages. I am Mracek. I was one of the few brave enough to volunteer for this duty."

"I'm glad to hear it." Malice removed her hand from the hilt of her knife. "Two requests, though."

"Yes, Lady Hunter."

Malice cringed. "Three requests. One, don't call me Lady Hunter. Malice is fine. Two, don't let Ruri hear you calling her my lady, she won't take it well. Three, where can I get some food?"

Mracek nodded seriously at each of her points. "Very well, Malice. But please inform the Heir of your choice of address. I don't wish to be punished for your informality. I am happy to conduct you to where you may break your fast. Please follow me."

He trotted ahead of her, easy to pick out in his tabard of pale purple and gold, colors that Malice now realized were the king's livery. She wondered what Corrigan's colors were and how she might find out.

Mracek led her down one corridor, then another, and another. Each was so different from each other that they might have come from a different castle. The height of the ceilings varied widely, as did the width of the corridors. Tapestries in bright colors decorated the walls of one hall, another was carved stone from floor to ceiling, still another had wood paneling halfway up the walls. The ever-present windows looking out onto the land with its continual sunset were enough to convince her they hadn't stepped through a portal into another fairy-tale palace.

She soon gave up trying to track their path. The twists and turns were baffling. Her direction sense was usually flawless, but from what she could tell, they should have made their way past her room twice now, yet there was no sign of it.

They occasionally passed members of the fae court who either ignored them completely or gave them a wide berth and stared at her as if she was a display at the zoo. She tried not to pay attention to the gawkers but quickly lost patience. When she bared her teeth at the next looky-loo, the creature's startled reaction was so gratifying that she repeated the look with the others.

The guards they passed were much more stone-faced. Malice also noted that they were mostly the same variety of fae as Corrigan, the Jaeger, and King Connall. They all wore versions of his livery, but ones more suited to martial action than Mracek's flimsy tabard. Their eyes turned to watch her, though none moved so much as a muscle to acknowledge her in any other way.

Finally, they arrived at a tall door. Mracek reached for the handle, but it opened toward them before he could grab it. He stepped deftly back and bowed low. He held the position as a trio of winged beings closer to the size of brownies flew past them. They noticed Malice. One looked at the other two and said something in such a high-pitched voice Malice thought her ears might bleed. They all laughed in a tinkle of bells that might have sounded pretty if Malice hadn't known she was being laughed at.

"Sylphs," Mracek growled after they'd passed. "Pay no mind to them. They're naught but a bunch of jumped-up pixies with no use for anyone without wings."

Malice blinked. "Noted," she said.

"I'll await you here."

"You don't have to do that." Malice glanced through the open door into the large hall beyond it.

"Will you be able to find your own way back to your chamber?"

"Well… No." The point was well-taken. Malice stalked through the door. Her hand settled on the hilt of her combat knife.

Fae flitted to and from between the long tables in the center of the room and those that lined the walls. The trestles against the unadorned stone of the walls were filled with so much food, Malice wouldn't have been surprised to see them sag in the middle. White cloths covered the tops of the tables, making it impossible to tell what they were made of, if anything at all. The whole thing had the look of a fancy wedding buffet. She tried not to snicker at the image but couldn't stop a muffled chortle from sneaking past her lips.

Once again, she was either gawked at here or discounted. It didn't matter. The smells of the food were distraction enough from the rudeness. She took a golden plate from a tall stack and made her way down the buffet, stopping when something looked vaguely familiar. If the smell coming off whatever she'd stopped to look at was reasonably unexotic, she snagged a small piece. Beyond the large trays of this or that roast beast, it was impossible to tell what might have meat in it. There didn't seem to be a meatless section. It was depressingly like the human world. The hardest part of being a vegetarian was eating out.

Once her plate was full, she went back through, pulling slices of meat onto a plate for Ruri. She'd almost made it back down the line when someone cleared their throat behind her.

Malice looked back over her shoulder slowly and with a look to do her nickname proud.

"I'm glad to see you preparing so well for the day, Hunter," said the Jaeger. "I too am preparing. I've received word of a scourge to the dawnward hills. Perhaps you'd be interested in joining the hunt?"

"Jaeger." Malice paused, uncertain which honorific to use, if any. "What's the saying? An army marches on its stomach. I don't see why hunters would be any different." Quickly, before he might assume she wasn't interested in the second half of his statement, she said, "And if I can be of aid, I'd love to help. When are you leaving?"

The Jaeger smiled. "Excellent. We shall set out at noon. Unfortunately, many of the hunt are bored nobles. They don't tend to rise at the same hour as we. The beast will likely give us some sport, but I expect it will be no match for someone of your capability."

Malice kept her face smooth, choosing not to rise to the comment of a being offering up sport. "We'll see. I'd like Ruri to come."

"Your paramour?" The Jaeger's left eyebrow climbed halfway up his forehead. "Does she have any facility for the hunt?"

"I'd say so. She'll be fine with whatever gets thrown at us."

"If you say so." His voice was doubtful. "Then you should both join us at noon. Come a bit early so I may assign you each to your mounts." He leaned forward conspiratorially after glancing around to see if anyone was close enough to hear them. "We hunt a hodag."

"All right." If she was supposed to be impressed, the Jaeger was going to be disappointed. Malice had a hazy memory of seeing a very large, vaguely reptilian-looking statue in one of the towns they'd driven through on their way to La Pointe. She thought that might be what he was referring to but wasn't sure how so ungainly a creature might exist in real life. "I'll be there," she said as he stood watching her, clearly waiting for something.

"I shall hold you to it," he said.

"Quick question before you go?"

"Of course." The Jaeger inclined his head to her.

"What did you mean by dawnward?"

"Ah, yes. It is no surprise you aren't acquainted with our cardinal directions. Dawnward is your east." He gestured to one side. "Duskward is west, while headward and tailward are your north and south, respectively." He pointed each one out as he said them. "Do you understand?"

"I do, thank you for the clarification."

"I shall hold you to that," he said, before giving her a half bow and leaving.

Everyone kept bowing, but Malice had no idea how to respond. Should she bow back? How long would she be able to get away with being a clueless human before one of the fae took offense? And what exactly was he going to hold her to and why?

The blood quickened in Malice's veins as it always did before a mission. She was going to get the chance to actually do something. If she was lucky, this would be a big enough boon that Connall would open the portals back up for them.

"What time is it?" she asked Mracek when she exited the hall.

He glanced out a nearby window. "Between eight and nine as I reckon it."

"Hold onto these for a second, would you?" He held out his hand and she passed over Ruri's plate of various meats as well as her own breakfast. She fished the phone out of her belt pouch and checked it. The clock on the face read 4:47, a far cry from the time Mracek had given her. Malice sighed. Clearly she couldn't rely on the device. At least the battery didn't seem to be running down. The notification of the voice message from Cassidy taunted her, but she couldn't retrieve it. Her attempts from the night before had been met with the frustrating wheel that spun as it tried to fulfill her request, but never went any further. The same had been true this morning. She shoved the phone back into the pouch with a frustrated sigh and reached for the plates he held.

"Back to your room?" Mracek asked.

"Yes, please."

"With pleasure." He led her back through the same halls and corridors. Nothing had changed about the demeanor of the fae they encountered, but Malice found it easier to discount them now that she had something to do.

* * *

Ruri opened her eyes and sat up as Mary Alice came through the door. Her hair stuck out at an angle on one side of her head. It was adorable. Mary Alice couldn't help but chuckle as she passed Ruri her leaning tower of meat.

"What?" Ruri asked suspiciously.

"You're super cute in the morning." Mary Alice leaned in for a kiss, which Ruri grudgingly returned. "Your hair is doing some exciting things."

"Oh." Normally Ruri was a morning person, but that didn't seem to be the case today. Mary Alice passed over the plate she'd put together, with its stacks of flesh. Her attitude brightened somewhat after she took a long, appreciative sniff of the food in front of her. She inhaled it with the same appetite she displayed when there wasn't something blocking her wolf. "Is good," she said through half a mouthful. "Thanks."

Mary Alice ate her breakfast more slowly, though not by much. She'd sneaked a couple of bites on the way up, but her stomach wasn't truly appeased until she'd cleared off half her plate. The lack of utensils didn't slow her down; she managed more than well enough with her fingers.

"The Jaeger has called for a hunt at noon today," she said when they'd come up for air from breakfast.

"Is that right?" Ruri licked some pink juices off her middle and index fingers.

Mary Alice tried not to focus on the movement of Ruri's lips and tongue around the tantalizing digits. "It is. I told him you'd be coming too."

"Why would you do that?"

"I thought it would be better than being stuck here by yourself." Mary Alice carefully kept her tone neutral. Ruri's response wasn't what she'd expected to hear.

"I suppose." Ruri looked up from her plate, unshed tears shimmering in her eyes. "I don't know how I'll be without my wolf."

"Oh, no." Mary Alice put down her plate and pulled Ruri back into a firm hug. "I'm sorry, baby. I didn't think of that at all. I was just thinking how maybe this could be the thing that gets us home."

"It's okay." Ruri scrubbed her palms into her eyes. She sniffed once. "I know you're not trying to be a jerk, and honestly I don't know what's going to set me off." She took a deep breath. "With the way I'm feeling, it's definitely a bad idea for me to hang out alone. I'll come along."

"Great." Mary Alice rested her chin on Ruri's shoulder. "It's okay if you don't want to. I'm not going to pressure you into anything you don't want to do."

"What's the matter? Are you out of C-4?"

"Very funny." Mary Alice nipped at the back of her girlfriend's shoulder.

Ruri's full-throated laugh sent a wave of relief through Mary Alice. She hadn't stepped in it too badly. She grinned and squeezed Ruri tightly against her.

"So what do you want to do until then?" she whispered into the pink shell of Ruri's ear. Slowly, she ran her tongue around the edge of the exposed earlobe.

Ruri didn't answer. Instead, she turned around and met Mary Alice's lips with her own.

CHAPTER TWENTY-ONE

The Wild Hunt's stable felt much more ominous when filled with dour fae who gave her and Mal sideways glances when they thought they weren't looking. A number of them sported moonstone in one form or another. So far, Ruri had noted a few necklaces, a bracelet, the pommel of a jewel-encrusted dagger, and even a ring. She was certain there were more. The reminder had her acutely aware of the crater of her wolf's absence.

The teens were there bringing beasts to various hunt members. They weren't treated with the same disdain, but then the riders barely seemed to notice them at all. Perhaps they were only accustomed to dealing with humans as servants. Not that she and Mal were exactly human, but they were certainly indistinguishable at the moment.

She stood to one side, trying not to feel too awkward. Mal was next to her, looking much more at ease. She exuded eagerness. Mal was at her best when she was aimed at a problem and ready to be loosed upon it.

"There you are" came the Jaeger's too-smooth tones. "I have a pair of mounts for you. I think you'll be pleased. This way." He made his way through the milling crush of fae and strange animals. A path opened in front of him like magic and closed as quickly behind him, leaving her and Mal to thread their way through them all.

The Jaeger stopped in front of a door that had yet to be opened.

"You," he called out impatiently to Carlo, who was clearly engaged in helping another fae saddle her mount. "Turn out these two immediately, if you please."

Carlo shrugged at the fae woman he was helping. She bestowed Ruri with a particularly dark look as her helper abandoned her. He hurried forward and threw open the door. Two horses of dappled grey stood in a pool of sunlight in the massive box stall.

Ruri was somewhat disappointed at the mundane appearance of the animals who regarded their sudden audience with mild curiosity. The other beasts had been much more fantastical. Hell, there was a horse with wings, for crying out loud.

Carlo led one of the horses out of the sun and her dismay faded. As it moved into the shadows, the horse's skin and muscles seemed to melt away until all that was left was bare bones. In each eye socket was a single burning coal.

Mal tensed next to her. "Jesus."

"You're not kidding," Ruri said.

"The pale horses don't often accompany us," the Jaeger said. "Many find them unsettling. Humans have historically viewed them as omens of death. They're not wrong." He laughed merrily. "You'll find them much like regular horses to ride."

"No problem." Ruri had grown up on a Minnesota farm in the latter half of the 19th century. This wasn't her first horse, merely the first she'd ridden in a few decades. She had no doubt muscle memory would serve her well.

"Oh, sure." Mal tried to hide her uncertainty with bravado, but Ruri still detected her unease. She doubted the Jaeger would be able to tell.

Carlo had lashed the halter of the first pale horse to a post while he worked to get it saddled and bridled.

"I assume you have no hunting weapons," the Jaeger said.

"All I have is my knife." Mal dropped her hand to the hilt at her waist.

"Is it steel?" the Jaeger asked.

"Yes."

"Take care not to wield it near the mounts. They can't tolerate the touch of iron or steel."

Ruri nodded. She'd wondered if that was the case. It had been a refrain mentioned regularly in her parents' tales.

"We shall get you kitted out while the boy readies your horses." The Jaeger drew them down the hall, away from the throng that was starting to make it way outside. A few stragglers rushed to get their own beasts ready.

The Jaeger pulled open one of the few non-barn doors to line the corridor. "Wait here," he said as he disappeared inside. Sounds of rummaging floated back to their ears. "Can either of you shoot a bow?"

"I've used a compound bow on occasion," Mal said. At Ruri's questioning look she leaned over. "Vamps," she whispered. "Wood through the heart works as well whether it's an arrow or a stake."

"It's been a very long time for me," Ruri said. "Do you have anything with a shorter range?" She peeked around the door to get a better view of her options.

The armory's interior was lit only by a small ball of light that hovered atop a sconce of dark metal. Its dim rays glittered off many metallic surfaces but did little to dispel the shadows. The metals were too warm to be iron, for the most part. Ruri thought perhaps they might be of bronze or copper. Much cooler metals glinted among them, but they were too shiny to be steel. *What is that?* she wondered. *Surely it's not silver.* The occasional would-be werewolf hunters who had attacked them with silver had quickly discovered how ill-suited the metal was to any kind of combat.

"There are options," the Jaeger said. "I have javelins, or maybe a sword would be more to your liking."

"The javelins will be fine, but perhaps a couple of knives instead of the sword."

"I'll take the sword," Mal said.

The Jaeger didn't answer, but sounds of movement redoubled. Ruri could barely make him out as he crossed the room and back. He finally came through the door, festooned with weapons. Mal moved quickly to relieve him of his burdens. She passed four short spears over to Ruri, followed by two knives in elaborately tooled leather sheaths. They looked and smelled like bronze, but their edges gleamed wickedly all the same.

"Do you have any armor for us?" Mal asked.

"Most of our number use enchantments for protection." He eyed them closely. "I may have something that will work." He was gone much longer this time, but when he returned, he held two thick leather shirts. Large bronze rings marched in even rows up and down the front and back of the armor, while smaller rings covered the arms.

"These should fit," the Jaeger said as he passed both to Mal, ignoring Ruri altogether. He stood to one side as Ruri helped Mal into her armor.

"Arms up," Mal said, as she returned the favor. Ruri tried to ignore the Jaeger as her mate dressed her, but his presence was difficult to disregard. She was certain he was judging them for needing physical protection.

Once the armor had been tied into place and the knives settled easily around her hips, Ruri picked up the rest of her armament. She had to juggle the javelins awkwardly as they made their way back to the pale horses.

Latawna had come over to help Carlo, and the horses were being finished up. Aside from their little group and the mounts, the hallway was empty.

"Mount up and join us in the courtyard," the Jaeger said. He strode past them and out the tall double doors.

Mal was eying her horse dubiously.

"It's just like any other horse," Ruri said, as much to her mate as to herself. She put her foot in the stirrup and grabbed onto the pommel. Her body remembered what to do, and she pulled herself up and settled into the saddle in one smooth motion. To her side, Mal was managing fairly well, though her skeletal horse looked back once as she was trying to settle her foot in the other stirrup. Latawna scooted forward and shortened the stirrups so Mal wasn't having to stretch to seat her feet properly. It was easy to forget that Mal wasn't exactly the tallest person in the world. Ruri was constantly surprised to find out she was taller than her mate, if only by a few inches.

It was strange to look down and see bones, but the horse didn't feel all that different from what she'd grown up with.

"Good luck," Latawna said. She handed Ruri the reins. "Try not to get dead."

"Um, thanks?" Ruri wasn't certain what to do with the off-handed good wishes. She dug her heels into the horse's side and clicked her tongue at it. To her relief, it moved forward, its counterpart pacing alongside.

As they emerged into the noonday sun, the bones disappeared, to be replaced with a smooth, dappled coat. There was nothing Ruri could see that would distinguish it from a regular horse. At their appearance, a trumpet cry went up from the front of the host. It was taken up by others, a brassy call that echoed from horn blower to horn blower. The host turned as one and cantered for the portcullis, leaving Ruri and Mal to follow along behind.

Once outside the castle walls, they wheeled to the east, ignoring the road in favor of open fields of tall grass bordered by stands of tall trees. Not every beast had the same gait, yet they managed to move in comparable rhythm. As Mal and Ruri drew abreast of the other riders, they were viewed askance. Mutters and whispers too loud to ignore but too soft to decipher reached Ruri. The tips of her ears burned as she tried not to listen for them. Instead, she concentrated on moving with the horse and on not noticing that it flickered between coat and bone when they cantered beneath the trees. When a spot of shadow hit the pale horse's coat, it looked like a hole had been bored through its skin, one that went down to bleached bone, without the gore of blood and muscle.

With a shudder, Ruri decided to pay attention to the countryside. Slowly, copses of trees became less frequent until rolling grasslands surrounded them. The only trees she saw were stunted things dotting the edges of small ponds or running along the banks of creeks and streams. Small creatures flew out of the grass as the riders' passage disturbed their resting places. Whether they were insects or some sort of fae, she couldn't tell. They were gone too quickly.

The sun slowly descended from its zenith. As they headed away from the perpetual sunset, Ruri tried to pretend they were somewhere other than Faerie. As long as she didn't look too closely at those riding in front of them, she was content to deceive herself. The illusion was ruined when they trotted past a picturesque cottage disgorging bright green smoke from its chimney.

The rolling grasses gave way to hills peppered here and there with large boulders that seemed to be forcing themselves free of the ground's grasp. A horn sounded from the front of the group and the beasts slowed to a walk.

"What's going on?" Mal asked quietly.

"If I had to guess, I'd say someone's sighted tracks of whatever we're hunting," Ruri said. "They're trying to determine which way to head, then we'll be off again."

The elf woman who Carlo had been helping looked over at her explanation and nodded in grudging approval. It was nothing too complicated to understand. The pack often employed similar tactics when they hunted together, but using barks and howls instead of horns. Ruri bit her lip as sorrow for her missing wolf and absent pack threatened to engulf her. There was too much about this that she knew deep in her bones, and yet she couldn't access it.

Ahead, the horn sounded and they picked up the pace once more. They didn't return to the ground-covering canter; instead they moved at a more sedate trot. Hills rose higher and higher on either side of them, and they were forced into a narrower and narrower file until they could barely travel two abreast. Ruri kept her eye out for Mal and made sure to keep her horse as close to hers as possible.

It didn't take long before Ruri noticed that all signs of wildlife had disappeared. Gone were the things that were being scared out of the grasses earlier. There was no sound of birds nor the rustle of larger animals in the dense shrubs that dotted the hillsides. She reached forward and loosened the leather wrap holding the javelins together in their carrying case on the saddle. The towering hills pressed down on her. Ruri glanced up at their tops. If something were to attack them down here, they'd have nowhere to go. It would be a bloodbath.

They moved too slowly for her taste. She would much rather have been on the heights in fur-form. The further they went, the tenser her shoulders and back got. She rolled them in a vain attempt to bring some relief to the tight muscles.

A disturbance up ahead pulled her attention. There was some hubbub coming down the line of riders toward them. There were no accompanying shouts or sounds to indicate an attack, though. Moments later, the terrier with the too-human eyes appeared. A sylph stood in the mount's stirrups, her wings beating rapidly. She spied them and dashed toward them. The terrier's legs moved so quickly they were almost a blur. More than once, the sylph ducked down and they darted beneath a horse's belly, seeming to take no mind of the massive hooves that could easily crush them. She pulled on the terrier's reins as she drew up to them.

"You two," she shouted in her piercing voice. "Take the right fork ahead. Orders from the Master of the Hunt." She looked around. "Everyone else not so ordered is to go to the left."

Murmured acknowledgments met her pronouncement.

The hunters continued to move forward. After a few minutes, the path split around a massive flat-topped hill. Most of the riders went left. Ruri and Mal joined the few swinging to the right. Moving more freely away from the crush, they soon rejoined the front of this much smaller collection of hunters, the Jaeger riding at its head.

He stopped them maybe five minutes later.

"We know the abomination is near," he said to them as they clustered as close to him as their animals would allow. "Its spoor is fresh. The other group will draw its attention and lure it toward a cottage ahead. The house is in a natural bowl and the hunters will contain it." He rubbed his hands together. "We shall confront it and deal it the death it deserves for trespassing into our lands. We will be as a hammer on an anvil, crushing it into oblivion."

"Yes, Jaeger," said a grey-skinned mountain of a man with stark black geometric designs marked into the skin of his bare chest and arms. He sat atop a large lizard with goggles over its eyes. His deep voice echoed among the walls of the hills like distant thunder. "It will be as you say." He cracked his knuckles. "Do we go now?"

"Patience, Lord Regin," the Jaeger said. "The horns will announce when it is time."

Lord Regin nodded eagerly. The motion was echoed around the group. Mal bobbed her head in assent. No one seemed to notice that Ruri had stayed still.

There wasn't much to do as they waited. The Jaeger stared at the top of the nearest hill without seeming to see it. His brow creased in fearful concentration on something, but Ruri couldn't see what that was. Other fae drifted into clumps of twos and threes while they carried on quiet conversation.

"How are you holding up?" Mal asked.

"My legs are doing better than I expected," Ruri said. "It's been a very long time since my parents' farm, but they remember what they're supposed to do."

"And the other?"

"I guess we'll see. I hope the knives are close enough to what I'm used to. How are you going to manage? That sword isn't exactly your katana."

Mal shrugged. "I should be all right. The balance is different and having two edges is a little odd. I wish I had time to practice with it, but I'll figure it out as I go. Don't worry," she said when Ruri raised an eyebrow in concern. "I'm a very quick study, especially when it comes to weaponry."

"Be careful, okay?"

"That goes for you too." Mal grinned. "And besides—"

"I'm always careful." Ruri joined in on the statement, one they had repeated frequently to each other over the past few months. Despite her concern with this place, these people, and this task they were undertaking with unfamiliar weapons, Mal still managed to make her smile.

The long blast of a horn shattered the still air. As one, each rider looked around to where the sound had emanated.

"We ride," the Jaeger cried, standing tall in his stirrups. He dropped back into his saddle and pressed his heels hard against the side of his mount, a dark grey horse with seaweed tangled in its mane and dark red fire in its eyes, and it leaped forward. The ground shuddered beneath churning hooves and paws as their group jolted forward.

This was no controlled maneuver. Each rider urged their mount forward, disregarding those to either side. Cries from the mounts merged with hollers and yells from the hunters, creating a din no beast could have missed. She and Mal ended up at the tail end of the group again, but Ruri was happy to be out of the way of chaos. Her pale horse matched the speed and direction of the hunters without her having to put her heels to it.

They surged down the narrow cut between hills, twisting and weaving with the terrain before spilling out into a deep bowl. Fae dotted the tops of the bowl, blowing their horns and crashing weapons against weapons or shields.

A recently quaint little dwelling sat in the center of the depression. One wall was caved in; the thatched roof sagged alarmingly. A long green tail covered with immense scales lashed out from the hole where the wall had once stood.

The door on the side of the house burst open and a small woman with brown skin ran out toward them, her hands outstretched.

"Help him!" she cried. "My man is still inside. The beast has him cornered."

CHAPTER TWENTY-TWO

"Excellent," the Jaeger roared. "The beast is occupied. Onward!" His mount plummeted down the rise toward the creature. He raised his sword high above his head. It reflected more light than it could possibly have collected. A handful of hunters followed him. The others spread out in a half-circle, unlimbering bows and pulling short spears and javelins from leather cases on their saddles.

"I've got her," Ruri yelled back over her shoulder. She leaned low over her pale horse's neck and peeled away from the group, heading toward the front door.

Malice had to pull on the reins to keep her mount from following. Instead, she stayed close to the hunters following the Jaeger as they galloped closer to the cottage. The first arrow shafts broke against the scaled hide of the hodag. The beast's tail didn't even twitch.

Someone threw a spear as they descended the slope toward the monster. It embedded into the hodag's tail, right where it met its body. The tail lashed. The Jaeger danced his mount back, but the two hunters coming in behind him weren't so lucky. One flew into the air as his mount was bowled out from under him. The other went down in an ungainly heap of hooves and wings. Her shocked cry rose over the thunder of their approach.

Before the hodag could react, the Jaeger slashed at its tail, easily opening a long gash in its hide. It howled and shifted, pulling itself around and trying to get away from the fae assaulting it.

The large grey fae, Lord Regin, rode in, leveling what could only be a lance at the hodag. The long pole collected shadows around it, motes drifting off like curls of the blackest smoke. The lance struck true, driving into the beast's side in a spray of ichor and shade before flexing and snapping in a small explosion of dark shards. As his massive mount galloped past the now-enraged hodag, it completed its spin and dropped a small body from jaws that dripped crimson. The rest of its body was as reptilian as the tail and haunches had promised and perhaps twice the length of the cottage it had been destroying. Long claws easily the length of Malice's hand came to sickening points. They dug deep furrows in the ground. Lord Regin avoided its bite only by twisting in his saddle. Immense teeth in a strangely flattened face clashed together behind him. It tossed its head, battering the next rider with curving white horns well over a foot long.

The sound of breaking bones accompanied the fae's scream, and he was flung from his mount. The group of hunters scattered to either side of the hodag, and suddenly Malice was the only one left. And she was barreling straight for the thing.

* * *

Ruri leaned out of the saddle and held out her hand to the woman. Though tears streamed down her face, the woman managed to see her and desperately grabbed hold of the lifeline.

"He's still in there," she sobbed. "We were eating, and there were horns. Then the wall came down."

Ruri settled the woman in front of her. "Let's get you safe, then I'll go back."

"Poor Trajan." Her shoulders shuddered and her belly heaved against Ruri's steadying hand.

Ruri cast about for somewhere to stash Trajan's wife. The hunters silhouetted at the top of the bowl looked down on them, never stopping their racket. A roar shook the ground. Finally, she noticed a small shed next to what had been a vegetable garden before something rampaged through it.

She urged the pale horse forward. It was reluctant to leave the hunt and she had to dig her heels in a few times before it would move on. "Don't worry," she said to ears that swiveled back toward her. "We're coming back." After her reassurance, the horse grudgingly responded to her commands. It took a few seconds to get to the ramshackle outbuilding.

"Wait here," Ruri said to the small brown woman. "I'll come back for you when it's safe."

"Get him back for me," she pleaded as she allowed herself to be transferred to the ground.

"I'll do what I can."

The horse wheeled around on its back hooves as soon as Trajan's wife was off its back. It plunged back toward the fray. Another howling groan shivered the air. Ruri couldn't see what was happening through the semi-circle of hunters around the shattered side of the home.

She urged the horse toward the front door, which was still hanging ajar on one good hinge. When they were within reach, she swung her leg over the horse's back and slid off without waiting for it to come to a stop.

"Join the others if you want," she called back to it. "I'm going in."

The horse shook its head and disappeared around the corner of the house. Ruri slipped through the front door and into chaos.

* * *

My god, those tusks are huge, Malice thought as her mount showed no sign of slowing. They were as long as the horns, though less curved and far too close. It was too late now to use her bow, and given the broken shafts that littered the ground around the hodag, there was little point. She worked her feet out of the stirrups as they pounded closer. *This is going to hurt.*

When her horse finally shifted to avoid running straight into the hodag, Malice allowed its momentum to throw her from the saddle. She tucked into a ball and hit the ground. Her dismount wasn't perfect. Fighting from horseback hadn't been covered in basic. Her shoulder blade hit the hard earth first, driving the air out of her lungs.

She ignored the sudden exhalation, riding the adrenaline spike with confidence born of far too much practice. She tumbled forward and gained her feet in front of the hodag's surprised face. It gaped at her for a moment, then swung its head, trying to gore her with massive tusks. Malice was already moving.

The hodag's breath washed hot against her back carrying along with it the smell of fresh blood and viscera. Malice dashed to the side, skirting its barrel-shaped chest. She dropped and rolled through the gap between its leg and the ground. There was just enough room for her to fit. She didn't often believe her small size was an asset, but today it certainly was. The hodag wouldn't be able to gore her there, not with the way its joints seemed to work. There might be some safety from its claws also. A distant part of her mind hoped she wasn't wrong about hodag physiology.

She was out of immediate danger along its flank, but there was no time to appreciate the breather. The hodag was already turning to face this new threat. Malice kept moving, staying ahead of teeth, tusks, and horns. If she could keep it going, it would expose its far less lethal flank to the hunters clustered outside the simple house.

Her foot came down on something wet and suddenly Malice's feet were sliding out from under her. She went down on one knee, then scrambled backward, only milliseconds ahead of the claws that raked out at her. She dodged away, avoiding most of them, but one caught her, digging a deep furrow across her back from shoulder blade to the top of her opposite arm. The hardened leather armor split with disappointing ease; the metal rings were no match for the hodag. Blood sheeted out, shockingly hot, to cover half her back.

The wound was grave, Malice could tell immediately. She ignored the spike of pain from being laid open, but she knew even with her body's enhanced healing powers she wouldn't be able to push past the physical effects of blood loss for long. *Time to change it up.*

Malice drew her sword and pressed her stinging back against the wall.

* * *

It sounded like the world was ending inside the cottage. Ruri had to duck to get through the door; the roof was only inches from the top of her head. The sounds of tearing wood and shattering crockery filled her ears, but still couldn't quite drown out the labored growl from the lizard-looking creature. It made for an unsteady bass line to the whole experience. Its attention presently was focused on the fae who bedeviled it from outside the dwelling. Ruri flattened herself against the wall to avoid its lashing tail. Spikes ran the length of it, and she didn't want to find out what it would be like to sustain a major wound without the wolf there to help her out.

She firmed her grip on the knives in her hands. That tail was moving awfully quickly. How should she attack it? Without the wolf, her reflexes would be slow, sluggish in comparison. The last time she'd been this way, Dean had been killed right in front of her.

A nearby rafter cracked from the impact of the beast's tail. Ruri flinched, once more seeing Dean's body lifted in the hands of the rogue Alpha who had attacked their pack and being powerless to stop it as the wolven brought Dean's body down over his knee, pulverizing the spine.

Ruri gasped, struggling to breathe. Her vision cleared in time to see Mal thrown into the cottage by the impact of a clawed foot. She bounced back up, quickly turning to face the beast, but not before Ruri saw where her back had been torn open even through the armor the Jaeger had provided. Blood pumped out of the long wound in a ragged sheet of shocking red.

Help her! Ruri screamed at herself. She took one step forward. Then another. And another. All instinct for tactics was gone. She had one goal: protect her mate.

* * *

The hodag didn't wait for her to get settled. Its flat face came in for a bite. Malice barely got her sword up and dodged to one side. She lifted her arm in a rising arc, seeking to slice open its nose or the closest thing it had to one.

The blade bit deep, sending a spray of black blood through the air. The hodag jerked its head back. Malice closed the gap, denying it space to recover.

Its body spasmed and it whirled, its tail taking out more wood and plaster. Timbers groaned as the small house was deprived of yet another wall. Malice sprinted to the side and used the beast's rough scales to climb onto it. She pulled herself up with one hand, pushing with her legs as she lurched onto its back.

The hodag roared in protest and Malice flattened herself against its back as best she could. The thick spines that marched in a proud ridge down its back made the maneuver tricky and painful to boot. Its tail lashed around, thudding into its side, narrowly missing Malice's leg. The tail whipped back the other way. A dull ache bloomed in her chest as she watched it make contact with Ruri's torso and toss her across the room. She landed with a thud Malice could feel, despite the rumbling around them.

A veil of red descended over Malice's vision. Ignoring the threat of the tail or anything else, she stood. The hodag's back wasn't the steadiest place to be. It pitched to one side. Malice tried to compensate but quickly realized the hodag wasn't tilting, but rather the cottage was in the process of toppling over.

She used her free hand to steady herself on the hodag's spines, then rushed forward. It couldn't reach her, but sooner or later it was going to realize it should shake or roll to dislodge her. She had to end this before that could happen.

She made her way to its shoulders.

"Hey, you green piece of shit," she yelled.

The hodag swung its head around to look at her, a moment of brief confusion in its massive, red-pupiled eyes.

Malice vaulted a large central spine, reversing the sword so its point faced down, then grabbing it with both hands. She raised it over her head and as soon as her feet made contact with the green hide, she pushed off.

The sword's tip pierced through the scales. Muscle parted before it. Malice used her weight and momentum to drag the blade down as she fell. The side of its neck split wide. Gore spilled from the wound, slowly at first, then in a spray as she bisected at least one major blood vessel.

The hodag howled, but without its previous strength. It sounded mournful, as if questioning how this had come to be. A wet cough shook its entire body before it slowly collapsed at her feet. Its muscles twitched once as if it were trying to stand, then all movement ceased.

Silence fell so quickly and unexpectedly that Malice wondered if she'd gone spontaneously deaf. The crash of the ruined cottage giving in to gravity convinced her she could still hear, as did the cheers of the Wild Hunt outside the destroyed cottage.

Ruri. She needed to find her girlfriend.

CHAPTER TWENTY-THREE

Hands held her, she could tell that much. They hooked under her armpits, pulling her along. The ground scraped past under the backs of her legs. Ruri was in more pain than she could ever remember. Every muscle ached, and there were too many points of agony to account for.

"Who dropped a house on me?" she asked.

Mal's laugh warmed her and some of the pain receded.

"That would be the hodag," Mal said.

"Is that what it's called? I don't think I knew that." She wasn't going to open her eyes. More pain lurked there; she could feel it.

"It's taken care of," Mal said. "If you give me a second, you'll be taken care of too."

"That sounds naughty."

"Not in that way." Mal laid her down carefully, her hands somehow knowing to avoid the places that hurt most. "Drink this."

Cool glass touched Ruri's lips. She opened her mouth. Liquid spilled into it. She swallowed instinctively. Whatever she was drinking warmed as it ran down her throat. It hit her stomach and the heat burst outward.

"Oh," she said, her eyes popping open without the agony she'd anticipated. The sensation was not unlike that of an orgasm, except that the pain dissipated ahead of the wave of pleasure. Some of her muscles crawled briefly in what she recognized as flesh knitting itself back together, but faster even than she could manage when her wolf was with her.

"That was interesting," Ruri said. She looked around. She lay in the open. Bright sunshine on a cloudless day warmed her. Lavender tinged the western sky.

"Yeah, it's a trip, isn't it?" Mal said. "I could get used to that."

"Careful, Hunter," the Jaeger said. "The tincture can be addictive to humans. Apparently your people can become enamored of the side effects."

"I can see why." Mal looked down at her, a small smile playing about her lips. "You came through in the clutch."

"Did you find Trajan?" Ruri asked.

"Who's Trajan?" Mal looked confused.

"The man who lives here with his wife."

"Oh." Mal's face closed down. She looked away. "No one else came out of that house alive."

"Oh no." Ruri's heart dropped to the bottom of her ribcage. "I promised her I'd get him out."

"I think he was dead before we got here." Mal placed her hand on Ruri's shoulder. "There was nothing you could have done."

"We'll take her back to the castle with us, if she wishes to go," the Jaeger said. "Brownies do well in service to others. She'll find some meaning to her life there."

"I'm sure she'd prefer to have her husband not killed by a…hodag." Ruri glared at the Jaeger. Either he didn't notice or he didn't care.

"She can't stay here." The Jaeger gestured behind himself at the collapsed cottage. "This will be best for her. Brownies are adaptable. She will adjust."

"I'm sure it's for the best," Mal said. "He's right. There's nothing to keep her here."

Ruri pushed away Mal's hand and sat up. "I'll talk to her. Wherever his body is, maybe cover it so she isn't confronted by it."

"The land will reclaim him soon enough," the Jaeger said. "He was a true subject of the king's. Now the hodag on the other hand, that we need to take care of."

"I'll be back," Ruri said to Mal. She ignored the Jaeger as best she could before she gave in to the temptation to pull off the armband and rip his throat out. The flippant way he talked about the brownie woman was more than enough to convince her that he cared nothing for those weaker than he.

She made her way back to the shed. There was no sign of her, so Ruri knocked gently on the door.

"Who's there?" The woman's voice filtered out to her.

"It's me, ma'am," Ruri said. "I dropped you off here."

"Ah." Crude hinges creaked as the rough door was pulled inward. She poked her head through the doorway, a hopeful expression creasing her face. "Did you get him?"

"I am so sorry." Ruri dropped down into a crouch so her face was level with the brownie's. "When I got back, he was already dead. I tried. We killed the beast. It's cold comfort, I know, but it won't take anyone else."

The brownie's face crumpled into tears. "He's gone? Trajan is gone?" Deep sobs shook her small frame. She sank in on herself and wrapped her arms around her knees. "Everything I had has been torn away."

Ruri reached out slowly. She clasped the woman's shoulder gently, unsure how the gesture would be taken. In her grief, the woman didn't seem to notice.

"What will I do?"

"You can accompany us to King Connall's castle, if you want," Ruri said. "I've been told there's a position for you there, if you want it."

The woman scrubbed her hands angrily over her eyes. "I don't really have much of a choice, have I?" She stood and looked past Ruri at what remained of her home. "The beast is dead, is it? What about the hunters who brought it to our door?"

"What do you mean they brought it?"

"There's only one way in. It was driven here. We heard the horns coming closer, before it tore through the wall. Then the racket above to keep it from continuing over. Our house was the only shelter."

"Is that so?" Ruri looked back toward the ruined cottage. Since it had collapsed, it was easy to see the Jaeger. The group of fae hunters seemed to shift, with him always in the center.

"I'm Ruri," she said, not taking her eyes off the Huntmaster.

The brownie woman followed her gaze. "Ylana," she replied. "Be careful of that one. He will always do what he thinks is right, no matter that others may disagree with him."

"Noted." Ruri looked down at Ylana. "They're dressing out the hodag, which will take a while. Is there anything you want from your house? I'll help you go after whatever you need."

"Blessings of Titania upon you," Ylana said. "I doubt much survived, but there are some items I'd like to keep. Some things of Trajan's too."

"Let's get on it then." Ruri headed down the incline toward the pile of a house.

She was able to steer Ylana away from the remains of her husband. For her part, Ylana refused to look in the direction of the body. The size of the cottage made sifting through the ruins a little easier. Certainly, Ruri was able to lift more than the brownie could, at least with her back. On a few occasions, when the pile was too big for Ruri to shift, Ylana glared at the offending heap. After a while, it would dismantle itself into neat piles of components. Then Ylana would rest for a few minutes.

True to Ruri's assumption, it took a long time to prepare the hodag for transport. As the pile of viscera grew, so too did periodic incursions from small bands of what Ruri now realized were pixies. They would swoop down in a group and wrestle a length of intestine off the pile, then abscond with it. No one seemed to care too much, and they grew bolder as the process progressed. Eventually, those tasked with the dressing had to shoo the pixies away from the carcass so they could continue their work.

Ylana finally said she'd done all she could stand. "Can we go somewhere else?" she asked. "If I spend much more time here, I'm going to be tempted to tidy this place back to its original state. I won't erase what's happened."

"Of course," Ruri said. "They're almost done, anyway. I'm sure we'll be on our way soon."

They didn't have long to wait. The hodag's carcass was suspended below a couple of long poles and carried between a couple of massive horse-shaped creatures. At least, Ruri assumed they weren't actually horses. Little was what it seemed here, and she was fairly certain nothing so mundane as an actual horse would be on the hunt with them. She didn't look too closely.

The ride back to the castle was a raucous affair with an almost carnival atmosphere. The fae laughed and shouted to each other. Though the clothing and weapons of some showed signs of use, there were no wounds to go along with the damage. Ruri thought they must have had the same drink she had. Alcohol of some sort seemed to be flowing. Ruri and Mal both refused the drinks that were pressed upon them from all sides. Some musical instruments had appeared. Music led to an increase in laughter and the hunters frequently broke into song. Occasionally a tune hovered on the edge of Ruri's memory, like she'd known it once but could no longer recall it.

Ruri, with Ylana on the saddle in front of her, felt like an island of sobriety as the group grew increasingly vocal. The hunters were much warmer to them now. Mal was eventually lost to a group of fae who wanted her to relive the battle with the hodag for their amusement. Ruri didn't begrudge her going off with them. Heavens knew she rarely got to share the afterglow of a successful hunt with anyone but Ruri. There was something about that shared experience that was exhilarating. Mal had as much right to indulge in that as anyone did. She didn't know the Jaeger had used people as bait.

The actual sun was starting to set when the castle finally came back into sight. Ruri understood why sunsets here were so striking. They were essentially doubled, the real one overlaid on top of the other to fantastic effect.

Fae packed the courtyard as they entered. A cheer went up from the crowd. Small winged creatures spiraled up from the throng, then disappeared into the castle's eaves. The Jaeger led the Wild Hunt to the center, then stopped. All eyes turned upward to a balcony some twenty feet from the ground.

It was empty.

The Jaeger kept them waiting. The crowd began to whisper and shift around them. Finally a lone figure stepped up to the railing.

"My Lord Seneschal," the Jaeger said. He didn't seem to be raising his voice, but his measured tones reached Ruri's ears easily, though she was toward the back of the riders.

The Seneschal heard him also. He bowed his head. "Jaeger," he said. "His Majesty regrets that he cannot greet your return as it deserves. He has decreed that a feast be held in celebration of the Wild Hunt for tomorrow evening."

"I am…pleased to accept my king's invitation," the Jaeger said. His voice was pleasant, but he sat stiffly in the saddle. He tugged on his mount's reins, wheeling his horse around without a word of goodbye to the Seneschal.

"He's not going to like that," Ylana murmured.

"The Jaeger?" Ruri said, taking care to keep her voice down.

"The king's Seneschal. The Jaeger was quite rude just now. The Tuatha put much stock in politeness. Those of the less exalted races are more likely to do something they consider offensive, but rudeness occasionally leads to duels between Tuatha."

"Thoo-a?" Ruri tried out the unfamiliar word.

"Tuatha." Ylana corrected her with a slight smile. "Humans called them the Shining Folk once. They're what your Tolkien had in mind when he created his elves. Our elves look quite different. Whatever you do, don't call one of the Tuatha an elf. They will demand satisfaction immediately."

"I'll try to remember that."

The hunters were following the Jaeger back to the Hunt's stables. Ruri turned her pale horse to follow. Now that no direct sun could reach her mount's coat, it had reverted to its skeletal self.

A moment later, Mal turned up at her elbow. "Let's go this way," she said, tilting her head to indicate the other side of the courtyard. The crowd was dispersing, which made it easier to cross the space.

Mal slid off her pale horse, then looped the reins around one of the many available posts.

"Geffron," she called as she entered the stable.

Ruri followed suit. Ylana slid down from the horse. It was a bit of a drop for her, but she managed without any difficulty. They trailed in after Mal.

An older brownie showed up from the back of the horse stables. He watched them curiously.

"You don't need a horse, do you?" he asked Mal.

"Not this time," Mal said. "I was hoping you might know how to help her out." She pointed at Ylana. "Her house was destroyed."

"Oh no," Geffron said. His eyes filled with tears. "Where is Uncle Trajan?"

Ylana simply shook her head.

"It was the hodag," Ruri said.

"It was quick," Mal added. "He didn't have time to suffer."

Geffron walked forward, his arms extended. Ylana flew into them. She buried her face against his shoulder and sobbed.

"I'll take her to the Matia," he said. "She'll be taken care of."

"The Matia?" Mal cocked her head to one side.

"She runs the household," Geffron said. "The closest human equivalent would be a housekeeper. I'd advise you not to use that title with her. Matia will cover it."

"I see. And thank you," Mal said.

Ruri nodded. She watched as Geffron shepherded the sobbing Ylana deeper into the stables.

"That was a good thing you did," Ruri said.

"I figured he'd know better than we would. I wish we could have gotten there a little sooner."

"I don't think it would have mattered. Ylana thinks the Wild Hunt led the hodag to their cottage. From what she said, it sounds like a real possibility."

"Huh." Mal looked troubled by the revelation. "That doesn't sound right. Why would anyone do that? I'm sure she misunderstood what happened. How could she even know if she was inside the house and they were outside?"

"I don't think anyone was trying to keep things quiet. Their whole strategy was to push the hodag in front of them. You can't do that by being quiet."

"We shouldn't argue about this." Mal spread her hands. "I'll speak with the Jaeger and find out what happened, but I'm sure she's misinterpreting it."

Ruri stared at Mal, unable to understand how she couldn't see what was going on. It wasn't right, and she was making excuses? "I want to be there when you talk to him."

"That's fine. I'm getting the horse taken care of, then heading back to the room to sleep for a week. Are you coming?"

"Of course I'm coming."

"Good." Mal reached down and took her hand.

They walked back out to the courtyard. Most of the fae were gone, opening an easy path to the Wild Hunt's stables. Ruri paced beside Mal, watching her mate and wondering what she would do if the Jaeger got his claws into Mal.

CHAPTER TWENTY-FOUR

King Connall's court was unrecognizable when Mal and Ruri stepped into the grand ballroom the following evening. The last time they'd been in there, it had glittered and shone. Now it was a place of gloom and shadow. Dim lights flashed as they drifted down from the ceiling at a languid pace. With a start, Mary Alice realized the flickering was from the light passing behind tree branches. A double row of tall trees lined the main carpet, heavy snow bowing the branches. Strangest of all, their breath steamed in the cool air. It was a good thing Corrigan had insisted on furs as part of their garb.

As before, music filled the room, but not the lively gavotte of their only other attendance at court. No, this music wailed, coursing past the edge of wildness into complete abandon. Mary Alice's leg muscles flexed, urging her to join in.

Somehow, she kept to the stately pace she'd been maintaining with Ruri. At the end of the long promenade was the king's throne or so she assumed. She was conscious of fae faces appearing between the trees, their eyes catching strangely in what little light there was. The music faded, not stopping, but sounding as if the musicians had moved away and were now barely within earshot.

The carpet ended in shadow. Mary Alice and Ruri stood arm in arm, uncertain where to look.

"Do you not bow before the king?" came the Jaeger's voice from the darkness.

All Mary Alice wanted to do was take a knee, but she refused though her muscles quivered to obey.

"I am happy to acknowledge King Connall as the king of this land, but I'd have to remind him that I'm not his subject, only a guest who I'm hoping has overstayed her welcome." Mary Alice paused, trying to find the right words, the proper combination of flattery and forthrightness that would allow them to leave. The pause stretched on. Screw it, she'd never been one who was pretty with words. "And besides, I don't even know if he's here. I'm pretty sure you know humans can't see in the dark."

A chuckle of chimes met her defiant pronouncement. The throne burst into view in a flash of light that seared into Mary Alice's corneas. She turned her head as her eyes overflowed with sudden painful tears.

"She is bold enough to be one of the Wild Hunt," the king said. "We see now how she was able to best the creature that despoiled our lands with its very presence."

Mary Alice opened her eyes into painful slits, allowing them to adjust to the brightness. The king's throne burned bright in a glade of birch trees. The branches wove together overhead in patterns that were neither natural nor easily followed with the eyes.

"There is no doubt about her bravery," said the Jaeger. He stood next to Connall's throne, only partially obscured by the many mirrors around it.

Mary Alice bowed slightly at the waist, dropping her eyes momentarily. Ruri mimicked her movements. When she stood back up, she took care not to look at the king directly. As was the case the last time, his dead lavender eyes watched her from every mirror.

"I had a hand in killing the hodag, it's true," Mary Alice said. "I wasn't alone. The other hunters did their part." Mary Alice had to wait for the deafening ululation that rose at her words to subside before continuing. "The Jaeger drew first blood."

He inclined his head toward her.

"But I couldn't have made my strike if Ruri hadn't attacked the hodag from within the house. She distracted it long enough to allow me to land the killing blow."

"Such modesty," the king said. "It will serve you well during your stay in our realm."

Mary Alice's heart sank. "Does that mean this boon isn't enough to open the portals back up to us?"

"You thought one little beast would earn you our favor?" The king's laughter was as brittle as it was beautiful. Mirth surrounded them as the gathered fae took up their monarch's jollity. He silenced them with the casual wave of one hand. "It is a start, nothing more. Given the depth of your insult, it will take much more to appease us."

They'd put themselves both in danger to try to impress this puffed-up man-child, and it had gotten them nowhere. Mary Alice's jaw tightened and she took a deep breath to tell Connall exactly what she thought of him. Ruri's hand on the small of her back stopped her. At her girlfriend's touch, her heart rate slowed and some of the adrenaline receded.

"I'll see what I can do, Your Majesty," Mary Alice said.

"Your start is promising," Connall said. "We expect great feats from both of you." His eyes left hers and slid over to the Jaeger for a moment before snapping back to her. "Perhaps you'll even come to eclipse our old friend. What do you say to two Masters of the Hunt in this court, Jaeger?"

"Your will be done, my lord." The Jaeger looked down. "It does sound a little crowded, however."

"Perhaps it does, at that. We shall think on it." The king looked away from Mary Alice. The lights around the throne dimmed and the music surrounded them again.

The Jaeger stepped out from his spot among the multitude of mirrors.

"This way," he said. "The hunters are past the receiving line with its various hangers-on." He smiled. "I want you to have a good time. Both of you. This feast is in your honor, of course."

"I thought it was in honor of the Wild Hunt," Mary Alice said.

"Of course it is, but were you not part of the Wild Hunt? Did you not strike the blow that felled the intruder? And my apologies, Lady Ruri. I hadn't realized your role in its demise. Lady Malice has kept many of the details to herself, it would seem."

"It's fine," Ruri said.

Mary Alice could hear the edge in her girlfriend's voice. There was no wondering at it. They still hadn't had the chance to talk to the Jaeger about how the hodag had ended up at Ylana's cottage. Still, she should cut him some slack. The Jaeger was giving Ruri the credit she definitely deserved.

"Here they are," the Jaeger said. Mary Alice's eyes were finally starting to adjust to the gloom. She recognized many of those they'd ridden out with. Lord Regin stood out in particular, towering as he did over the others.

A nearby table was mounded with food. Above it was the massive head of the hodag. A nearby bonfire bathed it in flickering light, causing it to look like its eyes were shifting to watch people as they moved and whirled around it.

"I'll leave you in the capable hands of your fellow hunters," the Jaeger said loudly. The group hollered its agreement with his statement. Hands reached forward to pull them into the revelry. As the Jaeger left, they were handed plates piled high with food and chalices brimming with frothy drink.

"To Malice," Lord Regin thundered. He raised a tankard bigger than Mary Alice's head above those gathered. "Hell of a fight!"

The group sent up a loud whoop. Around her, hunters were draining their drinking vessels. Ruri folded herself into a sitting position on the ground next to a log.

What the hell, Mary Alice thought. She took a long pull from the chalice. It was like drinking early morning sunlight, when the promise of the new day had yet to be spoiled. Somewhere between the first sip and the final gulp, Mary Alice had decided to finish the whole thing in one go. It was promptly replaced with another as those around her cheered on her efforts. Nothing could stop her. The evening would be fantastic, and nothing would stand in her way.

"Drink deep, Lady Malice." Lord Regin urged her on. "Drink while you can, for sooner or later the Hunt ends us all!"

"That's right," called another fae from the other side of the group. "Drink deep, eat to bursting, dance till you shoes come apart, and fuck until morning!"

"Or later," chorused the rest of the group. They fell into wild laughter and chatter. Their merriment included them and Mary Alice found her lips stretching into a wide grin. Her heart leaped. She grabbed the top item off her plate and bit into it. Warm juices dribbled over her chin. She wiped them off with her hand.

"Let's dance," she yelled to Ruri, holding out her hand. The sound of fiddles and something more visceral that moaned and wailed overtop the music could no longer be denied.

Ruri hesitated, a frown settling between her eyebrows.

"Come on!" Mary Alice waggled her hand. "It'll be fun."

Ruri reached up and allowed her hand to be grabbed. A circle immediately opened up around them. Mary Alice didn't know the steps her feet skipped to, but that didn't matter. Ruri had a harder time finding her rhythm. She tripped a couple of times, to the delight of the watching hunters. It wasn't long before Ruri begged off. Mary Alice let her go.

"I'm Freki," said the fae woman who jumped in to claim Mary Alice's hand.

"It's good to meet you," Mary Alice said. And it was. She'd recognized her voice as the fae who'd spoken out in the group. The fae woman was tall. She moved to the music, seamlessly mirroring Mary Alice's moves, almost predicting them. The music spun them faster and faster. Colors swirled past them, blurring together. The music climbed to a feverish tempo. Freki's hands were around her hips, lifting her off the ground, then setting her down again, only to lift her once more. When the music crashed to a stop, Freki released her grip on Mary Alice, sending her spinning through the air.

Mary Alice laughed at the exhilaration of it all. She landed in a pair of arms with an "oof" that made her giggle even harder.

"Whoa there," a deep voice said in her ear. "Watch where you're flying, little human girl."

"Apologies, Lord Regin," Mary Alice said.

"I'll decide what's needed to make it up to me," the grey fae said. "Won't you join me while I do?"

"I think I'd better leave the dancing for a while," she said. A new song was playing, and though her toes tapped out the beat, she thought a break was in order.

"And if it's a different type of dancing I'm wanting from you?"

"You won't get that from me." Mary Alice cast about for Ruri. "I'm taken." She glanced back over at him. "Besides, you're not my type. Too…" She mimed stroking over her crotch.

Lord Regin burst into coarse laughter. "A drink or two is what I'll claim then. Then after that, you tell us the story of your most challenging hunt."

"It's a deal." A drink materialized at Mary Alice's elbow before she'd finished her agreement. She raised the tankard toward Lord Regin and took a deep drink. Tonight was going to be fun.

* * *

Ruri watched Mal get whirled away in the arms of a tall Tuatha whose hair was twisted around in a complicated series of knots. She shook her head. Mal had certainly succumbed to the lures of this place. Had she not remembered any of Corrigan's warnings?

Not only had Mal taken a large bite out of something that was clearly meat, but she was also dancing. She'd never shown any interest in dancing before. Of course, the only club they ever went to belonged to the self-styled Lord of Chicago. There was tension between Mal and Carla, the head vampire and declared lord. They never stayed long, and everything between the Hunter and Carla was related directly to business.

"Your girl got pulled in by the music, didn't she?" Shejuanna Jackman said from behind her.

Ruri shot the teenage girl a glare. She'd picked this spot so she could watch Mal without having someone sneak up on her.

Shejuanna ignored the look on her face. "Your Malice will be fine. She's just a bit fae-touched right now." She tugged at Ruri's elbow. "Come hang with us. It'll be better than watching her have fun and moping about it." When Ruri hesitated, she rolled her eyes. "We're not that far. You can creep on your girlfriend from there."

"She's not my girlfriend—"

"She's not? Woo, girl, you really are stalking her!"

Ruri sighed. Cubs had too much energy and were prone to spend it jumping to conclusions. "She's not my girlfriend. She's my mate."

"Oh, okay. My mistake, that's a huge difference. You can still stalk your 'mate' with us." Shejuanna wiggled her fingers in the air.

"Anyone ever tell you you're a pain in the ass?" Ruri asked.

Shejuanna grinned crookedly. "All the time." She started walking away. "We're over here."

Ruri followed the teenager over to a small fire. Logs were laid out in a rough square. The rest of the kids were there, either sitting on a log or on the ground leaning back against them. A few other humans lounged with them. Ruri sat and realized the hard stone floor from the other day was gone. This was forest loam, so soft in places that it was almost spongy. She picked up a clump of moss and stared at it. Either this was an illusion or the marble from two nights ago was. Or they both were.

"Don't think about it too much," Carlo said. "You'll make yourself squirrelly."

"Just go with it," Latawna said.

"I don't know if I can." Ruri brought the moss to her nose and inhaled deeply. It smelled like moss all right.

"It'll make you crazy if you don't," Latawna said. The other teens nodded in solemn agreement. "We've seen it since we got here."

"I think I'll be all right." She took another whiff of the moss. It smelled of the woods. Real woods, filled with real trees, not this place with its fake nature. The skin under the armband itched and it took everything she had not to rip it off. She stood up. "I need a walk."

The teens didn't try to stop her. When Ruri looked back toward the hunters, she couldn't see Mal, but she knew her mate was off in that direction. She would be fine. If anyone could handle herself, it was Mal. She decided to see how far the illusion of the forest went. There had to be walls there somewhere. She turned until the fire was at her back and walked into the trees.

It didn't take long before she could no longer see the lights; the sounds of music and revelry abated until they were almost gone. They never faded completely. A slight breeze rustled leaves on branches. If the wind hadn't carried the smell of wildflowers on it, she might have believed she was back home. The illusion was a good one. She kept on, enjoying the feel of pine needles and dirt beneath the soft soles of her boots.

A light winked at her from the dark. Before long, she recognized the light as that of a bonfire. Figures capered around it. The fiddles grew louder. Ruri stepped out of the trees into a clearing around a fire. The music wailed around her, beckoning her to join in the dance. She was back in the thick of the party. Had she gotten turned around? That seemed unlikely. She'd been roaming forests for decades. Getting lost wasn't something that happened to her anymore. No, more likely was that the room had shaped itself around her and wasn't allowing her to leave. She could feel the invisible walls pressing in against her. The room with its vast forest was suddenly too small. She had to get out. Hopefully the way she was headed would take her back to the carpet. From there she could get out. If Mal didn't come back to their room on her own in a couple of hours, she would come back for her.

With the plan in mind, Ruri kept moving forward. She had barely made it back to the long carpet when the music cut out with no warning. Raised voices from the direction of the king's throne pulled everyone's attention. Like cubs to a moth, everyone moved toward the disturbance. Ruri allowed herself to be swept along. As she got closer, she realized the voice doing most of the shouting was a familiar one. She kept pushing her way through the crowd until she could see what was going on.

A tall figure knelt in front of the dais on both knees. She'd seen him before, and he held the same grace now that he had in the grove of trees, even in abeyance. Forced abeyance, Ruri realized. Two fae stood on either side of him. One held the back of his head, forcing it to look at the ground, the other stood with the butt of his polearm behind the figure's knees. He'd been forced to kneel. To one side and slightly behind was Sheriff Corrigan, looking every inch the elf. Or rather the Tuatha.

"You may be our heir," King Connall was saying, "but you do not speak for us. We have grown beyond weary of Nagamo's antics. He impedes the function and protection of our court."

Jaeger stepped forward. "The protection of this court is my responsibility. I beg leave to administer his just punishment. One commensurate with his crimes."

"Nagamo has a valid claim," Corrigan said. "And you forget yourself, Jaeger. You may protect the court from the beasts of the wilds and beyond, but Nagamo is no beast."

Nagamo muttered something, but Ruri couldn't hear it from her vantage. Some of the nearby fae could. They murmured among themselves.

"What was that, dearest Nagamo?" the king asked, his voice all honeyed sweetness.

"The only beast here is the one who won't release the soul of the hodag," Nagamo said loudly. He wrenched his head free of the guard's grip and stared directly at the king on his throne. "It didn't have to be killed. If you had let me know, I could have removed it with no harm to anyone."

CHAPTER TWENTY-FIVE

"A valid claim, is it?" The Jaeger's voice was silky in the silence of the great hall. "When he speaks to your king in such a tone?"

Ruri looked around at the fae gathered around the throne. They watched the action upon the dais without appearing to move. Was this what Faerie was? Explosive merriment that screeched to a halt the moment something more interesting presented itself?

"A valid claim." Corrigan's reply was steady and strong. "He trespassed only to do what was best for one of his people."

"His people?" King Connall asked. "'Twas nothing but a beast."

"He didn't know!" Nagamo said with raw vehemence. He tried to stand, but the fae to his side kept his grip around the back of his neck. He pushed down. Nagamo struggled briefly before giving up again. "He didn't know he was going through a portal," he said again more quietly. "All he wanted was food and warmth. You know as well as I do that this area is porous with all the portals your people have built between this kingdom and the mortal world. You took advantage of his ignorance and killed him for it, just as you took advantage of our forest spirits and bound them in eternal servitude."

"It always comes back to the dryads," the Jaeger said. "So much for the selfless service of your people."

"They don't deserve this," Nagamo said. "They need to be free. You promised to protect them in return."

"And do we not? Have any of those who swore to serve me lost their trees?" Connall sat back on his throne, looking down his nose at the kneeling fae.

"But for this long? You never told them they would be forced to remain in their trees for the length of their bargain. They need to roam."

"Poppycock," the Jaeger said. "Dryads are content to remain in their trees for hundreds of years. There are groves of dryadic trees in Europe whose dryads haven't left them in over a millennia."

"The Jaeger speaks truly," Connall said. "Those dryads are essential to the protection of the mound from humans. Until humans leave these woods, your former people must remain in their trees."

"Then they will be there forever."

"That is as may be."

"My lord, surely they don't all need to be inhabiting their trees at once," Corrigan said. She stepped forward, brushing past the Jaeger as if he wasn't there. She addressed the king directly, ignoring the mirrors to look him in the eye. "An arrangement could be made, some sort of rotation. They would still be able to fulfill their pledges but would have leave to wander as they must."

Connall sat back in his chair looking thoughtful.

"Impossible," said the Jaeger. "Our numbers outside the mound are thin already. If someone makes it this far, the dryads are our final defense."

"If we could treat with the other races, we would have more than adequate protections."

"The other races?" the Jaeger laughed, a beautiful sound that tinkled through the halls. "Surely you jest. The Unseleighe have neither the fortitude nor the endurance to act as adequate defenders. Can you imagine a hodag called up to defend these halls? It would as likely devour us as any attackers. As we saw."

"There are those who can control the hodag and others with more than enough power. What about Mami Wata?"

Ruri's ears perked up at the mention of the creature they'd already met. She'd suspected Mami Wata was some sort of fae, and it was good to have her suspicions confirmed.

"Mami Wata will never set foot Underhill," Connall said, drawing himself up. His eyes snapped with anger, a far cry from his usual dead-eyed stare. He looked every inch the king. The fires around the hall plunged into shadows until he shone like a beacon in the darkness.

"Let her wallow in the swamps casting her nets and weaving her schemes. That one fancies herself our equal when she is not fit to enter our hall."

He stood. "And this one has defied my authority for the last time." He raised one hand to the ceiling speckled with stars. His fingers glowed, getting brighter by the second as the light spread down his arm to encompass his entire body. Ruri had to close her eyes. The king's silhouette was still outlined behind her eyelids.

Her eyes popped back open at Nagamo's despairing shout. Ruri looked down to see him clinging to the edge of a hole that had opened beneath his feet. All she could see beyond him was blue sky. The edge of the hole was lined with the same white light as the glow that surrounded the king. She slid between two fae and out of the crowd. All Nagamo had done was try to protect those he called his own. That didn't justify plummeting to his death.

"Your Majesty," Corrigan said, her hands held out toward him. "Surely this is not necessary."

"That you think so tells me how necessary it is. This is still our kingdom, and you will bow to us." The king gestured at his guards with his free hand.

They moved toward where Nagamo dangled, polearms leveled at the dangling fae.

Ruri stepped forward and in front of the nearest fae soldier. He turned toward her and swung his pike. She easily stepped inside the swing and went nose to nose with him. She was too close for him to use the polearm. When he let go of the haft to grab her, Ruri grabbed his wrist. She pulled at him, using his momentum to swing him forward, then twisted and bent over at the waist. The fae flipped over her hip to land on his back on the ground. A gasp rolled through the crowd along with some scattered applause. Ruri let go and went after his partner. He was using his polearm to pry Nagamo's hands from the edge of the opening. She stepped over to him and jabbed a fist at his face. It shimmered and her hand went straight through it. When she tried to grapple his form, there was nothing to get hold of. An amused titter arose from the watching crowd.

The opening started closing around Nagamo's torso. He slid further into it as the butt of the polearm pushed him down. Ruri laid herself out on the ground and held out her hand, trying to reach Nagamo. She couldn't. An invisible hand closed over her forearm and hauled her back just as he was forced to let go of the edge, falling with an anguished cry as the hole closed over his head.

Ruri couldn't get her hand free, despite her best efforts. She struck with her other hand, trying to hit her invisible opponent, but a glancing blow was the best she could manage. Her hand struck something metal that rang loudly as her hand slid off it.

"Do not," said the Jaeger into her ear. She looked back for him but saw nothing. "If you don't wish to complicate your Malice's situation any further, you'll behave," he hissed.

She looked up. The fae she had incapacitated had gotten up and stood before her, his pike lowered. Three more had joined him. They stood around her in a loose circle, their weapons also aimed at her. The odds weren't good, but she thought she could take them if she could get the armband off. But what about Connall? He could open a hole under her feet and drop her wherever he wanted, it seemed. Why hadn't he? And where would that leave Mal? No, she needed to get a handle on herself.

Ruri nodded stiffly at the guards. The Jaeger's invisible hand let go of her. She became aware of the cheering. The fae grouped around them hollered like they were at a football game. On the dais, the king clapped wildly. A moment later, the Jaeger appeared next to him. On the other side, Corrigan didn't appear to have noticed his absence.

"That was quite a show, human girl," King Connall said. He was in high spirits. His cheeks were pink in the mirrors, and his eyes fairly shone with excitement. "There's nothing like watching a fight to get the blood going." He turned to the Jaeger. "Why did we stop bloodsports again?"

It was Corrigan who answered from the other side of the throne. "Because we can't afford to have too many humans go missing. Eventually someone comes after them. Like Lady Malice."

The king's eyes deadened until the lavender of his irises was swallowed by the black of his pupils. "Humans do not control us. We control them."

The Jaeger laid his hand upon the arm of the throne. "The Heir is merely concerned that we couldn't handle an incursion, given our current weakened state."

"Weakened state?" Connall sat bolt upright on his throne. "Reese the Hand!" he thundered. "Attend us."

Corrigan was right next to him, but she moved until she stood before Connall. She knelt, her fist pressed against the floor.

"You have doubted us for too long. You take the case of those who stand against us." The king stood and pointed at Corrigan with one finger, then spread his fingers so far his whole hand trembled. He brought the hand down slowly.

As he did so, Corrigan's entire body began to shake. She grimaced, levering against an unseen force to keep herself upright. It was too much for her. Her arm shook, then gave out. In a split second, she was face down on the floor.

King Connall stepped down from the dais. A solid slab of marble shot up from the ground to meet his foot. He moved forward and another step materialized beneath him. By the time he stood in front of Corrigan, a row of marble slabs stepped up behind him.

"We have discounted the counsel of others for too long when it comes to you, Reese, the Heir no more." He reached forward and undid the clasp of the heavy golden livery collar that spread across the sheriff's shoulders. It fell to the ground with a loud clang that should have been impossible to hear if it was indeed the forest floor it appeared to be.

The pressure holding Corrigan down seemed to have dissipated. She slowly pushed herself back into a kneeling position, not looking at the puddled golden links before her.

"I beg leave to continue to protect Your Majesty," she said. Her voice didn't waver in the least, though she kept from looking him in the face.

With a start, Ruri realized she was staring right at the king. She was close enough to make out the faint wrinkles at the corners of his mouth and the gauntness of his cheeks. They looked out of place in the otherwise flawless face, but they matched the heaviness she saw in his eyes. She looked down at the sheriff before he could notice her supposed rudeness.

"Of course you will protect us," Connall said. He made a hooking gesture with one hand. The chain unspooled itself from the ground, then floated through the air to wrap around his arm. "We expect nothing less. The human world would benefit most from your vigilance. The Jaeger will take on your protective duties at court."

The Jaeger inclined his head from his spot next to the throne. He hadn't moved a muscle since the king's confrontation with his heir. "I am honored, my liege."

"Of course you are, old friend." The king turned and ascended the marble stairs. As each foot left the one before it, the slabs retracted back into the ground. "We shall see who is worthy enough to become our next heir."

"Yes, my lord," the Jaeger said.

"We know you covet the position. Convince us you have the best interests of this court in your heart, and you may yet take it."

"My lord." The Jaeger put one hand over his heart and bowed deeply to the king.

The gathered fae murmured among themselves now that the action looked like it was over. The overall tone was one of shock. From the whispered bits Ruri could make out, the political shift was a seismic one. There were those who were smug at Corrigan's downfall and those who foretold doom in hushed but portentous tones.

"You are dismissed," King Connall said. The words might have been to the former heir, but the gathered fae took it as an order as well. The crowd dispersed rapidly. Some, though not many, made their way toward the exit. Corrigan stood and melted into the crowd.

That was more than enough for Ruri. It was time to make themselves scarce. There was no sign of Mal in the immediate vicinity. Music had started up again as if nothing had happened. Ruri took a deep breath and headed away from the throne. She was going to get Mal, then they were going to head back to the room and keep their heads down for a bit.

CHAPTER TWENTY-SIX

Mary Alice walked unsteadily, her arm draped over Ruri's shoulder. The stone hallway shimmered around her, the windows shifting as she turned her head. They left trails of light purple behind them.

"Dancing is fun," she said.

"I'm glad you had a good time." Ruri looked over at her and smiled briefly.

"It would've been more fun with you. Everything is more fun with you."

"That's nice to hear."

"Then I'll say it again." Mary Alice put her mouth to Ruri's ear. "Everything is more fun with you." She whispered the words, but Ruri still winced and pulled her head away.

"You're drunk."

"I don't think so?" Mary Alice kept her rubbery legs going in the same direction, which was no mean feat. She took mental stock. Her brain wasn't as muzzy as it had been the previous times she'd been drunk. It was quite some time since that had happened. Mostly she was in a fantastic mood and felt like she could conquer anything. Her right knee refused to lock and she lurched to the side.

Ruri righted her before she could topple over. "Sure you're not."

"My legs aren't drunk, they're tired only."

"If you say so."

"I do say so. I danced. A lot." To her horror, Mary Alice's lower lip began to tremble. "Without you." Tears began to roll down her face. Where a moment before, she'd felt unbeatable, now she couldn't believe that anything would ever be right again.

"Are you all right, sweetness?" Ruri's voice brimmed with concern Mary Alice didn't deserve.

"N-n-no," she choked out around deep sobs. "I w-was all alone."

"You're never alone," Ruri said. "I am *always* with you." She stopped them in front of a vaguely familiar door and said something to the frog-faced man Mary Alice had forgotten was with them, keeping Mary Alice upright in her grasp until he left them.

Her legs no longer felt like they were about to give out, but she couldn't seem to let go of Ruri's shoulder. The contact was all that was keeping her from falling apart. If she lost her grip, she was certain she would be lost forever. She kept crying even as Ruri ushered her over the threshold to their room with a tenderness she had no right to.

Every bad thing she'd ever done flashed through her head, and there were a lot of them. She'd emptied out her mom's piggy bank at the age of ten, then had spent it all on candy at the corner store. At fourteen, she'd shoplifted dirty magazines from the same bodega. To be honest, she'd gotten more of a thrill from the theft than she had from staring at pictures of naked women. She'd lied. She kept on lying. Her whole life was built on the lies she told to others. Those she didn't lie to, she killed. Stiletto's dead face stared at her from the darkness behind her eyelids.

"I should be alone." She pulled her arms away from Ruri, though it felt like she was ripping out her own heart in the process. "No one should be around me. It's not safe."

"I'm not going anywhere." Ruri sat on the bed next to her. She didn't touch her, but she was close enough that Mary Alice could feel the heat of her body.

"If you don't go, you'll end up like Stiletto." Mary Alice wrapped both arms around her head. "I killed her." It sounded so much worse out loud. "Oh god. I killed her."

Ruri went completely still. "You said she died in the fight with MacTavish."

"All he did was knock her out. I couldn't let her tell anyone about Cassidy, so I smothered her before she came to." She hadn't wanted to do it, but Stiletto was so damn by-the-book about everything. Keeping the existence of someone turned against their will from their superiors was against regulations, never mind that the someone in this case was Mary Alice's sister. It had been too much of a risk. Was it really the best way? Maybe she could have convinced her to keep it quiet. Now they'd never know.

Ruri's hand rubbed soothing circles between her shoulder blades. "Did she say she was going to tell?" Her voice was soft and low. Mary Alice heard no accusation in it, which somehow made things worse.

"She said she would have to include it in her report." Mary Alice sniffled, trying to clear her nose long enough to breathe through it.

"And what would have happened then?"

"Cassidy would've been taken to a facility for 'help.' Stiletto was all excited about how much could be learned from her. She's my sister, but Stiletto didn't care."

"Sounds to me like you did what had to be done."

Ruri's calm acceptance of her deepest, darkest secret was more than Mary Alice could bear. Grief poured through her. Grief for killing Stiletto. Grief at what Cassidy had been forced to endure, both at her hands and at the hands of MacTavish's wolves. Grief over what she'd done to Ruri by kidnapping and holding her against her will to help her sister. A thousand other points of anguish that had built up within her over the years threatened to drown her. Only Ruri's arms wrapped around her kept Mary Alice from succumbing. She cried until she didn't think she'd ever be able to stop. Finally, her body couldn't take the grief-storm any longer. She fell asleep between one self-castigating thought and the next.

* * *

The bone-deep sobs faded as Mal's breathing leveled into the regular rhythm of slumber. Ruri kept her arms clasped around her mate's torso, even as she hiccuped occasionally in her sleep. She waited until the hiccups faded and Mal was all the way asleep before letting go. A lock of hair had fallen in front of Mal's face as she cried. It was now soaked beyond belief. Ruri tucked the sodden lock behind Mal's ear and watched her mate's face relax. A persistent crease between her eyebrows was all that remained of the rictus of anguish her face had been locked into.

It was no wonder she was having trouble. She'd killed what was essentially a packmate, after all. Sure, she'd done it to save her sister, but Ruri knew from her own experience how much that hurt.

Poor Josephus hadn't seen it coming. He hadn't been in his right mind for days. Rabies was a hell of a disease to the wolven, much closer to how it progressed in animals than among humans. He couldn't have been allowed to infect anyone else in the pack, and it had been one of Ruri's first jobs to carry out as Dean's newly-minted Beta. She'd kept to fur-form for days afterward, in constant physical contact with others of the pack before she and the wolf had recovered some semblance of their old selves.

She moved her hand to trace the long scar that ran around the bottom of her ribcage on the right side and stopped. Instead of the ropey sliver of rough skin, her fingers encountered only smoothness. Ruri lifted her other hand to feel for the notch on her ear, but it was also gone. She bounded off the bed and in front of the mirror, opening her shirt as she moved. When she held it open and stared at her reflection, she was astounded to see that her scars had all vanished. Her skin was as flawless as a baby's.

Ruri stared, unable to believe that all the reminders of previous fights and scrapes were gone. Some of those scars had been a part of her for over a hundred years. Her breaths came fast and shallow around the hollowness in her chest. Losing them hurt as much as losing the tintype of her family. Without the scars to remind her, how many memories would fade? The skin on her shoulder itched. It was there that she'd been bitten by the wolven who'd turned her.

Jens Hagen had shown up at their farm one autumn afternoon and had talked her parents into having a photograph taken of the family, then had stayed the night with them. In the morning, they'd risen to find the first snowfall of the season had snowed them in. He stayed a few days until a thaw had cleared the road enough that he was able to get his wagon out of the barn. Despite the snow still clogging the roads and her hints that he could stay longer, he'd left.

To this day, Ruri still didn't know what had compelled her to follow him. Maybe it had been the argument she'd had with her mother about why she wouldn't consider going courting with the miller's boy. Or why she hadn't been interested in the son of the farmer to their west. Or any of the boys who had come to call. Maybe it had been the stories he'd told about the places he'd been and the people he'd talked to. Whatever it was, she'd snuck out of the house after everyone had fallen asleep and tracked him to his campsite. It was a simple task in the snow under the light of the full moon, and she wasn't slowed down by having to guide a wagon through the drifts.

She still remembered the way his small camp was set up, with the campfire next to the wagon, and the horses on the opposite side, away from the fire's heat. She remembered thinking that was strange, but then she'd been distracted by Jens stripping off his clothes next to the fire and dropping to his hands and knees. The flesh on his back had rippled and fur had come bursting through it in clumps. To her, it had looked as if his skin had melted away to reveal the massive wolf within him. Fear had frozen her to the spot, until the wolf had looked up with his molten gold eyes and held her gaze. And then she was running, but the wolf was in front of her. She tripped over something and fell heavily to the ground. Pain like unceasing fire had lanced through her left shoulder. She passed out and the next morning woke next to the burned-out remnant of the fire. The only sign of the itinerant photographer were wagon tracks in the snow.

She knew the legends. The next month had been spent eking out a living in the woods, and when she blacked out during its full moon, she knew what she'd become. The last time she'd seen any of her family had been when she crept back into the house and stole the tintype Jens had taken of them.

But she hadn't been alone. The sister of her soul had taken up residence. The wolf was with her from then on. Until now that was.

Ruri went back to the bed. Carefully, so as not to wake her mate, she pulled each item of conjured clothing off Mal. Each piece disappeared into a shimmer in the air and a drift of fine powder that floated away, leaving Billy's original components behind. All of Mal's scars were gone as well. She studied her mate for a while longer, then covered the sleeping Mal with blankets and slipped from the room.

Corrigan's door was down the hall. At least it had been the last time. Ruri hesitated in front of it for a moment, then knocked on it before she could lose her nerve. There was no answer. Ruri turned to leave then heard the latch click. The door opened and the sheriff stood in front of her. She was dressed in her uniform and looked human. In her hands was a light tan campaign hat. She ran her fingers nervously along the leather band above the brim.

"What is it, Ruri?" Corrigan asked. Her voice was almost monotone. She blinked up at Ruri.

"My scars are gone," Ruri said, feeling foolish.

"Did you take a healing potion? One that made you feel really good?"

"Yes, after the hodag hunt."

"Well, there's your answer. That particular tincture heals all wounds completely. How else do you think we can look so good for so long?" Corrigan's lips twisted in disgust as she gestured to herself.

"Are you all right?" Ruri asked. "What happened in the hall was rough."

"Rough." Corrigan barked out a sharp laugh. "That's one way to put being stripped of your rank and title and being humiliated in front of the entire court." She shook her head. "You might as well come in. This isn't a conversation I want to have where unseen ears might catch it."

Ruri thought about declining the invitation, but only for a second. "Why talk to me about any of it?"

"Why not?" Corrigan lifted one shoulder. "It's not like you'll tell anyone, not with what I know about you. The only people I can talk to here will either tell tales to curry favor or will be in trouble when someone assumes they know something and tries to extract it from them." She crossed over to a large chair and collapsed into it, throwing her hat down on the table. "Being the heir is incredibly difficult, but the realm needs one. What Connall has done is insanely dangerous, almost as dangerous as naming the Jaeger as his heir would be. Even that is only a matter of time, I fear."

"He doesn't seem to have the needs of his people in mind," Ruri said. In broad strokes, she filled Corrigan in on what had happened during the hunt for the hodag and Trajan's death.

"That's no surprise," the sheriff said. "It's how the Wild Hunt has operated for millennia, but they only used to ride in the mortal world. It's been over the past century that they've been confined Underhill. They have yet to adapt."

"I don't really see how it's better that they used to do that in our world."

"It isn't." Corrigan waved a hand wearily. "A lot of people here see it that way, though. They don't realize that the more we keep to the old ways, the more chance there is we'll be discovered. We won't survive that, not in any meaningful way." She blew out a long breath. "The Jaeger is all about the old ways. He wants to take the Wild Hunt out in your world again. He wants to cleanse what he considers undesirable elements."

"Humans?"

"Partly, though there aren't many around here."

"Who lives in La Pointe, then?"

"There are humans there, but the population is mostly fae in human guise and those of mixed blood. He's not very fond of those, but he dislikes the fae from further abroad even more."

Ruri shook her head. This crash course in fae politics had started a dull throb behind her left eye. "So he's okay with humans."

"As long as they're claimed by one of the Old World fae."

"And half-fae are all right."

"If one parent is an Old World fae. In his view they have at least some of the proper blood in them."

"But he doesn't like fae who…what?"

Corrigan smiled a bitter half-smirk. "He doesn't like fae who don't come from Europe. Those from Asia are barely tolerated. Those from Africa and the New World should never have come here. There are those in the court who label them Unseleighe. They call them dark and unclean and twist the original meaning of the word until it means something far different than it used to."

"Well, that's comforting."

"What is?"

"Knowing that you graceful, high and mighty fae have raving racists in your ranks also." Ruri grinned. "It's a little comforting to know racism isn't something humans have a lock on. It's also good to know your racists have the same logical issues ours do. How can the fae from here go back where they came from?"

"I think he would have more use for them if they'd done what was expected of them, but when they wanted to stay their own people and not become a serving-class for ours, he lost interest. You probably won't be surprised to hear the king shares many of his views." Corrigan shook her head. "I thought I could be a moderating influence on him, but as his grasp on this world weakens, the Jaeger has only gained more influence. Part of him still realizes the Jaeger as King Under Hill would be disastrous, which is why Connall didn't name him Heir tonight. I think. It's possible he's doing something tricky. It would have been like him a hundred years ago. Now I fear he's simply forgotten he needs an heir so this realm doesn't crumble to nothing if he dies."

"That's depressing."

"Isn't it? And I'm suddenly in a position to do very little about it." She picked up the hat and crammed it on her head. "But at least I can do my best to keep humans from noticing when our little world crumbles from within and explodes out into theirs." She stood. "I need to get back to work. I'll be back on occasion. If I disappear from court completely, the Jaeger will be free to do what he wants. The king still listens to me. Sometimes."

Ruri got up out of her chair. "So what do we do in the meantime?"

"Keep trying to figure out a way to get the king's favor and get out of here. If you can find a way to do that without the Jaeger's help, take it." Corrigan tugged at the bottom of her uniform shirt to straighten it. "Talk to Billy or Andra if you need me, but it had better be an emergency."

"Okay. Good luck, Reese."

The sheriff smiled at Ruri's use of her first name. "And to you. You need it more than I do."

CHAPTER TWENTY-SEVEN

Mary Alice cracked open one eye and blinked. Why was the room in shades of grey? She focused on Ruri's hair, spread out across the pillow in front of her face. No, not shades of grey, but everything looked washed out, nothing like the vibrant shades she'd seen last night.

Last night... She'd had a lot of fun, she could remember that much, but the particulars were choppy as if all she had to go on were photos of an event someone had snapped occasionally throughout the evening. There was a lot of dancing, some drinking. She smacked her lips at the remembered taste of a fizzy beverage. She wouldn't mind getting some of that again.

An argument. Had there been an argument or some sort of fight? The only image she could remember had to do with a man falling through the sky. That couldn't be right, could it? Mary Alice shifted, trying to get past the disturbing memory fragment.

Stiletto. She froze in the bed. Somehow, the squadmate she'd killed had figured into last night's events. That wasn't good. She tried not to move. She barely breathed as she sorted through the jumbled snapshots that were her previous night's memories.

There it was. Ruri and her, back in the hall, heading to their room. She was in tears and confessing all to Ruri, who was… Who was what? Had she been angry? Disappointed? Disgusted? She should have been all those things. Lord knew Mary Alice was.

She reached out a hand toward her girlfriend, needing to feel her, to steal some comfort before Ruri woke up and faced the mess that was the woman she called her mate. The thing that wasn't worthy of someone like Ruri.

Tears dripped off the end of her nose to land on the pillow with distinct plopping sounds. Ruri stirred, then turned over, reaching out to Mary Alice before she opened her eyes.

"Oh, sweetie," she said, her voice gravelly from sleep. She pulled Mary Alice into her arms, hooking one leg over her hip, molding them together down the entire length of their bodies. Neither of them wore a stitch of clothing.

Ruri's warmth seeped into her, chasing the tension from her muscles. She relaxed into her girlfriend's embrace, feeling at peace for the first time in months. Ruri rested her chin on top of Mary Alice's head. They lay there together for long minutes. Mary Alice was content to bask in her company. She was almost lulled back to a doze by the steady rise and fall of Ruri's chest. All the while, tears streamed down her face.

"So…" Mary Alice finally said. "I guess the hug means you don't hate me?"

"Of course I don't hate you." Ruri tightened her grip. "I take it you don't remember much from last night."

"Not really. Remind me to stay away from that stuff. I enjoyed it a little too much, I think." She sighed. It had felt amazing to get out from under all her cares, but chasing that kind of oblivion had done incredible damage to many in her cohort. It had led to the deaths of more than one, if indirectly.

"I can do that," Ruri said. "If that's what you want."

"It is."

"Then I'll remind you of that when you snap at me for it."

Mary Alice smiled. "I know you will. I like that you don't take my crap."

"Oh, I'll take it if I earned it, but I learned a long time ago not to take shit that isn't mine."

"I bet. So what did I tell you, exactly?"

"Not much, but enough, I think." Ruri paused before continuing. "You said Stiletto got knocked out in the fight and you finished the job before she could regain consciousness."

"That's about the size of it." Mary Alice sighed. "I didn't think it would bother me this much. I did it for Cassidy, which isn't as comforting as it should be."

"It's good that you're bothered by it," Ruri said slowly, picking each word with extreme care. "You worry about being a monster. If this didn't upset you, I think you'd be a lot closer to being one, no matter what kind of DNA you've got floating around in there."

"I should have been better. I should have figured out a way."

Ruri laughed, an incredulous edge to her amusement. "You were in a pretty textbook impossible situation. If someone gave a class on impossible choices, you and Cassidy's pictures would be front and center on the assigned reading."

"But—"

"But nothing. You made it out with Cassidy. You kept me alive. You took down MacTavish and helped free a dozen or more wolven from him. Yes, Stiletto didn't make it. Because you chose your family and mine. If that makes you a monster, then I'm one too, because I don't know that I could have made a different decision under those circumstances."

"You wouldn't have killed a packmate." Mary Alice knew Ruri would have found some way, any way, around it. "You would have figured it out."

"Maybe," Ruri allowed, "but the big difference would have been that I would have had support. You were on your own and still had the wherewithal to recognize you were in over your head. Without that, Cassidy would be dead. No, the reason Stiletto died is because your government brought you together as a pack and then destroyed your bonds. If the blame lies with anyone, it's with Uncle Ralph and the rest of those assholes. The only way out of an impossible decision is different choices. More voices. And they made damn sure that was never going to happen."

"If you say so." It made sense, but how much of that was because Mary Alice desperately wanted forgiveness for what she'd done, even if she didn't deserve it?

"I do say so, and it is so." Ruri held her back far enough to look Mary Alice in the eyes. "I fell for you because of the way you're bloody well going to protect those who belong to you. I've watched as you try to gather your pack and see it safe. I love you, Mal. I love you because you work so hard to build the bonds that were torn away from you, that keep being torn from you. And no matter how hard it is, you keep fighting for them. For me." Tears ran down Ruri's face now too. "For us. Even as you push me away, you pull me back in. That's not what being a monster is." She shrugged, then sniffled. "How can I not love you?"

"Oh, Ruri." Mary Alice ran her thumb under Ruri's left eye, then her right. The gesture did little to staunch the flow of tears. "I love you, too. It's impossible not to. You're the only one who could take what I did and figure out how to keep me from wallowing in it."

"Does this mean you'll stop trying to push me away?"

"'Fraid so. You're stuck with me now."

"Good." Ruri pulled Mary Alice in for a kiss.

It started out chastely, but it wasn't long before Mary Alice became aware of Ruri's bare breasts against her own. Her nipples pebbled, the puckered skin signaling her awareness of her girlfriend's proximity. Ruri grinned against Mary Alice's mouth. She bit down on Mary Alice's lip hard enough to send pleasure pooling in her groin. Mary Alice opened her mouth to moan, but the sound was quickly swallowed by Ruri's mouth completely covering hers. Ruri's clever tongue dipped into her mouth, darting against her tongue, teasing it with the tip once, twice, then withdrawing.

Mary Alice became aware of Ruri's hands in her hair. Ruri clenched her fingers, pulling on the sensitive roots and holding her in place. She kissed Mary Alice until she had no breath left in her, until her mouth had been possessed by Ruri, until Mary Alice had no thoughts except the desire in her belly and the woman holding her firmly in her place.

"Oh god, Ruri," she gasped when she allowed her to take a full breath.

"Mal." Ruri pulled away.

Before Mary Alice could do more than take a breath to protest the absence of Ruri's skin against hers, Ruri planted a hand between her breasts and pushed her backward onto the bed. She looked up at Ruri, who stared down at her with eyes bright with lust. It was odd not to see the brilliant gold of her wolf eyes looking down at her. Mary Alice didn't like it. Ruri's human eyes were beautiful and she loved looking into them, but that edge of excitement that came with knowing Ruri's wolf was in there and barely contained brought a little something extra to the experience, an edge of danger which was sadly lacking now.

Ruri shifted from staring down at her to holding herself up over Mary Alice's body, both hands planted on either side of her head. Mary Alice looked up at her, anticipation growing, coiling within. Her eyes flashed, then she leaned in, running the tip of her tongue up the side of Mary Alice's neck, leaving a path of goose bumps that spread down the left side of her body. She lifted her arms, wrapping them around

Ruri's neck. She lifted her hips, looking for some contact, anything to ease the empty ache between her thighs.

"Patience, love," Ruri said. She bit into Mary Alice's neck. Pleasure flared. Mary Alice gasped, her entire being focused on the delicious pain.

"God, Ruri," she moaned. "Please…" Her voice trailed off.

"Mmm." Ruri gently licked the site of the bite. "What do you need, baby mine?" She nibbled gently up Mary Alice's neck toward her earlobe, then stopped, bathing it with her breath.

Mary Alice couldn't concentrate on the question. "I…" She turned her head, trying to get Ruri to bite her ear. When her girlfriend obliged, she almost levitated off the bed. She grabbed Ruri's shoulders and pulled herself against her, glorying in the feel of her skin against Ruri's as sensation that she couldn't begin to describe flowed through her. The tension deep in her belly ratcheted up another level. She pushed her heels against the bed, legs roaming restlessly as she tried to keep herself from coming apart.

Ruri chuckled deep in her chest. The sound made Mary Alice bite her lip.

"So much for being patient," Ruri said, her voice low and rough. "I'm going to do such things to you."

"Oh, yes. God, Ruri, do it all to me."

Clever fingers wormed their way between bare chests already damp with sweat and gently caressed the outer edge of Mary Alice's aureole. She bit her lip again, this time so hard she was surprised when she didn't taste blood.

"You like this?" Ruri's voice rasped in her ear.

"You know I do."

Ruri squeezed her nipple gently, rolling it between her fingers. Mary Alice clamped her legs together, straining to find some friction for her clit. Ruri gave her nipple a final tweak, then ran her hand down over Mary Alice's torso. They tangled briefly in the coarse fleece at the juncture of her thighs. The hair was sopping wet, and her fingers slipped right on through. Mary Alice let her thighs fall open when Ruri's fingertips brushed lightly over her mound. Unashamed of the need and with no thought but satisfaction from the pure want that rode her like the cruelest of masters, she thrust her pelvis forward. Ruri rode the movement with her hand, not varying the light touch. She growled in frustration, but Ruri only laughed, a growl deep in her throat that sent more tension coiling through her core.

Ruri's fingertips spread Mary Alice's labia. Cool air coursed over hot flesh at once soothing and inflaming it. She cried out, beyond caring that she keened her arousal aloud for anyone to hear.

"Is this what you want?" Ruri skated her fingers over Mary Alice's swollen clit.

Her hips twitched. She had to swallow twice before she could answer. "Yes." She almost sobbed. "Dear god, yes. Fucking take me, Ruri!"

"Your wish…" Despite her words, Ruri kept her fingers where they were, making slow circles around her clit. Every revolution cranked up the pressure. Mary Alice held onto Ruri's back for dear life to keep from exploding before she got what she wanted. What she needed.

Ruri's fingers skated through one last revolution then dipped down, closer to the opening Mary Alice had to have filled.

"That's it," she said. "Ruri, please. Don't make me wait. I can't… I can't…"

"Well, if you can't…" Ruri's eyes gleamed amber, almost reaching the golden of her wolf's eyes. For a moment, Mary Alice stared transfixed at her girlfriend. A slow smile spread across Ruri's face. The smile was so wicked that Mary Alice thought she might come simply from the delights it promised.

Ruri pressed inside her with one smooth, quick motion, burying two fingers up to the last knuckles. The sensation of being suddenly filled, of muscles deep inside being stroked, of finally having what she'd been desiring for so long had Mary Alice digging her nails into Ruri's back. She threw her head back and cried out, then moaned with disappointment as Ruri withdrew. She cried out again when Ruri thrust back inside her, with three fingers, filling her up all the way, stretching her vaginal walls around those clever fingers that stroked in and out slowly at first, then picking up speed. She whimpered, her chest heaving as she breathed raggedly, swept away in a maelstrom of sensation. When Ruri crooked a finger inside her, skating it over exactly the right spot, she couldn't hold on any longer.

Mary Alice screamed, not caring who might hear. Her hips bucked once, twice, again before stilling as they became the focus of all the tension that exploded through her. Pleasure blasted her out of her body and over the horizon to float in pieces before slowly coming back to herself.

She opened her eyes to find Ruri lying next to her, head propped on her hand. Her girlfriend was more than a little self-satisfied, but a dangerous twinkle still lurked in her eyes.

"That was…" Mary Alice had no words. She stretched, luxuriating in how relaxed her muscles were.

"Glad to hear it." Ruri mimed looking at a wristwatch. "Don't get too comfy. We're not done yet."

"Oh no?" Mary Alice blinked innocently over at Ruri. "Whatever do you mean?"

Ruri gently tapped the tip of Mary Alice's nose with her fingertip. "If you have to ask, I guess I'll just have to show you."

"Oh. No. That sounds terrible." Mary Alice rested the back of her hand against her forehead. "Please. Stop. I beg of you."

"Oh, I'm going to get you for that." Ruri growled low in her throat and lunged over toward her.

Mary Alice met her with open arms, her leg sliding between Ruri's. She pressed her thigh up against Ruri's scorching center.

"Who's got who?"

CHAPTER TWENTY-EIGHT

Their exertions had left them peckish. The large dining hall had been fairly empty when they arrived. Ruri got the idea from Mracek that many fae were still in bed after a night that had been raucous even by the court's standards.

She'd been itching for some fresh air, perfumed though it might be, and had asked Mracek to conduct them to a garden, which was how they'd come to be standing outside, staring at light that darted and zipped beneath the placid surface of a well-manicured pond.

"What do you think those are?" Ruri asked Mal.

"They remind me of pixies," Mal said. She leaned closer to the water's surface. "If they'd hold still for a second, I could get a better look."

As the words left her mouth, the lights froze in place. They quivered slightly but didn't move. Mal bent forward even further.

"Maybe that's not such a good idea," Ruri said. She was on edge again, which was apparently her default setting here.

"I'd listen to your lady" came the Jaeger's voice from behind them.

They turned to find he'd come up behind them without making the slightest sound. He picked up a branch and joined them at the pond's edge.

"Nixies," he said. "As excitable as their forest brethren." He tossed the branch into the water. It sat on the surface for a second, then the water frothed violently as the lights converged on it. Water splashed as the branch was stripped of its bark and shattered into small pieces that were whisked beneath the surface.

"Oh." Mal stepped back from the edge, her hand going to the combat knife at her waist.

"Indeed," the Jaeger said. "You would likely survive, but not unscathed."

"Thank you for the advice." Mal smiled at the fae Huntmaster, then looked down at the lights flickering under the water.

"Yes, thank you," Ruri said.

"You have much to thank me for, Lady Ruri," the Jaeger said. His demeanor cooled perceptibly as he turned to face her.

"I suppose so," she said.

"Without my intervention last night, you might've gotten yourself and your lady in more than a spot of trouble."

Mal's head popped up. "What do you mean by that?"

"Your lady confronted the king's guards as he was disciplining an interloper." He shook his head, his eyes sad. "Fortunately, she managed to entertain King Connall in the attempt, but had I not stopped her continued efforts, you may be certain he would have taken offense."

"Ruri." Mal's voice was filled with disappointment.

"Not now, Mal," she said.

"Later then." The look in Mal's eyes said she wasn't about to drop the matter.

Well, if Mal wanted to talk, there was plenty to discuss, but not in front of the Jaeger. But there were things to talk to the Jaeger about.

"So, Jaeger," Ruri said, "I've been meaning to ask you about the hunt we went on."

"The hunt for the hodag?"

"Yes, that one exactly." She ignored Mal's attempt to catch her eye. "Wouldn't it have been better to herd the hodag toward somewhere uninhabited?"

"Ideally," the Jaeger said. His face grew somber. "The loss of that brownie was regrettable."

"Trajan."

"Pardon me?"

"His name was Trajan."

"Was it? Thank you for informing me." He inclined his head toward her. "But what you must understand about the hunt is that we had to act while the beast was within our grasp. Had we waited for another opportunity, more than one mere brownie would likely have died."

"Did your hunters check to see if anyone was home before driving it in? Did they try to get Trajan and Ylana out when they knew the hodag was coming?"

"Lady Ruri, I was with you. I can only trust that my hunters took all reasonable measures that time permitted in the pursuit of our quarry."

"But—"

The Jaeger raised his hand. "Your concern for the subjects of King Connall's realm is commendable. I suggest you spend more time with the hunt before misunderstanding our methods."

Ruri bit down on an angry reply. To insinuate that she was inexperienced when it came to hunting was so insulting she might have laughed if it had come from anybody else. The words came from him, however, so she settled for a tight smile and the stiff incline of her head.

"But that is not why I came to find you," the Jaeger said. "I trust I've answered your questions sufficiently?"

"Of course you have," Mal said. "What did you want to talk about?"

Ruri tried not to glare at her mate. They were definitely going to have words on this whole discussion.

"You were under the protection of the Heir," the Jaeger said. "As Reese the Hand is the heir no longer, I've come to offer mine in her stead."

"That's a generous offer," Mal said. Ruri was glad she'd filled her in on some of the evening's events so Mal didn't have to display any ignorance to the Huntmaster.

He glanced over at Ruri. "Indeed it is. While I have heard nothing to indicate she has abdicated her claim, it will become a liability. If it hasn't already. If you decide to stay on with the Wild Hunt, it's only sensible that I extend my protection to you. I'm not in disgrace, and no one will attempt to curry favor with the king by…inconveniencing you."

"What does that mean for Reese?" Ruri asked.

"A fair question, Lady Ruri. You will need to renounce her claim and accept mine for it to be binding. As she has yet to be formally banished or executed, her claim won't expire automatically."

"So we have to publicly disavow her," Ruri said slowly.

"That's correct."

"I don't have a problem with that," Mal said with a twist of her lips. "If it means we won't be messed with, I think it's a good idea."

"Very well, Malice. What say you, Lady Ruri?" The Jaeger's silken voice oozed reasonable concern.

"It sounds like it's for the best." By now, Ruri had brought her anger back under control. The Jaeger provoked it so easily. She hated feeling like he could manipulate her that way. How would Dean have handled the situation? It was funny; she'd never had any desire to be Alpha to any pack. She was strong enough, dominant enough to be one, but the external politics were the last thing in the world that she was interested in. If only she'd paid more attention to how her old Alpha had handled such things. The more time she spent with Mal, the handier that skill set appeared to be. She unbent enough to smile at him with something that hopefully resembled gratitude.

"Very well. I shall enter the new claim with the Seneschal before the day is done. He will have you brought before him to renounce the former heir's claim. Perhaps once that is handled, the two of you would like to join me for the evening repast. We will celebrate."

"Of course," Mal said, smiling and nodding eagerly.

It felt rude to refuse, and Ruri was certain that was what the Jaeger had been counting on. Or maybe he was only trying to be nice. She was so ready to believe the worst in him. Maybe he wasn't so bad after all.

A spike of pain behind her right eye turned Ruri's nodding smile into a gasp of pain. She clapped a hand over her face in a vain attempt to dull the sharp agony to a throb.

"Are you all right?" Mal asked.

Ruri pulled her hand away from her face and looked at it. There was no sign of blood. "It's just a headache, I think."

The Jaeger's brow creased in courtly concern. "Perhaps you should lie down for a while, Lady Ruri. I shall send a healer to attend you."

Mal put her arm around Ruri's shoulders. "I can take her," she said.

The Jaeger raised one eyebrow at the edge in her voice. Mal's face relaxed back into a smile.

"I've got her," she said pleasantly. "But maybe a doctor isn't such a bad idea."

"I'm fine," Ruri said. The pain was receding a bit. She unclenched her jaw. "If it doesn't get better in a bit, we can talk about a doctor."

"Are you sure, sweetie?" The concern in Mal's voice warmed her, but not as much as her willingness to be tender with Ruri in public.

"I shall leave you two, then," the Jaeger said. "Send me a message should you require a healer."

Mal nodded but kept her eyes on Ruri. "We should get back to the room."

Ruri was vaguely aware of the Jaeger taking his leave. The sharp stab of pain was dulling down to something she could handle. The idea of being cooped up inside was more unbearable than the pain.

"Let's stay here," she said. "I think it's easing up."

"Are you sure?"

"Yeah."

"You're the boss." Mal looked around, then walked her over to the base of a tall willow tree. Long tendrils hung down from the ends of its branches, brushing the ground with the breeze. She sat, bringing Ruri gently down with her.

"Here," Mal said, pulling Ruri down so her head was pillowed in Mal's lap. "Try to relax."

"Relax," Ruri said. "Right. Just relax in this messed up place with all the people we can't trust."

"We can trust the Jaeger, at least."

Ruri pushed herself up on her elbows and stared at Mal. "Are you serious? In what parallel universe can we trust that slippery bastard?"

Mal glared back at Ruri for a second, then gently guided Ruri's head back into her lap. "He's a hell of a lot more trustworthy than Corrigan is. She's the one who took your wolf away."

"Not for no reason. That so-called Huntmaster led a dangerous animal to an innocent family's door, then has the gall to pretend to be sorry when the completely foreseeable happens."

"Hey, I was right there when you called him on it. His explanation sounded reasonable to me. I've made that calculation more than once. It's not an easy call to make, but that doesn't make it the wrong one."

"You were there when he fae-splained how to hunt to me? Me? Who's been on more hunts in her life than she can remember." Ruri sat up. Her head pounded at the sudden movement, but she squinted through the pain at her mate. "I've never lost a bystander to a hunt, and I've been out there with newly turned wolven who have less control than a Norwegian farmer with a plate of lutefisk."

"What does that even mean?"

Ruri brushed away Mal's confusion with a wave of her hand. "He didn't answer any of my questions, and you happily went along with his empty words. What happened to my mate who doesn't take anything from anyone?" Ruri spread her arms wide. "Because I haven't seen her since we got here. You're going after a dangling carrot, letting the Jaeger and his twisted king string you along. The Mal I know would be looking for a way out, any way out, and certainly not the one she was offered."

"The Jaeger *is* our best bet. What else am I going to do? My special skill is killing non-humans, remember?" Mal jabbed her open palm with a finger. "If you have another idea, I'm all ears. But until then, don't you criticize the way I try to get us out of this jam."

"There it is." Ruri pointed up at Mal. "You. The way *you* try to get us out of this jam. I'm not even going to mention anything about how you're the one who got us into it—"

"Except you just did."

"It's always you. You decide this is the best way to go, and I'm supposed to fall in line. Never mind that I've been doing this for a hell of a lot longer than you have."

"Of course you have." Mal's lip lifted off her teeth. "You and your wolf. Forgive me if I don't want to take the word of someone who shares a brain with a dumb animal."

Ruri rolled over and stood, staring at Mal. Each word slammed into her like a body blow. "Oh. Well. That's…"

"That's right," Mal said jumped to her feet. She strode forward, so much anger around her that the air seemed to draw away from her. "I'm the one who can fix this. I'm the one who *will* fix this. You can accept that or slink off into the woods with your tail between your legs. Either you're on board, or you're on your own."

"If I wanted to be on my own, I would be. King Connall trapped *you* here. I can leave anytime I want to, remember? I don't need you, Mal, not for this."

"Then why are you still here?" Mal threw her arm out, pointing behind her. "Why don't you leave? Just go. I can handle this. Alone is what I do."

"For the love of…" Ruri shook her head and turned away. The pain in her head was nothing compared to the ache that threatened to hollow out her ribcage. She struggled to keep her voice from wavering under the strain of her emotions. "You don't need to. Not anymore. I keep telling you that. What's it going to take for you to believe it?"

"You have a hell of a way of convincing me." Mal turned on her heel and stormed back toward the castle. "I'm out of here. Don't follow me."

Ruri stopped in her tracks. She took a deep breath, trying to keep from breaking down completely. Mal disappeared from her view between two hedgerows, though she could still hear her mate's staccato footfalls on the paving stones.

"She'll be fine once she cools down," she said. It didn't sound any better out loud than it had in her head. If anything, it sounded worse.

They'd never had words like that, not even when Mal was locking her up in a metal box to take care of her sister.

How could she not know that Ruri was there at her back? By now it should have been obvious, even with the bonds Mal's employers had imposed on her, then destroyed. For someone who was so independent, she sure liked to take orders. There had to be a way to wean her off that. Mal shouldn't be taking orders. Though if Ruri was being honest with herself, Mal wasn't so great at giving them either. She had too much tendency to take it all on herself. No, Mal needed something else, but what?

Ruri sank down on a stone bench and buried her face in her hands. This morning had been so amazing. How had it fallen apart so quickly?

CHAPTER TWENTY-NINE

Mracek jumped up and ran after her when Malice stormed out of the garden.

"I don't need your help, Mracek," she spat over her shoulder at the confused page.

"Are you certain?" he asked as he automatically slowed to a trot.

"Of this, yes." She kept on walking forward. "But that's about it," she said to herself. *What's wrong with Ruri?* It was unlike her girlfriend to be so irrational about a situation. Usually Malice was the one flying off the handle or reacting inappropriately. How could Ruri not see that the Jaeger was their ticket out of this place?

"All right then." Mracek had stopped and his voice trailed off when she made no attempt to reply. He could stay and wait for her impossible girlfriend. *Whatever.* She didn't care.

Malice paid no attention at all to where she was going; she simply walked forward. She hoped someone got in her way. What she really needed was the chance to indulge in some extreme violence. She grinned. Yes, beating someone to a pulp would take the edge off.

Sadly, no one crossed her path. She was back in the courtyard. There weren't many fae there, but she recognized one from across the vast space. There was no mistaking the grey behemoth loitering near the Wild Hunt's stables. He would do.

"Regin," she called out as she approached him.

The fae turned around, a wide smile on his features as she drew closer.

"What happened to you?" she asked. "Did your mother mate with an elephant or something?"

His face grew darker as dense eyebrows drifted down.

"Or maybe she was the elephant." Malice stopped in front of him. She put her hands on her hips and looked him up and down. "You've got the build for it. And the face."

With a wordless growl, Lord Regin swung a massive fist at her head. Malice ducked it easily, not bothering to move her feet. She shifted her weight and allowed it to glide past her head. She didn't have far to duck; the fae towered over her.

"You move like an elephant too."

Lord Regin lunged, arms extended to grapple her. She was ready for it and ducked under his reaching hands. She slipped around to his back and nailed him twice in the kidney. Regin grunted at the attack and twisted to grab her. He was quicker than he had any right to be given his bulk. Malice managed to avoid his fingers, but one massive hand clipped her shoulder and sent her back a good five feet. Pain radiated from where he'd hit her, but it was nothing compared to the pain in her head when she relived the horrible things she and Ruri had said to each other.

Malice laughed. "That all you got, elephant man?" She didn't wait for him to answer. Instead, she ran at him. When he reached out for her again, she grabbed his arm and used her momentum to swing herself up and around the huge limb. As soon as her foot touched his upper arm, she pushed off it and launched herself at his head.

In the face of her unexplained and frankly stupid assault, Lord Regin took a step back. He tried to get his hands up to defend his face, but was too late. Malice put all of her weight behind her shoulder, driving her fist into the side of his face. Her hand glanced off his cheekbone, snapping his head back.

He closed his hands around her waist and threw her away from him with a roar. Malice hit the stone wall with a thud that jarred her all the way down to her bones. She slid down the wall to land in a heap. It hurt, everything hurt, but she still couldn't scrub the memories of her fight with Ruri from her mind. What was it going to take?

She started to laugh, a wheezing chuckle that blossomed into a full belly laugh. It hurt. Every agonizing breath was the only price she knew how to pay.

Lord Regin crouched beside her, casting her into the shadow of his bulk, his large face uncomfortably close to hers. "You done, or are we going to have another go of it?"

Malice tried to answer but couldn't get the words out around her attack of hilarity. She settled for clapping him on the forearm. He stayed next to her, watching her closely until she sobered up enough for the laughter to subside.

"Oh hell, that hurt," she finally said.

"Good," he grunted. "Want to explain why you tried to take my head off just now?"

Malice levered herself back into a sitting position. Another giggle escaped before she could stop it. "Oh, you know. I got into a fight with Ruri."

"With your lady?" He sat back on his heels.

"That's the one. Maybe. I guess we'll see."

"So you thought you'd take out what happened on the meanest whoreson who crossed your path."

"Something like that."

"Ah." Lord Regin stood up and held out his hand.

Malice considered it for a moment before grasping it and allowing him to pull her to her feet.

"If you want to take out some ill humor, I'm always willing to offer my service." A wide grin split Lord Regin's face. "I approve of the therapeutic benefits of violence, though I doubt you've worked it all out." He put a hand on her shoulder and steered her around the corner into the stables.

A half dozen or so members of the Hunt congregated inside. Two of them stood at the open door of one of the stalls. The others sat in one corner at a small table and chairs.

"What do you have in mind?" Malice asked.

"Something that's vexed us for a while," Lord Regin said. "But with you to lead us, a small group might just be able to accomplish it where the entire Hunt couldn't."

"That sounds promising." And it might kill two birds with one stone. She could blow off some steam and maybe earn Connall's favor. Getting out of here would be good for both of them. Of course, Ruri might have already left, since she wasn't stuck here. Malice bit her lower lip in a vain attempt to forget some of the stupid, hurtful things she'd hurled at her girlfriend. Ruri would be well within her rights to leave her. Malice hoped with every fiber of who she was that she hadn't.

He steered her over to the table. "Freki, Lopar," Lord Regin said to other two. "You'll want in on this." He leaned past Malice's shoulder toward the others. "We're going after the Bottom-Dwellers."

The other fae shifted toward him. "I'm up for that," Freki said as they joined the rest of them. "It's about damn time."

"Bottom-Dwellers?" Malice asked. "What, like catfish or something?"

"Nothing so elegant," one of the other fae said. "They come up out of the cracks in the ground to harass King Connall's subjects. Once-fertile grazing areas have been overrun with them."

"The problem is that they have excellent hearing," Lord Regin said. "The Wild Hunt has tried to ambush them more than once, but we are too many. We need a small group, but the Jaeger can't be spared from court to lead a small hunt. Now that you're practically honorary huntmaster, you can take us out after them."

Malice nodded. "I like it. This is exactly what I need right now. How aggressive are they? Are they going to put up a fight?"

"You can count on it," Freki said. "With a group this small, they might even try to ambush us."

"Why not make that a certainty?" Malice said. "We have a couple hunters lead them back to us, where we have our own nasty little surprise."

"I like how you think, Hunter," Lord Regin said. "Let's get the mounts readied. We can be out in mere minutes."

"Not too soon for me."

A few hours later, the small group of hunters was making its way through rolling hills. Malice was doing her best to rein in a restive kelpie. The Jaeger had been riding it the last time she saw it, and Lord Regin had insisted she be the one to ride it on this hunt. The horse-looking thing fought against her every step of the way and only seemed not to resent her presence when they were at a full gallop or when they were crossing a stream. Its dark grey coat was beautiful but constantly wet though there was no rain. She'd picked multiple pieces of seaweed from its mane, but there were always more every time she looked.

"How much longer?" she asked Lord Regin, who cantered at her side on his enormous lizard.

"We're almost there," he said.

"Really?" Malice looked around. The hills were lush and green, dotted with low trees and bushes. "When you said they came out of cracks in the ground, I'd envisioned something rockier."

"They cause the cracks to form," Freki said from her other side. "They pull people down, then they snap closed behind them. There's never any trace."

Lopar guided his mount closer to their small group. He couldn't get as close as the others, since his gryphon's impressive wings took up a fair amount of space. "Sometimes smoke and steam boils out of the crevice. Visibility gets limited pretty quickly when that happens."

"Does it seem to hamper them?" Malice asked.

"No one knows if they can even see," Lord Regin said. "Their eyes are completely white, without pupils. They're grotesque."

"And they kill the farmers who work this area?" She squinted at a nearby hill. "I don't see anything like fields."

"Mainly herders in this region," Lord Regin said. "Goats and deer, mostly. The Bottom-Dwellers started out stealing those. When the farmers tried to stop them, they began to disappear as well."

Malice nodded. She'd heard that story before, except it was usually rogue lycans or newly fledged vamps who were doing the killing. They often started with livestock in remote areas, then escalated to game more suited to their appetites. "We're going to need to keep an eye out for an ambush point. It's too bad the area isn't as rocky as I thought. A blind canyon would have been the perfect place to lure them to."

"We might still be able to do something similar," Freki said.

"Are you thinking the—" Lopar started.

"—bend in the Ayregad Sneethe?" Freki finished the phrase. "You know I am." She looked at Malice and explained. "They won't be able to open a crack under that, I bet. There's a horseshoe bend in the river less than an hour ahead. We could use that to box them in."

"That'll keep them off our backs on three sides," Malice said.

"You're riding a kelpie," Lord Regin said. He grinned when she stared at him blankly. "It's more at home on water than on land. You'll be safe as houses. Lopar has the gryphon. He can provide support from the air."

"That leaves you and Freki as bait," Malice said. "The others will stay with us at the ambush point."

"I can live with that." Freki's grin slashed across her face. "Let them try to catch me." Her mount looked more like someone had crossed an Irish wolfhound with a praying mantis. Malice had been trying to avoid looking at it since they started out. It wasn't the unusual build that freaked her out so much as the way it moved. It shifted between one motion and the next so quickly that it was almost impossible to see, and it held very still at other times. The jittery chunks of movement were hard to watch.

"Which way to the river bend?" Malice asked.

"This way." Lopar set spurs to the side of his gryphon. It squawked in protest and shot forward at a run.

Someone behind them blew a long brassy note on a horn. It was taken up by another horn, then another. Each was pitched to harmonize perfectly with the others. Together they sang a chord that stirred something in Malice's heart. Despite the pain she still felt, elation grew within her breast. She pressed spurless heels to the kelpie's ribs and leaned forward over its neck. Either it was following the gryphon's lead or the horns gave it the same excitement as they did her. It reared back, its hooves slashing through the air, exposing the fins on the backs of its legs. It bellowed, a loud drawn-out scream Malice couldn't believe was coming from its throat. It hit the ground so hard it trembled, then took off. The wind whipped past Malice, howling in her ears and tugging at the ends of her hair, pulling them back like a banner. They gained on the gryphon in no time, then passed it. Lopar urged it to keep pace, guiding their path with shouted directions and hand motions.

Malice didn't care. Fresh air filled her nostrils, powerful muscles bunched and relaxed beneath her thighs. This was freedom, to go where she wanted on a powerful beast with a host of armed people at her back. Nothing could stop them; only fools would dare get in their way. She laughed, releasing her mirth to the uncaring sky. The Bottom-Dwellers had no idea of the hell that was about to rain down on them.

CHAPTER THIRTY

The plan had seemed so simple while they'd discussed it, but now that Malice and the hunters were in place and awaiting their quarry, she'd begun to worry. For one, hanging out in the river on a kelpie's back was not as advertised. Her mount could breathe below the river's surface, but she couldn't. And so they were submerged up to her chin among the reeds along the river's edge. The water hadn't felt too cold going in, but the longer she stayed mostly under the surface without moving, the more chilled she became.

Lopar, on his gryphon, wasn't much better. They kept hovering above the scrub trees lining the river to get a better look, then flashing her the no-go sign. She could damn well tell nothing was happening, and she didn't need him constantly exposing himself to let her know. The other hunters were worse. One had taken the form of a seal and jumped in the water next to her. She was entertaining herself by nosing through the muck on the river's bottom, then depositing the "treasures" she accumulated in a growing pile on the riverbank. They looked to be mostly rocks and shells.

The remaining hunters had taken to the trees and were concealed there with their bows and javelins, but the constant movement of the boughs gave their positions away. It was all so unprofessional. Malice was unable to drop into the semi-meditative trance she employed when waiting for a creature to make the wrong move. She found herself longing for Ruri to be there. Her girlfriend was someone she could always count on, even with the fight they'd had only a few hours previous.

Why had they been arguing so hard? There was no point. She couldn't even remember what had started their quarrel. The words they'd said to each other ran through her head as clear as a bell, but the reason for it floated out of her grasp. Without any reasons, she was finding it difficult to stay angry.

So there she was, the top of her head sticking out of the water and getting colder by the second while waiting for people she didn't know or trust to get their work done so she could do hers. Perfect.

A brilliant star blossomed to life over the tops of the trees. It shimmered there for a moment and then blinked out, only to be replaced by another moments later. The trees where the fae had concealed themselves shook violently then stilled. The selkie's head popped above the water's surface next to hers.

"That looks like a signal to me," Malice said.

The seal head bobbed in agreement.

Malice firmed her hands around the kelpie's reins. She couldn't hear Freki and Lord Regin on approach yet, but she had no doubt she would soon enough.

The ground rumbled at the same time as another star burst into existence, this one right over their heads. If Fourth of July fireworks had been soundless and fully formed in one go, they might have looked like this. Malice wasted a moment wondering if the inventors of gunpowder had done so to imitate sights like this one. The rumble grew louder until the leaves of the trees and the water at the river's edge vibrated in time with it. The sound of branches snapping filtered back to her through the screen of reeds.

Freki was the first to come into view. She stood in her stirrups, watching behind her. A few seconds later, Lord Regin broke through the trees. The large lizard that was his mount moved quickly but wasn't nearly as nimble as Freki's dog-insect monstrosity.

Malice's heart tripped into overdrive at the scene unfolding behind them. A deep crevasse was opening at their heels. Trees unlucky enough to be too close shook, spasming violently, then listed sideways into the massive crack. Thick fog rolled from the opening in ominous clouds that obscured everything behind them. There was no sound except for that of breaking tree branches. The opening of the crevasse itself was completely silent.

Freki's beast juddered its way around the small clearing in front of the trees. Beyond it was the river and Malice. Lord Regin thundered up on his mount, then pulled the massive lizard about, holding his ground. He held a massive sword in one hand and the beast's reins in the other. As the crevasse rushed up to him, he howled at the sky in defiance. The earth split under his feet, and he plunged from view.

Eerie silence descended onto the clearing. They waited. Malice breathed slowly and evenly, knowing better than to hold her breath but wanting to all the same.

A howl split the silence. At first it sounded like Lord Regin's, but it quickly ran up through one octave, then another until it was an ear-splitting shriek. It was joined by another deep howl that ascended into something akin to a woman's horror movie scream. Then another joined it and another, until there were too many to count. Fog obscured much of the clearing, enough that Malice couldn't see the other side.

She urged the kelpie out of the river; water streamed off their backs as they burst forth. She readied her bow, the string miraculously dry. She didn't have time to think on the magic that kept it viable; instead she nocked an arrow and drew it. The kelpie took one step from the water and onto the bank.

The screaming stopped. The kelpie froze in the sudden silence.

A figure popped out of the crevasse. It was cloaked in the vapor that still billowed forth from the crack. The small and humanoid form moved slowly toward her, features becoming more evident one by one as it moved through the ground-bound cloud. It had skin the color of dark red clay. Hair stood about its head in a halo of white that was a stark contrast to its skin. Another being popped out of the crack and started toward her, but Malice was only vaguely aware of it. The first one was close enough that Malice could see crooked fingers that came to an end with long, off-white nails. They were thick and cracked and sharp as the pointiest claws she'd seen on any supra. Its eyes were wide and white, lacking pupil and iris. They took up half its face and never blinked.

Another figure climbed out of the crack.

The first, its companion not far behind, walked closer in a strange scuttling gait. Its arms didn't seem any longer than would be proportional to a human, but it hunched over so far its fingertips brushed against the ground. Its head lolled back and forth, exposing large ears that came to an exaggerated point.

Another climbed to the top of the crack and stayed there, head tilting back and forth.

Malice sighted at the closest one and let her arrow fly. The arrow hit the Bottom-Dweller's shoulder with a meaty thunk. It screamed, exposing a mouth of square grey teeth. They weren't the nightmarish rows of jagged edges Malice had been expecting. She had a second to wonder about that as she withdrew another arrow from the quiver on her back.

The scream was taken up by the others already on the surface and echoed out from the crevasse.

Malice drew and sighted in one motion, then let loose. She took the Bottom-Dweller in the throat, choking off its terrible cry.

As if that was the signal for the hunters to get off their asses, arrows and javelins rained down from the trees. The shots weren't terribly accurate, not with the obscuring cloud, but there were enough that the Bottom Dwellers suddenly looked like so many pincushions. They dropped where they stood, one toppling back into the crevasse. The nightmarish howls started again. At first screech, they were far away, but by the time they'd hit the highest-pitched scream, more were at the top of the crack. Mouths agape, Bottom-Dwellers poured forth in a wave of clay skin and white eyes. They spread across the ground, the white cloud shifting with them at the wind of their passage.

The ridges of her dry bow string rubbed against her fingertips. Magic. It was magic that had kept it dry. What else could magic do?

"Someone clear out that cloud," Malice yelled. There was no response. She tipped her head back to the sky, inhaled deeply, and bellowed: "Clear that fucking cloud out of there!"

Lopar shouted something from above and the wind came up, whipping the fog bank from the clearing. The Bottom Dwellers at the top of the crevasse froze in place when the sun suddenly swept over them. They were pushed forward and under by those who came behind and who froze in turn at the sun's rays. Those who'd been pushed down struggled to get up, but Malice watched as many of them were trampled beneath the feet and hands of those who were still coming. They piled up and up in a seemingly endless wave, only to be stymied by the sun and the weapons of the fae who awaited them. Malice loosed arrow after arrow into the churning pile of Bottom-Dwellers.

A deep howl emanated from the crevasse as the flow finally started to dry up. It wasn't the continuous rising tone of the Bottom-Dwellers. This one stopped and started and grew steadily closer. A Bottom-

Dweller flew out of the crevasse to land on top of the pile. It didn't so much as twitch, the side of its head cleaved open to expose dark brain matter and gore. Another body joined it. The Bottom-Dwellers who remained alive were filtering back into the crack, but they made a wide berth around the area where the raging howl seemed to be loudest.

A clawed foot grasped the top edge of the crevasse, then another. The howl was deafening. Malice raised her bow, waiting for whatever it was to expose itself.

"Don't shoot," the selkie yelled at her. She stood on the riverbank, her bow raised and without a stitch of clothing. A glossy brown pelt lay at her feet. "It's Lord Regin."

The goggled lizard-thing pulled itself the rest of the way out of the crack. Lord Regin sat on its back, a massive sword in each hand. He reached out and split the nearest Bottom-Dweller in half. It didn't have time to scream. The shocked gasp that left its lips could have been on purpose, or it could have been its final breath squeezing its way out of its ruined ribcage.

Lord Regin looked around, the cords of his neck standing out in stark relief as he looked for something else to kill. His harsh breaths rang across the sunny clearing. They were punctuated by the occasional sound of arrow striking flesh as the fae shot anything that moved. It wasn't long before there were no other sounds save the occasional crack and rumble from deep within the earth.

As the early afternoon sun continued to beat down on the scene of carnage, the bodies stiffened with subtle cracking noises. The sound reminded Malice of the sound of cereal in milk. She blinked, staring at the mounds of Bottom-Dwellers piled at the edge of the crevasse, which had ceased disgorging vapor. These corpses were already starting to stink, skin splitting open and streaks of black liquid running down the clay-colored skin.

Lord Regin's mount climbed to the top of one of the charnel mounds. Lord Regin looked around at those assembled, then tilted his head back, letting out a roar of triumph that was as loud as it was vicious. Behind him, the deep gouge in the earth's surface closed with a grinding snap. The pile shifted under the grey fae as Bottom-Dwellers were cut in half. His giant lizard surfed the shifting pile with ease despite the bodies that disintegrated messily beneath its bulk. Lord Regin continued to urge his mount forward.

The lizard beast moved toward the river where Malice still sat astride the kelpie, her bow forgotten in her hands, quiver empty on her back.

"Hunter," he shouted to her. He folded his trunk-sized torso into a bow from the waist. Freki's bug-lizard zipped into place next to him.

The trees rustled as the fae hunters dropped from the boughs to the ground. Lopar swooped down to join Freki next to Lord Regin. As one, they looked to her and matched Lord Regin's bow.

Malice had no idea what to do. She stared at the assembled fae as long, silent seconds ticked silently past.

"Thanks, everyone," she finally said when the silence became too heavy to bear. "Let's get this cleaned up and head back."

Lord Regin straightened and the other fae mirrored him with eerie precision. "You heard the Hunter," he said.

The fae jumped into action as he approached her. Next to her, the selkie pulled her glossy brown pelt around her shoulders as a half-cape. She moved to join the fae who milled about the piles of dead Bottom-Dwellers with purpose Malice couldn't quite make out.

"The bounty will be excellent for this hunt," Lord Regin said. He maneuvered his beast to stand next to hers and look out on the field of carnage.

"Bounty?" This was the first she'd heard of that.

"The left ear of each Bottom Dweller earns a token from the king," Lord Regin said. "No one has ever turned in so many in one day, I'll wager." He rubbed his hands together eagerly. "His favor will rain down on us all."

"Favor, is it?" Malice was tempted to copy Lord Regin's hand-washing motions. "I can use a bit of that." Finally, she and Ruri could get out of this place. They'd been here for…days? Or was it weeks? She was starting to lose track of time, and she still hadn't listened to that message from Cass. Anxiety prickled at the back of her brain, but she pushed it away. There were more pressing things to worry about. Cassidy would keep.

"How did you know the sunlight would harm them?" Lord Regin asked.

"Honestly, I was just trying to slow them down. I saw the giant eyes and figured if it was super bright out, they might have problems. That and someone said the fog usually rolls in with them. There had to be a reason." She took a chance and elbowed him in the side. It was like nudging a boulder. "Besides, I had to do something to save your ass."

Lord Regin laughed. "I was doing well enough in the hole. Took out more than a few myself." He leaned over and spat on the ground. "It's a shame I won't be able to turn in the ears on those, but they're deep within the earth now."

"So just account for some up here," Malice said. "We're splitting the tokens equally between all the hunters, aren't we? Last I checked, you're a member of the Wild Hunt."

"Huntmaster usually takes the first cut," Lord Regin said. "The hunters fight it out for what's left."

"That's ridiculous. We all did the work. We all profit."

"You'll be popular with the hunters, then. The Jaeger might take a dim view of all of it."

Malice shook her head. If that was the case, then she was disappointed in him. "He can take it up with me. My hunt, my rules."

Lord Regin hit his thigh with a resounding smack. A wide grin split his face. "They'll be lining up to ride out with you," he said. "I'd better get in there and make sure your wishes are followed. No one is to hoard the ears." He guided his mount a short distance away, then undid the straps holding him to the saddle and jumped down.

The fae had divided themselves into work groups. Some stood to one side, their hands outstretched. The ground below their down-turned palms was peeling itself open into a long trench a few feet deep. As they progressed on, other fae were rolling or carrying the decomposing bodies of the Bottom-Dwellers into the trench. It was a dirty job, made dirtier by the fae who were harvesting the left ears and tossing them onto one of a number of steadily growing piles. As Malice watched, discomfort began to gnaw at her belly. These were mass graves, and where she came from, those generally held very poor implications.

She tried to tell herself that collecting the ears was similar to the wildlife bounty system that existed in many states. Clearly these Bottom-Dwellers had been dangerous pests to the farming folk here. They'd been the ones losing their livelihoods, after all.

Two tall fae walked past, carrying a body between them. It was wearing a dirty white cloth that looked for all the world like a rude toga that was maybe a couple of steps up from being a loincloth.

"You two," Malice called out to them. "Hold up."

The two Tuatha stopped where they were and looked over at her.

"Is that a shroud?" Malice asked. "Did you put that on him?" At least she assumed it was a him. None of the Bottom-Dwellers had any secondary sexual characteristics that she could pick out.

"No," the one on the right said. The twist of her lips let Malice know what she thought of the Bottom-Dwellers' wardrobe. "It's what they use to dress themselves."

"Unseleighe savages," the one on the left said. He cleared his throat harshly, then leaned over to spit on the ground.

"Okay, thanks," Malice said. "I was just curious."

The Tuatha shook their heads, clearly confused by the odd questions the human was asking. They hoisted the body, settling it between them, then trundled off toward the burial trench.

Clothing wasn't a sign of simple animals. The disquiet in her gut churned into full-blown nausea. She might have made a terrible mistake. She needed Ruri. She could almost feel her presence, like a warm breeze that caressed the back of her neck. If only she could break away from this group and head back to her girlfriend. She would apologize for the awful things she'd said, then they'd work out another way out that didn't require hunting down the inhabitants of this twisted land. But she couldn't. She didn't know the way back, and getting lost in the attempt wouldn't help anyone.

So she waited, sitting atop the kelpie, hoping the fae would finish their dark business soon.

CHAPTER THIRTY-ONE

Ruri sat alone in their room. She picked idly at one corner of the elaborately embroidered bedspread. Mal was getting steadily closer. She'd felt when her mate had left the castle, the distance growing between them like a chasm opening in her chest. At first she'd been happy for Mal to go. Her presence had weighed Ruri down. That hadn't lasted long. Now that she was closer, Ruri felt like she could breathe again. They had to talk, to sit down and have a real conversation for the first time since they'd started dating or whatever it was they were doing. Mal was first in her heart, but Ruri had to know where she ranked in Mal's.

She shook her head. For the first time, she thought perhaps it was a good thing she didn't have access to her wolf. The wolf saw things so plainly. She didn't recognize shades of grey. So many things were a binary with her.

Mal, on the other hand, had no black, had no white. She was all shades of grey, mostly dark, but glimpses of lighter shades gave Ruri hope. There had been more of the light shades shining through of late, but not, it seemed, when that bastard the Jaeger was involved.

Ruri would be damned straight to hell and back before she would let some slippery fae asshole take her Mal away. But what if that was what Mal wanted? Who was she to stand between her mate and her mate's desires, especially when Ruri was the only one who had acknowledged the mate bond?

She let her head loll back to clunk against the headboard. How could a non-wolven acknowledge the mate bond? Could a non-wolven even form a mate bond? Was the answer in what Mal's employers had done to her? Did she have them to thank for this? She pulled her brain away from considering that line of thought too closely.

There was no point in sitting around and waiting. Ruri pushed herself off the bed and crossed to the door. As she'd hoped, Mracek still waited on the other side. He hopped to attention when the door opened.

"Where can I get a view into the courtyard?" she asked.

He opened a small book and thumbed through it. He flipped back and forth between a couple of pages, then closed it and tucked it away in a belt pouch.

"Promenade is on the other side today," he said. "I can take you right there, unless you want to go down to the courtyard proper."

"A view is fine, thank you, Mracek." She wanted to make sure Mal was okay, but she wasn't certain how happy her mate would be to see her.

"Very well." The page trotted off down the hallway, leaving her to follow along in his wake. As was usual, she quickly lost track of the twists and turns of the halls. Some seemed vaguely familiar and others she'd never seen before in her life.

"Does that book tell you how to get places?" she asked after they'd been walking for a while.

"It's enchanted to notify the bearer of changes to the castle's configuration." He shrugged. "They say one day I won't need it, that the castle will recognize me as one of its own and I'll simply know my way around. That hasn't happened yet." Mracek sighed. "There are younger pages who already have no need for it, but I have to rely on the book still. They say the realm resembles its ruler, so it may be that it will never recognize me."

"What do you mean by that?"

Mracek blanched and licked his lips. He looked around, then shook his head. "It's nothing. Just my own disappointment at not being a better page."

"I think you do a fine job," Ruri said. She reached toward him to place a comforting hand on his shoulder but stopped when he twitched it out of her reach.

"Your opinion doesn't count for much in all of this," he said. "But when the realm starts taking recommendations from humans, you'll be the first one I call in."

The words would have been easy to take offense at, but his tone was so sad Ruri simply couldn't. She stayed silent the rest of their way.

They ended up in a part of the castle Ruri hadn't been before. That in itself wasn't difficult. The castle was gigantic and ever-changing. Ruri was fairly certain that if she explored every day for months, she would still be stumbling across new areas. As they stepped out onto the long open walkway, Ruri realized she had seen this place, but always from the outside and below. The promenade ran the length of the courtyard with stately columns supporting a roof of impossibly fine stone worked into what she could only call a lace pattern. There was no railing between the delicate pillars. Anyone not paying attention would plummet the twenty or more feet down to the shining paving stones of the yard below. Across from them was the balcony where the Seneschal had met the returning Wild Hunt only two days previous.

As had happened that time, a crowd was forming. Ruri seemed to have underestimated how big a deal the return of the hunters was. There was no sign of them, but her sense of her mate told her that she and the growing throng didn't have long to wait. Lively music drifted up to her on the breeze. One thing she had to admire about the fae was their love of music. It seemed to accompany almost every aspect of their life, and they offered it freely. A lute and some type of curling horn she didn't recognize graced the walls of their room. She wondered what they would sound like when played together. She wasn't musically inclined herself and she didn't think Mal was either. If she was going to be honest with herself, she'd never asked her mate. It was amazing how little Ruri knew of her beyond the fact that she could decapitate a vampire in less than three seconds. Even so, she was willing to follow Mal anywhere, including through a strange door into a place that shouldn't have existed.

The excited buzz of the crowd intensified until she could no longer hear even the smallest snatches of conversation. Her sense of her mate informed her that Mal was close by. She strained to see the gatehouse, hoping for the faintest glimpse of her.

The chatter of the crowd ceased abruptly. Ruri looked back around to see if they were still there. It wouldn't have surprised her to find them gone, given how completely everything went silent. The fae were still there, but everyone looked up at the balcony in rapt silence. The king's gaunt figure stepped slowly across the wide space, then stopped at the marble railing. He was flanked a few respectful paces back by his Seneschal and the Jaeger. All eyes were trained upon them.

"This is a great honor for the returning hunters," Mracek said quietly from his place at her elbow. "King Connall rarely graces the Wild Hunt's return these days, not even when the Jaeger leads them out."

"I see," Ruri said, though she didn't. Dean had never attended to their return from hunts he hadn't been a part of, not unless someone had been injured. He'd always known if something had gone wrong and one of his wolven needed aid. The hunt was a part of life. Having him greet them would have been like getting a standing ovation for finishing lunch.

Unless someone was hurt. Suddenly stricken, she returned her gaze to the open portcullis. She hadn't felt anything that might indicate Mal had taken any wounds. Then again, without full access to her wolf, she didn't know if she would.

She didn't have to wait long. When the first rider appeared through the massive doorway, the crowd began to murmur again, despite King Connall's presence. The second rider through was Mal. She rode astride the Jaeger's wild-looking grey horse. Even from her vantage point, Ruri could tell it was pulling against her. Behind her was Lord Regin on his oversized lizard, but Ruri paid little attention to him. Her eyes drank in everything she could about Mal. Her seat on her mount looked decent, without the stiffness that might indicate she was in pain. Certainly, her skill with a horse, or horse-like animal, had improved greatly since their arrival. Most importantly, she had no wounds that Ruri could make out.

Mal turned her head this way and that, taking in the crowd. She took a long look at the balcony, then turned in her saddle. She craned her neck around, clearly searching someone out. When their eyes met and Ruri watched her mate's face light up, even all the way across the courtyard, she knew that someone was her. Mal didn't seem to be harboring any anger over their harsh words to each other.

I should be down there, she thought. *What am I doing up here?* She stayed put, though part of her demanded she head down to Mal immediately. It would be so much easier to get to her once the crowd dispersed. Ruri waved at Mal, feeling the matching smile spreading across her face. She hoped Connall would be brief.

"How was the Hunt?" All remaining crowd noise died away as soon as the king spoke. His voice traveled to all corners of the courtyard. It sounded to Ruri like he was standing right next to her and speaking for her ears alone.

"Reasonably successful," Mal said. "We were able to track down some Bottom-Dwellers."

"She is too modest," Lord Regin said from next to her. His voice boomed out, making the courtyard seem much smaller than it was. He raised one hand, displaying a small satchel which he then opened. Ruri thought he was being a touch overdramatic. He overturned the bag, pouring out a steady stream of something. She couldn't make out what they were, but each one was the same general shape and the same brownish-red color.

The crowd knew what they were and a collective gasp rose from their throats. The objects piled up rapidly, and there were far more of them than the size of the satchel would have suggested. The fae on the dais said nothing as Lord Regin continued to pour the brown objects onto the courtyard cobbles. By the time the pile was about two feet high, the flow from the bag had almost stopped. Lord Regin gave it an emphatic shake. A small rain of the things joined the others, then there were no more.

"An impressive display indeed," the king said. "Do you not agree, old friend?"

The Jaeger stepped forward to join Connall. He looked down on the small group of hunters.

"Quite impressive," he said. "I haven't seen its like, not even on the Hunts I've led."

"Nor we." King Connall turned back to the hunters. "We are pleased with the results and will award all the tokens earned against the bounty. You have truly earned our favor this day."

The hunters bowed low except for Mal who stayed defiantly upright. The king gave a quiet chuckle.

"Hunter Malice," he said.

The members of the Wild Hunt moved their mounts back almost as one, leaving her alone in front of their group.

"Yes, King Connall," she said.

"You have done our court a great service. Our actions in response to your previous hunt were wise, or you would not have been here to accomplish such a feat. You have desired our favor since that time, is that not true?"

Ruri became aware that she'd clenched her fists so hard her knuckles were starting to ache. This was it, the moment Mal had been working toward to get them out of this nightmare-scape of lavender and gold.

Mal nodded eagerly. "That's right, Your Majesty. I hope you can tell how hard I've been working to impress you."

"We can. Let it not be said that we are an ungenerous or ungrateful liege lord." The king raised both hands, holding the palms out toward Mal as if in blessing. "You have earned this boon. From this day forth, you also shall be known as Huntmaster of this court."

Murmurs rippled through the crowd. Ruri watched as Mal's face crumpled on the edge of what she knew was massive disappointment, but she wrestled her expression around to one of pleasure. Ruri's heart ached for her mate, knowing how much the announcement had crushed her. She reached out toward Mal as if she could touch her. Did the king know how badly he'd hurt Mal? Was this a deliberate act of cruelty, or did he actually believe that he was being the benevolent ruler?

"That is unprecedented," Mracek said. "I don't think I've ever heard of a human being offered a position so high in the court before, nor of a court with more than one Huntmaster. I wonder how the Jaeger will enjoy sharing his position with anyone, let alone a human. No offense meant, of course." He added the final bit hastily.

"None taken," Ruri said absently. Her eyes were on the Jaeger. If he was angry, it was difficult to tell. If she'd been able to smell him, she might have had some idea, but from their vantage, there was little to go on. He smiled and nodded as if in approval, and if he seemed a bit stiff, was that so different from how he normally carried himself?

"Thank you, King Connall," Mal was saying, her voice strong and betraying none of the shock Ruri knew she felt. "I'll do my best to…" Her voice trailed off.

"Of course you will," Connall said when it became apparent Mal was at a loss for words. "We celebrate the Hunt and your reversal of fortune tonight!"

The crowd erupted into cheers as if they hadn't had a feast only two nights ago. The king smiled and waved at the approval and excitement of his subjects. He raised one hand in benediction, then withdrew from the balcony, the Seneschal and the Jaeger in tow.

Mal looked up at her, their eyes meeting across the space. Even at their distance, Ruri could read her mate's pain.

"What's the quickest way down there?" she asked Mracek.

"Of course," he said. "This way."

Mracek led her off the promenade and through a series of hallways before opening the door to the courtyard. They didn't go down any stairs, but Ruri no longer expected the laws of physics to apply in this place. If they did, great. If not, she would manage.

The crowd had thinned out somewhat in the little time it had taken them to get down there. Ruri sought out Mal in the stable and found her stashing weapons in the attached armory.

"Hey," Ruri said.

"Hey yourself," Mal replied. Her response was light, but Ruri could smell the upset wafting from her, spiky and painful to the nostrils.

"Your hunt was…"

"Something else," Mal said. "Let me finish up here and I'll tell you all about it."

"I'd like that." Ruri waited, leaning against the wall and watching the bustle of the hunters as the human teens assisted them in putting up their mounts. The fae still treated the kids almost like furniture, with a kind of off-handed disregard unless they needed them.

"There we go," Mal said as she exited. "Let's go for a walk."

"After that we should stop by to see the Seneschal."

"What?" Mal asked.

"To take up the Jaeger's offer of protection, remember?"

Mal massaged the back of her neck. "Oh yeah. Sorry, I guess I forgot in all the excitement."

"It's not every day you get elevated to nobility."

"Thank god." Mal looked around to see if anyone else was nearby. "Mracek, how do we get on top of the walls?"

"The ramparts? I can take you, but not many people go for walks up there."

"It'll be perfect then," Mal said. "I want to clear my head."

He started off down the hall, pausing briefly until they followed once more in his wake, Mal on his heels and Ruri following her mate. She stifled a laugh at the image they must have presented of ducklings in a row. She noticed Mracek checking his book on the sly.

This time the trip was full of stairs. They climbed and descended enough to get to the ramparts at least three times over or so her legs tried to tell her. When they finally made it out the final door, Ruri was ready for a rest, never mind that she was in excellent shape.

"We'll let you know when we're heading out," Mal said to Mracek.

He nodded and took the hint, slipping back through the door to the final stairwell to wait.

"What happened?" Ruri asked. "You look spooked."

"You could say that." Mal ran her hand through her hair. "I think I might have done something terrible."

"Terrible? Like how?"

"You know all those ears that were dumped out of that bag?"

"Those were ears?" Stomach acid burned the back of Ruri's throat.

"Yeah. They were taken off the bodies of some fae creatures called Bottom-Dwellers. The others said they're bad news. Killed a bunch of livestock and some farmers, I guess. No one was able to farm in the hills where we found them."

"And you killed them."

Mal's eyes shimmered with unshed tears. "So many of them. But they were bad?"

"Are you asking or saying that?"

"I don't know." She took a deep, shuddering breath as the tears spilled over her eyelids. "I was told they were bad, but what if they were just living their lives? What if that was their own territory and we were the invaders?"

"Connall seemed pleased." Ruri kept her voice as neutral as possible.

"Yeah. Fuck that guy." Mal shook her head in a ragged, chopping motion.

"Agreed." Ruri put her hand on Mal's shoulder and drew in her unresisting body for a hard hug.

"He's just going to keep stringing me along. I had to kill hundreds of living things to get scraps from him. Scraps I don't want. I don't think I can do what it'll take to earn back passage out of here."

"I am so glad to hear you say that," Ruri said into Mal's ear. Her mate's tears were soaking the shoulder of her tunic. "It's time to look for a different solution."

"Past time. I can't believe how much time I've wasted already."

"That's why you need to listen to me more." Ruri squeezed her to let Mal know she was joking. Mostly. "I've been around the block a few times now. I know what I'm doing."

"I know." Mal heaved a deep sigh. She wiped the tears off her face. "It's only that most of what you say goes against everything I was trained to do."

"Which is why I cut you a little slack. Okay, it's actually a lot of slack. It's time you moved past your training. You outgrew Uncle Ralph a long time ago."

Mal laughed, a sharp hiccup tinged only lightly with mirth. "That's for sure."

"We need to be careful about what we do here, though. If we piss Connall off, our lives will get way harder. That means you should go to his feast tonight. You are the guest of honor."

"What about you?" Mal asked.

"I'm going to talk to someone about where to start with our little problem." Ruri hesitated, wondering if she should bring up the Jaeger. Mal didn't respond well when she talked against him. He was a problem. Better to leave it for the time being. She settled for rubbing her hand over Mal's back in soothing circles instead. "Are you all right now?"

"No," Mal said, "but I will be."

"All right." Ruri squeezed her tight, then let her go. "You smell like a swamp."

Mal's laugh was genuine this time. "A little rotting vegetation too stinky for your delicate nose? You should try riding something that smells like that for hours."

"Fun."

"Not really. My mount was the Jaeger's kelpie. It came in handy, but it stinks. Not too surprising for something that's more at home in water than on land, but it got old."

"That sounds about right." The words could also have described the Jaeger. Something about him definitely stank, and she was quite over him.

"Let's go back to the room," Mal said. "I want a nap, and maybe a little something extra." She waggled her eyebrows, a lascivious grin stealing across her face.

CHAPTER THIRTY-TWO

A nap had helped settle her almost as much as the extracurricular activities with Ruri. After that, they'd headed down to the Seneschal's office to officially accept the Jaeger's protection. The old man had been quite endearing. He'd reminded Mary Alice of her dad's father. She'd kept waiting for him to offer them hard candies, but sadly those never materialized.

Now she stood in front of the mirror back in their room as she waited for Billy, the brownie fashion king, to work his magic on her court apparel. She didn't care about being named huntmaster for Connall's court. All she'd been worried about had been impressing the king enough that he'd forgive her supposedly monstrous insult. The fairy king needed to grow a thicker skin.

Though she didn't care about looking good for him, she didn't see the harm in looking good in general. The look on Ruri's face when she was dressed to the nines was more than worth it. Her girlfriend leaned against the wall, her arms crossed as she watched Mary Alice being attended to. Interest still gleamed in her eyes, even after a vigorous couple of hours of quality time together. Even knowing about Mary Alice what she did.

A feeling swelled inside Mary Alice, pushing her breath out before it. She didn't deserve this woman who knew the worst of her and yet stayed by her side. Ruri supported her. She was a rock, steady and comforting. If Stiletto and the Bottom-Dwellers didn't make her run for the hills, then nothing would. Whatever Ruri was going to get up to while Mary Alice was putting in her time at the feast, she trusted it was for the best.

She caught Ruri's eyes and smiled, trying to infuse all the love she felt for her golden wolven. Ruri's answering smile was like the sun breaking through thick storm clouds. Mary Alice had no doubt about Ruri's love for her; it was almost tangible.

"Turn around," Billy said. He tapped her on the elbow.

"I'm sorry, what?" she asked. She didn't want to break eye contact with Ruri.

"If you're done making moon eyes at your lady, perhaps you'd like to turn around so I can make sure I didn't miss anything." Billy's words held an acerbic edge. "Unless you want to go to the feast with your rump hanging out. You'll certainly get a lot of attention, though I doubt your lady will approve."

"All right, all right," she said, wrenching her eyes away from Ruri's. "Don't get your knickers in a twist."

"I'm trying to spare you from that fate," Billy said. He motioned for her to turn.

She complied, turning in a slow circle.

"It's perfect as always," his daughter Andra said.

"You wanted to admire your handiwork, didn't you?" Ruri said.

"And you would all be so cruel as to deny a master craftsman this pleasure?" he asked.

"Of course not," Ruri said. When he motioned to her to take Mary Alice's place, she held up one hand. "I'm sitting this one out."

"Are you certain?" Andra asked. "Your absence is likely to be noticed."

"I doubt anyone will care," Ruri said. "I keep a low profile. Between us, Mal is the one who makes a splash."

Mary Alice tried to stifle a snicker. When that didn't work, she turned it into a cough instead. Yes, she was the one who garnered all the attention with her double life and the government's plausible deniability about her existence.

"You should wait before heading down to the feast," Billy said. "As the guest of honor, it's your prerogative to make an entrance."

"Do you think so?" Being flashy didn't seem so amusing anymore. The shadows sounded better than the undivided attention of the fae court. Every other time she'd had that, things had gone wrong.

"Absolutely." He grinned. "Then everyone will see and admire my creation. You are a stunning model for my work. The rawness of your humanity against the elegance of the fae…" His voice trailed off as he watched her critically. "It is a wonder more fae don't dress out their humans."

"Let's keep them from kidnapping humans for life-size paper dolls, all right?" Ruri said, her voice dry enough to burst into spontaneous flames.

"Tchah," he said. "More of your kind might help this place. Too much the same, all the time. There's an energy mortals bring, one that clears the cobwebs and shakes things up."

"Father," Andra said. "Watch what you say. You don't know who might hear."

"No one cares what I think." For all his cranky response, Billy still lowered his voice. "I'm a simple tailor, nothing more."

"A simple tailor who attended to the deposed heir," she hissed. "There are plenty who would look at you sideways for that fact alone, never mind the things you actually say. I don't wish you to be banished or, worse, cast over the silver falls."

"Yes, my dear." He patted Andra's hand. "I'll try to be more circumspect."

"Good." She nodded firmly.

"Good." He imitated her nod.

"You are a terrible father."

"And as daughters go, you're generally awful."

Mary Alice caught Ruri's gaze again as the brownies grumped at each other. Her girlfriend shook her head and continued to slouch against the wall while giving her a predatory look that made Mary Alice's insides flutter.

"They're doing it again," Billy said to his daughter. "We should go."

"Indeed we should," she said, then turned to Mary Alice. "If you must undress, make certain you don't turn any of the clothes all the way inside out. You'll still be able to wear them after."

"Before you go, I have a question for you," Ruri said. "Don't worry, I'm not about to lose control and rip Mal's clothing off in an uncontrollable fit of passion. You're both safe."

"Very well, what do you—" Andra's words were cut off by a tap at the door.

Mary Alice crossed the room to open it. She found the Jaeger waiting in the hall.

"Excellent, you are prepared." He peered around her into the room. "Is your lady not joining us?"

Mary Alice smiled to see him. He was frowning, the sides of his mouth pulled slightly downward without so much as a wrinkle to crease his smooth face.

"She's not feeling well," she said quickly, not wanting to disappoint him. "Another headache."

"Such a pity," the Jaeger said. "And on your night of triumph as well."

It was disappointing that Ruri wasn't going to be there. She flashed her girlfriend a questioning look, but Ruri shook her head, a grimace on her face.

"I'm on my own tonight," she said.

"Then I'm honored to escort you to the grand hall." The Jaeger extended his arm to her. It felt like the most natural thing in the world to take it.

"Don't wait up," she said to Ruri.

"Have fun, but not too much fun," Ruri said.

"I promise nothing." Finally getting the last word in on her stubborn girlfriend, Mary Alice swept from their room.

The Jaeger escorted her through the halls, her hand tucked in the crook of his arm, his hand companionably over it.

"The result of your hunt for the Bottom-Dwellers was most impressive," he said.

Mary Alice was happy to bask in the warmth of his approval. "Thank you. I was happy to do the king's bidding on this one." A little voice at the back of her brain tried to remind her that she'd been wrecked about the whole thing, but it was quiet and easy to brush aside.

"We're lucky to have you in our court," he said.

"And I'm lucky to be here. I hope you're not upset that I'm a Huntmaster now too."

"What?" The look he gave her was one of shock. "How could you wonder at such a thing? I'm happy to have someone who has rejuvenated the hunters. I've had them coming to my door all afternoon requesting to go out on the next hunt. With this level of enthusiasm, we'll be able to cleanse these lands of all the blights that disfigure it."

Mary Alice nodded eagerly. "I'm happy to help wherever I can."

"And that's why I can't be cross with you. Not when you've done me such a favor."

"We visited the Seneschal to formally accept your protection."

"I was informed." The Jaeger patted her hand. "I'm glad you took me up on the offer. To be quite honest, your new position offers some protection, but it makes you a target to certain dissident parties in Connall's court. There are many who believe humans have no place with us. The former heir, for example. As though humans haven't served us Underhill for millennia." He laughed loudly.

Mary Alice couldn't help but laugh along. What could possibly be wrong with humans serving here? She'd received so many wonderful opportunities while doing so.

"What can I expect tonight?" she asked.

"Nothing too elaborate," the Jaeger said. "The feasts are much the same, only the details change."

"So drinking, dancing, and general revelry."

"Quite so. We are nothing if not traditional."

"Full of tradition, but completely unpredictable."

"You've captured the essence of the fae, my dear."

"Finally," she said. "And to think you all were the supras I had the least experience with before I came here. Now I'm pretty much an expert."

He laughed and she joined in again.

The hallway they were in was the one she recognized as that outside of Connall's throne room. Guards lined the hall on both sides as they got closer to the tall double doors at the end. Each dipped the bill of their halberd as they passed.

"It's a sign of respect," the Jaeger murmured when she looked at the guards out of the corner of her eye.

She nodded but kept an eye on the Tuatha faces within their helms just in case. It wouldn't take much to whack someone's head off with one of the polearms.

"Go ahead," he said. "Order them to open the doors for you. It's your right now," he said as she hesitated.

"We're heading inside," Mary Alice said with a smile to the guard nearest the door.

"We'll work on that," the Jaeger said. His lips never twitched from his ever-present smile despite speaking through them.

She didn't want to work on it. She hadn't been an officer during her stint in the regular armed forces. Expecting people to jump at her slightest whim wasn't at all appealing.

She was saved from answering by her first glimpse of the grand hall. Where the previous feast had taken place in dark woods, this one opened up into rolling meadows under a starry sky. The stars sprinkled the sky so liberally and shone so brightly that she thought she might be able to touch them if she reached out her hand. A crescent moon hung low in the sky, its points oriented straight up so it looked like luminous horns minus their cow. Instead of fires, glowing pools collected here and there, most surrounded by dancing figures. Lights darted over and around the figures, as if the stars had chosen to leave the heavens and cavort among the fae. She understood why Billy had insisted on flowing fabrics, even though she'd tried to resist.

The breeze was warm, carrying with it the smell of wildflowers and motes of dancing light. Above it all soared the music, wild and free. It tugged at her, promising to please if only she'd give herself over to it completely.

"It's beautiful," Mary Alice said.

"King Connall will be pleased to hear it. He prides himself in creating the atmosphere for these events. I'm a little jaded, but even I have to admit this is one of his finer efforts. He honors you deeply."

"I am hella impressed." Everywhere she looked, there was something else to delight her senses. Here, hummingbirds hovered among the flowers, and there an unattended pool had attracted three deer-like creatures. Until she'd noticed the elaborate antlers wound about with ribbon and precious wire, she'd assumed they were from her world, but nothing like this existed there. This was yet another reason Faerie was preferable to her home.

There was no question as to the location of Connall's throne. All she had to do was find the moon in the sky and then look down. The moving points of light congregated there, then dispersed before moving back to dance ecstatically in his orbit. The cycle repeated over and over.

The Jaeger led her toward the king. They crested a small hill and were stopped by the herald.

"The Jaeger, Chasseur des Lapins, Huntmaster of the Wild Hunt, and Lady Malice, Ear-bringer, Beast Climber, Huntmaster of the Wild Hunt," he intoned.

Those wouldn't have been her choices for titles. Mary Alice wondered whose ear she had to bend to get those changed. So to speak.

"The masters of the Wild Hunt," said King Connall, his voice reaching out and touching the ears of every individual on the meadow. "Approach us, that we may properly honor Lady Malice."

The Jaeger kept them to a stately pace as they approached the king. "You are not of the common folk any longer," he said, using the same trick he'd employed earlier where his lips didn't move while he talked. "You need not hurry or risk losing his favor. Rank hath its privileges after all."

It was a strange privilege to gain. Mary Alice was certain there were others she might prefer, but none came to mind.

The Jaeger finally released her hand when they reached the king. He dropped to one knee in the dense carpet of lavender wildflowers surrounding the throne. Mary Alice made a deep bow, but again refused to kneel to the fae king. Was that the correct protocol now that she had a proper position in his court? No one had filled her in on the etiquette of the situation, so she did what seemed most natural to her.

"Rise, old friend," King Connall said. "There is no longer any need for that."

The music cut off and the Jaeger froze in the middle of getting to his feet. His gaze shot at the king, then he averted his gaze immediately before coming to his full height.

"My subjects," Connall called out. He stood tall before his throne. "Tonight we rejoice for more than the appointment of Lady Malice as Huntmaster, for you are heirless no longer. The Jaeger has served us, all of us, selflessly as Huntmaster for many long years. As we have someone to take on his mantle of responsibility, we are pleased to bestow upon him the title of Heir. Tomorrow we travel to the Heart of the Realm to invest him as he so richly deserves."

Cheers and capering around the reflecting pools met the king's pronouncement. For all the general feel of excitement, there were also those who stood by in silence.

"Come," said the king, "you will both join us at our side. This is now your rightful place." He motioned Mary Alice to his left side while the Jaeger took his place at the king's right hand.

He was never going to let her go now, the little voice at the back of her head said. That was just as well, since she didn't want to leave. She had everything she wanted right here: prestige, power, and access to those who would do her bidding without question.

CHAPTER THIRTY-THREE

"She's in there," Andra said, indicating the low door in the dimly lit hallway.

"Thank you," Ruri said. "I've got it from here."

"Are you sure you don't want me to wait? What if she's not home? You're pretty much useless when it comes to making your way around here."

"I figured that out already, thank you." Ruri bared her teeth in what she hoped looked a little like a smile. Not being able to make her own way had gotten old days ago, and she still showed no sign of improving. "I'll be fine. If she's not here, I'll wait."

"Suit yourself." Andra grinned. "I'll check back in a few days to make sure you're not still sitting here slowly starving to death."

"You're a good friend."

"Am I? I don't think such a thing exists in Connall's court." The last was said in a serious tone completely devoid of the traces of humor that had seemed omnipresent in her voice. Andra gave her one last look, then disappeared down the hall.

Ruri leaned down and knocked on the door. It only came up to her shoulder and lacked all embellishment.

"Who's there?" Ylana's voice filtered through to her ears.

"It's Ruri."

"Ah." Ruri heard movement from inside the room, then the shuffle of feet. A moment later the door opened and the brownie woman Ylana gazed up at her.

"What are you doing here?" The question was blunt.

"I thought I'd check on you, see how you're holding up."

"Indeed, and on the night of the king's feast?" Ylana raised an eyebrow.

"I have some questions too." Ruri looked up and down the hall. It was still empty, but she'd learned not to trust her eyes in this place. "Maybe I can ask them inside."

"Very well." Ylana stepped away from the door, pulling it open further.

Ruri ducked down and stepped into the room. Despite the plain door, the room wasn't rude; it wasn't even simple. A large fireplace took up one wall, the fire built up and burning merrily. A cauldron sat in the flames, and from the smell Ylana was making some sort of venison stew.

"You don't get a window?" Ruri was surprised. Practically every other room in the castle had at least one window, even when there was no logical way for that to be possible. She'd even been in closets that had windows, but there were none here.

"I asked not to have a window and was accommodated." Ylana sat down in a wooden rocking chair in front of the fire and indicated the worn sofa opposite it.

It looked like furniture for first graders, though most elementary school classrooms didn't include incredibly comfortable overstuffed leather couches. Ruri relaxed after she determined it would hold her weight and sighed at the feel of the furniture conforming to her body.

"Have you had dinner?" Ylana asked.

Ruri shook her head.

"Can't have that." She waved her hand and a wooden bowl levitated itself off the counter on the other side of the room. It crossed the room without the benefit of anyone holding it, then dipped itself into the bubbling stew in the cauldron. A second later a silver spoon floated after it, plunking itself into the stew, then both bobbed over to Ruri. She stared at them for a second, then reached out her hands. The bowl dropped the last inch into her palms. She instinctively closed her hands around it, but it had gone inert. Whatever had given it the power to float was gone.

"That was amazing." Ruri lifted the bowl to look at the bottom, but there was nothing unusual about it.

"A simple trick," Ylana said. "All it takes is a bit of magic, and I have access to plenty of that right now. The crown's way of apologizing for taking my husband, I suppose." Her lips twisted for a moment, then smoothed out leaving only the vestige of her scowl.

"Yes. I'm sorry." The smells coming from the bowl were making her stomach growl. Ruri dug the spoon in and pulled out a steaming bite. She blew on it, waiting for it to cool enough to eat.

"Don't take responsibility," Ylana said, her voice holding the sharp edge of warning. "There are those here who would take you up on that, whether you be the cause or not. I know where the blame lies, and it has naught to do with you."

"Sorry," Ruri said. She winced at repeating herself, then took a bite of stew. She chewed on the chunk of meat inside to give herself a moment before responding further. "It's a habit, a cultural thing, you could say."

"And one that has gotten your people in trouble with ours more than once over the centuries. What are you here for, Ruri? It's not for the food."

"It could be." Ruri had taken another bite of the stew, not caring that it burned her mouth a bit. She hadn't chewed enough to make the statement completely intelligible. What came out was a muffled mess. She finished chewing and swallowed. "This is fantastic." She stopped herself from shoveling another spoonful into her mouth. "You're right, though. I'm here to talk about the hodag."

"That beast." Ylana leaned forward and spat into the flames. "It's dead, and I couldn't be happier about that. I only wish the Jaeger would be there with it."

"I need to know where it came from. Do you have any idea?" She took another bite of the delicious stew.

"It came around for three nights before the Wild Hunt showed up." Ylana's eyes were vague as she peered into her past. "It always came in from the south. We could hear it snuffling around outside, but it didn't seem too interested in what we were up to inside the house." She sighed. "Trajan wanted to leave it alone. He said it wasn't bothering anyone, not even our chickens, so we should just keep out of its way."

"I'm assuming someone sent word to the castle then."

"Probably so. We certainly weren't the only crofters in the area, only the ones unlucky enough to have that ravening beast driven to our door."

"I-I know." Ruri caught herself before she could apologize again. "You said it came at night and over multiple nights, so wherever it was coming from, it had time to get there and back." She tapped one finger on the arm of the couch. "That's something to work with."

"What do you want with it?"

Ruri smiled. "I want to find the portal it used to get here. Someone said the realm is porous, so there must be gates back to our world that the king doesn't control. I assume he didn't let the hodag in or the other things he wants to keep out, like those poor Bottom-Dwellers."

"Ah, the Bottom-Dwellers." Ylana sighed and stared into the flames.

"What about them?" Ruri asked when she didn't seem likely to elaborate.

"They weren't hurting anyone," she said. "Not really. That land has been barren for decades. The worst they did was force the last few herders off it before they could die from their own fool stubbornness. It wouldn't have hurt the king to leave them to their own devices, but he and the Jaeger refuse to suffer the wrong kind of fae to live in our lands. Worse yet, they couldn't conceive of a way to kill them in more than meager numbers. Until your Hunter showed up, that is."

"I was afraid it was something like that."

"They came in on their own as well," Ylana said. "Though whether it was from your world or one of the adjacent fae realms, I don't know."

"But we do know for sure that the hodag came from my world, right?"

"That we do." She sat back and looked Ruri over with a critical eye. "You don't look near sturdy enough to take on whatever else might be lurking near one of those porous places. I hope you plan to take someone with you."

"I'll manage on my own," Ruri said. She wasn't going to be alone. "I can defend myself, if need be, but it's unlikely whatever is there will even notice my presence."

"If you say so." She pointed at Ruri's mostly empty bowl. It shuddered once, twice, then Ruri let go and it floated from her hands back over to the cauldron. "You're going to need something to coat your bones, then."

The bowl dipped out more stew, then made its way back to Ruri's hands. She applied herself to its contents again. They chatted between bites of delicious meaty goodness. Ylana was a charming hostess and she had a wicked sense of humor. As they grew more comfortable with each other, she took more opportunities to skewer Ruri with it. She laughed loudest when Ruri turned the pointed comments back on her. She was in the middle of a loud guffaw when someone knocked on her door.

They didn't wait for her to answer, opening it right away and sticking their head through. Geffron looked askance at Ruri, then over at Ylana.

"The king has announced the new heir," he said. He paused, licking his lips nervously. "It's the Jaeger," he finally said.

Ylana's face hardened between one instant and the next. She gestured at Ruri's bowl and it pulled itself from her grasp.

"You'd better get on looking for that portal," she said. "The realm is about to get very uncomfortable for a great deal many more people."

* * *

Receiving the fae was long and tedious. Mary Alice found herself in the same trance she used while on a stalk. It worked fairly well for this kind of situation. She could mentally disengage as she needed to, but when the king or the Jaeger said something that required a response, she could zone right back in. The night grew longer and longer, and still this or that Tuatha felt the need to come up and pay their respects to King Connall and especially his new heir. Very few of the other varieties of fae felt moved to do so. They chose to hang back and drink while shooting glances toward the throne when they thought Connall and the Jaeger were occupied.

The celebration grew steadily more raucous, the edge to the fiddles more desperate, and still Mary Alice's feet twitched to join the dance.

"We no longer require your presence, Lady Malice," the king finally said. "There are things we must discuss with the Heir before tomorrow's trip to the Heart."

"Thank you, Lady Malice," the Jaeger said. He smiled gently at her. "You've done well this night. I expect you'll do well tomorrow. The Huntmaster is expected to be present at major court functions and the coronation of a new heir is one of the most important. There are of course exceptions should you be leading a hunt, but I would counsel against scheduling one tomorrow."

"Of course, Your Highnesses." Mary Alice bowed her head, nodding to both of them. They smiled at her form of address. They weren't offended, not that she could tell, but she was going to have to get the forms down.

It was a relief to get away from the king and to stop having to watch everything she said. The music called to her blood. Ruri had said not to stay out too long, but surely it hadn't been more than a few hours. There was no harm in finding the members of the Wild Hunt and spending some time with them. She was their leader now. She owed it to them to get to know them.

Her mind made up, she made her way over to the pool with the loudest revelers. Sure enough, Lord Regin stood head and shoulders above the fae carousing around the source of gentle light. Other specks of light congregated there too. They whirled and spun through and past the dancers, only to return seconds later. The party had progressed far beyond any state she'd previously witnessed. Most of the hunters were missing at least one major article of clothing. Some were completely nude, the moon and starlight painting their skin until it looked as though it glowed from within.

They weren't only dancing on their feet either. As Mary Alice made her way closer to the center of the group, moans of passion and guttural groans of release reached her ears. Men and women were tangled together all around her, some in groups as large as six, and in all configurations of genders. Her gaze landed upon a fae woman with her head buried between the thighs of another fae woman, their skin so bright Mary Alice could still see their outlines for a second after she looked away. The eroticism of the scene coupled with the pull of the music had her own arousal building.

Maybe it was time to go back to the room and find Ruri. No, she'd made the decision that she would spend some time with her hunters. She had duties to attend to.

Mary Alice wended her way through the dancing fae, giving herself over to the music for a brief period. She dipped and whirled from one fae to another until her legs screamed for a rest. Panting and laughing, she pushed her way to the edge of the pool. When she looked down, she discovered that her jacket was gone and her tunic was unlaced almost down to her belly button. Her arousal had built to a fever pitch. Judging from the noises she heard in the corners of the dark, no one would mind or even notice if she added to them.

She loosened the ties on her pants and slid her hand down the front of them. Her fingers tangled in her hair, the strands wet with her desire. She couldn't stop her gasp when her fingertips skated between the folds of her labia then gently contacted the tip of her clit. Pleasure arced from her fingers into her center. She stroked once, twice, her hips twitching with each rub over the sensitive button that was the focus of her entire world. The music swirled around her, urging her to greater heights. She touched herself more forcefully, matching the tempo that pulled at her insides. Her center tightened, the universe narrowed down to a single slice, and she was in the middle.

She added another finger to the mix, running the tips on either side of her clit, doubling the sensation, coiling the tension in her center into a ball of hard, aching arousal. She panted, stroking herself faster, building to something amazing. The music promised her release would be like nothing she'd ever experienced. It pulsed around her, wrapping her up, demanding to be let in to please her as only it could do. Mary Alice put her head back. She bared her breasts to the crescent moon and inhaled deeply, pulling the wild notes inside her.

The undulating rhythms matched her heartbeat and then elevated it, sending it tripping wildly in her chest. Mary Alice placed a hand on her bare sternum, marveling at the strength of her beating heart. Her clit throbbed to the same beat, and her fingers twitched, grazing the pulsing organ tip. She moved her hand to her nipple, circling then squeezing it in rhythm with her heart, in rhythm with her clit, in rhythm with the universe and the music that all demanded the same thing. They wanted her release. They needed her release. They would tease and taunt her and send her ever higher until she could fly no more and would have to come crashing back down to earth, to this realm of sensation and chaos.

And beauty.

She grabbed her nipple and twisted, biting her lip and groaning in the back of her throat against the pain that mixed so deliciously with the pleasure until one blurred into the other and she could no longer define the edges of either. She twisted it again and cried aloud as her clit jumped beneath her fingers. She ground down on it with her fingers, but they weren't up to the task. They taunted when they should have taken. She pushed her hand further into her pants, rubbing the flesh of her palm against the swollen center of her pleasure. That was more like it. Twisting her nipple again, she ground down on her clit, chasing the pressure she needed and taking it for her own. The music caressed her insides, pulling her higher as she pressed harder.

The fiddles wound to dizzying heights, the drums pushing her forward. They demanded. She demanded, and when it all came to a head, she took. Her pleasure exploded from its prison of tension, obliterating everything else before it. She drank it in until she could consume no more, then released it outward. It scattered across the landscape, taking her with it.

She came back to herself on her knees in front of the glowing pool, one hand down her pants and the other cradling her breast gently. She stared unseeing at the sky before realizing those were real stars she was seeing, not just the sparkles of her release behind her eyelids.

The music had stopped, though she still heard the sounds of the faes' passion around her. There were softer murmurs too. She wasn't the only one who had just come.

A roar split the air behind her. "Huntmaster!" Lord Regin cried.

"Huntmaster," the hunters responded, those who weren't otherwise occupied.

Mary Alice smiled dreamily. Part of her supposed she should have felt some embarrassment or shame over her display, one that seemed not to have been particularly discreet, but she felt nothing of the sort. She felt whole and sated. Well, partially sated. She could definitely go another round, but not on her own. There was somewhere she needed to be.

"Hunters," she said as she got back to her feet. She turned to face them, not bothering to do up the laces on her shirt or pants. Why should she? They'd seen far more than the curve of a breast, and she'd certainly left nothing to the imagination about what she was up to. "Have a wonderful feast. I'm off after my own quarry."

She left to the thunder of their approval. The hall was alien to her eyes when she stepped into it. The guards were still there, and none of them acknowledged her as she sauntered half-clad past them. It wasn't until she made it to the chamber she and Ruri shared that she realized she hadn't needed Mracek's services. She'd navigated her way there unerringly, without thinking of it much at all. She'd had a destination and she'd gone there as if she'd known this castle all her life and it never changed configuration on its own whim. That was interesting, but not what she desired most. Ruri lay beyond the door, and she needed what her girlfriend could give her.

CHAPTER THIRTY-FOUR

It was barely past sunrise when Ruri tucked the note under Malice's combat knife. The note said she was going for a ride and would be back later. It was vague enough not to give away her intentions, but she hoped it would keep Mal from worrying as to her whereabouts. She let herself out, taking care to drop the latch with as little sound as possible.

As early as it was, the castle buzzed with activity. It was a big day, she supposed. Apparently, even the fae with their near-infinite lifespans didn't see a coronation regularly. She was happy to be anywhere else than to be a witness for the Jaeger's big day. It wasn't something he'd earned, of that she was certain. If everything else worked out, though, they'd be out of there soon enough.

She had to stop to ask for directions more than once to get down to the courtyard. Even when she tried following a scent trail through the castle, she ended up in odd places. She'd caught the smell of the stables at one point but had ended up in a massive library of floor-to-ceiling books that was at least three stories tall. As tempting as it had been to stay and poke around to see what the fae kept in their libraries, she'd kept going.

It took a bit of doing, but she eventually found herself in the courtyard. She stopped in the Wild Hunt's armory to arm herself with a brace of javelins and a couple of wicked knives as long as her forearms. The kids were up and seeing to the mounts. Jermayne nodded to her as she passed by, and Shejuanna gave her a tired wave. They knew something was up as well. So far it didn't seem that any hunters had come down to claim their mounts, but the air of tense anticipation had permeated even down to these halls. She left without claiming a mount for herself. Ruri was after a more run-of-the-mill beast today.

"I'll be right with you" came Geffron's harried voice from the back of the horse stables when she stepped in. Two Tuatha de Danaan were waiting around. Neither looked particularly happy about the delay. One sat on a low bench and tapped his fingers rhythmically on rude wood worn smooth, the other stared off into space chewing at her lower lip, a tiny crease between her eyebrows.

Geffron appeared from the back with a pair of tall, matched horses in tow. Golden blond with chestnut mane and tail, they jingled as each step set to ringing the dozens of tiny bells that festooned their tack.

Geffron gave her a harried look. "Horses at the back with no names over the stalls are free for anyone to use," he said on his way past. "Dress it with any tack hanging on the wall opposite." He smiled at the two Tuatha. "Lord and Lady DeMeere, Shallan and Tristan are ready to go."

Ruri made her way deeper into the stables. She wandered among the stalls before finding those that were unclaimed. There were many of them, and she hesitated before choosing one at random. Those stabled back here were definitely of a lower cut than the two she'd seen Geffron bringing out to the impatient fae. Her chosen horse was a little shorter, with a shaggy coat, one that would resist being brushed until it shone. A shock of coarse mane flopped in front of her eyes, and she flipped it out of the way to view Ruri as she moved closer.

It had been years since Ruri had dealt with horses. They'd been a way of life on her parents' farm, but after she was turned, horses would take one whiff of her then lose their minds from fear. Hopefully that wouldn't be the case. She might as well get some use from Reese Corrigan's damn bracelet.

The floppy-maned horse bent down to sniff at her proffered hand. She twitched an ear, then snuffled it more closely.

"I don't have any treats," Ruri said. "Sorry about that." Hopefully the shaggy mare would forgive her. It wasn't freaking out, so that was a plus. Ruri perused the available tack, then got down to the work of saddling the horse. She was hesitant at first, but muscle memory a century old helped move her through the process with steadily increasing confidence. In less time than she would have believed, they were ready to go.

"Thank you," she said to Geffron as she led her horse toward the front of the stable. "I may be out late, so don't worry if I'm not back until sunset."

"Do what you need to do," he called over his shoulder as he disappeared back into the bowels of the stable.

As she passed through the front, four more fae waited for mounts. A crowd of fae and their animals were already collecting in the courtyard. It was time to make her way out of there before she was remarked upon. A few more enterprising fae were already heading out through the heavy gatehouse, and she joined them. As soon as she passed under the portcullis, she cut to the east, following the trail the Wild Hunt had taken the only time she had joined them. She paid little attention to the tall trees and rolling plains as she and Floppy cantered toward their destination. The tall trees grew progressively shorter and sparser, while the grassy areas became wider and the gently rolling terrain steepened into hills. The area was familiar, and Ruri knew she was on the right track. Without a host of riders to slow them down, they made good time and it was only a few hours later that they found themselves in the bowl that had contained Ylana's home.

The house was gone, leaving only the stacked stone foundation. A lush area of wildflowers and mushrooms grew up in front of where the wall had been. Butterflies and dragonflies hovered over the wild patch of vegetation. With a start, Ruri realized it was about the size of Trajan's body. So that was what they'd meant when they'd said the realm would reclaim him. She carefully steered Floppy around the patch. The mare eyed it closely, but Ruri made sure she didn't nibble on the luscious clover that sprouted from the center of the jumble.

The house had been there, and the hodag had come through the dip in the hills. Ruri turned Floppy and headed back out of the depression. She retraced the steps of the Wild Hunt until the point where they'd picked up the hodag's trail. Fortunately for her, the hodag had been a large, none-too-careful animal. It was easy to track, even without the benefit of her wolf's senses and experience. Its claws had left deep rents in the sod, and she was able to follow it quite a way from where the Wild Hunt had encountered it originally. She shuddered when she saw the boulder with long scrapes and chips wrapping around it. The hodag had been an impressive beast, and they'd been lucky to have come away from it relatively unscathed.

She tracked it back for over an hour, as best she could tell by the track of the sun in the sky. A watch would have been nice, but she didn't have one of those. Mal's phone was managing to stay charged somehow, but the time displayed on it never changed. Her skills at telling time with the sun were a little rusty; the wolf was the one who generally remarked on the sun's position in the sky, and she refused to associate that point with the numbers of a clock.

Traces of the hodag grew fainter and fainter the further they got from Ylana's cottage. It had been a few days, and anything less than the largest and most obvious signs of its passage had been reclaimed by the land. That wasn't surprising, but it was straining the edge of Ruri's tracking abilities, which were considerable. When she lost the tracks altogether, she pulled Floppy to a halt and jumped down.

"Are you going to stay put if I drop the reins?" she asked the horse.

Floppy swung her head next to Ruri's and whuffed warm air into her ear.

"Thanks, but that doesn't answer the question." She looked around for somewhere to tie up the horse and decided that a low bush would have to do. She looped the horse's reins over the branches, making sure to leave enough length so Floppy could graze if she wanted to.

She turned in a circle, looking for likely candidates for portals. From what she recalled when Reese had been demonstrating that the portals weren't going to work for them, there would be something like heat shimmer. Did the portals need to be in doorways? Reese's had been, but that could have been for ease of use or even aesthetics. If the hodag had wandered through a portal without realizing it, chances were it hadn't been in a doorway, she reasoned. It could be something as simple as a cave opening or even a space between rocks. Hell, it could have been floating freely in the air. She couldn't count on it being configured in any particular way; she was simply going to have to look everywhere she could think of and hope she'd stumble across it.

There was nothing for it but to start. Ruri took a deep breath and started to walk a circular path with Floppy at its center. She stayed alert for anything unusual. Sadly, ordinary for here wasn't like ordinary for her own world. She wasted time investigating a natural fountain that sprayed crystal clear water twenty feet into the air without the use of a pump, but that turned up nothing but a handful of small fae with fish bodies and the faces of terrified children. A crack in the rocks had looked promising until she'd realized that the glow from within came from a vein of luminescent stone and besides that the crack was only four feet deep. Ruri pushed at that one for a while, convinced there had to be more to it but was forced to give up. Half a dozen other curiosities crossed her path. Normally looking into them would have been interesting, but today it was only an exercise in frustration. She had work to do, and the well-being of her mate hung in the balance.

Ruri dug a pebble out of the packed earth and bounced it idly in her hand as she ventured further and further from the mare. After the final dead end, one involving a tree with an honest-to-goodness door on it, she couldn't take it any longer.

"What is it going to take to find a goddamn portal around here?" Ruri yelled to the uncaring sky. She threw the rock as hard as she could at a hulking boulder that sat at the bottom of a hill.

There was no sound of pebble hitting stone. She swayed back on her heels, then leaned forward to stare at the large stone. There was nothing unusual about the boulder. It looked like so many others that she'd already passed in this part of the faerie king's realm. Ruri dug another rock out of the ground, this one about the size of her fist. It was a little paler than the boulder and would allow her to see exactly where it disappeared, or so she hoped. She wound up and let it fly at the place the first rock had vanished. This one vanished as well.

Ruri grinned. Things were finally going her way. She strode toward the place where the rocks had blinked out of existence, then stopped.

A woman's torso appeared in front of the boulder. A moment later her lower half came through. It was that of a giant snake.

"Hello again, little wolf," Mami Wata said. "The bones said I would see you again. I was starting to think they'd misled me, yet here you are."

CHAPTER THIRTY-FIVE

A persistent knock at the door roused Mary Alice from deep slumber. She was glad that it had. She'd been having troubled dreams. The spike of pain that jabbed through her temples when she opened her eyes was even less pleasant.

"What the hell?" she grumbled. "Ruri?" Her girlfriend didn't answer. Mary Alice's eyes popped open. She took in the room, trying to ignore the pounding at the door that conveniently matched the tempo of the pounding in her head.

There was no sign of Ruri. The covers on her side of the bed had been pulled up and tucked against her to prevent a draft from blowing down the covers. That was very her girlfriend. She always did that when she was the first to get up. Mary Alice was doing her best to remember to reciprocate, but it hadn't become habit yet and sometimes she forgot.

God, but her head was fuzzy. The pain was ebbing, but trying to think felt like swimming through molasses in February. The incessant knocking didn't help.

"What do you want?" she yelled as she sat up. She winced at the slight uptick of pain as she got upright, but it faded quickly.

"It's Billy" came the brownie's voice through the door. "Open up, we're already late!"

Late? For what? Mary Alice blinked at her feet, trying to get her thoughts in order. All she could remember was moonlight and ecstasy and Ruri above her, with eyes that filled her vision and fingers that filled her to bursting. Her groin pulsed at the memory, sending an echo of remembered pleasure through her center. Had it been a dream? Why did she feel like she'd had an audience? No, that was impossible. Her dreams were getting increasingly vivid the more time they spent with the fae. Still, she was all turned on, but there was no sign of Ruri to take the edge off, so she pushed the remnants of her reverie to one side.

"All right, I'm coming. Keep your shorts on." She pulled the top blanket off the mound of covers and wrapped it around her nakedness, then made her way over to the door. A folded piece of paper under her knife on the table by the window caught her eye, and she made a brief detour to snag it. She pulled open the door but didn't look up from the note.

Mal-
I'm going on a ride to check into a few things. I'll be back tonight.
I love you,
Your Ruri

That told her nothing. She leaned on the door and turned the paper over to see if there was a postscript or anything that might tell her what Ruri was actually up to, but it was blank.

"It's a good thing you're wearing next to nothing," Billy said as he swept past her, Andra in tow. "We need to move quickly to get you ready for the procession to the Heart of the Realm."

"Oh yeah." Mary Alice tried to blink away her muzzy-headedness. "That's today."

"Aye, it's today." He glared up at her, one eyebrow raised suspiciously. "Do you mean to tell me you'd forgotten about the most important event to take place here in two hundred years?"

"I had a busy night, so sue me. What am I supposed to do? And when is this happening."

"I only have three hours to get you presentable."

"Three hours? That's an insane amount of time. You usually get me done up in twenty minutes."

"For minor feasts of no particular consequence, yes. You are to accompany the king and the soon-to-be heir all the way to the Heart. You're going to be in the procession." He shook his head. "It's going to take all my art to prepare you, and your glamour will have to last beyond the normal twenty-four hours. The other court members of note have been three hours already in their preparation. There's no way you'll be where you need to be by the time the procession is to depart."

"But imagine the honor in the feat if you can pull that off, Father," Andra said. She placed a large roll of fabric on the dresser, then pulled two stools over to stand in front of it. "No one will ever be able to say you're anything but the preeminent tailor of this realm. Your fame will spread to neighboring realms." She unrolled the cloth, exposing what looked like the cherished collection of a five-year-old child with a penchant for collecting "interesting" items.

Mary Alice recognized feathers and some pretty rocks and glass, but other things were beyond her knowledge, including a section of jars filled with light and liquid. She reached a hand out toward them.

"Don't touch." Billy batted her hand out of the way. "Andra is right, of course. I am the best tailor in the realm, and I will prove that today. You will stand there, and you won't move or talk unless I say so. Understand?"

"Not really—"

"There!" Billy pointed to a spot in front of the long mirror. "No questions. We don't have time for your chatter. Not today!"

The brownie looked so fierce that Mary Alice moved before she'd quite realized it. Andra came over with a loose robe and held it out to her. Mary Alice tried not to grumble as she switched to it from the blanket wrapped around her shoulders.

They spent almost the entire three hours on her finery. She'd thought she'd been dressed nicely before, but those wonders were no match for the complexity and delicacy of her ensemble. And it was an ensemble. Layers upon layers of gossamer thin fabric draped her body. When she moved her arm, it looked like moonlight filtering through the waters of a pond to dance on the bottom. She was shadows and moonbeams, and at the very core of it all burned a steadfast light.

"That will do," Billy said. "You won't embarrass me completely."

"You've outdone yourself," Andra breathed, peering over his shoulder at Mary Alice.

"It's a small trifle," he said, but his lips curled into a self-satisfied smile. He glared up at Mary Alice. "Now take us to the stables," he ordered. "We must make certain your mount is adequately prepared. There isn't much time!"

Mary Alice wondered why she was letting this small fussy man hurry her along as she picked up her combat knife from the table and slid it onto her belt.

"I knew she wouldn't leave that behind," Billy said.

"Which is why you accounted for it in the design," Andra replied, a touch impatiently. "Clothes don't change the person, remember?"

"Don't quote my own words back to me, young lady." Billy started out the door.

Andra rolled the piece of fabric back up and scurried after him. They were moving quickly enough that Mary Alice felt like she had to hurry to keep up with them, despite their legs being half the length of hers. Somehow, she knew exactly where they were going. None of the twists and turns seemed unusual or unnecessary. This was new, though she had a vague recollection of making it back to the room on her own the previous night. Then again most of her memories from last night were vague. She thought about the throne room and knew instantly that she'd be able to make it all the way there on her own if she had to.

Billy gave her no time to experiment. He headed down to the Wild Hunt's stables with single-minded focus and snapped at her to keep up when he thought she was falling behind. They emerged in the long hallway that was the stable area. It was packed with fae, most of whom Mary Alice recognized from her first sojourn to hunt the hodag. A few were unknown to her, but she nodded at them when they nodded gravely to her.

The teens were running around to acquire mounts for everyone. Carlo jogged past, leading the pale horses, their coats flickering between skin and bones as they passed in front of the door.

"I guess I'm not riding one of them," Mary Alice said.

Latawna hurried up to her. "The kelpie will be ready for you in a few minutes," she said. "Hold on a few, and I'll get him taken care of."

"We will take care of it," Billy said.

"Do what you can to get everyone else outfitted," Mary Alice said at the same time.

Latawna blinked in confusion, looking back and forth between them.

"We'll get him," Mary Alice said a little louder. "Do what you need to for the others."

"Gotcha." She bounced on the balls of her feet and took a couple of deep breaths. "Good luck out there today." With that, she disappeared back into the crowd.

"You get your weapons," Billy said to her. "We'll make your mount presentable."

"Weapons?" Mary Alice looked from Billy to Andra then back again. Both brownies nodded solemnly. "If you say so." She moved down toward the armory, leaving the brownies to their own devices.

The room wasn't as empty as she'd anticipated. She wasn't the only one helping herself to weaponry. Lord Regin turned to her, a polearm twice as tall as she was gripped in one meaty fist.

"Huntmaster." He bowed to her. "I am glad to see someone has informed you of your duties for this occasion."

Mary Alice laughed grimly. "I'm just bobbing along here, trying not to get pulled under. No one's told me squat. The brownies showed up and decked me out in all this." She gestured down to herself. "I feel ridiculous."

"You dress to befit our king and his chosen heir." Lord Regin shook his head. "There's nothing wrong with that." He didn't look much different than he always did. His clothes seemed designed to allow freedom of movement and to show as many of his tattoos as possible. When she looked more closely, however, Mary Alice realized that his tattoos were different today. They shifted beneath his skin, small figures moving slowly from one bold patch of ink to another.

"I guess if you're done up for this whole thing, I can't object too much," she said.

"Indeed you cannot." He grinned at her. "Now find your weapons. Your other duty is to protect the king and his soon-to-be heir. We all will, for the good of the realm. If the king is killed before the heir is named, the realm will start to disintegrate, and unless the not-quite heir can appeal to the Heart, it will unravel completely, damning those who can't escape to nothingness eternal." He raised an eyebrow at her. "That includes you."

"I know it does." Mary Alice didn't try to hide the look of irritation that splashed across her face. No one had to remind her of her predicament. She pressed past Lord Regin and stood in front of a row of gleaming swords. There were no katana-type blades, which she thought was a strange omission. She picked up one and tested its weight and balance before putting it back. The rubies on the hilt were pretty in the light, but the balance wasn't right for her. It took her a few minutes to find something which was close enough to her katana that she didn't think it would take her long to become accustomed to it. It was a simple blade, with elegant scrollwork etched into the cross guard. A large milky-white gem with a dim glow stood proudly on the pommel, but those were the only elaborations to the weapon. She belted the sword around her waist, then set out to look at the bows. It didn't take nearly as long to find one she liked, and in no time at all she was making her way back to the enclosure with the kelpie.

Billy and Andra had been hard at work. The kelpie was outfitted with barding to match her clothes. Its reins looked like wisps of shadow, but when they were finished and she'd climbed astride the animal, they were completely solid.

"Thank you," Mary Alice said to Billy and Andra.

"You're welcome," Billy said at the same time as Andra. "Be careful out there." The last was Billy alone.

"I'm always careful." Mary Alice grinned, but it felt hollow. That was something she said to Ruri, but her girlfriend was nowhere to be found. She had the feeling Ruri was still in Connall's kingdom, somewhere to the east, unless she missed her guess. She would have felt better if she had been by her side, but girlfriend or no, she had work to do. She maneuvered the kelpie out of the box, ducking to fit beneath the top of the doorframe.

The hall beyond was still quite packed, but as she emerged everyone shifted toward the walls, opening a space wide enough for her to ride through. She urged the kelpie forward at a walk. Its eyes rolled from one side to the other, watching all around them. It stiffened as it drew even with some of the other mounts, but she kept it moving. If there was ever a day not to be in the middle of a fight between strange beasts, this was three of them. She kept the kelpie moving forward until they broke out into the sunlight of the packed courtyard.

All eyes turned to her and a loud cry went up from hundreds if not thousands of throats. The kelpie shuddered in place but didn't spook. She looked around, trying to make some sense of the chaos she found around her. Out of the corner of her eye, she saw Shejuanna, Jermayne, and Simeon grouped next to the stable doors. They shouted as loudly as anyone else. The cheer went on and she finally raised her hand to acknowledge those who called out for her. For a moment, the noise swelled, then it died down to the regular sustained clamor of a crowd that size.

Many fae watched from the sides of the courtyard, mostly those without mounts. The crush was ten to twenty people deep around the walls. Within that ring were dozens of fae on horseback or creature-back. Their mounts stood, some shifting restlessly, but they all faced the same way as though waiting for something only they knew was coming. What that was wasn't at all difficult to deduce. What Mary Alice couldn't figure out was where she was supposed to go.

"Lady Malice," said a familiar voice a few feet out into the crowd.

She looked over to see Mracek making his way toward her. He wended his way carefully between the beasts and their riders, the mounts paying far closer attention to him than their masters.

"Lady Malice," he said again when he drew up to her stirrup. He was a little out of breath and panted a bit before continuing. "The Lord Seneschal requires your presence by the King's Door."

"I take it that's over there?" She pointed in the direction the fae were standing.

"It is. The king's party gathers there to attend to him and the Jaeger when they emerge. It will be soon, from what I'm hearing, and you don't want to offend by being late."

"No, I don't." She tried to urge her mount forward but was blocked by a group of fae on horseback.

"I've got this." Mracek moved to the front of her mount, grabbing the kelpie's reins below its jaws. "Stand aside for the Lady Malice," he hollered, his voice hoarse from yelling. "Make way for the Master of the Wild Hunt!"

The fae looked behind them, then shifted to one side, bowing their heads to her. Mracek led her through the crowd, calling out the entire way until they emerged into an empty space in front of a tall pair of stone doors so close together she could barely make out the seam between them. The Seneschal beamed at her when she arrived as he hurried over toward her.

"You've done well, young Mracek," he said.

Mracek mumbled something and bowed, then scurried off.

"Lady Malice," the Seneschal said. "You are to ride at the front with the king's party, behind King Connall and his chosen heir." He looked at her soberly. "Are you prepared for this charge?"

"What exactly is the charge?" she asked.

"Why, to protect the king and his heir," he said, white eyebrows climbing almost to his hairline. "For the good of the realm, you will interpose your body between any danger that threatens them."

"Is the journey dangerous?"

"No more dangerous than any in Faerie. Our land is unpredictable, as are its denizens, but if both king and heir fall, we are all lost." He glared at her sternly. "I ask you again, are you prepared for this charge?"

"I am."

"Excellent." His entire body relaxed. Mary Alice hadn't realized how tense he'd been until he suddenly wasn't anymore. He patted her lower leg. "You'll do quite well. With a warrior of your prowess in his party, the king has little to fear."

"That's…good?" Mary Alice had no idea how to respond, and she cringed inside at her banal answer.

"It is." He drew himself up to his full height, looking ahead toward the guardhouse. "Array yourself there, behind the guards," he said, gesturing in their direction. "King Connall and the Jaeger will be joining us shortly, and you must be in position."

Mary Alice heeled the kelpie around and headed over to where the guards waited. She reined in and nodded to them, but they ignored her, focused as they were on everything else around them. Almost as soon as she'd gotten settled, a fanfare of impossibly sweet brass instruments went up behind her. She turned in her saddle and watched as the stone doors groaned open, the split yawning between them. The fanfare kept playing, even after the doors had opened all the way to reveal a bright light. Mary Alice wondered when the trumpeters took breath as they played on and on with no sign of movement within the even brightness between the doors.

The fanfare continued to some tempo only it knew, working toward its climax. The longer it went on, the louder the crowd grew until she could barely make out the instruments over their noise. Two dark shapes appeared within the light, and the crowd began to sing along with the fanfare, lending their voice to and around the notes, swelling into a song of such perfection that Mary Alice felt tears dripping down her cheeks. She wasn't the only one so affected. Many of the crowd around them and even some of the guards wept openly as well, though the guards never ceased watching.

The figures coalesced from the light into King Connall and the Jaeger. The fanfare finished with a flourish at the same moment as they stepped their mounts onto the courtyard's shining cobbles. The song of the crowd held for a note longer, then it deteriorated into cheering such as she'd never before heard in her life. The king stepped his mount forward, an impossibly graceful horselike creature with a single horn that spiraled from its forehead. Mary Alice tried not to gape at it, but that unicorns might actually exist hadn't crossed her mind, not even here. The Jaeger rode at his side, but a couple of paces behind. His beast of choice was a long dragon-like creature. It steamed as the warm air of the courtyard hit it, the layer of ice on its skin turning instantly to vapor. Swirls of frost were drawn and redrawn across the glittering scales on its hide, looking like Jack Frost himself was practicing his art as the dragon moved.

Mary Alice shook her head at her fanciful thoughts. Some protection she was, sitting there and thinking of fairy tales.

The king ignored her as he moved past, but the Jaeger smiled slightly at her and winked. The guards turned as one and were on their way; Connall never had to so much as slow his pace. She swung in behind the Jaeger and was joined by the Seneschal on a winged horse. It settled and resettled the wings that crossed on its back with a constant restless flutter. Mary Alice couldn't blame it; she would rather be flying too if she had the choice.

Their pace was slow as they proceeded from the courtyard. Fae lined every inch of the passage beneath the gatehouse and out onto the drawbridge. Music started behind her as the rest of the mounted fae moved to file into the procession. Mary Alice couldn't keep her eyes from scanning over those who watched and cheered from the sidelines. If there was a threat to the Jaeger, she would take it out.

He looked back at her. "It's a long ride, but the end is worth it. Be vigilant." He turned back around.

Mary Alice firmed her grip around the combat knife at her waist. Vigilant she could do.

CHAPTER THIRTY-SIX

They'd been riding for well over an hour, as best Mary Alice could tell. The road ran on before them, both sides lined with cheering fae, as it had been since they'd left the castle. She wondered where they'd all come from. She recognized some fae from the court, but the vast majority were unknown to her.

The constant cheers were giving her a headache, that and the need to be on the lookout for attacks while surrounded by possible assailants on all sides. The train behind them disappeared around the nearest bend, which had to be almost half a mile away. Music accompanied their progress and drifted over to her whenever there was a lull in the crowd noise. The gaps in shouts of praise and adulation never lasted long.

"Bit of a spectacle, isn't it?" Lord Regin said, raising his voice enough to carry to her ears, but not so loud that the king or the Jaeger might hear him.

"And then some." Mary Alice twisted in her saddle to look behind. It felt like a threat was approaching from that direction, though there was nothing to see when she checked. She turned back toward him. "How much longer is it?"

"We've only just begun, my friend," Lord Regin said with a grin. "The entire kingdom turns out for events such as this one. King

Connall feels strongly that his subjects should get the opportunity to worship—I mean, see—him. Sit back and enjoy the ride." He leaned back in his tall saddle and closed his eyes.

Mary Alice tried to match the grey fae's nonchalance, but she couldn't shed the feeling of danger. She tried to keep her eyes on everything, darting her gaze from one potential threat to another. She was accomplishing nothing but driving herself to distraction and she knew it. With a deep breath, she willed her adrenaline to drop and her breathing to slow. She was able to relax, though not to the level of Lord Regin, who was now snoring gently on the back of his giant lizard.

True to his words, the sun was well past its zenith and rapidly approaching the corner of the sky inhabited by perpetual dusk when the guards ahead began to slow from the steady trot they'd kept to the entire ride. The edges of the road had never cleared completely of the king's subjects, though when the procession had wended its way through the woods, the fae had been clustered between the trees so as not to get in its way. Now they were back to numbers similar to the ones she'd seen around the castle.

In the distance, a collection of tall crystals jutted from the ground, standing proud in a depression in the rolling grasslands. It took much longer to get there than Mary Alice had anticipated. As they approached, she realized how massive the crystals had to be to mess with her sense of proportion.

The facets of the crystals caught the lavender of the false sunset and refracted it into hundreds of brilliant purple shards of light that painted the grass. Mary Alice's vision was obscured with violet whenever she passed through one such patch. She felt nothing in particular, but the fae in her company murmured and looked to the sky when splashes of purple moved across them. Aside from her, only King Connall seemed unaffected. Even the Jaeger looked skyward.

When they finally reached the base of the crystals, Mary Alice was ready to get down. Her legs still weren't used to so much time on horseback. The muscles twitched with fatigue, and she knew that without a dip in the amazing baths, she wouldn't be moving very quickly come the next day. She looked around and realized no one else had moved, so she stayed put on the kelpie's back.

A moment later, fae dressed in the tabards of palace pages ran forward to grasp the reins of their mounts. The king dismounted first. As if that had been a signal, everyone else climbed down. Mracek held the reins of the kelpie but didn't acknowledge her. He seemed more interested in watching the Jaeger while appearing not to.

She jogged over to Lord Regin once she was down from the kelpie. "What now?" she asked.

"Only the king's party is permitted inside the Heart." He pursed his lips. "I don't think that's ever included a human before." His thoughtful look disappeared as he shrugged. "It takes care of itself, so we'll find out if it finds your presence objectionable."

"What does that mean?"

"I don't rightly know. Either you'll find out or you won't."

"That's comforting," Mary Alice grumbled.

"I do what I can."

She'd been in uncertain situations before. After all, there had been one after another since arriving in Connall's realm. At least now she knew there was the possibility that something dangerous could happen. The thought was oddly comforting. She slid her knife around on her belt so it would be easier to snatch up if she needed it. She wasn't certain how much use it would be against a pile of crystals, but she would find out if it came down to that.

The group that accompanied King Connall and the Jaeger toward the Heart was much smaller than she had anticipated, given the crush they'd come with. The Seneschal was there, and so was a woman Mary Alice assumed was either the king's bodyguard or the head of the castle guard. A wizened sylph woman she'd seen once before accompanied an elderly Tuatha man in flowing robes. Lights drifted around his head like a lazy crown.

Two plinths of pinkish crystal leaned against each other to form a triangular opening. The Seneschal moved to the front and they waited as he vanished into the darkness beyond. A moment later, the crystals burst into bright light from within. Layer upon layer of crystal shone with a pink light, overlapping and deepening the colors to a brilliant scarlet at the center.

A cheer rose from the watching fae behind them.

Connall took a deep breath, then let it out. He smiled, looking more relaxed than any other time Mary Alice had seen him. "Are you ready, old friend?"

"Beyond ready, my king," the Jaeger said.

"Then let us proceed." King Connall stepped between the leaning chunks of crystal. The Jaeger followed directly on his heels, then the guardswoman behind him.

Mary Alice stepped aside and let the others pass in front of her. It only seemed right that she bring up the rear to protect them against any threats that might choose now to strike. When she stepped into the tunnel beneath the massive crystals, a shiver spread through her body.

Mortal? A voice like slightly off-key chimes rang in her head.

"Uh, yes?" Mary Alice answered out loud. The aged Tuatha man looked back at her, both eyebrows raised.

Why do you come before the Heart of the Realm, human?

"I was invited. King Connall wanted me here to witness these events."

And why does the Head of the Realm invite a human?

"Because I've earned my spot here. I am the Master of the Wild Hunt."

The bells rang in her head. She was tempted to clap her hands over her ears to block them out, though she knew they wouldn't do any good. This wasn't her first mental intrusion. That had happened at the time of her first demon kill four years ago, not to mention all the times she'd sparred with Carla.

Curious, the voice finally said.

"I don't mean you any harm," Mary Alice said. "My job is to protect. I'm good at it. I won't let you or those who live in your realm come to harm if I can help it."

We shall see. The voice paused, the sound of chimes building up in her brain again. *Move forward, little human.*

The way forward was clear, but each step felt like she was pushing her way against fierce winds. She struggled on gamely, watching the backs of the fae, who seemed to have no problem at all. Her breath grated in her ears as she did her best to keep up. Ahead, the walls opened up into a chamber flooded by light of a pink so deep it was almost red. That was her goal. She watched as the fae entered the room one at a time, then they were no longer within her field of vision. Mary Alice took a step, then another. Her feet slipped on the smooth crystal ground as the invisible force forced her back. She growled and took another step. The force pushed back against her even harder.

She bit her lip and grabbed the hilt of her knife. Step by laborious step, Malice forced her way forward. She wasn't going to let some chunk of rock keep her from what needed to be done. When she finally stepped into the room at the end of the tunnel, she wanted to let out a roar of triumph. She managed to keep the instinct under control and instead grinned, conscious of the blood that dripped from her lower lip where she'd managed to pierce it.

"Now that all are here, it is time for the ceremony to commence," the Seneschal said. "We six shall guard against interlopers while the king and his heir perform the rite of binding with the Heart."

* * *

"What are you doing here?" Ruri asked. If Santa Claus had appeared through that portal, she would have been only slightly more surprised.

Mami Wata laid a finger alongside her nose and winked slyly. "Events are unfolding, so I thought I would see for myself." She moved away from the shimmer in the air that marked the portal.

A moment later, Reese stepped through in full human sheriff guise. She adjusted the wide brim of her hat, then glanced at the sky.

"Connall is still king," she said.

"He is." Ruri cocked her head at the sheriff. "Do you think that's going to change?"

"All signs point to it," Mami Wata said.

"And you want to stop that, I take it."

Both fae looked Ruri straight in the eyes with faces so blank it had to mean something.

"Are you engineering a coup?" she asked.

They were saved from answering when a third figure emerged from the portal and unfolded into the long frame of Nagamo.

"You're alive! But how?" Ruri had seen him fall. There was no way he could have survived. One of the wolven would have died from the impact, and they were incredibly resilient.

"I had some assistance," he said, glancing at Mami Wata.

"I'm glad for it. I thought you were gone for sure."

"Hopefully, the court of the king assumes the same. It will make what comes next much easier."

"What is coming next?" Ruri spun on her heel to stare at each of the fae in turn. "Why am I in the middle of this reunion?" She stopped facing Mami Wata. "And why are you looking at me that way?"

"How has your Malice been?" Mami Wata asked.

"What does that have to do with anything?"

"It's important," Reese said. "Has she seemed oddly attached to anyone? Has she forgotten things related to them? Negative things especially."

Ruri looked back and forth between the sheriff and Mami Wata. "Why do I get the feeling that you want me to answer in a certain way." She split her glare between them. "My people don't make good lapdogs."

Mami Wata laughed. "Or coursing hounds, which is why we're talking to you." She moved to one side, the heavy coils of her lower body sliding with dry susurrus over rocks and dried earth. "Do you know how most fae interact with humans?"

"From what I've seen, it's mostly trickery and deceit." Ruri glared at Mami Wata. "You said you didn't know anything about the kids from the camp."

Mami Wata shook her head. "I said I knew nothing of dead children. The children you were talking about weren't dead. My answer was completely truthful."

"Maybe technically, but the spirit of it was…"

"What use had I of the spirit? You were the ones who burst into my home and threatened my acolytes. I did what I had to protect those who are mine."

Reese cleared her throat. "Charm," she said. "The fae are very good with charm, so good we tend to forget other strategies exist. Oh, certainly, some of our less savory cousins use fear, but you can argue it all stems from the same place. We're manipulating your perception of us to create a desired emotional response."

"And why's that then?" Ruri asked.

"Fear mostly, and some pride," Mami Wata said. "Our kind ruled this world for so long, then humans lost their reliance on us. We are so much less than we once were." She sighed deeply. "I once had hundreds of followers on the sunny shores of a wide sandy-bottomed river, but as the ages rolled on, my followers dried up, as did the water. Now I have three acolytes on the oft-frozen shores of a tiny lake. Were we as adaptable as humans, our pride would be less of an issue, but there are those of us who would rather die than change. And they have, many of them at the hands of your brethren."

"That's all well and good," Ruri said, "but what does it have to do with Mal and me?"

"Not much, except to explain why we strongly suspect your Malice has been charmed," Reese said. "When you were under my protection, I would have felt any major charm magics and could have exerted my authority to stop them. Now that I'm not, I fear the Jaeger has nothing to stop him from sinking his claws into your mate."

"You said 'major,'" Ruri said. "Does that mean you wouldn't have felt some things?"

"Sadly, yes. Charms can be exceedingly subtle, especially in the hand of a master manipulator like the Jaeger."

"That does explain a lot." Ruri paused, rolling the idea around in her head. As much as she would have preferred it to be otherwise, it made sense. "I haven't been able to figure out why she's been so hot and cold on things. She says one thing to me, then does another as soon as I'm not around."

"She doesn't have your natural protections," Nagamo said. "The Tuatha have powerful abilities to charm. My own people fell prey to it."

"But she does have you." Mami Wata slithered closer behind Ruri and put her hands on her shoulders. "True love is a powerful counter-charm, but it only works in the presence of one's love. When you're there, your Malice can think without the Jaeger's influence clouding her mind, but when you're gone…"

Ruri shifted her shoulders, but Mami Wata kept her hands resting on them. They didn't feel bad, nor did Mami Wata seem threatening.

"We're here to help you with that part," Reese said.

"So that I can help you, I imagine." Ruri made no attempt to soften the edge of cynicism in her tone.

"Nothing in either of our worlds is free," Mami Wata said.

"And those gifts which seem freely given carry with them the biggest obligations," Nagamo said. "Which is why we approach you openly."

"You're going to have to break this down for me," Ruri said. "I'm not doing anything for anyone without knowing what's at stake and why."

"I told you she was going to be stubborn," Reese said to the other two.

"You did," Mami Wata replied. "This would be so much easier if she was susceptible to our magics." She took a deep breath. "The Jaeger is in possession of a prophecy wherein he becomes the king of this realm. The major sign that the prophecy was coming to fruition is the Wild Hunt having two masters."

"So even though he shared the huntmaster title with Mal for less than a day, that was enough?" Ruri asked.

"Yes," Reese said.

"And now that this prophecy is underway, there's no way to derail it?"

"We don't wish to derail it." Nagamo leaned forward, a dangerous glint in his eye. "We wish to expedite it."

Ruri shook her head. "Then why do anything at all?" If this was them being straightforward, why was she working her way up to such a headache?

"King Connall is no longer an effective leader of our people," Reese said. "Thoughts of his last days fill his mind and have made him vulnerable to the influence of those who hold tight to our old ways, to the point of endangering the people they claim to protect. Down that path lies our ruin."

"The Jaeger will be worse," Mami Wata said. She tightened her hands on Ruri's shoulders. Her fingernails pricked through Ruri's tunic and shirt and into her skin. "His ways will bring the notice of humans down upon us."

"And you want to keep him in power?" Ruri flexed her shoulder muscles and Mami Wata eased up on her grip.

"His is the last gasp of a way of life long past. We hasten its final expulsion, with the aim to replace it with that which will see our people—all our people—continue."

"It's a setup." The words were out of Ruri's mouth as soon as everything fell into place in her mind.

"Perhaps." Reese grinned. "Think of it as drawing an infection to the surface before operating on the festering wound."

"What's in it for me? What's in it for Mal?"

"Malice will be free of her obligation to the realm and will be able to return to your world," Reese said.

"That's great." Ruri eyed the sheriff closely. "I get your word on that, right?"

"Of course you do," Nagamo said. "We will all swear to it."

"Fantastic." Ruri rubbed her hands together. "Now what's in it for me?"

The fae exchanged looks.

"What more do you want?" Reese asked.

"You needed Mal," Ruri said. "You used her. Us. Getting us out of the situation you dumped us in is a start, but that's all it is. You owe us, and I want assurances that you'll repay what is owed." She stared Reese straight in the eyes, then transferred her glare to Nagamo. "A favor. A boon, if you prefer. That's what you owe me. Maybe I won't collect on it, but if I do, you better be prepared to deliver."

"Done," Nagamo said. "The fae of this realm and the counties which claim fealty in your world are in your debt."

Reese winced a little but nodded. Ruri got the feeling that Nagamo had agreed more broadly than the sheriff would have liked. She didn't care. The anger that had been building slowly within her when she realized they'd been pawns in fae political machinations told her they owed her. There was only one way to go now, and that was forward. But that didn't mean she was going to forget who'd gotten them into this mess in the first place.

"What's next?" Ruri asked through gritted teeth.

"We solve the problem of the charm over your mate," Mami Wata said. "We don't want Malice telling the Jaeger about your true identity, after all."

"Oh." She hadn't considered that. "No, that would be bad."

"For you and for her," Mami Wata said. "She still has her part to play. The king's wishes won't permit her to leave, even through portals not of his making."

"It seems to me since you have us trapped here so easily, circumventing the Jaeger's charm is the least you can do."

"Indeed." Mami Wata turned her around to face her. "And we shall, but first I need your wolf."

CHAPTER THIRTY-SEVEN

"My wolf?" Ruri stared up into Mami Wata's dark eyes. "You can't have her."

"I don't wish to have her," Mami Wata said. "I wish to make use of her." She held up a beaded string with a wooden charm hanging from it. On closer inspection, Ruri realized the wooden form was the stylized shape of a wolf's claw, remarkably similar in size to her own.

"How is she supposed to help?" Ruri was proud that her voice didn't tremble at the question. Part of her was tempted to tear off the armband and call her wolf to her now that she had the slightest reason to. It had been so long, and she yearned to be reunited with the other half of her self. The rest of her knew the temptation was reason enough to resist. Wanting something so badly made her easier to manipulate, and she would be damned if she would hand her wolf over if it might mean danger to them.

"The talisman isn't complete," Mami Wata said. "It must be quickened. Some hanks of your wolf's fur will be perfect and will permit Malice to resist the Jaeger where you are concerned."

"That's it? That's all you need? And you promise that's all there is to this?"

"Yes, child." Mami Wata fixed her with an imperious look. Ruri felt like her mother was pushing back at her for being too demanding.

"That is all I require. That is all I will take. I swear to you on the lives of my young attendants. Should I be untruthful in this, may I lose them and the last of the power that keeps me here." The air around her darkened as she spoke, shadows gathering around her form. Her eyes glowed from within. Ruri could make out little except her general outline in the darkness and her glowing white eyes.

"Is that sufficient, child of the druids?" Her voice boomed out and surrounded Ruri.

She firmed her jaw and straightened her back. "It is." Her voice didn't waver in the least. She would not be intimidated.

Without breaking the lock their eyes had on each other, Ruri removed her tunic. She followed it with the shirt, dropping them to the ground without looking where they landed. She had to look away from Mami Wata to remove her boots and pants. Warm air caressed her skin which sprouted gooseflesh immediately. Her muscles tensed, recognizing the imminent change.

"We should be brief in this," Reese said. "I can no longer access the land to keep your secret from the moonstones."

"Brief or not, you'd better move back," Ruri said to the fae. "I have a feeling she's going to be cranky."

Reese and Nagamo exchanged looks, then moved back about ten feet.

"Keep going," Ruri said.

They stepped back further, stopping at about twice the distance.

"You too," Ruri said to Mami Wata.

"I've seen your wolf before," she said. "I will be safe."

"It's your funeral." Ruri reached up and wrapped her fingers around the armband. The metal was cool beneath her fingers. She ran one fingertip over its raised patterns. This was it, what she'd been yearning for for days.

She took a deep breath and skimmed the armband down over her elbow, then past her wrist and over her hand. She barely heard it clang to the ground. Pain, instant and unrelenting, gripped her body, sending her up on her toes, then hunching over. Her muscles seized and she was toppling over. A howl exploded into her mind as her wolf rushed back into her body. Fur sprouted from her skin in an explosion of fluid. Her limbs trembled and bones snapped as her body forced itself to conform to the wolf's will.

The howl wasn't in her head for long. Seconds later, Ruri sat in full fur-form, head tilted back and howling at the strange sky above her. She dug her nails into the hard-packed earth, feeling it give before her powerful claws. She dragged deep furrows in the earth as if to say "I'm here, I've made my mark, and you'll have to throw me out if you don't like it." The heavy scent of flowers filled her nostrils, blocking out more natural scents of dirt and sweat, but a little still came through, something dry and old. Snake scales and the heaviness of time.

They turned to survey the fae woman who swayed before them. She appeared disinterested, but her scent told them she focused on little else.

We need to be careful with her, Ruri thought to the wolf. *Her goals are not our goals, but we can work together. For now.*

The wolf contemplated the strange fae creature, this Mami Wata. She yawned, flashing her teeth and displaying a lack of concern over her presence. It was all show, to be certain. Mami Wata was someone to watch, like all who weren't pack, but she wasn't the one who had trapped her and shoved her away deep in the recesses of her other half's weak human body. That one was still here. She could smell her.

Ruri looked around and caught sight of the two fae who watched carefully from a little way off. The tall one smelled of the deep woods and its secrets, the other smelled of easily doffed humanity and of leaves warmed in the sun. The tall one might look human to some, but Ruri saw his true form. He towered high above them, touching the sky with long limbs tipped with leaves. The other stood beneath the graceful boughs. A crest of red hair stood proudly on her head, uncovering pointed ears and golden skin that moved with sunlit dapples though there was no shade.

That one. The one of sun and unseen shadows, she was the one who had trapped the wolf, caging her in human skin for far too long. A growl rose deep in her chest. She stalked away from the snake woman, her lips pulling away from massive teeth. This one would pay in blood and its final breaths.

Hold on! Ruri screamed at the wolf. She tried to exert some control, but the wolf's hold was too tight. This was what she'd been worried about. The wolf had been gone for too long and she wasn't going to allow anyone to cram her back into Ruri's flesh prison until she'd had some time to be herself.

The wolf ignored her, stalking them closer and closer to Reese, making no attempt to hide. She wanted the sheriff to know they were coming and to tremble before them. As an intimidation tactic, it seemed to be working. Reese paled and stepped back, trying to maintain some distance between them, but the wolf kept closing. She was out for blood, and she wouldn't stop until it painted their muzzle and coated the inside of their mouth and nostrils. The death of their enemy was the only thing that could satisfy her.

Ruri felt her control slipping, felt herself slipping into the wolf's righteous rage. She was right, she was more than justified in her feelings, and the consequences she demanded were not only reasonable, they were just. Reese Corrigan, Reese the Hand, human sheriff, Tuatha de Danaan, former heir of the realm of King Connall, had to pay for her crimes. She would pay for her crimes.

They moved forward as one, muscles bunching beneath them to send them springing toward their prey. They bounded forward, devouring the ground between them and their quarry. The scent of fear filled their nostrils and they snarled in terrible anticipation, mouth agape, waiting for that moment when teeth would pierce flesh and they could demand the oldest justice of all.

Something reared up in front of them. They didn't have time to move around it. Instead, they ran into the unyielding surface. Strong arms wrapped around their torso, and a fleeting pain bloomed between their shoulder blades. The wolf whined, not understanding what was happening. The whine turned into a roar as cold metal was shoved over their paw. Ruri convulsed as the wolf was forced back within her, howling the entire time. Her fur coat retracted, her muscles twisted in on themselves, forcing her bones back into straight human lines. Whatever had been holding her dropped her, but she couldn't force her protesting arms and legs to do anything to cushion to blow as she hit the ground. The air in her lungs was pushed from her in a rush. She turned from her side onto her back, trying to breathe but could only gasp as her body tried to contend with two shocking transformations in less than a minute.

Mami Wata's head moved into her field of vision. She held up a handful of tawny fur. "I got what I needed." She tilted her head. "Are you all right?"

"That. Was. Not. Nice." Ruri panted.

"Nicer than what you had planned for poor Reese. It was longer than I would have liked. Hopefully our distance from the castle will be enough to keep your presence secret a little longer." Mami Wata extended her hand, and Ruri took it, pulling herself to a seated position.

"I told you she wasn't going to be happy." She rotated her head on her neck, trying to work out the numerous kinks in the muscle. "Do you need her for anything else?"

"No."

"Good, because I don't think we'll be getting me back anytime soon the next time she comes out." Ruri stood up, looking around for her clothes.

Now that the wolf was gone, Nagamo and Reese were approaching carefully. Ruri moved off, ostensibly to get dressed, but also because she could still feel the echoes of the wolf's terrible rage toward the former heir. She didn't trust herself not to act on it. Mami Wata handed the handful of wolven fur to Reese, who pulled a small spindle from one pocket. Ruri watched as she spun the fur into a short length of golden wire, then handed it back to Mami Wata. For her part, Mami Wata wrapped the wire around the wolf-claw charm. She beckoned Ruri over.

"Hold it hard in your hand," Mami Wata said. "Prick your palm with the tip and think of what you love about your mate."

Ruri took the strange charm. She turned it over, then gripped it tight. Mal's face jumped into her mind, with the little crease she got between her eyebrows when she was concentrating. Then how her face cleared and lightened when Ruri talked to her or when Mal spoke of her family. She pressed the tip of the claw into the delicate flesh of her palm. There was the slightest pinprick of pain as it pierced the skin. She closed her eyes and thought about Mal moving below her as she pressed her fingers deep inside her, giving Mal pleasure and the release she couldn't get anywhere else. She thought of Mal's strong profile and the determined set of her chin when she'd decided on a course of action. She remembered the comfort of Mal's arms around her and of knowing that the Hunter had her back against all comers, despite their differences. Or maybe because of them.

A flash of light emanated from between her fingers, bright enough to see even through her eyelids.

"Yes, that quickened it nicely," Mami Wata said.

Ruri looked down, but the glow was already gone.

"Give it to your mate and make sure she wears it whenever you are not around. It will protect her mind and keep you both alive long enough to see this through."

"If anything happens to her, the three of you are the ones I'm going to get my pound of flesh from," Ruri said. "I hope you realize that. It's in all your best interest for Mal to survive this intact. You haven't seen what I can do, and you don't want to." She didn't often dwell on her losses of control. It had been decades since she'd last slipped up, but when she had, the incidents had been beyond messy. What happened to the three conspirators would be as violent, but it wouldn't be an accident. "If there's nothing else, I'm heading back."

"I have some things to take care of," Reese said. "They don't require anything from you. You may go."

Ruri bared her teeth at the sheriff. She'd long since lost any ability she might have had to control Ruri's movements.

"Nagamo, shall we?" Reese headed off into the hills. He nodded to Ruri, then stretched his long legs to catch up with the Tuatha in a few steps. They disappeared around a boulder.

"Child of druids," Mami Wata said. "The route we are on is best for my people and yours. I hope you'll understand that when this is all over."

"That remains to be seen." She crossed her arms across her chest. "Next time try being a little more upfront about things. It'll go better."

"That's as may be." Mami Wata turned and made her undulating way over to the shimmer of the portal in the air. "It can't be changed now." Her form wavered for a moment as she moved through the portal, then she was gone.

Like that, Ruri was by herself. She was alone with her anger, which now that it had no focus was rapidly diminishing into something resembling anxiety. She wasn't a control freak, certainly not like what Mal aspired to much of the time, but there was so much about the situation that she didn't know. Talking to the fae left her so many more questions than answers. All she had were the reassurances of people who admitted they preferred charming humans to dealing with them on the level. She held up the counter-charm, taking a good long look at it. There was nothing threatening about it, and if it helped, then that was all to the good.

She pinched the bridge of her nose and took a deep breath. It was time to go back to the castle and give Mal the trinket Mami Wata had whipped up, then figure out how to get them out of their current predicament in one piece.

CHAPTER THIRTY-EIGHT

The center of the crystalline structure that housed the Heart was shaped like a six-pointed star. The Seneschal guided Malice to the point where she would stand her post. Lord Regin was somewhere to her left. She could hear his massive bulk moving around, but with all the sharp angles, she couldn't see him. She couldn't see anyone.

Connall and the Jaeger had entered the Heart through a gash that had opened in the face of an enormous chunk of crystal. It had sealed up behind them without any indication that there had ever been an opening. Malice had no idea how long the ceremony was supposed to take. She prepared to be on her guard for a protracted period. She drew her sword and grounded the point, then wrapped her hands loosely around the hilt and concentrated on each breath, ignoring time as it passed around her. For an untold time, her little area stayed much the same with its pinkish light. Then something changed. Her pulse raced, excitement surging in her chest. She blinked, her eyes darting around to see what it was that had pulled her from her trance. There was no sign of movement in her vicinity and it took her a moment to realize what had brought her fully back. The glowing white stone on the hilt of her sword had brightened.

"Lady Malice?" Lord Regin's deep voice came from her left. "Do you see this? Do your moonstones glow bright?"

"Is that what the white stone on my sword is?"

"Quite so." Malice heard him moving.

"What are you doing?" The Seneschal's voice echoed back to her through the cramped halls. "Get back to your post."

"The moonstones are glowing," Lord Regin said. "That can only mean one thing. There is a cur nearby."

A cur. They were talking about Ruri, though they didn't know it. What had happened to make her take off her armband? Mary Alice watched the bright shine of the moonstone on her sword. It shone steadily, with a light markedly brighter than the dim glow it usually gave off.

"It's been centuries since a werewolf made its way Underhill," the Seneschal said to Lord Regin. "It's likelier that the stones are responding to the magic of the Heir's introduction to the Heart. Our magic works strangely here, so close to its source."

"Are you prepared to bet their life on it?" Lord Regin growled.

"You're young," the Seneschal said, his voice low and soothing. "You don't remember when these were developed. Normally, the glow waxes with the beast's proximity. However, the Heart does strange things with distances and time. With a moonstone this bright, one would have to be in here with us. Perhaps one is among us, or perhaps it lurks on the edges of the realm. Or the Heart is reacting to the presence of one from the past or the future. Or there has been a surge of wild magic from within the Heart, and there is no cur in our lands now nor will there ever be. If there is one here, which I very much doubt, it would have to contend with all the king's subjects outside and you staunch defenders inside. There is no threat to King Connall or his heir."

"Are you certain?"

"Of course I am." The Seneschal's voice turned peevish at having to defend himself. "There, you see? The stone has faded."

The light dimmed in front of her eyes. For a moment, Malice thought it might reignite, but there was nothing. She was fairly certain Ruri was all right, though she didn't know how she knew. Her heart rate and breathing slowed, returning to their normal steady pace.

"What do we do?" Lord Regin's deep voice was puzzled.

"We stay here and protect the king," the Seneschal said. "With the light gone, there is no way to track the glow back to determine if a cur was even here. As I said, it's likely a byproduct of the powerful forces of the Heir's introduction."

"Very well," Lord Regin said. His heavy footfalls echoed back to Malice as he took his post once more.

For her part, Malice wished she had a way to contact Ruri. Something had caused her to take wolf form. If it was just Ruri going for a run after being cooped up as a human for too long, why was it so short? The Seneschal might have been prepared to write it off as a freak occurrence, but she knew better. She stood still, torn between her duty to the task she'd been set and her need to check and see if the woman she loved was all right. There was part of her that still insisted she was fine, but what did she have to go on except a gut feeling? Was she prepared to risk Ruri on a hunch?

Of course she wasn't.

She turned to go back the way she'd come. Everything looked the same in here, but she knew how she'd entered.

"Where are you going?" Lord Regin asked as she walked past him.

She froze. It wasn't like she could tell him she was worried about Ruri with the whole moonstone thing. She hadn't thought this through.

"Nowhere, really," she said. She stretched, throwing her arms wide, then turned to face him. "How long does this normally take? I'm getting antsy."

"I know what you mean." He glanced down at one gauntleted hand. Malice would have put money on the pale stones around the edge being moonstones. "I don't rightly know. I've never been present for this ceremony. I was out in the crowd the last time, so who knows how long the king and Reese the Hand were in here. Lord Seneschal," he called out. "Is the wait normal?"

"Quite normal," the Seneschal replied. "Our vigil is to be carried out for as long as it takes. In silence. In our assigned spots."

"So no chatting then," Malice whispered to Lord Regin.

"It seems not." He shrugged, then assumed a wide-legged stance not too dissimilar from the one she'd taken.

Malice went back to her spot. Without knowing if Ruri was in trouble, she had no good reason to leave that wouldn't betray her girlfriend's true nature. Corrigan hadn't been straight with them on a number of things, but it didn't seem she'd exaggerated the depth of animosity the fae held for the wolven, not if Lord Regin's reaction was anything to go by. Only the Seneschal's contention that the magic in this place was somehow affecting the moonstones kept Ruri safe, but how long would that last?

She resumed her post, sword point grounded against crystal again, and tried to send her mind back into the same trance. Her anxiety refused to allow her back in. What was Ruri thinking, taking the armband off? She gritted her teeth, trying to concentrate on something other than her worry, but her brain continued to yammer at her.

She'd finally managed to achieve some clarity of thought when she felt like she was being yanked sideways through space. She staggered, working to keep her balance. As quickly as the spell had come on her, it stopped. She looked around wildly, expecting to find disintegrating walls of crystal, but there was nothing. There wasn't even the slightest bit of dust in the air.

"What was that?" she called out. "Did anyone else feel it?"

"I sure as stars did," Lord Regin said. The others called out in the affirmative, all except the Seneschal.

Malice became aware of the sound of hurried footsteps.

"Lord Seneschal," Lord Regin called. "What is amiss?" His voice receded as he walked rapidly in the Seneschal's direction.

Something was up. Mary Alice hastened through the crystal halls toward them. Another shift hit her. She was being pushed in the opposite direction, but nothing around her moved. She froze in her tracks. Knowing she wasn't moving didn't stop her from feeling as if she was hurtling to one side. When the force stopped, she took a couple of involuntary steps in the opposite direction before everything settled again. It was like stepping off a merry-go-round and still feeling the world spinning, though she'd already stopped.

From the hubbub of noise from the fae, she wasn't the only one to have felt it. She ran to where the Seneschal and Lord Regin stood outside the crack that had allowed the king and the Jaeger access to the Heart. The rest of the fae arrived seconds after she did.

The Seneschal stood staring at the crystal wall, his face slack with shock, his mouth moving as he said something too quietly to make out.

"What is it?" Lord Regin was saying to him. "What's happening in there?"

"No, no, no," the Seneschal was saying when Malice was finally close enough to hear him. "He didn't do that. He can't have done that. No, no, no…" He carried on, repeating the phrase like a mantra.

"Lord Seneschal?" Mary Alice said.

The white-bearded fae looked at her, not seeing her for a moment, then his eyes focused. "The ceremony is complete," he said. "But…" His voice trailed off.

The crystal wall split in two with a loud, grinding snap, forming a narrow crevice in its shining surface. It was dark down inside where before the Heart had shone with scarlet fire. A figure moved toward them and into the light from the hall. It carried a slender form in its arms. With horror, Malice realized it was the Jaeger carrying the body of King Connall.

"The king did not survive the ceremony," the Jaeger said, his voice thick with grief. "He collapsed as it was completed." He shook his head and stared down at the pale body he carried. There wasn't a mark on either of them. "He was my friend. How did it come to this?"

"Lord Jaeger," Lord Regin said. He stepped forward, then stopped. He dropped to one knee, his head bowed, one fist pressed against the hard crystal floor. "Your Majesty," he said.

"The king is dead," said the Seneschal in tones of deep mourning.

"Long live the king," Lord Regin said.

"Long live the king," Malice echoed with the gathered fae. The Jaeger was king now. Surely he would grant what she wanted.

"May I take him?" Lord Regin asked.

The Jaeger nodded and carefully passed Connall's body over to the mountainous grey fae, who handled it with ease.

"We must lay him to rest where the sunset touches," the Jaeger said. "He must go to the Summerlands."

It was a somber group who left the Heart. Mary Alice trailed after the Jaeger—no, the king. She was going to have to get used to thinking of him that way. The new king was accompanied by his Seneschal and the head of the king's guards.

"What happened in there, Your Majesty?" the guardswoman asked.

"Indeed," the Seneschal said. "How did King Connall end up dead during the ceremony when only the two of you were present?"

"What is it you imply?" the king asked.

There was a short pause before the Seneschal answered. "Nothing, Your Majesty." His voice was studiedly neutral. "It is only that others will wonder and I want them to know the truth."

"This is the truth," the former Jaeger said. "He collapsed moments after the Heart accepted me." He shook his head. "There was a spike in the magic, something about it wasn't quite right. It was…wilder than usual."

"We observed that out here as well," the Seneschal said.

"Then you understand." He looked over at the head of the guards. "I know you served your liege for a long time. Will you be able to transfer your loyalty to me?" He raised a hand before the guardswoman could open her mouth. "I don't need your answer right away. Think on it and let me know. Until you do, there are those who will watch over me." He turned his head and looked back at Malice.

"Of course, Jaeger," Malice said. She paused, her face heating up. "I mean, Your Majesty. I have your back for as long as you need me at it." It was her privilege and her pleasure to serve him. She had no doubt he would be an excellent king.

The king laughed. "You have no idea how that puts my mind at ease, Lady Malice."

At the front of the group, Lord Regin stopped in front of the narrow tunnel that led outside. Everyone slowed down to keep from running into him.

"How do you want to do this?" Lord Regin asked. "Everyone will want to know what happened. They'll already know something is amiss."

"We will take him to the Cliffs of Dusk," the king said. "Seneschal, you will go out and instruct the assembled as to what has happened and tell them we take King Connall to the traditional place of leavetaking. Lord Regin will follow with his body. Lady Leanan, you will see he is wrapped up and laid over his mount. We, along with his subjects, shall accompany him to the place where he leaves us for his final journey. It is as he would have wanted." The king snapped off the orders without thinking. He was clearly getting accustomed to being in charge.

The guardswoman inclined her head. "Thank you for permitting me to accompany him one last time, my lord."

"Of course," the king said. "Lord Seneschal, we await your return."

The Seneschal opened his mouth as if he wanted to say something. He thought better of it and gave the new king a stiff bow instead. He disappeared through the narrow corridor that led outside. There was no door on it and the murmurs of the crowd filtered back to them as they waited. They heard the mass intake of breath from the watchers when the Seneschal appeared. He began to speak. His words were met with silence as he described King Connall's final moments to the best of his ability.

The former Jaeger had his arms crossed and was tapping his fingers on his opposite forearm. He rocked on the balls of his feet, giving every indication of someone who was ready to get going.

"The king is dead," the Seneschal said to the gathered fae. His pronouncement was met with cries of horror and fear. "Do not be afraid," he cried over the din, "for we have a new king. The Heir completed the ceremony and is now lord over us and the realm. All hail King Tedrick!"

Silence draped over the crowd, then slowly dissipated with scattered chants of "King Tedrick!" Slowly, the cries grew more numerous and rhythmic until the new king's name was being bellowed over and over.

Malice was surprised to hear the former Jaeger's first name. It hadn't occurred to her that he might actually have one and not simply a title.

The Seneschal entered the hall. "My lord," he said, "your people await." Whatever reservations he might have had, he seemed resigned to his new reality now.

"Thank you, Lord Seneschal," King Tedrick said. He turned to Malice. "Should I require your skills, I don't want you too far from hand."

She accompanied him from the crystal structure that housed the Heart. The first thing she noticed was that the sunset had lost its glorious hues. The sun itself had brightened considerably, but the colors painting the clouds looked almost monochromatic compared to the previous evenings she'd witnessed. It took her a moment to realize that the setting sun that had perpetually marked Connall's reign was gone.

They watched as Lord Regin laid the king's body on the grass. Lady Leanan gestured to one of the guards, who hurried over to the head of the procession. He hauled down the banners that had fluttered from the lances of the guards who had lead the parade. She knelt on the ground, not heeding the stains to her pants. When he returned, she took the banners and wound them about Connall's corpse. She tied them to him using golden cords, then lifted the shrouded body, cradling it carefully in her arms. The unicorn stood and allowed the corpse to be draped across the saddle he'd ridden in maybe a few hours before.

Malice was having problems keeping track of time. It seemed like more time had passed within the Heart than out here. When they'd entered, the sun had barely started to set. They'd kept their vigil for hours, but the sun had only just slipped below the horizon when they came out.

The only sound that broke the profound silence was the wind. It was as if the realm still breathed, though the rest of them could not. The wind whistled as it moved over and through the cracks of the Heart, pulling mournful sounds tailor-made for the general mood.

King Tedrick moved forward toward his mount. Malice stayed close behind. When he was mounted, she went to the kelpie, mounting him and moving it next to the king. Now that the sun was down, night was coming on quickly. Small globes of cool light sprang into existence above the heads of some of the guards. Malice glanced back and saw similar orbs in the crowd of fae who had come to witness what was supposed to have been a joyous occasion.

The host moved on from the Heart, away from the castle. Malice kept to the king's right side, while Lord Regin stayed at his left. Lady Leanan's horse paced somberly next to the dead king's unicorn. The bells on the harnesses which had sounded so bright and cheerful hours before now sounded jangly and harsh. With a start, Malice realized her bells were the only ones still ringing. The others had done some type of magic to muffle theirs, leaving hers to sound much more sprightly than the occasion called for. There was no way she could reach them all to pull them off. The Seneschal moved his horse next to the kelpie and ran his hands down the reins. He couldn't reach all the bells either, but whatever he did served to dispel their noise. She nodded gratefully to him as he moved away again.

The pace they kept now was glacial even compared to the slow pace they'd kept on their way to the Heart. This was a plodding walk, and she had no idea where they were going. Night fell dark around them, the sky devoid of moonlight, with only the twinkling of distant stars to light their way. She could see enough and hear enough to keep pace with the king's horse, but that was all.

After a while, Malice noticed snaking lines of light moving through the grasses, coming toward them.

"Your Majesty, what are those?" she asked. "Are they dangerous?"

"Quite to the contrary," Tedrick said. "Those are Connall's subjects. They're joining his funeral train. We shall see him off together."

She squinted in the darkness. When they got close enough, she could see that they were indeed fae, many of whom were carrying more of those glowing orbs. Smaller lights moved among the larger fae. It seemed pixies could demonstrate emotions other than manic excitement. The movement of the lights seemed somehow restrained and dignified.

And so they kept on through the night. Her eyelids should have been drawing down over her eyes as exhaustion set in, but she never tired. Night finished its slow plod into day with a steel grey sunrise. Low clouds covered the sky, threatening rain. Malice couldn't recall seeing anything other than occasional clouds whipping past at high speeds, never such cloud cover. The terrain had changed around them in the night. Gone were the rolling hills and occasional trees. Flat grasslands spread out as far as her eyes could see. Malice squinted into the distance. There was something wrong with the horizon. It appeared to double. She blinked and looked again, then realized she was seeing the edge of a long cliff. They were approaching the end of a massive plateau. The sky was lightening at their backs. The clouds prevented shadows from forming among the dry grasses.

They kept on until they were just short of the edge of the plateau. When there was no further to go, they stopped, the king in front, the unicorn with Connall's body barely within his reach. They waited, looking down onto the plains below. The drop was vast, the details so far away they were impossible to make out, except that the plains were golden as if lit by a sun different than their own. There was no way anyone could survive a fall from the edge of the plateau down to the ground so far below. Malice thought perhaps a winged creature could fly down, but it seemed as likely that even wings would give out from fatigue before they could land.

They waited, eyes on the golden plains. Malice glanced over at the former Jaeger to see if she could get any indication over what came next, but he had eyes only for the golden lands on this strange double horizon. She looked the other way and watched as the accompanying fae fanned out and stepped up to the edge of the plateau in a long line stretching to either side of them. As she watched, more arrived, a seemingly endless flow of people who came to that boundary line between earth and sky, then stopped to stare past the beauty of a land they could never touch. And still they came. They came until there were fae as far as her eyes could see and further.

There were no words, here at the edge of the world, only the mournful wail of the wind with nothing to stop it. The keening was appropriate, as if the land mourned with its people. Given what she'd been told of the king's relationship to the realm, perhaps it did.

At a signal Malice couldn't see, the new king slid off his white-blue mount with curls of steam that were whipped away by the omnipresent breeze. She was the only one who looked toward him. The fae kept their eyes forward as he approached the unicorn. It shifted away from him, but he grabbed its bridle of gilt and glass and held it in place. He murmured soft words into an ear that was laid almost flat. The ear didn't prick up, but the unicorn ceased its sidling. King Tedrick dropped the reins and undid the cords lashing the old king across the saddle. He stepped back, the wrapped body grasped in his arms. With infinite care, he laid Connall's body on the ground, then undid the wrappings, pulling them aside to reveal the king's still form. Already, Connall seemed smaller than he had in life.

A shaft of light broke through the low, grey clouds. It wasn't golden like the light that shone on those faraway plains nor was it the colorless shade of early morning light that hinted at the limitless possibilities of the day before reality and time darkened its hue into something more concrete. It was palest lavender, shot through with motes of dancing gold that twinkled and spun around each other. The light landed on Connall's body, bringing life to his cheeks, coloring the pale flesh until it looked like he might sit up and start ordering his subjects about. It was a false life. Connall lay unmoving, but as Malice watched, she realized she could see the wrappings through his body.

The golden flecks of light landed on his skin, covering it until there were more lights than skin. The wind came up, scattering the motes, blowing over the edge and taking the king's body with it. His body disappeared in a shower of sparks that kept his vague outline for one breath, then another. A final gust of wind scattered the sparks, down to the land below in one final exhalation, like the sound of a dying man's last breath leaving his body.

Mary Alice became aware that her face was soaked with tears. She hadn't known the fae king well and what parts she had known she hadn't liked, but there was something beautiful about his final sendoff. There was a peace to it, one she suspected she would never be privileged to feel, though she came close when she was in Ruri's arms. The land below them beckoned. It was gorgeous and peaceful. She took a step toward the edge but was halted when a large hand reached out and grabbed her forearm, pulling her back toward safety.

"That's not for you," Lord Regin said. "Nor any of us yet. One day, perhaps."

"Right," Mary Alice said. "One day." She turned her back on the promise of golden fields. There was work yet to be done.

CHAPTER THIRTY-NINE

The ride back to the castle was one of the eeriest Ruri had experienced. Despite dire warnings from palace fae about the dangers of being out too late, she'd seen no sign of life. She'd been so wrapped up trying to find a sign that would indicate that all the realm's fae hadn't spontaneously disappeared that it had taken her a while to realize Connall's sunset was gone. She suspected that meant the king was dead but had no way of knowing for certain. Her sense of dread wasn't alleviated when she arrived at the castle either. She'd seen livelier tombs.

While she was removing her borrowed horse's tack, she realized she hadn't smelled wildflowers for quite some time. She paused while lifting Floppy's saddle off her back and inhaled deeply, but the only scents to reach her nostrils were those associated with the stable. No amount of sniffing was going to bring anything to her except straw and horse dung.

She finished rubbing down Floppy and headed into the keep with the idea of going right back to the room she shared with Mal. As usual, the castle had other ideas. She wandered in circles through halls she barely recognized and those she didn't know at all. Why Connall needed a corridor whose ceiling displayed realistic—and she suspected real—underwater vistas while the windows looked out onto a night sky devoid of bonus sunsets, she didn't know. The entire time she paced the halls, she saw nobody else, not even the usually ubiquitous guards or scurrying servants. When she finally recognized the hall as the one where her room was located, Ruri's feet and legs ached from walking.

The room was much the same as it had always been, save for the sunset-less view she'd already seen through the other palace windows. It felt as empty and lifeless as the rest of the castle. She peeled off her clothing and dropped them where she stood, then rolled into bed. There was little chance Mal would be joining her. Ruri's sense of her mate was faint and off to the north somewhere. She was moving, but beyond that, Ruri could tell little about what was going on with her.

Tired though she was, sleep was elusive. The sense of loneliness intruded upon her, pressing in like an unwelcome watcher's gaze, heavy and intangible. If she hadn't been so exhausted, she might have laughed at the irony. Instead, Ruri tossed and turned, trying to get comfortable without Mal next to her. When she finally drifted off, her sleep was fractured and filled with uneasy dreams where large snakes slithered after her, calling her name and saying her job wasn't done yet.

She came awake slowly, which was unlike her. Her eyes were sandy with fatigue and her mouth tasted like she'd spent the night sucking on pennies. With some effort, she pushed herself up from the very welcoming mattress and stared out the open window. A grey sky greeted her, not exactly the kind of scene she needed to get going.

Ruri's stomach growled loudly, reminding her that it had been quite some time since she'd eaten. There was no food in the room, but she didn't know how to get to the dining hall on her own.

Screw this. She swung her legs over the side of the bed. *I can catch my own damn food.*

She stomped over to the wardrobe and pulled out clothes suitable for spending the day outside. She stepped out into the hall. All she had to do was make it out to the courtyard; surely that couldn't be too difficult.

The castle apparently wanted her to eat her words. It took much longer than it should have before Ruri found herself coming through a door at the bottom of a spiral staircase that had never, to her knowledge, opened into the courtyard. She stood outside the door, hands on her hips and glaring out over cobblestones that managed to shimmer despite the lack of sun. The courtyard was as empty as it had been the previous evening.

She made her way over to the Wild Hunt's stables and hauled back on the door.

"Jesus!"

The loud exclamation on the other side had Ruri jumping straight into the air.

"Holy crap," she said, putting out a hand to steady herself.

"Why don't you watch where you're going?" Shejuanna grumbled. "You almost scared the piss outta me."

"Like you didn't to me?" Ruri crossed her arms. "You're the first person I've seen all day."

"Yeah, same here. Aside from the others, this place has been dead since yesterday's big procession that we weren't invited to."

"No one came back after that?"

"Nope. It was weird. Like there were some fae around, but right around nightfall, they all up and left." Shejuanna licked her lips as her eyes shifted to one side then the other. "The animals got all squirrelly too at about the same time. They calmed down after a few minutes, but Simeon got hurt pretty bad before they stopped fussing." She eyed Ruri warily. "I don't suppose you'd take a look at him and see if he'll be all right?"

"I'm not a doctor." She'd had some experience with patching up basic wounds, pretty much every wolven did, but as Beta, she'd ended up handling a lot of triage for the pack. She knew her limitations. "How is he hurt?"

"He got a hoof or something to the side of the head."

"That's not usually a good thing."

Shejuanna shook her head. "No shit. So you gonna come see him or not?"

"I'll take a look."

Without another word, Shejuanna led Ruri through the stables of the Wild Hunt to a plain door just past the last holding box. The corridor the door opened into was cramped, the roof a bare foot above Ruri's head. Some of the taller kids must have had to duck to make their way down there. The walls were unpainted stone that needed maintenance; piles of sand and rock chips littered the edges and corners of the floor.

The room at the end of the corridor was much nicer than the trip there had suggested it might be. It was a long room with fireplaces at either end. Beds lined the walls, but the teens had taken the effort to string up dividers of canvas or similar heavy cloth. It reminded Ruri of the barracks at the camp the kids had taken off from, but with a decidedly more rustic flare.

"He's down here." Shejuanna led Ruri past the beds to the one closest to the fireplace at the far end. Someone was sitting on the edge of the bed running a wet washcloth over the face of the young man tucked into the sheets. The rest of the teens perched on chairs or sat on the floor. They looked up as Ruri and Shejuanna approached.

"So we're not the only ones," Carlo said. His voice was muted, and he looked back at the bed with Simeon and Latawna right away.

"No, I was going to go hunting," Ruri said. "Ran into Shejuanna on my way to the armory."

"Oh."

"Are you going to help him?" Latawna asked.

"I'll do what I can," Ruri said.

"We have soup if you're hungry," Jermayne said.

"I can use a bite, but first let me take a look at Simeon."

Latawna scooted off the bed, taking the washcloth with her. Ruri sucked in a deep breath at the ugly bruise that mottled Simeon's left temple. The skin was swollen and marred further by a nasty cut that someone had taken the time to clean out. The bed gave under her weight as she sat down, shifting the boy a bit, but he gave no sign that he was aware of her.

"Has he said anything since he got hurt?" Ruri asked. She gently placed her fingertips on his neck, seeking out his pulse. She found it, but it was light and thready, not the strong and steady rhythm she would expect from one his age.

"He was complaining a bit, then he stopped talking," Latawna said. "He asked for his momma before he fell asleep. We tried to wake him since Jermayne said it's dangerous for people with concussions to fall asleep, but he won't open his eyes."

"I need a phone," Ruri said.

"What for?" Shejuanna asked. "You can't call anyone."

"I'm not going to call anyone. I want to see the flashlight." She held out her hand. "Come on, I know at least one of you still has one of the damn things."

They looked at each other, then fished in their pockets. Ruri had four phones to choose from. She grabbed the nearest one and felt around it to find the power button. It flared to life in her hand, bathing her fingers in cool blue light.

"Where's the flashlight? These things usually have one, right?"

Shejuanna snatched the device from her hand and fiddled with it for a second. A pinpoint of bright light blinked on.

"Don't you have your own phone?" she asked as she passed it back.

"Mal has a phone," Ruri said absently. "I've never seen the need for one."

"You and my grandma," Carlo whispered. The others snickered but couldn't hide the nervous tinge to their laughter.

Ruri left the comment alone. They were worried about their friend, and it wasn't like she was about to explain to them that technically she was old enough to be their grandmothers' grandmother.

She shone the light into Simeon's right eye. His pupil was blown out, taking up all but a thin sliver of iris. The pupil stayed fixed, even with the bright flashlight glaring into it.

That's not good. Ruri pulled up his other eyelid. The pupil looked the same and didn't move when she shone the light in.

"I can't do anything for him. There's something wrong with his brain." Ruri sat back, then handed the phone back to Shejuanna. "I'm sorry."

"Shit," Jermayne said. Carlo clapped a hand on his shoulder and gave it a quick squeeze.

"The fae might be able to help him," Ruri said. "They gave me something to drink that fixed me right up."

"We can ask the Matia when she gets back," Latawna said.

The kids nodded.

"Whenever that is," Ruri said.

"Do you know what's up?" Jermayne asked.

"I have an inkling, but I don't know if it's right," Ruri said. "Better that we operate on the assumption that they'll be back at some point, which means keeping Simeon alive until then. Have you been feeding him?"

Jermayne shook his head.

"Let's get some water in him. Then we'll see if he can keep down some soup." That might help. Humans were so much more fragile than wolven. If this had been one of her packmates, time would have been enough to heal whatever was wrong with his brain. Unfortunately, humans didn't work that way. "There's one other thing you might want to consider."

"What's that?" Shejuanna eyed her with suspicion.

"Take him back to our world. Get him to a hospital. The doctors might be able to save him. They have a much better chance at it than we do."

"No way." Shejuanna brought her hand down in an emphatic chopping motion. "That's never going to happen."

"You should think about it," Ruri said. She turned back to Simeon. He hadn't moved. "If it could save his life…"

"And what kind of life does he have back there?" Latawna asked. "What kind of life is waiting for any of us? We made this choice. All of us."

"They threw us away," Carlo chimed in. "He don't wanna go back to that. No way."

"Besides, they think we're dead," Shejuanna said. "We're better off with them thinking that. What would we do? Roll his body out onto the sidewalk in front of an ER? How would they deal with a guy who's dead not being dead?" She shook her head. "No. He wouldn't want to go back there."

"I won't try to force you," Ruri said, "but you needed to think about it. Just make sure you're opting out for the right reasons."

"It *is* the right reason," Jermayne said. He nodded firmly. "It's the right call."

"Then I guess we wait."

Ruri spent the next hours at Simeon's bedside, helping his friends care for him. They were able to get some water into him, as well as the broth from the soup, but his condition never changed. There was little discussion, and the teens would leave the room in ones or twos, then come back. From the smells they brought back with them, Ruri surmised they were looking after the mounts.

It was late morning when she heard the first signs of life that weren't the teens or the beasts of the Wild Hunt. She made her way out to the courtyard and watched as the fae streamed in. It occurred to her that this was the first time she hadn't heard any kind of music accompanying them. Their faces were drawn and exhausted.

Ruri stood by, watching until she saw a familiar face in the crowd. She darted forward, weaving her way between members of the court until she drew abreast with Mracek.

"What happened?"

"King Connall is dead." He stared at her with eyes dulled by fatigue.

"I thought maybe that was what the sunset meant."

He nodded. "We saw him off to the Summerlands. The Jaeger is now King Tedrick."

"That's not good."

Mracek shook his head violently. "You can't say things like that." His eyes flitted about as he looked around him. "His wishes are reality now."

"Got it." She scanned the crowd. "Where's Mal?"

"With the royal party." Mracek had been quite animated a few moments before, but now he looked seconds from rolling into bed. "They're further back at the end of the procession."

"Dammit." She needed to get the counter-charm to her before the Jaeger—Tedrick—could solidify his hold over her. "What about the Matia?"

Curiosity warmed his dull eyes. "Why would you need to see her?" He yawned widely.

"One of the human kids has been injured. He'll probably die if he doesn't get help. She oversees them along with the regular fae servants, doesn't she?"

His tired nod was the answer she wanted. "Be warned however, she may not be able or willing to help. At any rate, she rides with the royal party. She was present at the Heart."

"More waiting then. That's awesome."

"I'm afraid so." He turned to leave. "Is there anything else you require? If there isn't, I'm going to go sleep for a week."

"That's all for now. Thank you, my friend."

He raised a weary hand in her direction, then shambled on.

Ruri found herself a vantage point where she could watch the courtyard and wait without getting in the way. Her sense of Mal told her that she was getting closer, but moving slowly. It would be a while yet. The temptation to go and meet her pulled at her guts, but she had no desire for their reunion to be under the eyes of the new king. Better by far to wait it out, no matter how twitchy the idea made her. She settled in and watched the gate for the first sign of her mate.

CHAPTER FORTY

The trip back to the castle couldn't be over too soon for Mary Alice. Everything moved so slowly. The march had seemed stately and solemn for a bit, but it hadn't been long before it simply felt slow. No one talked. Instead, the fae all seemed to be contemplating or meditating on something she didn't see or care about. The guards were on alert, and Mary Alice tried to pass the time by watching for threats, but that excitement waned rapidly. Her usual poise had left her, washed away in the haze of the events of the last day. She didn't want to think about them, but all she had to distract herself were groups of fae peeling off from the pilgrimage every time they reached another fork in the road.

By the time the castle walls appeared in the distance, Mary Alice had been ready to cheer. Then she waited some more as they made their sedate way closer and closer to the palace. All she wanted was Ruri, their bed, and a long nap.

When they finally arrived in the courtyard, the tail end of a train too long for Mary Alice to wrap her head around, they were met with tired but still scurrying pages. The lavender and gold tabards in King Connall's colors had already been replaced with the burgundy and grey of King Tedrick. She squinted at the top of the nearest tower. Sure enough, the pennants were also Tedrick's colors.

A subdued Latawna came forward to take the kelpie from her. As Mary Alice was turning to leave, King Tedrick called out to her.

"Lady Malice, I shall require your presence in the morning. We have much to discuss."

"Yes, uh, my lord." Mary Alice folded herself into an awkward bow.

"Rest now," he said. "I shall send a page for you after dawn." He walked away, already in deep conversation with the Seneschal and the captain of the king's guard.

Since their group had been the last to enter the castle, the courtyard was much emptier than when they'd left it what felt like a lifetime ago. She thought about the room she shared with Ruri in the west wing of the castle and knew she should enter the southern door to get there. She felt something else also, a warm presence that approached her from behind.

"There you are," Mary Alice said, turning and opening her arms wide.

Ruri stepped into them and gave her a tight squeeze. "It's about time you got back. I've been waiting a while and a half."

Mary Alice leaned forward and pressed her lips to Ruri's in a quick smooch. "I'm glad to be back. That was something else. I don't even know how to explain it all. Or even part of it." She looked around, then lowered her voice. "There was some serious shit that went down. I'll tell you about it when we get some time."

"And I want to hear it all, but there's this thing I need to do first, and I think I need your help for it, since you're all high and mighty around here now."

The lure of the bed and getting to finally lie down tugged at her. Some of her annoyance at having to wait must have showed on her face.

Ruri stiffened in her embrace, then pulled away. "If it's too much to ask, I'll just figure out how to talk to the Matia myself. It's fine."

Mary Alice opened her mouth to snap back, then thought better of it. She was tired, but something was definitely eating at her girlfriend.

"I'm sorry," she said, pulling Ruri back toward her. "I'm tired, but obviously this is important to you. I can keep my eyes open a bit longer. What do you need from me?"

"I need you to take me to the Matia so I can ask her a favor."

"Who's that?"

"The sylph woman you rode in with." Ruri gave her a disbelieving look. "You spent hours riding about ten feet away from the woman and you don't know who she is?"

"There was way less time for talking than you'd think." Mary Alice let Ruri out of the hug but snagged her hand. She got up on her tiptoes to see if she could make out the old sylph woman. She thought she saw her close to the entrance to the servants' quarters. "This way."

Ruri followed her willingly, allowing herself to be towed around the groups of fae who still lingered. Her head turned to watch a larger group. Mary Alice followed her gaze and realized it was a group of Wild Hunt members gathered around the large figure of Lord Regin. They noticed her watching and nodded to her.

"Lady the Matia," Mary Alice called out when they were close enough to get the sylph's attention. "A moment of your time, if you don't mind."

The Matia turned their way. Two younger brownie women accompanied her. Their eyebrows climbed their foreheads at her words and form of address. Mary Alice ignored them.

"Have you met Ruri?" she asked. "She's my…partner, and she has a question for you."

"Lady Malice." A slight tightening around the corners of her lips was the only indication of displeasure. "I have not met the Lady Ruri." She looked them both up and down, then very obviously didn't curtsy. Instead, she regarded them steadily in the eyes.

Mary Alice grinned. Whatever the Matia thought she would gain by not adhering to the arcane politeness of fae high society, it was completely lost on them.

Ruri stared right back at her. "Simeon was kicked in the head by one of the Wild Hunt mounts. He's dying."

The look of concealed disdain vanished from the sylph's face immediately. "One of the human stablehands?"

Ruri nodded.

"Tell me where he is."

"Over this way." Ruri walked away. "He's still in their room off the stables. He hasn't woken up for a while. I think he's got some trauma to the brain."

The Matia waved her hand. "I'll make sure he's taken care of." The wings on her back blurred into life with a soft buzz. She lifted off the ground and darted in front of Ruri. "There's no need to accompany me. Humans usually find this rather disturbing."

Mary Alice and Ruri shared a glance, then lengthened their strides to keep up with the sylph. They almost jogged across the courtyard trying to keep up with her. When they entered the Wild Hunt's stables, the teens put down the cleaning tasks they were engaged in and followed them.

The Matia knew where she was going. She buzzed her unerring way down the unfinished corridor and into the coziest barracks Mary Alice had ever seen. It was easy to see who needed help. Simeon's still form lay on the bed. Carlo, who had looked up when they came in, leaped up from where he'd been sitting at the edge of the bed.

"You did it," he said to Ruri.

Mary Alice didn't miss the tight-lipped smile Ruri gave him.

"Let's see," the Matia said. Her wings slowed, then stilled when her toes touched the floor. She settled herself on the other side of the bed from where Carlo had been sitting. She placed a hand on his forehead. "Oh dear," she said, then moved it to his chest. "We don't have much time." She shook her head at whatever she found there. "We don't have much time at all. If he is to survive this, it has to be now."

"All right," Carlo said.

"Survive what?" Mary Alice asked at the same time.

The Matia didn't answer. She placed her hands on Simeon's temples and closed her eyes. Nothing happened.

"What's going on?" Shejuanna asked Ruri in hushed tones.

"I have no idea," Ruri answered.

A low hum filled the room. The sound wasn't constant. Rather, it ebbed and surged with intensity in no pattern that Mary Alice could discern. Bits of light and shadow detached themselves from the objects in the room, including their group. Of all of them, only the Matia was untouched. The bits of light adhered themselves to the edges of Simeon's still form while the scraps of shadow disappeared into him. Faster and faster, light and shade were drawn to him until his body glowed and pulsed from within in time with the hum, shadows showing through shifting lights with each throb.

The Matia removed her hands from Simeon and sat back. Whatever she'd done didn't stop and kept gathering light and dark. The hum settled into a steady rhythm. The pulsing light and darkness sped up.

It stopped. The light on Simeon's outside contracted and intensified while the shadows rushed outward. Tears streaming down her face, Mary Alice turned her head. It was impossible to watch. When she looked back, in Simeon's place was a large bird with feathers in hues ranging from red through orange and into bright yellow. A dim glow clung to its feathers, and sparkles drifted from the edges of its wings and tail. It cocked its head at them and blinked strange eyes.

For a second, Mary Alice couldn't place what was so odd about the bird, then she realized what was giving her the chill that was creeping down her spine.

Its eyes were still human.

"Where's Simeon?" Latawna's voice was high and uneven.

"That is Simeon," Mary Alice said.

"There was nothing else I could do for him." The Matia stood and smoothed her skirts with trembling hands. "Now his soul stays intact and he may continue to serve our king, which is the best any of us could ask." She eyed the strange bird. "Who knew he had that in him? Now, if you'll excuse me, it's past time I was in bed." She brushed past their stunned group.

Silence lingered in her absence. Ruri moved to close the door, pulling Mary Alice along with her.

"That's such crap," Ruri whispered. "What about the potions they used for us when we got hurt going after the hodag?"

"It would have been less of a hassle than whatever that spell was." Mary Alice blinked, then realized the kids were watching them closely. "Maybe this isn't the best place to talk about this."

"Why not? Because of them?" Ruri had stopped trying to keep the volume down. "They should know they're getting screwed over. They were lured here, treated as glorified stablehands, and then what? Turned into mounts for the pleasure of the fae?"

"Of course we're getting screwed over," Jermayne said. "Better here than there."

"So you're okay with this?" Ruri asked.

"Not really," he said. "We all thought we'd have longer. They told us it would happen after we got old."

"We get to become one of them," Latawna said, her eyes shining. "He's beautiful." She held her hand out toward the massive bird.

"So even if there was another way, you're okay with this one, the one they're choosing for you." Ruri turned to look the rest of the teens in the eyes.

They avoided her gaze uncomfortably.

"I can't deal with this place." Ruri turned on her heel and left, the sound of her footsteps echoing loudly through the narrow hall.

"That's not..." Mary Alice couldn't think of a reasonable way to end the sentence and allowed it to trail off.

The teens grouped around Simeon in his new form. The bird tilted his head to watch them. He settled his feathers but didn't look alarmed. When Jermayne reached out a hand to him, he gently rubbed the side of his beak along it.

There was nothing else to do here. As it had been since they'd gotten there, the kids had made their decision. Short of tying them up and tossing them through a portal, Mary Alice couldn't do anything to change it. She slipped from the room and closed the door quietly behind her, then went after her girlfriend.

Ruri was nowhere to be seen when Mary Alice emerged into the stables. Mary Alice wondered where she could have gotten to and realized that she could sort of feel where she was, much like the way she'd become aware of her room or other rooms in the castle. It was handy that she'd come to be able to navigate the halls of the place, especially since they constantly moved and shifted. It was even handier that apparently that knowledge extended to Ruri.

Mary Alice allowed a yawn to crack her jaw, then went after Ruri. She wanted to be in bed, but there was no way she could leave her girlfriend to wander the halls of the castle. Besides, she would sleep better if Ruri was around.

It didn't take her long to track Ruri down. She'd somehow ended up near the keep's massive kitchens. It was warmer in the wide halls with their low ceilings and spare decorations. Ruri came striding determinedly toward her. When she saw Mary Alice, she stopped.

"How did you?" She turned to look behind her. "I was heading toward…and there was a door that…" She clenched her fists by her side. "I hate this place so much!"

"I know you do." Mary Alice walked up to her and tucked a stray lock of hair behind her ear. "It has to be hell keeping your wolf inside all the time."

Ruri leaned into Mary Alice's touch. "It's not just that. It's what this place does to the people who end up here. Those kids are fine with what was done to Simeon. They think these damn fae are doing them a favor, but they're not."

A fae servant walked past them with a silver tray piled high with dishes. He watched them from the corner of his eye but didn't stop.

"This isn't the place to talk about it," Mary Alice said. "Let's go back to our room. I know the way."

"How do you get around here? My direction sense is usually on the money, but this place keeps changing on me and I can't wrap my brain around it." She allowed Mary Alice to lead her away.

"It clicked one night and I've been able to kind of feel where the room I want to go is located." She shrugged. "It's weird, but I'm not going to question it."

"See, that's it right there. This place is weird on weird and after a while we get so ground down that we go along with things, even when we know they're not right. You know what I mean?" Ruri watched Mary Alice intently.

"I guess so." It made a certain amount of sense, though she didn't think she'd indulged in that kind of behavior too much. What she'd done was because it made sense or because the Jaeger had asked it of her. Those were both good reasons, neither of which was born out of apathy.

Their room wasn't far, but it was in the direction opposite the way Ruri had been heading. Ruri was quiet on their way back and she chewed at the corner of her mouth the way she did when she was thinking. Every now and again she would glance at Mary Alice. Each time she looked over, Mary Alice smiled in what she hoped was a reassuring way, between deep yawns.

"Told you I knew how to get back," she said when the familiar door to their room came into sight down the corridor.

"That you did." Ruri pushed open the door and sat on the edge of the bed.

Mary Alice walked past her to the other side and began stripping off the layers of finery Billy had spun for her. He'd been right to extend the duration of the glamour. Her boots were real and the hardest to strip off. She struggled with the ties.

Ruri walked around the bed. "What are you doing?" She knelt down in front of Mary Alice. "How did you get these in a knot that big?"

"You try keeping the laces in order when you can't see them for a day."

"Good point." With careful precision, Ruri managed to get Mary Alice's boots unlaced. She pulled the right one off.

Mary Alice groaned at the feeling of her foot no longer being encased in leather.

"So the Jaeger is king now." Ruri moved over to the left foot.

"Yeah. I guess Connall died during the ritual. Oh, that feels good." She wiggled the toes on both her feet, marveling in their newfound freedom, then collapsed backward onto the bed.

"Does that mean his curse is gone and you can go through the portal back to our world?"

"Huh." Mary Alice raised her head to meet Ruri's serious eyes. "You know, I completely forgot to ask about that."

Ruri tilted her head and looked at her steadily.

"What?" Mary Alice propped herself up on her elbows. "You don't understand how crazy it was. Things happened and I got kind of pulled along with it. I'll make sure to ask him soon."

"Next time you see him?"

"Yes, the next time I see him."

"Good." Ruri stood up from where she'd been kneeling and climbed onto the bed. She looked down at Mary Alice without saying anything, then threw one leg over Mary Alice's pelvis and settled her weight across her hips.

"Whoa there," Mary Alice said. "I don't think I'm in any condition for shenanigans."

Ruri reached forward and fluffed the pillow under her head. "I'm helping get you ready for bed, you perv."

"Sure you are."

Ruri grinned, the right side of her lips pulling slightly higher than the left.

As usual, Mary Alice watched entranced as her slightly elongated canines were exposed. She loved the way amusement or joy transformed Ruri's face. It was easy to think she was a very serious person indeed when her face was at rest, but smiles turned her into someone who looked like they'd never seen a day's worth of hardship in their life. She knew better, but it was easy to believe it when Ruri looked at her like that.

"I, uh, have something for you," Ruri said as she watched Mary Alice with intent eyes.

"Really?" Mary Alice yawned again. The softness of the bed under her was pulling her closer and closer to sleep. "What is it?" Her eyes drifted shut.

"A bracelet."

Mary Alice felt something being tied around her wrist. She tried to open her eyes to look at it, but that was a lot of work. "I don't usually wear jewelry."

"I'd really like you to wear it. It's been made just for you."

"Will it make you happy?"

"Very much."

"Then I can't see why I wouldn't wear it."

"And that is why I love you."

Mary Alice felt Ruri lean forward, then warm lips brushed her forehead. That was fine. It was better than fine, it was wonderful. She smiled and allowed sleep to roll her under.

CHAPTER FORTY-ONE

"Ah, Lady Malice," King Tedrick said. "Join us."

Mary Alice looked around as she stepped into the room. She'd never been here before. All of her interactions with King Connall had taken place in his throne room. A large table dominated the center of the space. It was easily twenty feet along the side. She thought it might be a dark wood, but if there was a grain, it was so tight it was hard to tell.

She recognized Lord Regin immediately. He stood head and shoulders above the rest of the fae in the room, most of whom seemed to be Tuatha. He'd donned a tabard in Tedrick's colors, though it was richer by far than those worn by the pages. He stood to one side of the king. The only other person she knew by name, or rather by title, was the Matia. She'd seen the others before—they were all members of the Wild Hunt—but she knew most only by sight.

The top of the table held forests and plains. In one corner was the castle. Along the far edge was the range of upside-down mountains where she and Ruri had first appeared. She watched in awe as clouds scudded over the castle. The sunlight in the room dimmed.

"Is this in real time?" Mary Alice leaned in for a closer look.

Lord Regin cleared his throat.

"Oh shit, I'm sorry." She bent at the waist in Tedrick's direction. "Your Majesty."

Tedrick held up a hand toward Lord Regin. "It's all right. She isn't my subject, more of a consultant, if we want to adopt mortal terms." He eyed her. "That doesn't mean you can act so familiarly in public, you understand."

"Of course, King Tedrick." She grinned. "I think my track record proves I can be discreet."

"Indeed." He motioned her attention back toward the table. "This is the realm. Connall had ceased paying close attention to it, which is something I plan to rectify with your assistance and that of the Wild Hunt. Take a look there." He pointed to a spot among rolling hills split through by a meandering silver river.

"That's where we faced off against the Bottom-Dwellers," Mary Alice said.

"Very good." Tedrick waved his hand at the general area. "Do you see how everything is darker over here?"

It looked like the area was shaded by clouds though there were none visible on the projection. Mary Alice nodded.

"It means my influence is weaker there. I don't have enough fae who have sworn fealty to me living there to be able to clearly see what is happening. You'll notice there are more areas like this throughout the realm." He leaned forward, bracing his arms on the edge of the table and glaring at the offending spots. "I need to encourage my loyal subjects to move back to these areas. Each one contains groups who won't swear fealty, but who live on lands that belong to me. My job for you…" He looked around at those gathered about the table. "For all of you, is to clear those areas out so they can be resettled." He looked directly at Mary Alice. "You will spearhead those efforts."

"Me?" All eyes were upon her, and not all of them felt well-inclined toward her. "Surely you have people better suited to leading a campaign like this. I'm more of a lone operative. I don't really command groups."

"Yet you led the party that wiped out more Bottom-Dwellers in an hour than anyone has managed to do in months upon months of hunting them." King Tedrick pushed himself away from the table. "You are the best choice for this task."

"I'm not from here. How do I know which fae belong and which don't?"

"I will fill you in on each area. For now, I want you to finish the job with the Bottom-Dwellers. They'll be on their back foot after the blow you struck and we should capitalize on that."

"If that's what you want." Mary Alice tried not to think of the piles of Bottom-Dweller corpses rotting in the sun. "I'll get on that right away."

"Excellent." King Tedrick smiled at her.

Mary Alice felt the warmth of his regard all the way down to her toes. She straightened up to her full height.

"I knew I could count on you." He looked over at Lord Regin and nodded.

"That's it, everyone," Lord Regin said in his bass rumble of a voice. "The Huntmaster will meet you in the stables to go over your plans. When will that be?" The last was directed at her.

"Let's say in four hours?"

Lord Regin raised an eyebrow. "Are you asking or ordering?"

"Four hours, everyone. Be there."

"You heard her." He walked toward the gathered hunters, shooing them toward the now-open door to the corridor.

Mary Alice turned to leave with them, but Tedrick caught her elbow.

"Not you," he said. "We have more to discuss, but away from the ears of others."

She stood and waited while Lord Regin closed the door and turned back to them.

"Clearing those areas for my subjects to settle is vitally important," Tedrick said. "I want you to work on that, but I also need you to do something for me."

"Of course," Mary Alice said. "Whatever you need. You're in charge."

"The Lord Seneschal informed me of the lighting of the moonstones during the Ritual of Binding in the Heart. The former Seneschal was of the opinion that it was a result of magical fluctuations brought on by the ceremony. There is a reason they call it Wild Magic, after all."

"Former Seneschal?" Mary Alice asked.

"He has retired," Tedrick said. "It seems the death of the old king was too much for him. Lord Regin has agreed to take his place."

"Congratulations," she said to Lord Regin.

The grey fae inclined his head gravely.

"I need you to track down the cur that set off the moonstones," the king said. "It can't be allowed to roam here. Who knows how many of my subjects it will devour."

"I'll get some of the Wild Hunt on it." It would be easy enough to let them wander the countryside looking for a werewolf that was back in the castle.

"No. I want you and you alone to handle this. No one is to know."

"So what you're saying is that you want me to track down one creature while also overseeing the group that goes after hundreds of Bottom-Dwellers? I don't mean to be rude, Your Majesty, but how am I supposed to be in two places at once?"

"If the court finds out there was a cur in my realm, they'll panic. You underestimate the danger even one of those things represents." He leaned forward, jabbing his finger against the edge of the table for emphasis. "You're the one with the experience against these animals. You will take care of tracking this one down."

Mary Alice straightened her spine and placed her hands behind her back. "The moonstones aren't bright anymore. That means it's gone, doesn't it?"

"If it got in once, it can get in again," Lord Regin said. It was a shock to hear him enter the argument after staying silent so far. "There are areas of the realm that are leakier than others. The edges, for example. It's how we could see into the Summerlands. My guess is it came through a random portal, then went back the way it came. There's nothing to stop it from entering any time it wants."

"I'll see what I can do," Mary Alice said.

"If there's anything else you know about our little werewolf problem, I expect you to tell me," Tedrick said.

The urge to tell him about Ruri squeezed in around her brain. Mary Alice studied the table with its upside-down mountains and the tiny castle which somehow still held enough detail for little pennants of maroon and grey to flutter atop the towers. She leaned against the table. The room's light focused and caught the gold wire wrapping the wooden claw charm on her bracelet. It winked at her.

"I'll make sure to keep you updated on my progress, my lord." Hopefully there hadn't been too long a pause before she answered.

"Of course you will." Tedrick stared through her, then looked over at Lord Regin.

The grey fae walked over to the door and held it open. The implication was clear. Mary Alice bowed stiffly to the king and made her way from the room. The bracelet on her wrist felt strange. She wasn't used to wearing jewelry, and she had no idea how it would affect her combat abilities. Ruri had been so adamant, though, and she hadn't been able to turn her down.

It was hours before she was supposed to meet with the members of the Wild Hunt to discuss their campaign against the Bottom-Dwellers. She could have headed back to the room she shared with Ruri, but that didn't feel right either. Her interaction with the king wasn't sitting right. Part of her wanted to run back and tell him all about Ruri, but the sane part of her knew that instinct was foolish in the extreme. But where was it coming from?

She needed to get her head on straight, and there was one way she knew to do that.

Mary Alice headed down to the Wild Hunt's stables. A few of the hunters milled about, one of whom she recognized.

"Freki," she said. "What are your opinions on a friendly bout?"

"A bout?" The fae woman lifted one of her eyebrows quizzically. "What were you thinking?"

"Just some sparring. We can keep it bloodless if you like."

"Bloodless?" Freki grinned. Her teeth took on points for a brief moment, then disappeared so quickly Mary Alice thought she must have imagined them. "Where's the fun in that?"

An answering smile tugged at the edges of Mary Alice's mouth. "Perfect. Do you have any preference in weapons? I'm thinking a sword for me."

"I can work with that." Freki pointed down the hall toward the courtyard. "There's a training salle next to the horse stables. I'll meet you there as soon as you're ready."

After a quick stop at the armory to choose a sword, Mary Alice found the training salle without issue. She warmed up, running through her katas while ignoring the stares and whispers of the fae using the salle. When Freki arrived, they wasted no time in climbing into the ring at the salle's center. The fae hunter was quick and she handled her long spear as if she'd been born with it in her hands. Malice smiled. This was going to be fun.

They were evenly matched, and their sparring took on an edge that attracted a crowd of fae to them. Back and forth they went, the fae shouting encouragement to Freki with only a few appreciative yells for Malice's success. This went on until Malice sidestepped a lunge from her opponent, then slid down the length of the spear, ending up inside the reach of the weapon with the tip of the sword leveled at Freki's gut. The hunter froze as Malice pushed forward enough for the sword to barely pierce her clothes. A small spot of blood appeared on her white shirt.

"First blood." Malice stepped back, a wide smile crossing her face. She ran her thumb over the wire-wrapped wolf claw at her wrist. It hadn't gotten in the way at all. In fact, touching it made her feel even closer to Ruri, which would never be a bad thing.

"Congratulations, Huntmaster," Freki said. "You kicked my ass."

"You kept me on my toes."

"Not enough." Freki shook her head ruefully, soaked locks swaying with the movement of her head. "You're not even sweating."

"Yeah, well." Malice turned away. She wasn't about to explain her physiology to anyone here who didn't already know. A nearby fae handed her a towel, which she tossed to Freki.

A commotion rippled through the gathered watchers. Someone was forcing their way through the crowd. By the curses and exclamations, the fae weren't too thrilled about it. When Ruri and Jermayne appeared at the side of the ring, Malice could see why.

"The drake took her!" Jermayne yelled.

"What?" Malice started toward him.

At his side, Ruri was keeping back any fae who tried to get too close to the distraught teen.

"The icedrake. The one the king rides." He was panting, looking up into the faces of the fae on either side. They stared back at him without expression.

Malice knelt at the edge of the ring. She grabbed his shoulder and pulled him around to look at her. "Slow down and focus. The drake took who?"

"Shejuanna. It got out of its pen. When we tried to herd it back in, it grabbed her and took off. Someone left the stable doors open." Tears stood in his eyes and he struggled not to shed them. "It got out the gates. It's gone and it has her!"

Ruri shoved an impassive fae out of the way and looked up at her. "Mal, we have to go. We have to get her back."

"Yes, we do." She looked around at the fae. "Anyone who wants is free to come. We're going on a drake hunt!"

Silence met her words. She looked over at Freki, but the fae woman didn't meet her eyes. Malice looked up, seeking out the hunters she knew in the crowd, but no one would look at her.

"For fuck's sake, people," Malice said. "A kid's life is in danger."

"A human child," someone yelled from the back of the crowd. "Against a drake? It's likely dead already."

"You would have us go against an icedrake for the sake of a human?" called another. "It's folly without worth."

When Malice tried to pick out the hecklers, she couldn't. It could have been any of them.

"That's a hell of a thing," she said. She squeezed through the ropes and dropped down next to Jermayne. The fae moved away from her as if she were radioactive. "A hell of a thing. Come on," she said to Jermayne. At least she knew she could count on Ruri. She didn't have to check to see if the wolven was coming to save a human.

CHAPTER FORTY-TWO

The pale horse Ruri rode flickered from coat to bones and back again. Mal rode next to her, the reins from Ruri's horse in one hand while Ruri leaned far out of the saddle to watch the ground. The icedrake had left obvious signs of passage, so tracking wasn't difficult. Large gouges of earth from its impressive claws told her they were on the right track. Chunks of wet bark told her they were falling behind. When they'd first started out after Shejuanna, those signs had still been frozen.

The terrain was familiar on the occasions she looked up. She'd been through it more than once. It seemed they were headed toward the hodag's old territory once again.

The pale horse kept up its canter, moving tirelessly beneath the canopy. That was one advantage of the beasts. The only reason they weren't galloping was that Ruri couldn't read the ground for tracks at that pace.

She wasn't about to let this place claim another of the kids. That thought and the comforting presence of her mate by her side kept her focused. Ruri knew Mal would lead her true.

Sure enough, the patches of ice and water eventually dissipated and she was no longer able to depend on them. The furrows of earth torn up by the drake's claws were still fairly easy to locate, but the beast was so long that there was a fair bit of distance between gouges.

"What's wrong?" Mal demanded when Ruri reached forward and pulled back on the reins, slowing them to a walk.

"Nothing yet," Ruri said. She didn't look up. "Just trying to see where… There it is." She touched her heels to the pale horse's side and it lurched back into a canter.

"What's the matter?" Mal asked the next time Ruri reclaimed the reins to slow her mount.

"The trail is getting trickier to follow. Maybe don't ask every time I need to slow down, okay?"

"Fine. It's just that I really don't want to lose her."

"I know. I'm doing the best I can here. I can't control that it's moving faster than we are." Ruri spared a glance up and a brief smile. "You know I'll give you a heads up if something is really wrong."

"Got it."

"And so do I." Ruri urged her mount forward faster to follow this new set of tracks.

They had a few minutes of panic when they lost the tracks on the far side of a river.

Mal chafed visibly at their lost time while Ruri cast about for signs of the drake's passage. She didn't say anything, but Ruri could feel the anxiety rolling off her in waves.

"Found them," Ruri said when she spotted the long trench halfway up the side of a steep dirt embankment. The drake hadn't headed straight across. Instead it had allowed the water to push it downstream a ways before crawling out the other side. Though now that she thought of it, it was likelier it had waded in and formed an ice floe around itself, which had been pushed downstream before it could emerge. She hoped Shejuanna hadn't been injured in the attempt.

She noted a bush that sat precariously at the top of the slope. They would make their way back to it and continue from there. "We need to find a way up. There's no way the horses can make that climb."

"Are you sure?" Mal eyed the dirt slope. "I think I could make it."

"Unless you want to carry it on your back, it's not getting up this way."

"If you say so." Mal urged her pale horse into a trot along the water's edge.

Ruri followed along. She'd taken back her reins while they were looking. It was ten minutes while they looked for a way up and another ten minutes as they scrambled to the top of the embankment, then again as long to make their way to where the drake's tracks picked up.

She tossed the reins to Mal, then bent low over the pale horse's neck as they picked their way onward. This side of the river, the trees thinned out and the hills became more angular. Large boulders and exposed chunks of bedrock littered the landscape, replacing the majestic trees they'd ridden beneath before making the crossing. She'd been here before. Occasionally, a fresh scrape from the drake would cross an old one left by the hodag. Those became more numerous as they got closer to the hodag's lair.

"This area looks familiar," Mal said.

"It should." Ruri gestured past her. "Ylana's cottage was that way."

They were in a narrow ravine between two hills. As they came around the corner, Ruri recognized the entrance to a cave.

"It went in there," she said.

"Are you sure?" Mal stared at the narrow slit between massive rocks.

Ruri looked at Mal, her arms crossed over her chest.

Mal's cheeks flushed a delicate red. "Of course you are. Let's go." She jumped down off her mount.

Ruri lowered herself to the ground. "There's one thing you should know about this place. I'm not sure what it means or if it's relevant, but this is near where the hodag came through. It could be the one it used, but it seems small for that. I think there's another portal to our world around here somewhere."

"How do you know all that?" Mal held up her hand before Ruri could answer. "You know what, fill me in on it after we get Shejuanna back. I'm sure you had a good reason." She drew her sword and started toward the cave entrance.

Ruri stayed put behind her. She fingered the silver armband through the thin fabric of her shirt. They should have stopped for some armor, at least for Mal. Fortunately for her, she wasn't going to need armor or weapons, but the same couldn't be said for the Hunter. Maybe leaving with just their mounts and what they had with them had been a little short-sighted.

"Are you coming?" Mal asked when she realized Ruri hadn't followed her.

"Yes, but not like this." She stripped off her shirt and tossed it to Mal, then bent down to unlace her boots.

"Are you sure that's a good idea? It might give us away."

Ruri kicked off her boots, then started to shimmy her breeches down over her hips. "That thing isn't going to go down without a fight. Better that I shift now than in the middle of it." She dropped to her hands and knees, then looked up at Mal. "Bring my clothes along, please. I'll need them again after." She pulled the armband down over her hand.

The wolf rushed into her like the warm spring wind over winter's barren landscape. Ruri surrendered to her without thought. The shift, which occurred in the space of mere heartbeats, toppled her onto her side. Scrabbling to her feet, she nosed at the silver band on the ground. The wolf tried to kick dirt over it, but Mal came over and rescued it before it could be buried.

There's a youngling in the cave, Ruri told the wolf. *We have to get it out, but it's guarded by a fearsome beast.* She brought an image of the icedrake to mind, detailing its sinuous length and the vapor that rose from its body as ice hit warm air. She lingered on the sharp claws and even sharper teeth. It didn't take long before she felt the wolf's assent. This was a worthy task.

She joined Mal at the entry to the cave. Mal apparently thought she was going to lead the way, but Ruri nosed past her into the narrow tunnel. Taking point made sense given her ability to see through glamours, something Mal lacked.

The tunnel was barely more than a crevice. The stone ground and walls were scored by claw marks, some much deeper than they had any right to be. The air drifting from the cave smelled of dry cold. Such smells were to be expected while out on a frigid winter's day, but not here. The cold of a forest was unconcerned with those who went about their business. It didn't care about much and floated past them. This cold was very much interested in them. She could feel its gaze.

Despite a chill that grew steadily more intense, Ruri pressed on, Mal close at her heels. The wolf was happy to know her mate was nearby; her presence was like a warmth at their back.

It didn't take long once they'd entered the passageway before the light had almost completely vanished. Mal was navigating pretty well, but it wouldn't be long before both of them were blind. The dark did nothing to allay the feeling of being watched.

The terrain was rocky and unforgiving and the deeper they ventured into the cave, the icier it got. It took everything Ruri had and judicious application of her toenails not to slide all over the place. Mal was having a much harder time of it. She'd already taken one nasty fall. Ruri had a faint ache along her cheekbone, one that throbbed in sympathetic time with the rapidly purpling bruise on the side of Mal's face.

Staying on her feet required so much concentration that it took Ruri a moment to realize the interior of the passage was growing subtly lighter. By the time the crevice finally widened into a cavern about thirty feet across, pale blue light made it possible to see that every surface was glistening with a thin layer of ice.

The cold's sharp interest became razor-edged. Something slithered over a hard surface in one corner of the cave. She turned her head to follow the sound of scales on ice as it shifted to a large boulder, then to a broken column against a far wall. Slithering filled the space as the walls of the cavern shifted around them. Those ice-covered rocks cracked and coiled. Ruri turned, placing her rump against Mal's leg, covering her mate's back.

The blue glow in the cavern's far corner brightened, then drifted closer. As it came nearer, Ruri made out a head lit up by the bright blue flame of its eyes. It was easily five feet across with a pair of unwinking blue orbs now trained upon them. That was its body that coiled around the edges of the cavern, scales sliding over each other. Ruri watched, horrified as her mind made sense of the moving body parts surrounding them.

* * *

The thing was bigger than Malice could have believed, far larger than it had looked when King Tedrick had been riding it. When she'd last seen it, it had been maybe eight or nine feet long. Now it was maybe twice as long as the hodag had been. She couldn't keep all of it in front of her. Pure instinct had her back to back with Ruri, but the wolf slipped away suddenly, leaving her exposed in the center of the cavern.

The icedrake hissed, a surprisingly melodic sound of cracking ice and brass. It lunged forward, its massive head striking toward her. Malice dropped into a roll and bounced back up, her sword in front of her. The drake's beak-like muzzle snapped together where her head had been. She wasn't sure how much damage she could do with a blade, not when it seemed the size of a toothpick compared to the bulk of the beast crawling toward her. She thought longingly of the shotgun in the back of her pickup truck. The mortal world had never seemed so far away. She would have given her left arm for a flamethrower.

Ruri was still out there, and if Malice knew her girlfriend, she was trying to get the drop on the drake. It was up to her to keep it focused completely on her.

The drake struck at her again, trying to take a chunk out of her torso. Malice had been expecting a move like that. She dropped to one knee and swiveled to the side. As its head streaked past her, she brought the long sword down on it, aiming for where its head met its neck. The blade bounced off the heavily armored neck. Instead of recoiling, the icedrake swept its head into her. It was like getting hit by a boulder that radiated bone-chilling cold. The blow carried her halfway across the cavern.

With a snarl, Malice tried to get her feet under her and lunge back toward the beast. Her feet slipped about until one caught enough purchase to propel her in the direction she wanted to go. She slid toward it, her sword hand trailing along the ground, barely staying upright. With her other hand, she grabbed hold of the bony projections on the icedrake's neck, the same gnarled plates that had prevented her sword from biting into its flesh. Icy cold flashed through her hand. She wished she'd thought to grab some gloves or any kind of protective gear. Her muscles were one concentrated ache of cold, but she forced her fingers to keep their grip, gritting her teeth against the pain. The drake paused, looking around for her, and she took advantage of its confusion to pull herself fully onto its neck. Cold leached into her from every place her body made contact with its skin. Ruri was still out there. Malice brought the hilt of her sword down on the top of the icedrake's head.

"I'm right here, asshole," she shouted at it and reversed the sword in her hand.

The massive head swiveled and one intensely blue eye stared at her. Its pupil was in the shape of an X, she noticed with abstracted bemusement. Sprays of blue and white emanated from the intersection of its pupil in a constantly shifting field that reminded her a bit of science fiction movies when the heroes traveled at hyperspeed. It had been a long time since she'd watched any sci-fi and Mary Alice wondered if Ruri would be up for it. They could cuddle together on the couch and watch it on the laptop. Not that her superiors would be overjoyed at that use of government property, but she figured they couldn't bitch about it too much. After all, she was always on. Her mission didn't afford her any time for leave, not when a supra could go rogue at any moment and she was the only one there to cover her area. Who had thought it was a good idea for one Hunter to cover fifteen states, anyway? The wisdom of her superiors was definitely suspect in that area, not that they'd had much choice in the matter, not when half the cohort they'd been training died during the process. And that didn't take into account those who had died while performing their duties. How long until she was the last one standing?

A sharp scream interrupted her train of thought. Mary Alice shook her head, trying to focus through the haze of unconnected thoughts. What was going on again?

The ice-covered cavern snapped into place around her. The icedrake's eye was closed, its mouth agape as its roar of pain thundered on and on. She slid to one side as it thrashed out its agony. Desperate to keep from being thrown, Malice stabbed the sword into the beast's neck, aiming for a gap between two bony plates. Ruri was close, below her.

The sword tip slipped on the plate, scratching a shallow groove into the blue-tinged bone. She threw her weight behind it nonetheless, praying it would hit something with some give. The blade skittered, then caught. It slid into the drake's neck, behind the bone-frilled jaw. Not daring to let go with her other hand, Malice leaned into the thrust, using her body to drive the sword in all the way to its hilt. Ice flashed into place over the handle, freezing over her hand, trapping it and the blade against the creature's scaled skin.

The drake reared back, rising to its full height. Malice looked up in time to see the ceiling rushing at her. She threw herself to the side, trusting her body's weight to break her hand out of its icy prison. She tumbled off the beast's neck as it slammed into the roof of the cave. She landed on her back without any chance to protect herself. Chunks of ice and stone rained down on her, but she scarcely noticed them as she worked to get some air back into her shocked lungs.

CHAPTER FORTY-THREE

Ruri kept her grip on the underside of the beast's freezing neck. Her jaws were locked and nothing short of a massive crowbar being wielded by an even more massive being could have pried her free. Blue blood dripped into her mouth, so cold it burned wherever it touched. The beast was trying to shake her off, but she kept her grim hold, no matter how her body shook and flew.

Mal was doing something up there, but she couldn't see what. She could feel her determination, almost as cold as the scaled beast she fought. Her mate would be fine; she couldn't spare another thought for her as she clung, the drake's flailing growing ever more desperate.

It reared up, smashing into the cavern's ceiling. Mal tumbled to the side, landing on the cave floor with a thud. Ruri kept steady, but the wolf tried to push her aside. She wanted to get to Mal. For a moment, the wolf won out and she released their hold. They dropped to the floor next to their mate. She lay on her back, gasping like a landed fish.

Satisfied that Mal would be fine, the wolf launched them back at the drake, but it had already recoiled, shielding the horrible wound on its throat.

That was too bad. Ruri tried to get the upper hand, but the wolf was too entrenched to permit it. They circled, dodging and weaving as they looked for an opening in the drake's defenses. It followed them, its head keeping up with every movement. They shifted away from Mal, keeping the drake's eyes on them while she recovered.

Its eyes darted over to their mate, and they took the opportunity to attack. They dashed toward a clawed foot and bit down on one of the toes.

The icedrake roared, sending icicles crashing down throughout the cave. Blue blood flooded into the wolf's mouth. The first splash numbed their tongue and gums, but the wolf held on, biting through skin and scales until they hit bone. She flexed their jaws and their teeth ground into the bone. The drake flailed, shaking its foot with all its strength. The toe gave and they flew off into the back of the cave, the massive toe still between their teeth. The drake screamed as the digit was ripped free of its body. It surged after them as they tumbled to the ground in a jumble of limbs. They rolled once, twice, then couldn't stop the pained yelp as they fetched up against an ice-covered wall. There was no time to take stock of what was hurt. The icedrake's maw yawned in front of them.

They scrabbled against the slick floor as the drake inhaled. Finally, their claws caught something not covered in ice and they pushed themselves forward. It wasn't an impressive bound; they'd had very little traction. But it was enough to get them out of the nightmarish cone of sleet and howling wind that burst forth from the drake's mouth. Their back end didn't quite make it, and their tail and one leg went numb after an incredible flash of pain. One back leg was still enough to keep moving, especially since the drake's head had turned to follow them. They kept careening forward to stay ahead of the horrible breath until it finally stopped.

The icedrake stared at them, its sides heaving. They didn't stop, but they were breathing heavily also.

The drake's head whipped away from them.

"That's right, you piece of shit," Mal yelled from across the cavern. "Leave her the fuck alone!"

They scooted around to get a better view of her. She stood next to the beast's flank, armed with nothing but her combat knife. The hilt of her sword winked from between two large plates. It didn't seem to be troubling the drake too much. The knife dripped slowly with blue blood that froze as it fell. Shards hit the floor and shattered with a sound like ringing crystal. Mal lunged forward, driving the knife through one of the massive scales that armored the beast's belly. It sank in with little resistance.

The drake whined, more in disbelief than in actual pain. The squeal that followed when Mal twisted the knife was definitely one of anger. It reared back, filling its lungs with the cave's glacial air.

The wolf struck. The wound they'd inflicted on the underside of its throat had already iced over, so they aimed at the side of its neck. They bounded forward as it inhaled even more deeply. The wolf surveyed the expanse of neck before sinking their teeth into the base where it met shoulder. Their powerful jaws snapped scales and sank into the muscles beneath them. The drake cried out, coughing gouts of ice as it writhed.

When its head was close enough, they let go and propelled themselves toward it, latching on to the softer skin behind the bone-protected jaw. The skin parted like paper. The drake howled again. It whipped its head back and forth, trying to slam them against the wall, doing everything it could to shake them off. The wolf refused to yield. She had a job to do.

The drake flailed its entire body, tossing Mal away from it in a desperate paroxysm of agony. They felt Mal's pain as she impacted something. The wolf took advantage of Ruri's distraction and pulled on their combined strength and bit down with all their might. Their jaw trembled with the strain, then the remaining scales on the beast's neck snapped. Thick muscle gave under the onslaught of tooth and might and a chunk of the drake's neck disintegrated in a splash of blue liquid.

They disengaged as the beast collapsed. As soon as their paws hit the slick ice floor, they scrabbled away from the tumbling corpse. Its blood froze as it hit the air, coagulating into a spiky fountain the color of the clear sky on the coldest days.

Ruri was already casting about for Mal before they'd cleared the crush zone. She hadn't been far from them when she'd disappeared from view. It was hard to smell much of anything in here, frigid as it was. She whined in quiet disappointment, then closed her eyes.

Mal pulsed as a warm spot in her mind on the far side of the cave. The pain they'd felt when she was thrown clear had faded. She healed almost as quickly as the wolven, and she had all their ferocity and more. Ruri pulled herself up. The numbness in her hindquarters was gone, pushed away by the burst of warmth and energy that had filled her with the drake's death. It didn't feel like she'd been through a battle. It felt more like she'd just come back from a particularly rejuvenating run with the pack. Ruri only had one pack member now. Mal didn't feel too injured, but she had to make sure. A warming wind from the cave's mouth increased as she made her way across the floor. Already, puddles were forming as the ice brought by the drake was melting.

Mal was on her feet when she found her. She spared a moment to drop to her knees and throw her arms around Ruri's neck, not caring that her fur was liberally coated with the blue ichor. She was painted with more than a little bit herself. Ruri's shoulders relaxed as she gave her mate a quick once-over, smelling her, checking for signs of wounds that adrenaline wouldn't let her feel but that would bleed nonetheless. To her relief, she found nothing. It appeared Mal had escaped the battle more or less unscathed.

Mal let her go, then went back to searching between the rocks of the cave's edges.

The youngling, Ruri thought to the wolf. It was the whole reason they'd come here.

The wolf leant her nose to the search. It didn't take long to find her squeezed in between a couple of massive slabs of rock. She was far back between them, well out of the reach of the wolf's muzzle. The girl tried to squeeze herself further in when she saw the massive wolf's head coming for her.

"I'll get her," Mal said. "I bet she's about ready to go home."

*　*　*

"Are you all right?" Malice asked Shejuanna after coaxing her out of her hideyhole.

The teen sported some long scratches along her arms and a particularly deep cut on one cheek. None of her wounds was bleeding, though the amount of frozen crimson blood on her face was mute evidence that it had bled for quite some time.

"I think so," Shejuanna said. Her breath left large clouds of vapor in the air. It was warming rapidly in the cavern as the icedrake's body decomposed, but it was still damn cold.

"I'm sorry, but we didn't think to bring any extra clothes," Malice said. "Let's get you out of here so you can warm up."

Ruri moved away from her side.

Shejuanna's gaze followed the massive wolf with her golden fur. Now that there was no drake to be terrified by, it appeared she was transferring her fear to Ruri.

"It's all right." Malice recognized the stance the wolf was taking, with her legs braced and her tail and head down. "That's Ruri. She's a wolven—a werewolf."

"Werewolves?" Shejuanna stared at Ruri in fascination. "Those don't exist."

"No more than fairies," Malice said. She scanned the cave for signs of further danger. Ruri was at her most vulnerable during the change.

"Yeah, but I've seen those."

"And now you've seen her." The shadows were clear, as best she could tell. The melting ice made it a little difficult to get a bead on things, but nothing in the cave pressed against her skin. Nothing except the warm spot she always got from Ruri in her wolf form. Heat flared along that spot as her energy spiked and Ruri shifted.

Mal had seen the transformation more times than she could count, but it was different being there with Shejuanna. What must she have been thinking watching muscles writhe beneath tawny fur? The crack of bone being forced into place while the fur receded to reveal pink flesh happened gradually at first, then all at once. A moment later, Ruri crouched before them, the skin on her back covered in a sheen of sweat. Steam rose off her. At least this part of the change was much neater than the other.

"Holy balls," Shejuanna breathed.

"Not really," Ruri said as she straightened her back. She made no attempt to hide her nudity, but she rubbed her hands briskly over the skin on her upper arms.

"I'll be right back." Malice hurried off to gather Ruri's clothes from where she'd dropped them in the tunnel leading to the cave mouth. "Here." She handed them over. "How was your wolf?"

"She's not happy about any of this." Ruri snatched her clothing and hurriedly donned it. "I had to talk fast to get her to agree to go back, especially knowing this is going back on." She held up the arm band that had been wrapped up in her pants, then slid it up her arm.

"I'm glad you're back," Malice said. There was so much more she wanted to say, but not in front of Shejuanna. "Let's get her back to the castle."

"Agreed." Ruri picked her way carefully around still-icy patches of ground, stopping at a boulder to lace up her boots before heading toward the cave mouth.

Malice took the time to retrieve her sword. It still stuck out of the icedrake's neck, but the skin had receded from around it. She pulled it out easily, then wiped the blade off on a relatively unsullied patch of its hide before settling it back in its scabbard. The blue glow from the icedrake's eyes still lit up the room, but it was fading. Much longer and they'd be in the dark. She met up with the other two at the mouth of the tunnel. Ruri started into the crevice as soon as she joined them.

"Go ahead," Malice said to Shejuanna.

The teen followed close on Ruri's heels. She watched her closely, as if Ruri might turn on her at any moment.

Malice shook her head. She took up the rear, keeping her wits about her to make sure they weren't ambushed from behind. It seemed unlikely, but she wasn't going to lose someone to an assumption.

They made their way slowly through the tunnel that connected the cavern to the outside. The light behind them faded, and the tunnel got dark enough that Shejuanna pulled out her phone and turned on the flashlight so she could pick her way around the larger boulders and sharp chips of stone that littered the floor of the passage. Eventually, daylight from the opening of the crevice made the phone unnecessary. Shejuanna tucked it back into a belt pouch. The light dimmed for a moment as Ruri stepped through the opening.

"Uh, Mal," she said, "we have a problem." Her voice filtered back unsteadily to Malice.

Shejuanna looked back at her, eyes questioning.

"Stay put," Malice said as she tried to maneuver past the teen. "Don't come out until I call for you by name."

"Okay." Shejuanna squeezed to the side to allow her to pass.

"What's going on?" Malice asked when she stepped back into the sunlight. "Oh."

Mounted fae surrounded the cave mouth. More looked down on them from the heights. She had no doubt that if she looked behind them, she'd see more fae there as well. These were those she recognized. Lord Regin sat astride his giant lizard. In the same bunch was Freki on her dog-insect thing. The rest she recognized from their hunts.

They all pointed weapons their way. Malice couldn't count the number of bows and spears that were leveled at them.

"What brings the Wild Hunt out here?" Malice asked. She stepped forward to stand next to Ruri, who had her hands raised.

"Oh, Lady Malice" came a familiar voice from the ranks of hunters in front of them. They parted to reveal King Tedrick astride the kelpie. He guided his mount forward. "The moonstones quickened again. Imagine my surprise when we discovered you at their source."

CHAPTER FORTY-FOUR

Ruri kept her eyes on the ring of fae surrounding them, but her attention was focused on the fae king. He ignored her completely while he glared at Mal, who had stepped forward and angled her body so it was between them.

"I don't understand what you're saying," Mal said.

Tedrick laughed, a harsh sound that contained none of the musical qualities King Connall's had. It reminded Ruri of the harsh cries of scavenger birds.

"Come now, Lady Malice," he said. "You've been playing me for a fool this entire time. I have to hand it to you. Your performance has been nothing short of masterful, but you really shouldn't have worn your totem in front of me."

"Totem?" Mal glared at him. "What are you even talking about?"

"Do not play your games with me." He stared back at her expectantly.

Ruri lowered her arms, then crossed them. No one said anything; they paid attention only to her mate.

"Was your plan to take down the realm?" King Tedrick's lip curled. "Was that it, cur?"

Mal shook her head. "I've never wanted to take down this place. All I wanted was to go home, but Connall wouldn't let me." She took a step toward the king.

Tedrick shook his head and raised a finger on his right hand. Two fae stepped forward and interposed themselves between Mal and the king. "I knew the cur in my realm had to be one of the humans who had most recently arrived." He smiled, a malevolent grin that twisted his lips but never touched his eyes. "My loyal steed took the girl, and you followed her as I expected you would. Humans clump together like filth. It is really too bad you had to kill my icedrake." He shrugged. "But his mate sits on a clutch of eggs. I'll be able to replace him soon enough."

Ruri stared at the fae king, the bottom dropping out of her stomach. They'd killed that drake thinking it had snapped and gone after the kids. Acid churned in her belly. It had been a pawn, its death no more necessary than that of the hodag.

"I knew it had to be you when you shook off my charm spell," he said.

"Charm spell?" Mal's voice was quiet; Ruri had to strain to hear it. "You charmed me?"

Ruri took a step back toward the mouth of the cave. Nothing good happened when Mal's voice got that quiet.

A shimmer started in the air to their left, then rippled out from the center, growing wider by the second.

The ripple seemed to spread to the gathered fae as they noticed the shimmer.

"King Tedrick," Lord Regin said, "a portal is opening. Your guards!"

Four Tuatha materialized out of the crowd and descended on Tedrick to form a protective square. The king scowled and tried to wave them away, but they ignored his direction. He craned his neck to see around the two armored fae in front of him.

Ruri took a few steps back. No one was paying the least bit of attention to her. She ducked inside the cave and started yanking on the ties of her boots. The rest of her clothing would tear as the wolf forced her body into its other form, but boots were made of sterner stuff.

"What's happening?" Shejuanna spoke in a harsh whisper from right behind Ruri.

"Stay put," Ruri said as she peeled off the boots.

"If you don't tell me what's going on, I'm going to check for myself."

Ruri sighed. "The king and the Wild Hunt think Mal is one of the wolven. They were confronting her about it, but a portal is opening and now they're more worried about that."

"Why do they care if Lady Malice is a werewolf?"

Ruri cringed at the slur. "We're called wolven. And the fae don't get along with my kind. Apparently it's some ancient beef about wolven being created to protect humans from the fae, but it's so long ago that I don't remember it."

"So what you're saying is they don't like you."

The considering tone in Shejuanna's voice had the hairs on the back of Ruri's neck standing on end. She looked back at the teen.

"No, they don't," Ruri said. "But how much do they really like you?" Shejuanna opened her mouth to answer, but Ruri kept on talking. "Simeon could have been healed, did you know that? When Mal and I fought the hodag, they gave us a drink that healed our wounds up completely. Why didn't they use that on him?"

"Why on you then?" Her words were hot, pushing against Ruri in pained accusation.

"They had another use for us." Ruri tilted her head. "How many mounts in your stables have creepy human eyes?"

The question took the heat out of Shejuanna. While she was struggling with it, Ruri pressed on.

"Why did just the two of us come after you? If they care so much, there should have been a big group of us. They simply were not interested."

"That can't be right. What about the others?"

"They were told to go back to work. Jermayne came close to punching someone."

"Sounds like him." Shejuanna deflated, the bravado seeping out of her before Ruri's eyes.

Ruri felt bad for being so blunt with the teen, but the last thing she needed was for her to attempt to curry favor with the fae while Ruri was trying to pull her mate out of the fire.

She had no idea what was going on out there. She crept to the cave mouth to find out.

* * *

Malice glared at King Tedrick behind his wall of guards. They wouldn't be able to protect him for long. She'd already calculated four different ways of getting to him. She was having issues wrapping her head around ways to actually kill him. Her mind skittered away from those scenarios.

Charm her, would he? The manner of his death would be a surprise to both of them.

She took one step forward, but some of the hunters had still been watching her. Half a dozen bows lifted and pointed her way. She couldn't feel Ruri's comforting presence at her back. She must have taken advantage of the distraction to get back inside the cave. Malice grinned. The hunters and their king were in for one hell of a shock.

The shimmer of the portal was now large enough for a normal-sized person to pass through. Lord Regin would have had some trouble, but the rest could have passed through easily. The fae knew it also.

"You lot," Lord Regin bellowed. "Weapons on her. The rest of you, take care of whatever comes through that portal."

They waited in tense silence. The moment stretched as the portal remained, but no one stepped out. Finally, a dark-skinned woman's head and torso appeared among the shimmers in the air. She bent down and through. Scaled coils followed her body, then Mami Wata turned and looked at the king.

"Ah," she said. "My old friend, the Jaeger. How fare you these days?"

"Old friend?" Malice said. "You two know each other?"

"Oh yes." Mami Wata shifted forward on sidewinding coils. "Well, for a time. He was quite interested in what I had to say a few years ago. He wanted the 'Witch of Lake LaBette' to tell him how he could become king."

Two of the guards protecting Tedrick shifted to sneak looks at their ruler. So too did a number of the hunters. Lord Regin's eye flicked back and forth between Malice and the snake woman.

"Is that true?" Malice recognized Freki's voice.

"The time of two Huntmasters was the sign you'd been waiting for, was it not? Did you have to talk good King Connall into making you heir, or was that his idea?"

"I never spoke to him of it," Tedrick said. He picked his words with obvious care. The gathered fae muttered amongst themselves.

"Have you found your cur yet?" She swayed in place.

Tedrick's eyes followed her. Sweat stood out on his forehead, a sickly sheen that Malice could see from where she stood.

"I have." He pulled himself up to his full height. "She's right here." He pointed an accusing finger at Malice.

Mami Wata's face twitched and writhed before splitting in a huge grin. She threw her head back and guffawed, the beads in her hair clicking merrily against each other in rhythm with her mirth.

"You really think the Hunter is the cur that summons your downfall?" she finally said. "Your reign will last until a cur leads the Wild Hunt, that is what I told you." She shook her head. "I'm beginning to think you don't have the intelligence to govern our people."

"*My* people," Tedrick growled. "You are not fit to live among us."

"So say you, but you are not fit to be king. If the Hunter was your cur, your reign would have ended before it began, instead of merely teetering on the edge of ruin."

"You forget, witch." His eyes glowed with triumph. "I control the Wild Hunt! I alone name the Huntmaster. If she isn't the cur, then I'm safe."

"So tell us more about how Connall died when you'd finally maneuvered yourself one step away from ultimate power," Mami Wata said, her tone silky. "Nothing about the prophecy I gave you said you had to kill him."

"I will not start my reign under a cloud of suspicion."

"Then maybe you shouldn't have murdered poor Connall. He was headed for the Summerlands sooner than later. All you had to do was wait, but that was beyond you. Such impatience does not befit a king."

Tedrick ignored Mami Wata's comments and kept on as if she hadn't spoken. "I am king now. My wishes are what guide this realm, and it is my wish that you be gone." He stared at the snake woman as if expecting something to happen.

"I'm afraid that won't work on me." Mami Wata slithered closer to the king, a bland smile on her face. "I'm not one of your subjects, remember? I doubt you've managed the control over the realm your predecessor had. It's a pity he died before he could impart that to you…"

"There's more than one way to wield power." King Tedrick cocked his head in Mami Wata's direction. "Kill her."

Two of his guards started forward. They lowered their polearms in the snake woman's direction. The two who stayed by him were the ones who'd looked back when he'd been accused of Connall's murder. They stood between Tedrick and the snake woman, but stoic faces couldn't completely mask the doubt in their eyes.

The portal shimmered again and Corrigan—no, Reese—stepped through. She was covered in mail that shimmered crimson and silver. In one hand, she wielded a long sword and in the other she carried a cloth-wrapped bundle the same red as her mail and a little shorter than her sword. A simple helm that gleamed too brightly to be steel covered her crest of red hair. Despite its brilliance, remnants of past battles crisscrossed the helmet in darker lines. This was someone who was no stranger to a fray.

"Usurper," the former Heir thundered. Her voice reverberated off the hills and crashed around them in a deafening wave of sound. "I claim my right to combat. You murdered my uncle after poisoning him against me. You are no more fit to rule than you are to take breath. Face me!"

"I don't think so." Tedrick looked up at the hunters surrounding them. "Kill them all," he shouted, then raised both hands to the sky. Darkness boiled above him as clouds formed from his hands and coiled around each other in a steadily widening funnel that reached to the heavens.

The shocked silence was punctuated by growls of thunder.

"Here!" Corrigan tossed the bundle to Malice, who caught it easily. The sheriff swung a large shield off her back and held it up before her in a defensive crouch.

Malice recognized the hilt through the wrapping. She tugged the fabric away to reveal her katana. She grinned.

Light streamed from points all over the hunters and their king.

"She reveals herself," he cried over a crack of thunder. "Attack them."

The hunters raised their bows and released a volley. Arrows whistled through the air toward them. Corrigan raised her shield to intercept those headed her way, but Malice had no such protection. She fell back on what she knew. When defense was impossible, the only other option was in-your-face offense.

She darted forward, hoping to work her way beneath the arcing rain that plummeted toward her. There weren't nearly as many arrows as there should have been. Not everyone had followed the orders of their king.

She managed to avoid most of the arrows. They landed behind her, burying themselves in the ground or hitting the sheriff's shield with solid thunks. They bounced off an invisible barrier around Mami Wata with hisses like water hitting a hot pan.

Malice swatted one arrow out of the air with her katana an unthinking extension of her hand. Fire roared through her shoulder as one arrow flew true. She couldn't stop the cry that forced its way past her lips. She stumbled, but only for a moment. She was halfway to Tedrick, close enough to see his eyes widen when she took another step toward him, the arrow sticking out of her shoulder.

"Again," he cried, then redoubled his efforts to fill the sky with storm clouds.

The guards who had been heading for Mami Wata adjusted their attack and struck out toward Malice.

A howl split the darkening sky. The cries from the hunters were tinged with fear and anger. Those shouts grew louder and more arrows flew from their bows.

"I told you it wasn't me," Malice yelled at Tedrick. "My mate is the one you should have been worrying about, and she's going to make you eat those words!"

She raised her sword, turning away a thrust by the nearest guard. It was a good thing she'd worked out against Freki so recently. Spears were tricky, up until you got inside their reach, and polearms were merely glorified spears. Pain spiked through her shoulder and chest. The damn arrow was in the way. She danced out of reach long enough to grasp the shaft and break it off.

Though she kept her eyes on the guards, the pain was enough to grey out her vision. When it cleared, the guards were closing again. One was already swinging his weapon down toward her.

Malice braced herself for impact.

CHAPTER FORTY-FIVE

At Tedrick's command, Ruri dropped to the cold stone floor of the tunnel and pulled the arm band off.

"What are you doing?" Shejuanna hissed.

Ruri didn't answer. Couldn't answer. Her jaws seized with familiar cramps. The change was slower this time. The wolf demanded to know what was happening. She could tell something was amiss. They'd already shifted recently and the energy for a quick change simply wasn't there.

Ruri groaned. A quick change was excruciating, but over in a hurry. This one lacked the same edge, but she felt every muscle shift, felt the bones bend before snapping into place. Even the fur sprouting from her skin itched with a fire she couldn't quench.

"Are you all right?" Shejuanna hesitated, looking like she wanted to get closer, but anxiety spiked through her scent.

Ruri shook her head and tried to keep from snapping when the teen reached out to her. She lifted her lips in a snarl. Shejuanna snatched her hand back, her scent flashing from anxiety straight into fear.

A wave of echoed pain rippled through her shoulder. Her head snapped up toward the mouth of the cave. Mal. Their mate.

Fur rolled over her and liquid drenched the floor beneath paws that already churned to propel her out of the cave. She ran raggedly, her lungs burning from the effort.

It was much darker outside the tunnel than it had been a few minutes ago when Ruri had reentered. Storm clouds churned over King Tedrick's head, connected to his hands in a long rope of darkness. Two fae closed on Mal.

She let out a howl of rage and pushed herself across the rock-littered ground. Arrow shafts stuck out of the grass at odd angles. As she ran, more projectiles dropped out of the sky. Ruri bounded back and forth in a crazy zigzag pattern. Her muscles vibrated on the edge of exhaustion. An arrow just missed her as a back leg gave out and she tumbled to the side in a jumble of limbs. She pulled herself to her feet and kept on.

As the gap between her and her mate closed, she saw the arrow protruding from Mal's shoulder. She put on a burst of speed, digging her toenails into the hard ground and pushing forward with all her might. The erratic pattern was taking too long.

Another pain echo rippled through her as Mal broke off the shaft sticking out of her shoulder. Mal wavered and the two fae facing off with her jumped on the opening.

Ruri was close enough to smell the triumph coming from them and to hear the grunt of effort as one pulled his long axe back to swing at Mal. The other drove forward toward her with the tip of his axe-thing.

She leaped using a final burst of energy, crashing into the lunging guard and sending him toppling over into the other. She grabbed the guard's throat in her teeth and pulled it out with a quick shake of her head. The guard had time enough to look surprised before the light went out in his eyes. Vigor pulsed through her veins. She got to her feet slowly, eyes never leaving those of the remaining guard.

The guard scrambled away from her, terror on his face. He moved impossibly slowly and it was cub's play to shift around the body of his partner. He fumbled at his belt, trying to draw his dagger from its sheath. His eyes never left hers.

A blade flashed over her shoulder and into his neck, separating his head from his body.

"It's time to run," Mal said to the fae king.

"This is my realm," Tedrick cried. He raised one hand toward the clouds above, then brought it down sharply. In a blinding flash, a bolt of lightning descended. It struck the ground between him and Mal and

Ruri with a deafening roar. The scent of ozone pricked her nostrils. Dirt and small rocks geysered up from the strike and rained down around them, trailing plumes of black smoke. "Mine!"

"He is a usurper and a traitor to the throne and the realm." Reese strode up to stand beside them. Ruri admired her bravery in standing so near a target of lightning while covered with all that metal.

A bellow met her statement. Across the field, a large grey fae on a massive lizard lumbered toward their little group.

"To me, true fae of the realm!" Reese rotated the gleaming sword in her hand. She ran toward the king, but Lord Regin urged his mount forward on an intercept course. Reaching down, he ripped the goggles off the lizard's eyes, then threw them in Reese's direction.

She raised her shield immediately and lowered her gaze but never stopped running toward the king.

The wolf sent a querying thought Ruri's way.

I'm not sure, Ruri thought back at her. *It can't hurt to follow her lead.*

The lizard closed on Reese. In its wake came more hunters. They hollered and whooped, but not in a cohesive group. A sword flashed and a hunter fell, cut down by her compatriot. More weapons rose and fell among the packed hunters. Before long, only a handful of fae followed Lord Regin, but whether they were there to help or hinder him, Ruri couldn't tell.

"Cover the sheriff," Mal yelled. "I'm going after the bastard." She dashed away, leaving Ruri and the wolf to stare after her. The wolf wanted to follow along and cover her, but Ruri insisted on following their mate's orders. She'd only ever fought against a handful of enemies at once, and those had been other wolven. Mal was the expert here. With poor grace, the wolf conceded, and Ruri loped across the hard ground to catch up to Reese.

Reese arrived at the same time Lord Regin did. He directed his mount straight into her. Somehow, she stood her ground but turned and deflected them past her. She kept her head down behind the shield the entire time.

As Ruri darted to one side to cut Regin off, she happened to look the lizard in the face. It stopped in its tracks, locking eyes with them. Cold fire reached down into Ruri's soul, holding her immobile and insensible before it. She was helpless to do anything but stare into eyes that blazed with white fire. They grew to encompass her vision. The sound of battle diminished around her until she floated alone in a sea of white, devoid of anything. She couldn't feel her wolf. She couldn't feel Mal. It was all gone. All of it. *Forever*, a voice whispered in her mind. Mercifully, everything faded to black.

* * *

Malice stalked toward King Tedrick and his inadequate guard contingent. The guards firmed their grips on their weapons, then exchanged glances. One cocked his head at the other who nodded. As one, they stepped back, leaving the path to the king open.

"What are you—" Tedrick backed up a step upon seeing his defenses evaporate. "Attend me. Guard me from her!"

They ignored him and melted into the crowd of hunters who milled about behind their king in confusion. Tedrick raised one hand and brought it down, again calling lightning from the clouds above.

Malice threw up one arm over her eyes to protect them from the bolt that hit the ground between them. Its concussive force jolted through her like a heavy punch to the sternum. She paused, crouching low to keep from being bowled over, then looked back at the so-called king.

He snatched at the sky. The hairs on the back of Malice's arms and neck lifted slightly and her scalp tingled. She braced herself for another strike, but nothing came of it.

Tedrick reached both hands up to pull down the lightning, but beyond a bit of a tingle like muscles on the edge of falling asleep, Malice felt nothing.

"Having problems getting it up?" she called out to him. She had a sister. She knew exactly what kind of edge to add to her tone to get under the skin of another.

He ignored the dig. "Stop her," he ordered the hunters at his back.

A few stepped forward as she closed the gap even further. More hesitated behind, then joined their compatriots, leaving a third contingent who seemed content to bear witness but forbore getting involved. The fae confronting her had bows. Malice broke into a run to render them useless. Her shoulder still throbbed where the arrow had sunk into it. The head and what was left of the shaft plugged the wound, so she was in no danger of bleeding out. The only thing she had to contend with was the pain. That she'd wrapped up into a neat mental package and shoved into a distant corner of her brain.

She was fast. She saw it in the surprise on the faces of the fae as she closed on them. Some had already started to raise their bows to fire. One loosed a shot that went wide when she dodged it. Malice grinned at them.

A flash of fire seared her brain. She was turning to find Ruri before she realized what was happening. She could feel her mate on the battlefield, over where Reese and Lord Regin traded heavy blows with their swords. The sound of metal on metal rang through the air. The tawny wolf slunk around the front of Regin's lizard mount. It followed her with glowing eyes that Malice could see from where she stood.

But Ruri was gone. Time slowed as she tried to make sense of it all. The wolf was there, but the warmth that she associated with her mate was gone.

Sharp pain across her left calf pulled Malice back into her own situation. She whirled to confront her attacker, a lithe fae woman who danced back at her sudden movement. Whatever was going on with Ruri, she would figure it out after taking care of her own mess.

Malice flowed forward, transitioning from one stance to another, always in response to what was happening around her. The hunters landed small hits upon her, but for every cut they managed, she returned the favor tenfold. Her katana cut gaping slices into their flesh with the barest touch. Whatever magic they'd used as protection wasn't helping them now. They avoided the sword as if it was radioactive, giving it a wide berth. They couldn't keep up with her. She slipped among them, leaving carnage in her wake, while they jostled each other in their attempts to reach her.

Eventually, crowding was no longer an issue. Only three hunters remained standing. Those who could do so had removed themselves from her corner of mayhem. They ignored Tedrick's increasingly frantic commands to get back in there and finish her off.

She circled in place, keeping an eye on the last of the hunters. These three were seasoned, she could tell from the way they hesitated to rush in. They closed on her methodically, pushing her within range of the others.

"Kill her. Kill her now!" Tedrick's voice rose above the moans and cries of the wounded, above the sounds of weapons clashing together, and above the muted rumbles of thunder that issued from the clouds still seething above their heads.

To their credit, the trio ignored him and continued their measured pace around her. Malice pivoted to keep them in view. Her foot came down on something soft and rounded. It rolled under her weight, and she shifted to keep her footing. The nearest hunter, a tall Tuatha woman with hair in a stiff green crest, flashed forward, a long knife in either hand.

Malice managed to dodge one swipe and deflected the other, but the hunter kept coming. Her hands were blurs of wickedly sharp metal, flicking at Malice's head, then cutting her arms when she dodged. She almost managed to stick one in Malice's side, distressingly close to her kidney. Malice contorted her torso out of the way; she hadn't known she could move like that. The potentially lethal stab wound became instead a painful, but survivable slash along the ribs.

She couldn't stop moving. The other two fae were within range and kept herding her back toward the hunter with the knives. This wasn't going according to plan, which meant it was time to change it.

Malice turned to face Knives, panting hard enough to be sure the fae would see it. She favored the leg with the slash to the calf. It hadn't been deep and was already starting to close, but Knives wouldn't know that.

Sure enough, the fae redoubled her efforts while doing her best to avoid contact with Malice's katana. She rushed back in, a whirl of blades. There was something about the way she moved and attacked that reminded Malice of Stiletto. She shoved the image of her squadmate's face out of her mind and dropped to one knee, snatching the combat knife from the top of her boot. She whipped her hand out and to the side.

Knives pivoted to follow her, then froze. She looked down at her belly and raised a trembling hand to touch the hilt sticking out of her abdomen.

"I'm sorry," Malice said, unable to look away.

The fae dropped to both knees. The remaining hunters had stopped moving. They stared at her, then back at Knives. One looked around at the bodies of the other hunters who had failed to take her down.

"Run, maybe," Malice suggested helpfully.

They exchanged a quick look, then started to back away.

A prickle started along Malice's skin, starting at the base of her neck, then moving down her spine and up her scalp. The hairs on her arms lifted. She'd felt this before. She looked up at the menacing clouds above and cringed when she saw the brilliance flickering in their depths. She had no shelter, nothing and no one to protect her.

It was a poor defense against the worst nature could throw her way, but she had no other recourse. Malice raised the katana with both hands, the claw-shaped charm on Ruri's bracelet tapping the sensitive skin on the inside of her wrist. There was no way she could parry lightning. She wished she could say goodbye to her beloved Ruri one last time, to see her eyes flash molten gold in the moment before she climaxed, to feel her hand rubbing soothingly on the small of her back when she was ready to strangle Cassidy, to feel their arms wrapped around each other, Ruri grounding her when she felt like she might lose herself to the rage and fear that dictated all of her existence. All of it, that was, except the corner Ruri had insinuated herself into. She was her mate; they belonged to each other. It was the most natural thing in the world, but it felt like a revelation decades in the making. Her mate, who would be alone.

Tears streamed down Mary Alice's face as she waited for the hammer to crush her.

CHAPTER FORTY-SIX

Ruri came back to herself to discover the wolf had her jaws wrapped around the lower half of the lizard's snout. The wolf pulled away from it, forcing the jaw open far past its natural angle. Slowly, the sides tore and the lower jaw bent back as the wolf ripped it off the lizard's body with terrible deliberation. Their sides and flanks stung from more scrapes than she could count. Ruri was certain they'd lost multiple patches of fur.

A flash of recognition from the wolf welcomed her back. The lizard continued its now-muffled scream, its tongue hanging down through the gaping hole where its mandible had been. Lord Regin's answering roar was cut short by the flash of a silver blade that pierced into his breast and out his back. The sheriff yanked her sword out of him before his slumping body could pull it from her hands.

"Are you all right?" Reese called. She jumped down from the lizard's back as it slowly listed to the side, its terrible screaming having faded to a muted gargle. In a moment, that too was gone. "Basilisk stare would turn most to stone."

The wolf shook herself to dislodge some of the blood and tissue that had ended up in their fur during the fray. She didn't care what had attacked them, so long as it was dead. The name of the creature was familiar to Ruri, but now wasn't the time to dwell on it.

Members of the Wild Hunt still moved toward them, but cautiously since witnessing the carnage.

"Lead them off," Reese yelled.

Lead them off? Energy raced through their veins, an artifact of the kill magnified far beyond what they were used to feeling. They glanced over at their mate. She was almost impossible to see in the throng of hunters who were trying and failing to kill her. How much longer would she last? If they could get the hunters away from this place, there would be fewer to try to kill Mal.

There was no way to answer the sheriff. Instead, they pushed and loped toward the gathered fae. Shoving matches and contained scuffles broke out, were put down, then broke out anew. The bodies of those who'd been on the losing side of those disagreements dotted the slope behind them. That all stopped when they noticed Ruri's wolf hurtling toward them. Whatever trouble was between them was forgotten when presented with a common foe.

A javelin arced out of the sky toward their torso. The wolf jerked them to one side, but kept running. The javelin parted their fur as it flew past.

A squat fae with a pair of hand axes stepped toward them. They easily dodged his blades, then reached out their muzzle to hamstring him. He went down with a shout and a spray of blood, his leg no longer capable of supporting his weight.

Their opponents were so slow. They had no chance of catching them, not alone, and they didn't have the numbers those kobolds had had to overwhelm them. Every dead fae meant renewed vigor. Every mouthful of fae blood gave them energy to spare. They gloried in the death and maiming of those who would have kept them imprisoned. A trail of fae bodies piled up in their wake, and they kept shoving ahead, buying every forward pace with fae blood.

And then they were free of the crowd. They spun about and danced backward, their mouth open, tongue lolling to the side in a ghastly and mocking lupine grin. The wolf raised their muzzle and tested the air. She tilted their head all the way back and released a long howl.

The bell-like call galvanized the fae horde. They pushed forward, over and against each other, to get to them. The wolf held the call as the fae drew closer, then cut it off. She stared at their pursuers until they were within inches of touching the long guard hairs of their coat, then turned and bounded off.

The fae howled back and the ground trembled as they threw themselves after Ruri and her wolf. Glowing points of cool white light accompanied them as they ran. It didn't take long for the wolf to gain the heights while the fae chased them. When they glanced back, they saw that some of the hunters had mounted their beasts and were closing the gap.

Behind them, lightning flashed and almost simultaneous thunder rent the air.

* * *

The light was so bright it smeared across her vision even behind tightly closed eyelids; it threatened to wash her away. The heavy crack drove Malice to her knees, but she managed to keep the sword raised. It went on for eternity. It was over in an instant.

She cracked one eye open, not daring to believe she'd survived. She knelt in a blackened crater. The ground smoked around her, its acrid char searing itself into her nostrils. Against all odds, a small patch of green grass survived beneath her. Her ears rang and her vision blurred around the edges, but she'd emerged relatively intact.

Tedrick stared at her, his mouth agape. He sat on his ass, the kelpie nowhere to be seen. If Malice had to guess, she would have assumed it wasn't any happier about having lightning slung around than she was. The beast was smarter than her. It had taken off. Malice was still here.

"Not what you thought would happen, was it?" Malice said. She pushed herself back to both feet. Her voice sounded far away, like it was playing on a TV in a neighbor's apartment. "Where did your lackeys go?"

Tedrick was surrounded by the dead and dying. The hunters who'd faced off against her hadn't been as lucky as she. One lay on her back, empty, smoking eye sockets staring at the uncaring clouds. She—at least Malice thought the fae had been female—was only a few feet away from her. She tore her gaze away from the body. This was one that would come back around in her art; she could already feel the hold of the fae woman's death on her psyche.

"What's the matter?" Malice rolled her shoulders to loosen them up, then started picking her way over the rubble-strewn ground toward the king. "Did your people take off after you slaughtered them to get to me? What the hell, man! They were your people. Yours!"

He said something, but the words couldn't penetrate the hum in her ears. It was just as well. There was no excuse for what he'd done. You didn't kill your own people. Her face grew hot at her own hypocrisy and she shook her head.

Tedrick scrambled to his feet as she closed on him. He reached to the sky to pull down more lightning. He felt like the brush of nettles against her skin. For a moment, the itch flared to life. Malice gritted her teeth against the sensation and raised the katana in a defensive stance, but there was no response from the clouds. She had until his magic recharged to kill him. She had no problems contemplating being the author of his demise now. Whatever charm he'd seen fit to lay on her seemed to have well and truly evaporated. Trying to melt someone with a lightning bolt apparently had that effect.

Her lips pulled back from her teeth. Malice didn't know if she was smiling or snarling. She didn't much care.

He said something else she didn't catch.

"I'm going to kill you, you know." Malice took another step toward him. "You can go down swinging or looking. It's up to you." Her father had said that a lot. He'd swung at everything, for all the good it had done him. It would do Tedrick even less good.

His face firmed into something resembling resolve. He drew his sword. It should have gleamed, but all it had to reflect were the dark clouds above and the brilliance of the moonstones on his gauntlets. He leveled the sword at her and shouted something in defiance.

Malice shrugged.

Tedrick howled, his rage spilling out in an inky blot. Malice blinked. She hadn't expected that. Still, he was going to die and she would be the one to deliver the killing blow. It was refreshing to confront someone who so obviously needed to die. The world would be a better place for his absence.

The darkness came at her. Malice ran to meet it. Her first step into the cloud rendered her blind. She'd fought in darkness before, but that had been with her hearing intact. Right now it was anything but. She could still feel him, a presence that scraped against her skin. He was somewhere before her, but swinging around to her right. She pivoted to keep the discomfort in front. Would she see him when he closed? Best not to rely on the possibility.

They hadn't much practiced fighting while relying only on their sense of others during Hunter training. It was the least understood of their enhancements. Based on discussions she'd overheard between their trainers and the techs in charge of monitoring them, the new ability had been something of a bonus. Beyond some cursory "training" that had more closely resembled testing, they'd done very little with it. Malice cursed their lack of foresight as she waited for the fae king to close on her.

The nettles flayed deeper into her skin. Malice twisted to one side and lunged, trying to reach Tedrick with her sword. She found nothing. She'd moved too early and he'd dodged her clumsy attack. The fae had been the leader of the Wild Hunt for a very long time. It was too much to hope that he'd have few skills in tracking or the blade. If she'd had centuries to hone her skills, she would be unstoppable, but she only had seconds to gauge his position. It would have to be enough. She would make it enough.

She could feel him circling her. Once again she pivoted to keep him in front.

"What are you going to do if you somehow manage to kill me?" Malice asked. "Your subjects know what you are now. Do you really think they're going to allow themselves to be ruled by a waste of oxygen like you?"

He might have answered. She still couldn't hear much. Occasionally, a rumble of thunder would make it through the ringing in her ears, but that was it.

Still he circled. Could he see her? It was his darkness and his land. She supposed she had to operate as if he had every advantage. Better to be pleasantly surprised. Malice shifted her grip on the katana's hilt. Battle was no place for assumptions.

"So what do they do to rulers like you here?" She kept her tone conversational. "Do you they throw you down a well? I imagine you couldn't get up to too much mischief down there."

The pressure increased again. Malice waited. She gritted her teeth to keep from acting too soon. Then, when it already felt too late, she struck. He was trying to slip past her so she turned with him and slashed for where she knew the largest mass would be.

Her blade bit into something. Malice cried out in triumph at the same time his sword found the top of her shoulder. He carved a line of fire down the front of it and halfway across her chest, her tunic doing little to stop the slice. She bit off a shout of pain and disengaged.

The itch on her skin lessened as he did the same. Malice bit down on a growl of frustration. This was all taking much too long. If she'd been able to see the asshole, he'd be dead by now. Ruri was off somewhere to the west. She could feel her again. Her mate was whole and if she'd received any wounds, she couldn't tell. It was time to take the fight to him.

She moved toward the feeling of Tedrick, deliberately at first, then faster when he didn't move. She was up on the balls of her feet, moving as silently as she could with no feedback to tell her if she was successful. She closed until it felt like she was right on top of him, and he showed no sign of realizing she was there. Instead, he continued the deliberate circling he'd been doing. At the last moment, he stopped. Malice dropped to one knee and extended her blade toward him. The hairs on top of her head were tugged then sliced through with the force of his swing. Her blade swung true. It sliced through Tedrick's skin and muscle as easily as through water, the kiss of cold iron splitting him open with little resistance. His cry of pain came through her still ringing ears. He shouted at her, indistinct words of anger.

Again, the itch burned. Her hands trembled with the effort of not scratching at the area of aggravation. He was calling the lightning again, and based on the answering itch she felt in the clouds above, they were ready to answer. She could feel his form on her skin, traced around in a halo of prickling fire. It told her that her katana had sliced through the top of his thigh, almost at the hip. She brought the blade around and jabbed it into his abdomen. The blade lit up with the same mental fire she felt around him. She stood, slicing upward through his belly. The blade barely slowed as it sliced through his ribcage.

The darkness dropped away, blown away by a gust of wind so strong it pulled at her hair and set the edges of her clothes to flapping. The charm on her bracelet smacked against her arm. Still, she pulled the blade up. Blood sprayed from Tedrick's mouth and he struggled to raise both hands to the sky. Malice kept on pulling. Her blade came up and out of the top of his chest in a bright arc of crimson. His form blazed in her mind's eye, even as it slumped to its knees, his arms still above his head.

Malice raised the katana high in the defensive position she'd been in the last time he dropped a lightning bolt on her head.

Brilliant light arced down toward him, not her as she'd assumed. She barely had time to get the blade down between them when the energy flashed out from him in a wave of blinding white. It caught her like a freight train, sending her sprawling backward. She landed on her ass and rolled to one side to keep her head from cracking into the ground, for all the good it did her. Nothing moved; her vision was awash with light. She felt nothing. She couldn't have protected herself if she'd wanted to.

CHAPTER FORTY-SEVEN

The wolf raised their head from the mangled body of the fae under their paws. She inhaled deeply, testing the wind for signs of nearby hunters. The blood on their muzzle and in their mouth masked other scents. Her ears twitched at the crackle of imprudent feet crossing dried leaves. It was time to move on.

They raced the wind, pulling their pursuers further away from Mal. At least they were out of reach of the storm cloud that still grumbled fitfully. The occasional column of cloud-to-ground lightning still split the air, but it was mostly on the edge of being dormant.

Their ears swiveled at the sound of hooves on hard-packed ground behind them. The wolf listened closely, measuring how close their pursuers were. The mount's hoofbeats were uneven, nearly flagging. Their own pace was still strong and sure. Ruri had lost count of how many fae hunters had fallen to their jaws. The wolf didn't keep score.

A jagged boulder loomed out of the ground in front of them. They sped toward it, listening to the sounds of those who presumed to harry them. There was no change in the labored cadence of the hoofbeats.

Perfect.

The boulder stood some ten to twelve feet tall, but the back side was cracked and jagged. Smaller stones had crumbled off it and a small pile of rubble sat at the base. Climbing it was almost as easy as running.

They scrambled to the top, the wolf doing her best to make as little noise as possible. Once up, they slunk over to the opposite edge, then peered over. Two fae, each astride a horned creature, were picking their way up the slope toward them. They'd wisely slowed down and were treating the boulder as a possible ambush point.

They weren't wrong, but they underestimated their foe's abilities.

The wolf backed up to the opposite side of the huge rock, then charged at the edge, launching them through the air. They hit the ground not five feet in front of the mounted hunters. Before they could react, the wolf had hamstrung one mount and sunk their teeth into the thigh of the hunter on the other beast. The first horned creature's terrible screams unnerved the other. It reared back, but the wolf wouldn't relinquish their hold on its rider. For a moment, the wolf hung in the air, but the beast came back down with a shuddering thud. The hapless hunter started to slide from her saddle. She clung to the saddle horn, but to no avail. She tumbled down in a flurry of cloak and limbs. The wolf didn't wait for her to recover before tearing out her throat. Fresh blood filled their mouth, the taste of iron and something else bringing them renewed energy.

The other hunter had already run halfway down the hill. The wolf growled deep in her chest, ready to go after this new quarry.

Let them go, Ruri thought. *They'll only slow us down.*

The wolf shook their body. Her lips lifted back from her teeth while she considered the fleeing fae.

Time to remind the others that we're still out here. The Wild Hunt can still turn on Mal.

The wolf's deep howl was at once agreement and repudiation of the idea that the hunters might attack their mate. Distant shouts sounded. Too distant.

They climbed back up the boulder and stood on its edge, fully visible to those who would track them. The wolf tipped back her head and keened again to the sky. Another wolf would have heard it for the challenge it was and stayed away, but the fae who followed them were stubborn to the point of stupidity. They crested a far rise and paused to point and shout at the wolf. They waited, unconcerned as the hunters urged their mounts forward or ran closer on their own feet.

Another far-off peal of thunder rumbled toward them. It was followed quickly, unnaturally, by a flash.

They had time to wonder what this new magic was before a muted force punched into their body. This time the shock wave of pain was so strong they stumbled and only the wolf's natural reflexes stopped them from slipping over the boulder's side.

The towering storm cloud that had been visible on the horizon was gone. So too were all the other clouds and the blue of the sky. The heavens above were featureless, a smooth grey color that never varied in tone. It was aggressively neutral, neither dark nor light. It was nothing.

The hunters appeared on the ridge where they'd been only moments before, then disappeared from view, heading the other way. None of the stragglers had even a glance to spare for them.

Mal. They were headed back toward Mal.

The wolf jumped down from the boulder and hit the ground already in a full lope. Whatever had just happened, Mal was right in the middle of it. Their mate needed them.

* * *

Malice stood over Tedrick's corpse. His eyes stared up at her unblinkingly. They carried none of the accusation Stiletto's had, or if they did, it was nothing she would take to heart. He'd gotten what he'd deserved.

She bent down and used an unstained edge of his tunic to clean the blood off her blade. A touch on her shoulder sent a pulse of alarm through her body. She grabbed the offending hand and spun, sending the potential attacker up on their toes.

"Hey there," Reese said, her voice tense. "It's just me. Would you perhaps let off the pressure?" Her blade was smeared with the remnants of blood hastily wiped away. Her armor no longer shone. Instead the silver and crimson blurred together in a Jackson Pollock vision of gore and worse. The helmet had gathered new scratches and dings, and within, Reese's eyes were hooded and distant.

Malice let go of the fae woman's hand without answering. She looked around to see if Ruri was nearby, but nothing moved in the vicinity. They stood in a field of the dead. The silence was near absolute. Wild strikes of lightning had snuffed those voices out. Tedrick had a lot more to answer for than had been laid before him.

Malice's head snapped up when she realized there was no wind, not even the faintest breeze. The winds had whipped at her when she'd confronted the king. It was completely unnatural for them to be gone so completely. A leaden sky devoid of any characteristics lay over their heads. It felt disconcertingly close. Malice kept herself from reaching out toward it.

"We don't have time to stay here," Reese said. Her voice was tight, overly controlled like she was working hard at keeping it level but was on the edge of failing. "I can send you out through the portal I came in, or you can come with me. Either way, it has to be now."

Malice shook her head. She couldn't leave without Ruri. "What are you talking about?"

"The king died with no Heir. Our realm is unraveling." She gestured to the sky. "That's the first sign. Our connection to the Summerlands will already be broken. The edges of the realm are being eaten by the nothing between worlds. If I don't get to the Heart and convince it to accept me again, those who can't make it to a portal in time will be lost."

Reese turned away from her and headed for one of the pale horses. Someone had tied it to a scrubby bush. There was no sign of the other one.

"I don't have time to convince you. Come or stay. It's up to you."

Malice hesitated for only a moment, then trotted after the sheriff. She hated being forced into things, and that's what Reese was doing. On the other hand, the sky was ominous in a way she couldn't identify. Its sheer lack of character or variation spooked her so viscerally that she had no explanation for the terror she was barely keeping at bay, but it was there nonetheless. She still had people here, beyond even Ruri. From what she'd seen, it was unlikely anyone would think of the teens. And what about Mracek and Billy and the others whose lives had touched hers? And even those who hadn't but didn't deserve this.

"Glad you could make it." Reese untied the pale horse. With no sunlight, the horse was all bone. Red fire burned in its eye sockets as it watched them. It shifted nervously, tossing its head in discomfort in the same fashion as a normal horse.

Reese patted its spiny neck reassuringly, then climbed into the saddle. "We're going to have to ride double. It's a good thing pale horses don't tire like mortal horses do. Grab my cloak." She pointed at a crumpled piece of red cloth in the middle of the blood-soaked battlefield. Malice recognized it as the wrapping for her katana.

"What am I supposed to do with it?"

"Lay it behind the saddle, then get up. It's not going to be very comfortable, I'm afraid."

"Good to know," Malice said under her breath. She picked up the cloak, which was mostly untouched by gore and spread it out, hoping it would give her some protection from the bony protrusions of the horse's spine. The fabric seemed to hover above the bones as if the muscles and skin were still there, but invisible.

"What about Shejuanna?" Malice asked when Reese reached out toward her. "We can't just leave her here if the world is falling apart."

"She is already gone," Reese said. "Mami Wata took her out through the portal while the king clashed with you. Now come, we don't have time for this."

She took Reese's hand and was pulled up behind the fae. Reese didn't wait for her to get settled, but moved them forward at a rapid clip. In no time, they'd reached a gallop. Malice had no way to move with the horse since she didn't have access to the stirrups. She flung her arms around the sheriff's waist to keep from sliding off. The mail's cold rings were coated in ichor in too many places. She quickly realized she would have to put up with having her hands coated in drying blood.

They passed a group of hunters heading back the way they'd come. The fae paid no notice to them.

Malice leaned forward and shouted into Reese's ear. "Aren't you worried they'll double back and attack us?"

Reese shook her head and replied in kind. "They're likely heading to the portal I came through. It's the closest one they would know about. They're like animals before a forest fire. There are no conflicts more important than the need to escape. We'll see more, I'm sure." Malice picked up what she said over the sound of hoofbeats and wind.

"So everyone's heading out, but we're staying in."

"That is exactly it." Reese turned to watch her out of the corner of her eye. "If you want to head back to the portal, I can let you off now. Mami Wata will be watching for stragglers. She'll guide you through until the area is eaten by the nothing."

Malice firmed her grip around the sheriff's waist. "Not a chance. There's work to be done. Besides, it's nice to save lives instead of taking them, for once."

"Good. I'm glad I don't have to do this alone." Reese paused, choosing her next words with care. "Even if it's with someone I normally wouldn't work with."

"Likewise."

A laugh shook the sheriff. "At least we're finally on the same page, even if it is at the possible end of my realm."

"Better late than never, as my dad would say."

"Indeed."

They rode on in silence, the sheriff alternating between a ground-devouring gallop and a canter. As she'd predicted, more groups of fae passed them. Another group of hunters headed back toward the icedrake's lair. A few families were heading in the direction of the castle.

"There are more known portals there," the sheriff said when Malice asked. "The hunters are the only ones who now know of the portals by the drake's cave. At the very least, they know of the one we came through. Furthermore, the castle and the Heart will be the last places to go. The hunters will have to hurry. That area is close to the outskirts of the realm. It'll be gone soon if it isn't already."

Malice nodded, then turned to look west. "Heads up, we're going to have company. Ruri's coming." She'd been able to feel her mate moving around and knew she'd been all right. It would take more than a few fae to slow her down. Pride expanded in her chest.

"Good to know." Reese firmed up her grip on the reins and slowed the pale horse to a trot.

The gait was uniquely uncomfortable with no saddle or stirrups to help cushion Malice's pelvis on the horse's back. She did her best to shift with the animal, but her efforts were ineffectual at best.

"There she is." Malice pointed out the flash of golden fur on the ridge line ahead of them.

The horse slowed down and tried to turn as Ruri's wolf form dashed down the hillside toward them. The sheriff kept a firm hand on the reins. The flames in its eye sockets flickered between a dimness that was almost impossible to make out to bright flame that licked the top of the sockets.

Ruri didn't seem to notice the pale horse's discomfort. She ran up, her ears back and lips curled up to expose sharp teeth. Her growl preceded her, sending the horse into another series of efforts to be anywhere but there.

"It's all right," Malice called out to her mate. "We're heading to the Heart to fix this place before it falls apart."

Ruri cocked her head. Her golden eyes locked with Malice's. Doubt ate at the back of Mal's head, but it didn't feel like her own. That was a new sensation and a handy one. Would they always be able to communicate like this while her mate was in wolf form? She hoped so.

"I'm up here because I want to be," Malice said. "We don't have much time!" She tried to project as much urgency as she could. Ruri had to believe her.

The wolf gave an awkward nod with its great shaggy head. She retreated up the slope a ways and waited. Their mount needed little urging to break into a gallop again. It stretched itself out to get past the wolven watching it from higher ground. When Ruri followed them, the horse pushed itself even harder. Eventually, Ruri fell behind far enough that the horse wasn't going at a constant gallop. It might have been the fae version of a regular horse, but it certainly seemed to share many of a real horse's instincts.

They kept on under the unrelenting grey sky. The hills lost their jagged edges, smoothing into rolling slopes covered in lush grass and wildflowers. They found the road and maintained their grueling pace, passing more fae hurrying along to the palace. Malice's legs and behind ached. When one part would get beyond discomfort into pain, she would shift until the new group of muscles protested, then she'd go back to the first.

It was a wonder Reese didn't have sharp words for her constant shifting, but the sheriff had a singular focus. Malice realized Reese was cycling back and forth between gallop and canter for their sake, not the horse's. The pale horse showed no sign of flagging. She caught glimpses of gold fur flickering through the trees, sometimes on one side of them, then on the other. Ruri's presence was a great comfort to the tension she felt from the sky above and the nagging feeling of becoming unmoored.

In an abrupt movement that sent the pale horse into a stumble, Reese yanked on the reins. Malice clutched at her to keep from sliding off the horse's back.

"What's going on?" Malice peered over the sheriff's shoulder. "Oh."

A grey hole with ragged edges obliterated the road through the woods.

CHAPTER FORTY-EIGHT

The wolf moved through the trees as the pale horse tripped and shuddered to a stop. It had been clear to them that the skeleton horse was put off by their presence, a fact the wolf found ridiculous. It wasn't as if there was enough meat, any meat, on its bones to make it a worthy morsel.

They stopped, not wanting to spook Mal's mount. The wolf raised their nose and sniffed. The air had a peculiar dead flavor to it, a deadness that lacked the stench of decay. They should have smelled pine needles and decaying leaves, but what came to their nostrils was almost sterile. They skulked forward along the road, slipping from tree to tree, then concealed themselves under the dense branches of a young conifer. It was there they spied what had stopped their mate and the human-not-human sheriff.

A cutout hung before them, blocking the road. Its center was grey and flat, so flat it was difficult to discern its edges. They squinted, trying to determine where the nothing ended, but were unable to tell.

"Ruri!" Mal called to them. She was watching them and motioned them near with a wide sweep of her arm.

They kept an eye on the horse as they crept closer. Ruri wanted to leap into the air from joy. Mal had seen them even as they disguised their presence. She'd looked right at them. Somewhere in everything that had happened, she'd acknowledged their mate bond. The connection between them practically hummed as Mal was finally able to use it as it was meant to be used. No longer would they be hobbled with half a bond. This was how it was supposed to be. Everything that had happened to them finally felt worth it.

As long as they could get out in one piece.

The former Heir had gotten down off the horse and was weaving together a plait of green sticks. Mal slid down behind her, then crouched in the grass. As they got closer, Reese said something and the sticks shone with a sourceless metallic reflection, then returned to their original appearance. She placed the plait over the pale horse's head. Immediately, the horse quit shying away from Ruri and the wolf. It paid them no attention whatsoever. Ruri didn't doubt that if it had had a working digestive system, it would have started grazing.

The wolf trotted them even closer, but the horse still paid them no mind.

"It sees you as part of the forest around us," Reese said. "Right now it's more worried about that hole of nothing than about where you might be." She shook her head. "Frankly, so am I. This shouldn't be here."

"How do you know?" Mal asked. "It doesn't sound like this happens too often. Have you ever been through one?"

"No... But everything I've heard says the realm disintegrates from the edges."

The wolf nosed her way forward. The closer they got to the disconcerting emptiness, the more the land's scents faded. When there was nothing left to smell, they stopped. The packed dirt under their feet seemed stable, but in front of them it grew steadily more indistinct.

"It's continuing to spread," Reese called out to them. "Don't get too close to the edge or it could swallow you."

That sounded bad to Ruri. The wolf agreed, but before they could back up, the grey grew more intense. The wolf blinked and jerked back, sending them onto their hindquarters in an ungainly sprawl. They looked down at their front paws. Everything was intact, which was good. But no, they weren't completely intact. Two claws on their left foot were gone. They ended in a sharp edge. The fur around them had been shorn back almost to their skin. The wolf crept back from the edge of the nothing, eyeing it the entire time.

"We can't get through here," Reese said. "The terrain is too tangled to cut through, but the most direct detour is through lands the kobolds hold. As I see it, we don't have a choice or the time to argue.

Maybe they'll be gone, fleeing ahead of the nothing." She dropped to her knees next to the wolf.

Ruri and the wolf looked up into her eyes, surprised she would get so close to them.

"We can't slow down while we're going through there," Reese said. "Our time is already too short. I need you to keep the kobolds from us."

"That sounds like a terrible idea," Mal said. "You don't have to do this if you don't want to." She put a hand on their shoulder. Warmth bloomed along their side, and they leaned into her, taking additional solace from their mate's touch.

Would Mal stay behind with them then? The wolf didn't think so, neither did Ruri. She smelled determined and they both knew she was impossible to budge when she'd decided on a course of action.

They looked back at the patch of nothing. It had expanded again. The stretch of road where they'd been sniffing at it was gone. Their missing toenails seemed to throb, reminding them of their absence. It was past time to get moving. The wolf grabbed Mal's hand lightly in her jaws. Whatever was coming their way, they would face it together as mates.

"All right then," Mal said. She turned to Reese. "Let's go."

* * *

The ride only got harder. Since they'd found the nothing hole in the forest, Reese had stopped varying their pace. They'd been galloping for over an hour. Malice's thighs and pelvis screamed at her when she bothered to listen to her body's complaints. Since she could do little about them, she chose to ignore the occasional twinges of agony.

Ruri paced them, never too far from the pale horse they rode. Since the sheriff had worked her magic, it paid little attention to the wolven.

Again and again they'd passed fleeing fae. One woman had stopped and called out to them, asking what was happening.

"To the castle," Reese had shouted over her shoulder. "Make your way there and out!"

The road had started sloping upward and the trees were thinning out. Malice still kept her eye out for threats but couldn't help noticing strange geometric shapes through the branches. They were headed toward the upside-down mountains again. She hated those things. They represented everything that was wrong with this place.

"We don't have to travel far through them," Reese said as they headed up through a pass. "It's a finger of the range that extends toward the grasslands. This shouldn't take long."

No shadows were cast by the massive inverted triangular shapes, not even the soft darkness they might have seen on a cloudy day. Ruri had made it to the heights. There was no wind to ripple through her fur. It hung curiously limp, except when she was running. Everything was quiet. It had Malice's hackles up. Her gaze darted from one crevice to another, watching for threats. She strained to hear anything that might be coming over the lonely ring of their hoofbeats on stone. Aside from the squawk of the horse's tack and the noises of its passage, there was nothing.

"That was easier than I hoped," Reese said.

The pass was behind them and rolling grasslands filled the landscape ahead. There was little to block their view. Reese reined the horse in to a stop.

"That doesn't look good," Malice said. Without trees or steep slopes in the way, she could see dozens of nothing holes. They littered the landscape, blurred around the edges and difficult to make out. They ranged in size from larger than a house to one not far from them that was only a couple of feet in diameter. In the distance was a glowing speck. The road had once led right to it, but it was no longer whole.

"Not good at all." Reese nudged the horse forward at a walk.

Some of the tears crossed the road. At least the terrain made them much easier to navigate around. Malice blinked as a hole seemed to pop open in their path. Was it a new one, or was it simply that they were so difficult to make out? She understood why the sheriff was moving so slowly, but she chafed at the need for it. From Reese's hunched shoulders and tight grip on the reins, she wasn't happy either. It was like holding on to a sticky statue. The blood was drying slowly and had gotten tacky. It didn't smell like human blood; the stench of iron was missing and replaced by a metallic scent she couldn't name.

"Ruri," Malice called out. She could feel her mate's presence off to one side.

Ruri's golden head popped up out of a shallow depression to the left. Her ears pricked up toward them.

"Can you get through here?" Malice asked, knowing her voice would carry to the wolven's ears. "Are you able to tell where those holes are?"

Ruri slunk in front of them. She lifted her head, sniffing at the air. That wasn't what Malice had expected. She'd thought Ruri might be able to see the holes better. It hadn't occurred to her that they might smell different.

A pulse of confidence shot through Malice's chest. Ruri took off at a trot. She swerved to make her way around a smallish bit of nothing, then picked up the pace.

Reese urged the pale horse forward, picking up speed until they matched Ruri's pace. It wasn't a full gallop, more of a canter, but better by far than the walk they'd been forced to keep.

"Does she know where we're going?" Reese asked.

"I doubt it. She wasn't there during the Jaeger's ritual with the Heart. You'll have to direct her. Just yell, she'll hear you."

"That seems a little rude."

"Your world is ending, and you're getting hung up on niceties." Malice shook her head. "You might as well drop us off at the nearest portal then."

"Ruri," Reese shouted. "A little to the west, if you please. Head for the light on the horizon."

Ruri glanced back at them, one golden eye winking at them over tawny fur. She adjusted her trajectory after skirting yet another pocket of nothing.

"Look at that," Malice said. "You got it done and you were polite. I'd say you're ready to be Queen of Canada."

Reese stiffened. "Urgency is no reason for rudeness."

"Relax, I'm just giving you crap. I don't have anything else to do." She patted Reese awkwardly on the shoulder. "If I don't get to do something soon, I'm going to explode. I guess it's making me into a sarcastic bitch."

"Oh." Reese's back relaxed. "Don't count on nothing to do. There's still plenty that can go wrong."

"That is fantastic to know." She kept her voice dry so Reese would know she wasn't being serious.

They wound their way through the tall grasses toward the Heart. Every now and again the sheriff would call out course corrections to Ruri, always making sure to couch them as polite requests that would have been more appropriate at high tea. It was slower than a straight shot would have been, but still much faster than it would have been without Ruri's guidance.

Malice decided she actually liked this version of Reese. She wasn't so sure of herself, which was refreshing after dealing with so many of the other fae.

The area was starting to look as familiar as it could with the points of nothing turning reality into Swiss cheese. They mounted a rise and looked down into the bowl that held the Heart. It looked much the same as it had before, except now the top crystals glowed brightly, sending up a beacon. There was a distinct lack of tears in the fabric of the realm around the Heart, but the space was far from empty. The beacon had done its work.

Hundreds of shining eyes cloaked in shadow looked their way.

CHAPTER FORTY-NINE

"So that's where they went," Reese said.

"They don't look hostile." Malice eyed the gathered kobolds. It took her a moment to realize they weren't the only fae there, simply the largest group. Flashes of light she knew by now were pixies zoomed about above their heads. Birds and other winged creatures lined the crystals that glowed against the indifferent sky.

"Not yet." Reese clicked her tongue at the pale horse.

Step by reluctant step, it made its way toward the throng of fae. Ruri paced along beside them. The pale horse fought the sheriff every step of the way as they rode down the incline. When they were ten feet from the mass of fae, it stopped and refused to take another step. The fae watched them without moving. Malice wondered if they were even blinking. If they were, she had yet to catch it.

"Looks like we walk from here," Reese said.

"I guess so." Malice eyed the crowd. She wondered how many of them she could take out before they were overwhelmed.

Reese shifted and Malice realized the sheriff was waiting for her to get down. It took her a moment to do so. She'd been back on her feet for less than a second before Ruri came to join her, pressing her massive body along Malice's legs. She angled herself so she stood between Malice and the silently watching fae.

Malice carefully drew her katana. Some of the nearest kobolds shifted away from them when she bared the steel blade. She dropped her hand to her side, shielding the sword from their eyes.

"Careful waving that around," Reese said as she got down from the horse. She slapped it on the side of its neck bones. It shuddered once, then walked away on stiff legs.

"Last time I dealt with those things, they almost killed us. You had to rescue us." Malice knew which part of that was the worse crime. She should have been able to take on more of them.

"Things are different now. There's a bigger threat. We need them focused on that, not on you."

"Then say something to them, but I'm keeping the sword out." Malice flipped her free hand toward the crowd. "You want to be queen, so get royal on them."

"They barely treated with King Connall. I doubt they'll take my word for it. Let's see how far we can get without bloodshed, shall we?"

Reese took a few steps forward and the kobolds gave way. When Ruri joined her, the fae moved even more quickly. Malice joined them, keeping her katana down but at the ready. This would be fun.

* * *

The kobolds and fae parted around their little group. Ruri and the wolf took the lead, their head constantly moving from one potential enemy to the next. The fur rose on their hackles the further they pushed into the crowd. The only noise came from the movement of the fae in the tall grass as they got out of their way. As they drew closer to the glowing crystal pile, they could hear the scratching of clawed feet on crystal and the settling of wings. Occasional muted bell-like tones whispered from the Heart as the creatures moved.

The fae who gathered here seemed to be on the more bestial end of the spectrum. Ruri saw no Tuatha or brownies. The wolf whined when Ruri came to that realization. It felt too close to the abandonment of pack members to both of them. As stewards of this land, the Tuatha were falling far short. Where were the other fae to organize some sort of evacuation? Why would they leave these fae to fend for themselves?

At least Reese was trying to fix things. Or so she'd said.

The creatures above cocked their heads to watch them as they came closer. One had human eyes that looked out of place in its avian face. Simeon. Sparks of light drifted down from the end of his orange and red tail. More dripped slowly from the tips of his wings. The rate of sparks was much less and somehow dimmer than they'd been in the teens' barracks.

A crevice between two crystal monoliths led into the Heart's glowing interior. Ruri strained to see down the rough hall, but it ended at a junction. Without going inside, there was no way to see what might wait for them in there.

Every eye turned to them when they made it to the Heart. The closest kobolds took half a step toward them. A growl rumbled from the wolf's throat and they stepped back again.

"I don't think it's a good idea for Ruri to go in," Reese said.

"You can't leave her out here with all of them," Mal said.

"She was made to destroy us." Reese looked down toward Ruri and the wolf, her hands spread as if in apology. "There's no telling how the Heart will react to her."

"Okay." Mal stepped forward to stand beside them. "We'll keep an eye on things out here."

"Have you been inside?"

"The Jaeger had me as a guard during the ritual."

"So the Heart recognized you?"

"I think so?" Mal didn't sound completely certain. "It talked to me. I think it was reserving judgment."

"Then you're going to have to come with me."

"Not without my mate."

The wolf let out a peculiar whine as Ruri exulted in their head. Not only was Mal acknowledging the bond to herself, but also to others. If she'd been in human form, she would have burst into tears.

Reese grabbed Mal's arm. "Didn't you just tell me we don't have time for politeness? I need you to anchor me. If you don't, I may not be able to make it back. It's why the binding ritual for the Heir calls for two people."

Mal yanked her arm out of Reese's grip. "I'm good out here."

"If I can't find my way back, I can't stop this. We all go away then."

Ruri nudged into Mal's hand with their muzzle.

"What is it?" Mal asked.

They leaned against the back of her legs, pushing her toward the Heart. There wasn't time to argue. Scents were thinning down here too, growing stretched and verging toward indistinct.

"I can't leave you." Mal dropped to a crouch in front of them.

They stuck their nose into the hollow between her neck and shoulder and inhaled deeply. The scent of their mate coursed through their nostrils and deep into their lungs. They held the scent in, pulling it deep into their body, into their blood. Mal was always with them. She was them. They were her. Even if it all ended here, nothing would ever change that.

Mal threw her arms around them. She dug her hands deep into their fur, burying her nose in the crook behind their jawline. Tears soaked through their guard hairs and into the downy undercoat. Moisture trickled down to their skin.

Always, Ruri thought with every fiber of her being. She hoped Mal could feel her conviction. *Always, and again.*

The wolf opened herself to Mal and for a brief moment, it felt as if their mate occupied the same space as the entwined souls of the wolven. They fit into a perfect whole, balanced and equal.

"I get it," Mal whispered.

Their bond resonated with the depth of her feeling. It was a well, deeper and broader by far than what little she showed on the surface. Ruri felt it and poured the same depth of regard back into the link they shared. She watched in amazement as moisture welled up in Mal's eyes. As her stoic mate allowed the tears to fall without making any effort to hide them from Reese who watched them from the side.

Mal squeezed their neck and withdrew, wiping the wet tracks off her cheeks as she stood.

"Watch our back," Reese said to Ruri and her wolf. "I don't know how this will go or if the Heart will try to protect itself."

They watched Mal and Reese proceed under the leaning stones into the Heart. They disappeared around a corner. The wolf moved until they stood in the center of the opening. They set their paws against the ground and braced themselves. Nothing would get past them while they stood.

CHAPTER FIFTY

The Heart was much as Malice remembered it. She followed Reese down a corridor of rough-hewn crystal that followed the curve of the outer walls. When they'd made a half circuit, they came upon another crevice that led deeper into the Heart. The last time she'd been here, the Jaeger and Connall had disappeared down that narrow hall, but only the Jaeger had come back alive. To think, she'd been so proud to be included in this momentous occasion. How much of that had been his magical manipulation and how much had been her own pride at finally having someone recognize her skills? She worried it was too much of the latter.

"Is the Heart speaking to you?" Reese asked in hushed tones.

"I'm not getting anything."

"Neither am I." She plucked at her lower lip while staring into the tunnel leading to the Heart's inner chamber. "That has me worried. If the nothing has spread too far, it will lock itself away from the realm. This and the deepest essence of the castle are all that will survive." She sighed. "One day, other fae may stumble upon it and rekindle the realm, but it will be too late for those of us who remain here now."

"What are you waiting for, then?" Malice gestured toward the narrow hallway. "Get in there and reintroduce yourself."

"It's not that simple. There are forms, rituals. And we have nothing of what we need to start those."

"Fuck form and ritual." Malice stalked toward the crevice. "This is an emergency. I think the Heart will forgive you a little rudeness. Exigent circumstances, and all that."

"You can't go in there!"

"Then you'd better come and stop me."

Malice lengthened her stride until she was moving just short of a run. She swiveled her shoulders to clear the narrow entrance. Reese's footsteps sounded on the crystal ground. It sounded like she was being chased by a bell. Malice ducked down and broke into a jog. The hall couldn't be that long; the Heart wasn't that big.

The interior of the crevice was dim. The walls glowed dimly but did little to dispel the shadows inside. Fortunately, the floor was worn smooth. There were no chunks of crystal or cracks and dips to trip her. Reese picked up the pace, and Malice sped up to stay ahead of her. At the rate they were moving, they should have been at the center chamber already. The walls were lightening around them, but so subtly that at first Malice thought it was that she was getting used to the dim light. The walls were widening also. No longer did she have to maneuver her shoulders to keep from touching the sides.

She kept on. Ruri was back there, alone. They had to fix this. If they couldn't, she needed enough time to get back to her mate, to be with her as this world ended around them.

Malice chided herself. This was no way to think during an op. As much as it pained her to do so, she took hold of her emotions and compressed them into a neat mental package, then tucked them down in a buried corner of her mind. She hadn't needed that particular exercise for years, but it still helped. Time to focus on the task at hand.

Reese came up behind her, then next to her. Malice was already in a full sprint. She ignored the sheriff, but Reese didn't seem interested in stopping her anymore. She matched Malice's punishing pace. Together they ran down a steadily brightening hall.

It felt like they'd been running for hours when they finally arrived in the central chamber. By that time, the walls were so bright that all shadow had been obliterated. The hall was a massive construction that echoed their footsteps back to them. It was far wider than the exterior of the Heart had been. Malice tried not to think too much about that.

The chamber was massive, maybe a hundred yards or more across, though it was difficult to tell. The center of the chamber was filled with radiance so bright that Malice couldn't look at it directly. Her eyes already watered. She looked away and over at Reese.

"Now what?"

"I go talk to the Heart."

"That's all there is to it?" Malice grinned. "Easy peasy."

"By myself." Reese took a deep breath. "I haven't done this before."

"Didn't you do the Heir ritual?"

"Yes, but Connall was the one who spoke directly to the Heart. All of my communication was through him."

Malice took Reese's shoulders in her hands. She turned the sheriff so she faced the blinding brilliance of the Heart. "You've got this. Ruri believes in you." She shoved Reese forward.

"If I call out, come and get me. Talking to the Heart is disorienting and I won't be able to see. If I get lost in its presence, I won't be able to put down the nothing."

"You can count on me. Now get to it."

Reese laughed and raised a hand in farewell. "Yes, milady." She walked forward.

The edges of her form blurred in front of the intense light as she receded in Malice's vision. Malice watched her as long as she could. She had to glance away every now and again to clear her vision. Eventually, when she looked back, she could no longer see Reese.

"I guess that's it, then." Malice settled herself into a crouch leaning against the wall next to the entry. The wound across her shoulder ached. She didn't have to touch it to know it was scabbed over. It was probably close to half-healed already, though not enough to be completely pain free. She placed her unsheathed katana across her knees. What there was to fight, she had no idea. Maybe there would be nothing, but if there was, she would be ready. Besides, she always felt more at ease with a length of steel within easy reach.

* * *

The mass of kobolds and fae stood still, so still Ruri couldn't tell if they breathed. She split her attention between them and the grey that was spreading like a blot along the top of the rise around the Heart. The patches blended into the grey of the sky and it was difficult to tell where the blots ended and the sky began, but flickers at their edges gave them away. Every now and again, a fae creature would make its way between the spreading holes and join the throng in front of them. Fewer were coming even as more gaps opened.

It was the only movement this deep in. A pair of deer-like creatures that walked on their hind legs made their way down the hill toward the center of the depression. When they joined the others, they stopped moving.

Tension was the only constant. The fae didn't move, but they didn't relax either. That terrible strain rooted itself in them. They were all waiting. Waiting and wondering.

The wolf didn't wonder. When they were gone, it wouldn't matter any longer. She had no doubt of what waited for them and she went willingly knowing Mal would be there with them. Ruri sighed. She would have liked more time with Mal.

A murmur spread through the crowd. They looked back at the outer edges of the depression. A patch of nothing had opened halfway down the hill. It was small. It widened slightly, then diminished before widening again. The edges of the nothing vibrated for a moment, then it pricked out of existence like a popped soap bubble. Whatever was protecting this area from the nothing was still in place, but it was weakening.

The gathered fae pressed in closer on the Heart. What gaps there were between creatures disappeared as the entire group compressed. The wolf growled at nearby kobolds. They stopped short of touching their fur, but it was a near thing. All it would take to snatch one up in their jaws would be for the wolf to reach out their head. There wasn't room for all these fae in the Heart itself. They would have to keep them out. The wolf licked their lips, pre-savoring the taste of fae blood. Mal was counting on them.

CHAPTER FIFTY-ONE

Nothing changed. Malice stared at the walls, then closed her eyes to give them a rest. She had no idea how long she'd been there. The semi-meditative state she was used to didn't really allow for awareness of time passing. That was pretty much the point. Her phone was useless. The clock hadn't changed in days. She knew that, but she still broke out of her trance twice to pull it from her belt pouch and check. She was certain she'd been there long enough to become hungry, but she wasn't. That was something.

Something from outside pulled her out of the trance. Malice blinked, tears streaming from under her eyelids as she suddenly exposed her eyes to the chamber's unrelenting brilliance.

"Lady Malice!"

There it was again. Reese's voice. She was calling out to her.

Malice surged to her feet. "Where are you?" She squinted into the brightness but couldn't see anything.

"Lady Malice." Reese's voice was further away. Was she headed the opposite direction?

"I'm coming!" Malice dashed forward. The light swallowed her. She turned, trying to make out the chamber's exit, but couldn't see it. "Reese!"

"Malice?"

She oriented herself on Reese's voice. First step was getting to the sheriff, then they would figure out how to get out. It was an awkward game of Marco Polo. Reese kept on sounding further away. Malice found herself running to try to catch up to the sheriff.

Her legs weakened quickly as if she was running into gale force winds. She set her shoulders and lowered her center of gravity, forcing herself onward, toward that receding voice. The light was growing impossibly brilliant. She had to find her, she felt it in her bones. Without Reese, they had no other chance. This was it. She had to do it. She had to.

"Reese!"

"...Malice?"

* * *

More holes opened to the nothing. Ruri had thought there was no space between the fae before, but now they were crushing together, trying to get to the relative safety of the Heart. All was still quiet, the silence growing more eerie as the fae pressed in against each other without so much as a word or utterance between them. Those against the crystal of the Heart shifted to avoid being crushed, their faces stoic despite the crush.

The ground dropped out from underneath them. The wolf spread their legs to keep their balance. They blinked, then were back on solid footing. They hadn't moved. The fae weren't any more worked up than they had been.

Something was wrong. They felt lost. The only point that felt solid was the pull of Mal from deep within the crystalline pile. They looked out over the unmoving throng. Reese had said to stay here, but Mal pulled at them. She needed them.

There was no contest.

With one last glance at the fae, they turned and ran into the Heart. The way forward was clear, and they stretched into an all-out lope in no time. It took only seconds to make their way down the hall to the T-junction at the end. Mal's scent lingered to the left, so they followed it, allowing their mate to draw them deeper inside. Mal was somewhere further within. Their sense of her shifted as they followed the corridor around. She was always deeper within.

On the opposite side from where they'd entered was a crack going further inside. The wolf and Ruri were of one mind. They didn't hesitate. There was no discussion between them. Mal was somewhere in there. They had to find her.

They plunged into the crack, shouldering their way through, only to find that it widened almost immediately. Though it was dim inside, their eyes had no problems making out the walls that sloped toward each other and met far above. There was no real ceiling, just where the walls met. The hall lightened considerably as they ran down its length. The wolf narrowed their eyes into slits so they could see. They ran on and on and on, never stopping or slowing. Their heartbeat was an urgent knell that spurred them forward. It tripped to Mal's name, a rhythmic tattoo that compelled them to move as fast as they could.

Somehow, they made it into a chamber as massive as it was radiant. Mal was nowhere to be seen, but they could feel her. It wasn't much further now. If it hadn't been so cursed bright in there, they might have seen her. It felt like they should have been able to reach forward and snag the hem of her tunic with their teeth, but when they moved forward, there was still no sign of their mate.

They pushed on, the air flowing away from their face as they made their way to where they belonged.

* * *

Malice struggled forward, her hands reaching out. Was she trying to block out the light that threatened to sear her retinas or was she grasping at it? Beams of brilliance lanced toward her between fingers and tears streamed down her face in pain and frustration. As much as she tried to get to Reese's almost indistinct cries, she couldn't. Something was holding her back, working against her. She groped forward another few inches, but her fingers caught at nothing.

Even nothing had weight here.

"...Lady...Malice..." Reese's words floated to her between beats of her heart. It thundered in her ears, yet she didn't dare stop striving. The harder she worked to get to Reese, the louder her heart beat and the harder it was to hear her, but when she let up for a moment, Reese's voice still receded. How it hadn't gone silent by now, Malice didn't know, but she wouldn't stop as long as she still heard it.

Something collided with the back of her legs. The force working against her vanished and she tumbled forward. Her hands and knees took the brunt of her fall, but it was awkward. Pain sprang up one arm as her wrist buckled. She rolled to one side to stop from mashing her face into the cold, hard floor.

Whatever had hit her moved up her, sniffing along the length of her body until it got to her head.

She knew who it was before she opened her eyes.

"Ruri."

The bright light couldn't obscure the eyes of molten gold that gazed down at her. She reached up and wound her fingers through the thick fur of Ruri's ruff. Renewed energy coursed through her veins. Reese's voice sounded out as if she was standing right next to them.

"Malice!"

She pulled herself up, using Ruri to help. The terrible force that had threatened to crush all resistance out of her parted.

"That way." Malice pointed into the brightness.

Ruri bounded forward, pulling Malice along beside her. She kept her fingers tight around Ruri's fur. Whatever had tried to keep her at bay seemed to be no match for her mate.

A figure appeared to one side of them. It wandered aimlessly, arms out, feeling for objects it would never touch.

Of course it was Reese. Who else could it be? Malice pointed at her and Ruri reoriented herself without any words of direction. She simply curled around in a loose arc, and then they were loping toward the sheriff.

"Reese!"

She turned their way, squinting against the light. Her eyes widened when she saw them and she ran forward.

"You found me." Reese looked down at Ruri.

"I wouldn't have been able to without her," Malice said. "There was a force. Something. It kept me from coming to you."

"I guess the Heart has made up its mind about you. I doubt it approves of you killing Tedrick." She shook looked down at the golden wolf who stood with them and shook her head. "I'd never thought about what might happen if one of her kind made it to the Heart of a realm. It can't seem to affect her. I'm grateful, but also…" Reese's voice trailed off.

Malice shrugged. "It had to be done. Speaking of that, are we good now?"

Reese smiled. "Almost. The Heart had accepted me. It took a bit of explaining, but I got it sorted. Now I need to get to the Heart's peak." She looked around. "Which way is out?"

The sea of unrelenting white around them offered no answers. Malice strained her eyes, but saw nothing but white. As far as she could tell, there were no walls and certainly no exit.

Ruri huffed. She panted up at them, tongue lolling from her mouth in a lupine grin.

"If you know the way, let's just go." Malice tightened her grip to let Ruri know she wasn't nearly as crabby as her words might sound.

Ruri gave another deep whuff of amusement. She pivoted, then trotted toward a point that Malice couldn't see. Reese jogged beside them. Malice sneaked a look at her. She didn't look any different, but then neither had the Jaeger. Whatever power she'd gained wasn't visible.

For as long as it had taken Malice to get to the sheriff, they were back at the chamber's perimeter in next to no time. The comparable dimness of the corridor out was one of the most beautiful things Malice thought she'd ever seen. Ruri let out a questioning whine.

"After you, of course," Malice said.

"What was that?" Reese asked.

"Nothing. Just glad we're about to get out of this place."

"And get out we will." Reese smiled.

Ruri kept them moving forward. The hall went dim almost instantly. Malice's eyes were so blown out by the brightness of the central chamber that she could barely see. Ruri kept going without slowing. Her confidence was palpable through her skin. Malice closed her eyes and kept on, Reese closing in on their tail. When she opened her eyes again, she could see, if barely. The walls were closing in. She shifted her shoulders to keep from scraping them against the crystals outgrowths. Ruri slowed down so Malice didn't have to let go.

The outer ring of the Heart was darker still, but her eyes were finally getting used to a reasonable amount of light. She allowed Ruri to continue pulling her forward, though. She didn't want to let go, to break that connection.

Outside the Heart was a mass of neutral grey. The fae had turned to watch the nothing coming for them. They took no notice of the small group that had made its way out of the Heart.

Malice tried not to watch the holes of nothing. Some had opened in the crowd, melting gaps into the throng. The fae gave it as wide a berth as they could, but none seemed willing to abandon the dubious shelter of the Heart's walls.

She turned to the sheriff. "What are you—"

Reese was gone. She was already halfway up the side of the Heart. The massive crystals looked like they should have been too slick to climb, but she managed. Pools of radiance rippled to life in her wake. Everywhere she touched the Heart, whether it was with hands or feet, there was light.

Some among the fae noticed her ascent. Murmurs began to trickle through. The noise awoke the crowd to something other than stoic acceptance of approaching doom. One by one, they turned, a new emotion seeping through the collective mask of disinterest. It was hope.

Hope as Reese leaped from one massive crystal to another.

Hope as the winged fae creatures shifted or flew out of her way to clear a path to the top.

Hope as she shimmied up the massive crystal that was the Heart's peak.

Reese stood alone at the top. She raised one hand and almost touched the uncaring sky. She wavered for a moment and a collective gasp rippled through the watchers. Malice found herself holding her breath. She let it out slowly but never took her eyes from the sheriff.

Reese crouched, wrapping both hands against the needle tip of the crystal peak. Her lips moved, but whatever she was saying was whipped away as the wind came up.

This was what the crowd had been waiting for. Jubilant whoops rang out. The crystals on the roof burst into light that would have seemed bright had Malice not just spent far too much time in a room that was nothing short of blinding. The fae birds launched themselves from the roof in a wave. They trailed curtains of light behind them in an ever-expanding pattern into the sky. Bits of bright blue trailed after them, holes to something opening up in the nothing their wings silhouetted against.

The wind howled, pushing out from the Heart. Malice kept her grip on Ruri, who held tight to the ground. A glance behind her told her that the nothing was still there. Blue sky was showing above, but there was no sign of grass or the hill that led down into this depression.

"Enough!" Reese shouted. Her voice cut through the howling winds. The crystal peak was now too bright to look at. It waxed ever brighter, then something gave in a wave felt as much as seen. A swell crashed over them, then soothed them in its wake. It roared in Malice's ears in a soft whisper. White light blasted out her vision while never obscuring it.

When she could see again, Malice looked out onto a landscape transformed.

Green grass covered the hillside. Closer to them were fields of wildflowers with curious gaps in them that were filled only with blades of tall greenery. They bent before a gentle breeze, swaying back and forth.

Above, the winged creatures still climbed, the web of light between them growing gossamer thin, but not fading completely. They flew out in all directions and the sky opened up before them. It was a beautiful summer day. The sun warmed them as fluffy white clouds scudded across an expanse of the purest blue she'd ever seen. It smelled of warmth and the promise of a cool evening. If there was a more perfect summer afternoon, Malice had never experienced it. She somehow knew she never would again.

There was a thud as someone landed on the ground next to her.

"I think that about does it," Reese said. She put her hands on her hips and surveyed the area. "Yes, I think this will do."

CHAPTER FIFTY-TWO

"Are you taking anything back?" Ruri asked Mal.

Her mate looked around the room where they'd stayed the past couple of weeks. "There isn't much I want."

"No special memories to cherish?"

Mal stuck her tongue out at her and sent a pulse of amusement through the bond they shared. She was getting much better at that. "I'm keeping the sword. Does that count?"

"It's not the keepsake most people would go for, but I'm not surprised."

"I have my phone. That's all I really care about. It's been…hard to remember a lot of what's happened." Her face twisted for a moment, then relaxed when Ruri used their bond to send her a wave of love. "Maybe that's just as well. The Jaeger did a real number on me."

"You'll get to check your message, finally."

"Oh god, yes!" Mal held the phone up and looked at the face. "Cass is going to be pissed that I haven't called her back yet. She finally gets in contact with me, and I blow her off. I'm never going to hear the end of this."

"Just explain you've been trapped in a fairy kingdom. I'm sure she'll be fine."

"Oh yeah, because that sounds like a real thing."

Ruri shrugged. "She's seen some weird shit."

"Not this weird." Mal shook her head. "Do you have everything? Want me to carry something?"

Compared to Mal, Ruri had ended up with an embarrassment of riches. She thought Sovereign Reese might have oversold her contribution a bit when trying to convince the fae court that the wolven in their midst wasn't dangerous. While nothing she'd said had been untrue, the glowing picture she'd painted had led many fae to shower her with gifts.

Her wolf thought the whole thing was hilarious. She didn't understand that declining the offers could be a very bad idea. Ruri had no desire to accidentally offend any of the fae only to find herself under the thrall of an exotic curse. Some of the gifts, such as those from Ylana and Billy, she would always treasure. Others were actually useful, if a little odd. The pile of wolf-themed items was a little much. She liked wolves, that was obvious, but she'd never seen a need to surround herself with their likenesses. Why did she need a wolf statue with glowing moonstone eyes when she had the real thing inside her?

If there had been a way to keep the fae from finding out about her after Reese reclaimed her realm from the nothing, she would have, but the arm band that had confined her wolf was long gone. The wolf shifted inside her, a sharp prickle of fur against the underside of her skin. She wouldn't have permitted Ruri to put it back on anyway.

Ruri laughed to herself. Really, who was she kidding? She was so glad to be whole again. It was worth any amount of wolf tchotchkes to have the sister of her soul back.

"Hey." Mal took Ruri's hands in her own and pulled her in front of her. "Where did you go?" Her mate gazed into her eyes with gentle concern.

Ruri blinked, then leaned her forehead against Mal's. "Just spacing out. It's been an interesting couple of weeks. Or so."

"Interesting is right. I'm glad we're heading home. Finally." Mal squeezed Ruri's hands, then let them go with regret she could feel. She picked up a wooden trunk. "This is going to take a few trips."

A knock sounded at the door. Ruri hastened over to it. Shejuanna stood in the hall.

"Oh," Ruri said. "It's you."

"You don't have to sound so surprised," Shejuanna said. "Can I come in?"

"Of course." She stood aside to let the teen through. "What's going on?"

"We know you're leaving." She lifted one shoulder in a half shrug. "Thought we should say goodbye. I volunteered."

"The others too cool to come say it themselves?" Mal asked.

"They're a little freaked out about the whole end of the world and her being a werewolf thing. I tried to explain it wasn't like that, but they had a really fucked up time when all that was going down. Most of the fae just took off through the portals, no one thought of them. They just hunkered down in the stables with the remaining mounts, without knowing what was going on. Not that I know what that was like. Mami Wata took good care of me, and I got to hang out with her people. It's weird thinking I was away eating chips and drinking Coke while this world was almost wiped away." She shook her head, looking inward. "But I'd rather remember that than…what happened before."

"That must have been scary," Ruri said. She couldn't imagine how that must have felt.

"You can say that." Shejuanna gave her a crooked grin. "They'll get over it. I'll get over it. We get to live in fairyland, what could be better?"

"If you say so."

"We do say so. None of us changed our minds."

"As long as you're sure," Mal said.

Shejuanna sighed. "Sure as we can be. Anyway, have a good trip and thanks for coming looking for us. That means more than you probably think."

"I know." Mal's voice was quiet, but Ruri felt the intensity behind the words.

Another knock sounded on the door.

"Okay then." Shejuanna sidled toward the door. "Guess that's my cue." She pushed it open.

Mracek stood on the other side. Waiting behind him was a bevy of pages. Shejuanna gave them a small wave and slipped out between the waiting fae.

"We're here to move your possessions to the portal," Mracek said. He avoided looking her in the eyes. Apparently there was a legend about catching the gaze of a wolven. As effusive as the fae had been in their thanks, it was clear it would take much more time than she and Mal planned to spend there for them to get truly comfortable with her.

"Mal," Ruri said over her shoulder. "The transportation problem seems to have solved itself."

Mal popped around the corner, still carrying the chest.

"Good." She tried to pass it off to Mracek.

Two young pages scurried forward to intercept Mal. They snatched the box away from her, then trundled down the hall with it dangling between them. They also avoided looking directly at Ruri.

As if that had been a signal, the rest of the pages flooded into the room. They snagged the remaining luggage and fled down the hallway.

"This way, if you please," Mracek said. He followed along in the wake of the servants.

"Is the castle back to its usual self yet?" Mal asked.

Mracek smiled. "It's getting there. The pantry is adjacent to the training salle this morning, and the Grand Hall has developed a new set of windows looking out into deep woods."

"That's encouraging," Ruri said. When they'd first returned, the castle had been distressingly mundane. As nice as it had been to be able to make her way around, it felt like some vital piece was missing from it.

They passed through an area of hall where the pattern of the stone on the walls was gone, leaving an artificially smooth face behind. A large chunk was missing from a tapestry that sat on the edge of the blank spot. It simply ended as if the missing part had never existed.

When Reese had convinced the Heart to accept her claim on the realm, the bits of nothing had all filled back in, but not perfectly. What came back was almost a generic version of what had been there and only for simple objects. Ruri looked down at her hand. She was still missing the nails on her index and middle fingers. They were gone as if they'd never been. No one knew yet how many fae had been swallowed by the nothing. They were still trickling back in from the mortal world.

"Here we are." Mracek gestured toward a familiar doorway.

The last of the pages disappeared through the open door.

"The Heir's rooms?" Mal asked.

Reese stuck her head out the door. Mracek immediately folded himself into a deep bow. She flipped a hand at him.

"Enough of that," she said. "Do you see a crown on this head?"

"Ah, no, Your Majesty." He stood straight, trying to appear relaxed, but darting eyes betrayed his discomfort.

"Come on in," Reese said. "This is the closest portal to your rooms, so we decided to send you off here."

"Can't wait to get rid of us?" Ruri asked.

"It's been exciting, but I have to work on putting the realm back together. Please don't be offended, but your presence has been more than a little distracting."

The rooms still held the same basic shape as they had the last time Ruri and Mal had been there. The quiet lakeshore with its sandy beach butting up against tall reeds through one doorway was new. So was the hole in the ceiling that let the sun pour through onto a pile of furs, despite Ruri knowing that there was another floor above them.

The pages had piled their luggage and chests next to the door with the lake through it. They left the room in a silent file. Ruri tried not to snicker as they did their best to pretend that she and the nearly seven-foot-tall woman with the lower half of a snake also occupying the room were anything less than perfectly normal. Common even. Her teenaged attendants padded around in one corner. Someone had outfitted them with soft robes of brilliant orange and deep red. They were rearranging something. Rabbit glanced over her shoulder and gave them a cheeky grin before getting back to her work.

"Is she—" Mal stopped herself, then started over. "Are you the new Heir?"

"I will be," Mami Wata said. "We need to make the trip to the Heart, but once I am invested, it will be official." She swayed closer to them. "I expect this means Reese will reign forever. No one will dare assassinate her knowing I'm waiting in the wings."

"Hardly," Reese said. She flopped down on the edge of the piled furs. "This sovereign business is exhausting. I miss being sheriff of La Pointe already. Once they're used to you, I'm heading back to the mortal world."

"As I said," Mami Wata said dryly. "Her reign will never end. There has never been a non-Tuatha sovereign before. There are many in the court who may never be prepared for that change."

"I don't care who's in charge," Mal said. "Just make sure you keep everyone in line. I don't want to make another trip out to the woods to investigate fae mischief." She smiled as she said the words, but Ruri could feel the undercurrent of seriousness behind them.

"Where's Nagamo?" Ruri asked. She'd looked around the room, but there was no sign of her friend. A small pang of sadness resonated through her chest at the thought of not finding out what had become of him.

"He's rather busy," Reese said. "He was able to get most of his people out before the nothing could claim them, but they're having some problems adjusting to being able to come and go as they please. He told me that it's like they've been in decades-long hibernation, which they don't usually do."

"I'm glad to hear it. I was worried he might not have made it. It's too bad he didn't get everyone out."

Reese nodded gravely. "It is, and that's a burden I'll carry for a long time." She sighed, then clapped her hands together. "But I'll tell him you were asking after him. That should lift his spirits."

"Please do," Ruri said. She hesitated a moment before continuing. "I have one more question before we go. The Jaeger said that your prophecy had him as king until I led the Wild Hunt. If the prophecy was true, how were we able to kill him?"

Mami Wata smiled wide, far wider than human lips would have been able to stretch. "The One-Day King made many mistakes, starting with seeking me out for the prophecy and ending with the assumption that his interpretation of my words was the correct one. You did lead the Wild Hunt."

"No way. The Wild Hunt would never follow me…" Her head snapped up as Mami Wata's meaning suddenly became clear. "Oh!"

"I still don't get it," Mal said.

"When they were chasing me, I *led* them on it. He assumed it meant a wolven would be in charge of the hunters. It probably sounded like a 'cold day in hell' kind of thing to him, but that wasn't it at all."

"Got it." Mal shook her head. "He was an idiot." She dusted her hands off. "Now that we've established that extremely obvious fact, can we get out of here? I have a voice mail from my sister to listen to." She held up her phone.

"Of course." Reese stood and crossed over to the portal. She touched the side of the doorway. The image of the lake flickered then changed. Rows of cars under bright sun took the place of the idyllic scene. "I had your truck impounded." Her voice was apologetic.

"I'm not paying for a ticket," Mal said.

"Of course not. They'll allow you to leave without issuing a citation."

"Good."

Mal and Ruri shoved the small stack of luggage through the portal.

"Stop by if you're in Chicago," Mal said.

"We'll see what happens," Reese said.

"That sounds wonderful," Mami Wata said. "I would love to see Lake Michigan again."

Mal held her hand out to Ruri, who took it. They stepped across the threshold and into the parking lot.

Moist heat hit them like a wet washcloth across the face. The portal winked out behind them.

"What the hell?" Mal glanced around, then looked at her phone. It was vibrating as though trying to free itself from her grasp. Ruri leaned over her shoulder and watched as notification after notification filled the screen. The date jumped from January to July, then the phone went dead.

"Oh no," Mal said. She looked over at Ruri. Panic skittered down the length of their mate bond. "Six months! How in the hell did we lose six months?"

Bella Books, Inc.

Women. Books. Even Better Together.

P.O. Box 10543
Tallahassee, FL 32302

Phone: 800-729-4992
www.bellabooks.com

Printed in the USA
CPSIA information can be obtained
at www.ICGtesting.com
JSHW082149140824
68134JS00014B/145